ALSO BY SENA ANDEO

Eulogy: A Tale of Terrial

I0653948

TIDES OF
GAFFORAH

Tides of Gafforah
Blood of the Gods: Book 1
Copyright © 2021 Sena Andeo
Nef House Publishing
www.nefhousepublishing.com

All rights reserved. Without limiting the rights under copyright reserved alone, no part of this publication may be reproduced, stored in or introduced into a retrieval system, or transmitted in any form or by any means (electronic, mechanical, photocopying, recording, or otherwise) without the prior written permission of both the copyright owner and the above publisher of the book.

This is a work of fiction. Names, characters, places, brands, media, and incidents are either the product of the author's imagination or are used fictitiously. The author acknowledges the trademarked status and trademark owners of various products, brands, and/or restaurants referenced in this work of fiction, which have been used without permission. The publication/use of these trademarks is not authorized, associated with, or sponsored by the trademark owners.

ISBN: 978-1-948374-62-0

TIDES OF
GAFFORAH

SENA ANDEO

NEF HOUSE PUBLISHING

For Dad, who is my number one supporter through the editing process.

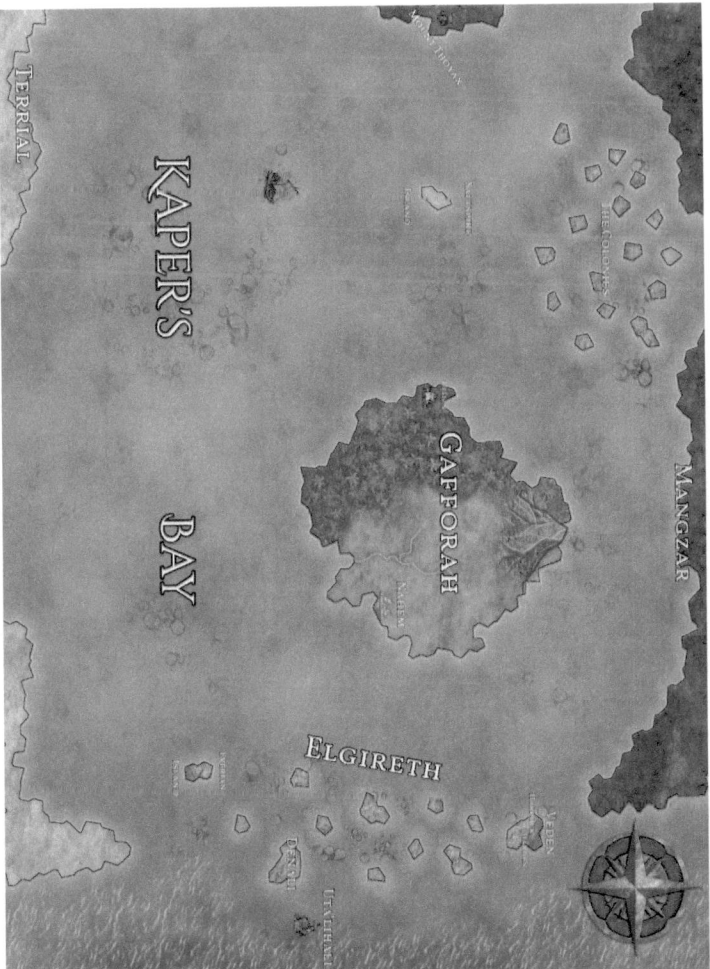

~ 1 ~

KEYRA

Hardock is unimpressive as far as port towns go. Its streets are crowded and muddy, the distinct scent of marsh mud and the sea impossible to escape. Kaper's Bay stretches to the west, a mirror-like expanse of still waters and splashes of color from reefs nestled beneath the surface. To the east, across the island of Veden dotted with settlements smaller than most mainland families, is Hardock's sister town, Harden. It borders the East Sea, a roiling ocean of dangerous tides and hidden menace with borders yet to be explored. It is to Veden that merchants come from the southern islands of Qan and lands such as Nath'iki, Waheth, Lizaq, and countless others. Veden's neighboring islands make up the chain known as Elgireth, a natural barrier that protects Kaper's Bay from the elements and blocks large seafaring vessels from crossing through. To reach Gafforah and the eastern shores of Terrial and Mangzar across the bay, larger ships are forced to dock at Harden and rent local wagons to trek their goods to Hardock where they use skiffs and shallow barges to maneuver the rest of their path. For playing such an essential part in the eastern sea trade, Hardock itself is nothing more than a bed for a tired sailor. The native tradespeople build and rent out bay boats, while the rest of the citizens are forced to scramble for any coin they can earn—or steal—from sailors.

Today, like every day, the ports are crowded with merchants in makeshift stalls clinging to the docks where barges wait to be rented. Their goods are painted in lively colors that mimic the surrounding coral reefs in hopes of catching a passing eye. In contrast, their own homes are nothing more than rock and mud huts or dark wood scavenged from those who think they can make it through Kaper's Bay in their ocean ships.

Children shove fried foods in the faces of first mates in line for rentals while their captains drink the island dry. Most are overwhelmed by the dazzle of color and life after hard journeys at sea. These are the easiest victims, willing to trade a few jewel shards in exchange for a few moments of peace as the Elgir swirl around them. They grow frustrated as jewels disappear from purses while they purchase mysterious meat on sticks, only to have their food snatched from their hand while they search for the currency thief. The Elgir have mastered this game, knowing exactly where the sailors' attention is—or isn't, at any given time. Those experienced with Veden stand in line with cotton stuffed in their ears and purses stuffed in their boots, pretending not to speak the language.

Keyra is too old for the exhausting ploys. She has been a seamstress in Hardock for more time than she cares to keep track of, until her thick black curls turned gray and her brown skin turned leathery. Her once-bright hazel eyes have become cloudy and long, thin fingers have stiffened. She cannot flash brightly colored cloth in the faces of sailors or speak so rapidly they will agree to anything to shut her up. Her fingers can no longer pinch from bags with one hand while doing a card trick with the other. She and the other elderly of Elgireth have their own methods, setting up stalls amid the hubbub where they can sit and gossip while stitching worn sailors' clothing, ships' sails, flags, and anything else a needle can repair. Their craft draws customers out of necessity.

Today, however, she finds herself lingering in the board house she shares with the other elderly women of Hardock. She can tell it is going to be miserably hot. There must be a storm brewing in the ocean, pushing the humidity ahead of it. "Ilyin woke up an hour early," Keyra's neighbor says as she gathers thread and a collection of various sized needles from her things. "She was stitching up a mainsail last time I saw her. Better get going if you want to catch the rich ones."

Keyra mutters inwardly as she dons the long overtunic traditional to the Elgir people. Layers are necessary even in the brutal summer as the weather can take a turn within moments. She packs up her materials, sewing needles and thread. She and her fellow tailors are always in high demand. While most sailors are adept tailors, often the low-priced services of a local appear more attractive when comforts long forgotten are only a short walk away.

Outside the board house, the sun beats down mercilessly on the sparsely vegetated island. The only relief comes from the many canopies stretched across the streets in the most densely populated areas. They do more to stifle the air than keep away the sun in her opinion, holding down the heat from the churning crowds and yelling vendors. Keyra's stall is a small tent between two docks, a short walk down the street from her door and located where she can catch a slight breeze most mornings. She had dawdled too long this time, she knows that. She is losing valuable business. Her weary bones don't push her upright as fast as they used to. A handful more years, and her fingers will lose their mobility as well. She can only hope she has saved up enough to survive her retirement by then.

She lowers herself creakily into her chair and scans the prospective customers. The first sailor off the vessel to her left wears Gaffori pantaloons and a silver chain about his neck. She recognizes him as a ferry captain from their island neighbor to the west. His black-and-silver flag waves proudly at the top of jagged sails. He gives Keyra and her wares a side eye before going on his way. He is wisely suspicious of Elgir vendors and will not prove a patron.

A prospect distracts her. A cabin boy ravaged by sunburn from the harsh ocean sun stumbles drunkenly into a merchant stall. Chaos ensues and the seller begins screaming at him in a language he does not understand.

Keyra is between them just as the shopkeeper pulls a spiked paddle from beneath the counter. Sometimes her body forgets her age and she sprints like she is twenty again. "Let me have this one," she tells him in their own tongue. "I'll owe you a beer at the Brains, Isah. He won't want any of your pastries anyways."

The graying man's face relaxes. "Two beers and I'll make it convincing for his friends."

Keyra notices the cluster of green sailors watching the unfolding events with bated breath. "Fine. But if I catch you giving one to Zephy Hazir again, I'm going to beat you in an arm wrestle while your friends watch."

Isah screams in answer, raising his weapon above his head. The young sailors scatter but Keyra holds her ground. She lifts her hands and takes up a fighting stance, fingers spread wide.

The easily two-stone merchant stops mid-swing as though gripped by an invisible force. Exclamations of disbelief give Keyra the encouragement to take her act a step further.

She shouts a command and Isah flies back against his stall. "You owe me an entire night of beers for that show," he says as though they are his dying words, arms outstretched pleadingly towards his attackers. He goes limp amid gasps from the audience.

The gaggle of foreign spectators are stunned into silence. Keyra bows to the sailor boys. The Elgir applaud until the boys follow suit. If there is one unspoken rule on Veden, it is that the natives play along with each other's ruses. Gains for one are gains for all. Already, pockets have been picked by children that flicker through the shadows of the crowd.

Keyra shuffles to the cabin boy as the rest dissipate back to their lives. His eyes are glazed. "Sorry if you were frightened, boy. That pastry owner has a particularly sour temperament. Thankfully for you, magic is a powerful force here. You would be wise to protect yourself."

"Are your flags magical?" He points a curious finger to the samples hanging from her tent. The flags she sells are nothing more than a colorful distraction for the less-experienced sailors. They are overpriced and made from cheap fabric.

Keyra shakes her head sadly. "Everything in Elgireth is magical, including my flags. However, they are too expensive for your silver moons. We deal only in jewel shards here. Too many passing world currencies can create confusion on our small islands. Perhaps with your friends' help, we can reach an agreement."

They whisper amongst themselves. The cabin boy turns back to the merchant, his face flushed with ego. "We decided that instead of buying your pathetic excuse for a cheap trick, we're going to take all the money you have and allow you to keep your life and colorful scraps." He places his hand on his weapon and the sailors behind him follow suit. His eyes dart to Isah, who is watching despite the fact that he's supposed to be severely wounded.

Keyra sighs. Children are always ruining her fun. "You are Andrieli, correct? Nath'iki by your accent and the darkness of your hair. You are a cabin boy but the quality of your sword hilt and the sigil on your ring speak of wealth. Do those sailors serve your father? Grandfather? Why then would you threaten an old woman in a foreign land over pennies? You know nothing about me and my people, yet you choose threats and violence as a first resort."

The young one smiles cockily, half drawing his sword. "I'm someone who doesn't appreciate being taken for a fool. I don't need to know anything about your culture. You have none. You are a chain of islands so small they can't support themselves except as a privy break for sailors headed to Gafforah. All I've seen so far is a hunched old woman who thinks she can rob me blind over some pathetic dyed fabric scraps with a little help from her cohort." He motions to Isah, who is brushing rubble off his tunic and assessing the damage to his stall with a miserable expression. Keyra will have to remember that when it comes time to pay their tab.

The cabin boy is inches from Keyra's face at this point, but she does not back down. Her lips twitch with a smile. "Look up, little lordling, and see what kind of culture we are."

Everyone in the area is watching the unfolding events. All have hands on weapons, whether drawn or not. Suddenly, Isah is mere feet away with arms crossed over his chest. The unsettling silence says more than any threat she could make. The game is up. "Go home," Isah demands in halting Western.

The boy opens his mouth to protest, which may have been effective back in Nath'iki. He wisely chooses to shut it again and turn away from Keyra. "It's getting late, boys. This grandma isn't worth the trouble anyways." They head for their ship without another word, betraying the fear they tried to hide. The Gaffori sailor Keyra had spotted earlier laughs gruffly from a bench. Isah snaps his attention to the stranger. "Got something to say, outsider?"

The sailor flips the merchant a rather brilliant gemstone. "Neighbor, my friend. We are neighbors, not strangers, and I am no fool. I come here for booze and a bed, not trouble." He takes his leave with a salute and business returns to normal.

Keyra nods her thanks to her friend and heads for her stall. The day may have just started, but she's already looking forward to that drink.

~ 2 ~

BETA
&
THE BOY

B eta stares into the still waters of Kaper's Bay, frowning at the face that looks back. Her green eyes are large in a small face framed by thick waves of long brown hair. Her sandy skin is several shades lighter than the native Elgir islanders, making her stick out in a crowd. It's none of these features that she focuses on, but rather the orange scar that runs from just above her eyebrow down across her eye to the middle of her cheek. Even in the distorted water, it glows in the muddled reflection clearly.

She leans back, turning her attention to the expanse of water that stretches in front of her. Beta may not look like many of her fellow Elgir, but she is just as drawn to the still beauty of the bay as they are. She stirs the polished rocks beneath the surface with a toe, wondering just how deep the layers go.

"Beta, are you joining us for break?"

She's distracted from the question by a splash deeper in the bay. There it is again, the glitter of wet scales and the smack of a massive tail on the surface. She stands and squints, afraid to move lest she frighten the creature away. "Did you see that? Tell me you didn't miss it. It *has* to be a seaqueen."

Rolith hops down from the rock where he and his companions have spread a blanket. He offers her a slice of apple sprinkled with cinnamon. "A seaqueen? Most of us stopped believing in those when we were children, Beta. It was probably just a shore shark."

"No, shore sharks aren't violet colored." She breaks the apple into smaller bits and tosses them into the water as a sacrifice to the seaqueen.

"Everything is violet colored this time of day. Stop wasting our food, seaqueens don't eat apples." He snatches the remaining fruit from her hand like a frustrated father. "Why don't you forget about the fish people and fetch your scroll before it floats to Gafforah." He motions to the forgotten schoolwork, now soaked through as the waves playfully tug at its ancient corners.

Beta groans and shakes it dry as best she can. The writing has run and turned Namen's Prayer to clumps of ruined ink. She pouts and pulls the water from the scroll with a motion of her hand and a tingle of energy between her and the bay. While the water comes free, it takes the ink with it and she is left with a torn, blank piece of paper. She tosses the gray droplet into the ocean and watches it disappear. "So much for passing religion. Don't tell Brielle, she'll have my head for ruining her favorite prayer."

Rolith hops to the boulder to rejoin their group and offers her a hand. His long, dark hair falls over his gray eyes, giving him an innocent and sheepish look. Beta knows better than most that it's a deliberate ploy to disarm attractive girls, not an act of nature. He doesn't need it. His crooked smile and strong features are enough to flutter even Beta's heart. "Forget about that old bookworm. I promise she won't even notice it's gone. Come have some proper food, maybe it'll wipe that sour look off your face."

Beta wrinkles her nose and ignores his offered hand. She calls a gust of wind to pick her off her feet and drop her on the boulder like a stray leaf. "Maybe I like looking sour. It keeps my crazed fans at bay. I could use some wine, but I suppose fish and bread will do, if that's all we have." Rolith scoffs and runs his fingers through his locks. He and Beta have always played this game, flirting casually when they don't have anyone else's attention. Both know they never intend to take it further than that.

The rest of her companions lounge on top of their favorite study boulder. Malvin has coppery hair that he keeps tied in a topknot, a face freckled by the tropical sun, and black eyes that look unnatural in an otherwise bright face. He's not as attractive to Beta as Rolith, but it's his abrasive personality that repels her the most. He is a stone mage, like Rolith, a gray scar striping over his eye. He sits across the blanket from the others, juggling upwards of twenty pebbles with intense concentration in his scrunched face. His scrolls lie wrinkled and forgotten to his side, left to the mercy of the sea wind. When he hears Beta's comment, he reaches in his bag to pull out a wineskin, offering it to her after taking a hefty swig himself while the pebbles rain around him, forgotten. Beta accepts it gratefully.

Peynter is more studious, a water mage with a blue scar who has his notes carefully organized and in different colored inks to better remember certain topics. He is not as gifted in his magical abilities as his study mates are. He replaces his ineptitude with hard work, both in studying and in physical exercise. Despite his best efforts, he is lanky at best, with a shaved head he hopes will make him look more intimidating. It doesn't achieve the sense of authority that he may have intended, but Beta will be the first to admit the shaved head suits his dark skin and sharp eyes. He also claims to have a beard coming in, though Beta has yet to see proof of that. He only looks up when the wind Beta uses to carry herself scatters some of his work.

"Watch it, battlemage! Some of us care if we get good marks in Professor Quinden's class. The old cooch has had it out for me ever since that acid accident."

Rolith snickers at the memory. He is also a stone mage, and a year ahead of the others. Supposedly he is the head of their study group although Beta has had servants that were stricter than Rolith. He is handsome with dark hair and brooding eyes. Most are intimidated by his appearance; although a few moments in his company is enough to realize his heart is still that of a child. "All those fancy notes won't save you from Quinden's wrath. He can't read them thanks to you and that failed acid experiment of yours. Beta, don't hog the skin!"

Peynter winces and stacks his papers huffily. "It wasn't my fault the assistant got the labels mixed up!" He watches the wine skin pass from student to student disapprovingly. "You really shouldn't be drinking while studying, it dulls the mind."

Beta nudges him playfully, ignoring her own notes which are still in her bag except for the unfortunate prayer scroll. "I've learned more than you have in our year here. Like, that water mages are one of the most common sorcerer types and arguably the weakest."

Peynter holds up an indignant finger. "Now wait just a moment, missy. First of all, you grew up in the Citadel, so I would hope you've learned more than I have. Secondly, it's not my fault the ocean doesn't like the sound of my voice. Clearly sorcery powers aren't reliant on personality, or I would be the prodigy and not our resident charmer, Malvin." He glares at the stone mage in question, who is making a rock dance to the tapping of his foot.

"What can I say, the rocks love me! I'm practically a battlemage."

Beta laughs with the rest of them, knowing full well he can never know what it's like to be a battlemage. Kaper's Bay sorcery allows the user to speak to elements that are otherwise shut off to communication. Water mages speak to the ocean, fauna mages to the animals, and so on. There are even those who can speak to time and the minds of others. Those that practice and learn the language of their element can create bonds, allowing them to manipulate the world around them with ease. There are those that have a natural gift and hardly need to convince their element to cooperate, like Malvin, and there are those who struggle creating a connection and largely have to rely on their gained knowledge, like Peynter. Then there is Beta, and her incredibly rare abilities. Battlemages have no need to create bonds and request interaction with the world around them. They *demand* it, with a thought, a brush of their hands, and the elements mold to their will eagerly. There were stories that the battlemages of old could raise their arms and the earth would split beneath them, yearning to please, or that groups of them could summon gales from clear skies. She will never experience such power herself, though. She and her mentor are the last battlemages in existence.

"I heard it helps water mages connect if they swim often." Beta changes the subject, watching Peynter scribble out something on his scroll. Malvin catches the look Beta gives him and Rolith pretends not to notice. Malvin and Beta grab Peynter by the arms, tossing him into the sea before he can so much as squeak his disapproval.

One by one they join the water mage, laughing with joy and forgetting their troubles for the moment. They are oblivious to the eyes watching them from the neighboring island, too small to be named, from the top of the long disused lighthouse.

The boy presses a spyglass to his eye from the window. He knows them all by name, as he does most of the students. They come to the beach by his island often to study and relax. He cannot help his eyes as they stray to Beta, her wet clothes pressing tightly against her lithe body. Rolith is dunking her head underwater and acting more like a child than a supervisor. The two of them seem to be enjoying themselves. He hates that. Rolith is far too old for Beta. There must be rules at the Citadel against the kind of horseplay he is witnessing.

The boy records the scene in his notebook and slams it shut before the ink can dry. He has tortured himself long enough. He sighs and turns to the portrait on the wall beside his bed. It is his most prized possession—a depiction of Beta done over the years of observing her from a distance. Everything about it is perfect; from the way her sun-kissed locks cascade around her petite face to the look of wonder in her bright green eyes hooded by dark lashes. She truly is exquisite. He touches her charcoal lips with the familiar yearning in his soul. Only then does he turn away and head down the spiral staircase to the leisure area below.

"Twenty-three minutes," a slurred voice calls from below. He hesitates on the third step. "How many times can you pleasure yourself in an hour? Not drooling over that sorceress, are you?"

The bottom of the lighthouse always reeks of homemade barley beer. The kitchen is a wreckage of unwashed dishes and the scavenger bugs that feed from them. The single other occupant is the boy's father, hunched over in his stained, overstuffed chair by the dying fireplace. He was once the lighthouse keeper, assigned with the task of protecting the lost ships and representing the islands. That was before the Citadel lit their own light from their taller, brighter tower, and the lighthouse keeper had turned to brewing to occupy his time. Now the lighthouse is no more than a crumbling monument to the man's uselessness. He seems to recognize this and takes it out on the boy whenever he gets the chance.

"You'd better be down here to do some chores. This place would make a pig sty look like Wight's Keep. And get some food. I'm wasting away down here while you're spying on that poor, innocent girl."

The boy silently heads straight for the door before his father can hurl more demands. He has his own business to run, and he won't let the slurred beratements bring him down.

He heads down the precarious stairs to the bridge that will take him across the water to the next nondescript island, and then the next, until he reaches civilization. The lighthouse's island is little more than a pile of slick rocks rubbed by the ocean daily. He is careful to skirt around the outcrop that hides the apprentices on their beach. He has no interest in being hassled by the boys while Beta watches with a smirk. She may not take part in his torture, but she does nothing to stop it.

"Hey, Mumps!" The name stings worse than any belt lashing. He keeps his head down and ignores Rolith's jeers. He isn't fast enough. The sorcerer stands on the edge of the boulder, towering over the boy, taking a hero's pose. Why is it that attractive people always assume the most confident stances? The boy will never know, as he has never been considered attractive. "I'm talking to you!" The boy pauses on the bridge, keeping his eyes on the rotted boards beneath his feet.

Behind Rolith, Beta claps her hands together to dry instantly. The water mage, Painter, or whatever his name is, grits his teeth as he communicates silently with the water over his body. It leaps off him in odd little spurts before finally running down his legs and onto the rock. The boy hates how easily they control the elements as extensions of themselves, using energy to move and influence nature as easily as their own bodies. The stone mages are left to use towels as best they can. The sorceress jabs Rolith playfully in the ribs. "Leave him alone, he's got a shit enough life as it is." The boy wants to tell her the truth, that Rolith's insult targeted one of the boy's most obvious flaws and therefore shows a lack of creativity that embarrasses only himself. Perhaps something more impressive would be targeting his deeply hidden psychosis or that he is unable to relieve himself standing up. That would have hit its poorly aimed mark. Insulting his pock-marked skin, scarred from disease in his childhood he could not control, is cheap.

Rolith and Beta begin debating light-heartedly and he seizes the chance to make a quick escape while their attention is diverted. His days are long enough without her sea-foam eyes boring into his back with disgust cleverly disguised as pity.

Jagged rocks give way to cobblestone after the third bridge, and civilization begins to unfold. While the business of the northern islands like Veden are based on incoming merchants, the southern islands belong to a different economic system. The shallows between Elgireth and the East Sea are home to the last large settlement of leemoahs, thanks to its unique and isolated location. The humanoids of the sea prefer to build their cities in shallow waters between land and open ocean where they can travel quickly or trade with landwalkers. While Veden belongs to the sailors, the leemoahs have claimed Dunlin for themselves.

The leemoahs are scaled creatures, with faces that resemble the long snouts of horses with short fangs. Their eyes, like their scales, come in every variety of ocean color, from soft violet to deep blue, to vibrant green. They have webbed hands and feet and a fin that runs from the top of their head to the tips of their rudder-like tails. They are the only known species to boast feathers despite being primarily an underwater species. The material is highly sought after by the magical community for its unique waterproofing properties. The feathers range in a rainbow of colors and can be nonexistent or as thick as human hair. From the boy's experience, those with more head feathers are considered superior to their bald counterparts. All adorn themselves with piercings from shipwreck-scavenged precious metals.

The leemoahs offer their own unique commodities at their stalls: metal forged by submerged volcanoes, recognizable by the pockmarked, bubbled texture that makes it so valuable on land. Baubles are created to hold pockets of air beneath glass imperfection. These pockets hold spells to protect the wearer or trinkets of sentimental nature. The boy himself has one of these, an amulet from his mother that has a bubble holding her last breath. Island magic will give him strength through it, or so the old leemoah cleric who watched his mother die had claimed.

"Oi, foam face." A wrinkled human hand beckons him from the shadows of a water tower. "Your pops been brewing lately?"

He sighs and approaches. "No more, Dest, you still owe me from last time." With his father too busy perfecting his recipe to worry about trivial matters like food or jewel shards, the boy often carted the excess to Dunlin to sell to the locals. The human population in an otherwise majority leemoah community are always looking for something to drink besides the salt ale preferred by the locals.

"I gave you those magic seeds, didn't I? You owe *me* as far as I'm concerned."

The light casts strange rays on the old man's rigid face. Decades of stormpox spurred by alderwine has left him more sea monster than person. Luckily for him, the boy is above bringing up his bully's 'foam face' appearance. He shook his head definitively. "If they were magic, perhaps. All your valuable seeds sprouted were brown bushes and disappointment."

Dest snarls. "I hope you didn't let them die. They're an investment, you know. Would have brought you good luck in a year or so."

"Well you didn't mention that before, and I certainly owe you nothing if that's how much work I had to do to get anything out of them. Jewels or precious stones. That's the only currency recognized on Elgireth."

"Or perhaps you'd take some pox cream for your face," Dest screams as the boy walks away. Again, with the less-than-intelligent insults. Are there no clever minds left in Andriel?

He approaches the woodworker's hut where his second income comes from. While no trees grow farther south than Veden, there is more than enough driftwood washing up on shore from the bay and the sea to create gray furniture for those with an expensive taste. Most patrons are sorcerers looking for desks or chairs for offices in their high tower.

Inside the hut, the air is choked with sawdust and the smoke from the constant fire fueled by unused chips. The woodworker, Baldur, hones a knife and whistles cheerily to himself. His good mood dissipates as the boy walks through the door. "Waves be damned, boy, I told you not to come in today."

"I need work. Dad's already drunk so there's not much else for me to do." He stands, awaiting instruction in the doorway.

Baldur wipes sweat from his forehead with a greasy rag and waves the boy away. "Not enough business, kid. Interest in wood furniture has gone down since Gafforah started exporting for cheaper. I can barely keep this place running for myself. Why don't you see if any of the fish people around here need help? There's always demand for their bubble metal. Aryet knows why."

The boy stays where he is. He knows as well as Baldur that the leemoahs will not hire a landwalker when there are unemployed among their own tribes. With no income, he may as well take up brewing and drink his days away with his father. "I can't sweep the floors for today? I'd take some fresh water or bread as payment."

The muscled woodworker throws his rag at the boy. "Get out, poxface! I told you I don't have anything for you."

The boy has had enough of the insults. He snatches a carved piece from the table at the side of the door before bolting. He can hear Baldur's screams behind him, but years of dodging hurled objects have made him quick on his feet. He ducks down a side alley and holds his breath until he can no longer hear his pursuer. Once safe, he inspects the stolen object. It is a sort of amulet carved from well-oiled black wood. There's a luminous sea stone the size of an eye set in the square frame and a miniscule latch that opens a secret compartment on the back. It has to be worth quite a few jewels. Good. The boy dons the necklace and heads back for the lighthouse, hoping to snatch an unwatched hunk of bread or fish on his way to stop his stomach from screaming.

~ 3 ~

WENDWYNN

Jagged slabs of granite, set afire by hell sparks, filled the sky with the burnt stench of inevitable doom. The clouds were eerily beautiful, lit from below, their tops casting eerie shadows in the night sky. The soldier found himself focused on this heavenly show instead of the chaos around him. It made it easier to tune out the screams of the dying.

He had done his share of screaming but his vocal chords were raw and useless now. The remaining strength in his body was conserved for the weak heartbeats that pushed his lifeblood from his body. Breathing was a burden, and any medical treatment was a laughable concept. Already, three healing mages had passed him by, assuming him dead. They were right, of course, if not slightly ahead of themselves.

"*No!*" Six glistening knights appeared as though summoned by the shout. They were menacing through the chaos, their armor gleaming beneath bloodstains. They circled the dying soldier with weapons pointed out.

A woman fluttered into the protective circle, wearing unimpressive armor and a helm that hid her face. He knew who she was before she removed the gear, by the chains draping from her shoulders to her collarbone. Only one woman in Gafforah wore such finery. The soldier's labored breathing paused for a painful heartbeat. He could not stand, much less bow. He could do nothing but acknowledge her presence with a blink. Her wild, dark curls had been pinned back from a round face with high cheekbones and a wide nose. Her skin was the color of polished bronze and her angular eyes were an especially bright blue in contrast with the soot and blood around them. She was a goddess, taller than most men and exuding an undeniable aura of greatness. "Syfer, stay with me."

Were those tears? Could the queen truly be mourning his passing? He must be hallucinating. They had never been close in life. He assumed she only knew him by his family name. "Your Grace, we cannot remain here much longer," Sir Embyr said with a tremor in his voice. The enemy had noticed the abnormal cluster of royal guards and would be converging soon.

The queen handed her great sword to a knight whom the soldier recognized as Captain Nalag in favor of a curved dagger. The boy couldn't keep his eyes off of the massive blade, six feet in length with a channel running half of the length and the infamous blood-red stone of Hearthslayer. He wished he could have seen her cutting through the enemy frontlines as part of the vanguard, but he had been in the flank, supposedly safe as his father insisted. The queen placed a warm hand on his forehead as she drew the dagger's blade across his neck, mercifully quickening his death.

The woman, Wendwynn, stood and retrieved Hearthslayer from Nalag, who was struggling beneath the bulk of the war sword. She was back in the fray in the next heartbeat. She fought with a new ferocity, determined to end the conflict before more children died. Syfer had been fourteen, she knew that much about him. She glimpsed his father across the field, fighting with the terrifying speed House Seran was known for. He was oblivious to the death of his middle son. There would be time to drown their sorrows in ale later.

Sir Embyr deflected a war axe with a clang of metal. The queen was reminded there was no time for tears. She had a war to win.

From the cliff sides, one of the catapults crumbled, bits of flaming tinder raining on the combatants below. Pieces of building collapsed with them, making her grateful they had evacuated Uldin earlier. "Your Grace, they've broken through the east wall."

The queen's eyes turned to the messenger. He was no older than Syfer. "Thank—" She was cut off when an arrow pierced the boy's throat.

"Where is Frejith?" she screamed. The sorceress was wasting precious time they did not have. Wen's guards followed her like bloodied ducklings as she fought her way towards the stairs that wound up the beach to Uldin, high above. Hearthslayer sang a strong baritone as it swiped spears and swords aside like wheat beneath the scythe. "Come on," she whispered. Anytime now.

There it was, a brilliant flash of green fire from an arrow shot into the clouds. Amidst the ruins of the east wall, a man with green-gray skin and matte black armor screamed for his men to stop fighting with panic in his throat. Wen knew he was seeing horrible visions thanks to Frejith's magic. From what she had heard others describe, he saw massive, twisted snakes of fire alive and hungry in the sky, spewing fear and lava among the ranks of the enemy. The man called for a retreat and his soldiers looked to him in confusion. The moment's distraction was more than enough for the queen's army to make the final push. The queen laughed and swung her blade with renewed vigor. Her soldiers echoed her efforts. Their war cries were louder; their swords hit harder and found more flesh. The tides were changing.

"Gafforah, to me!" She raised her great sword so it caught the orange glow of the night sky in all its battle glory. As one animal, her warriors adjusted so the enemy had to either face their weapons or be pushed into the frigid bay waters. The man in black armor screamed in agony as he clawed at his eyes, desperate to make the visions stop. There was nothing he could do. They were in his head, as part of him as his thoughts.

Wendwynn's enemy, the Mangzarians, were confused, but ever engulfed with their thirst for blood. It would be their undoing. They were oblivious to the changing formation as most could see nothing but red battle lust. The weakness of their leader would make them fight harder, but with lack of restraint or watchfulness. Everything was in place. The queen raised her hand and grasped the token in her fist with white knuckles. She could not naturally use magic, but there were always loopholes for those willing to look for them.

There was a sound like the splitting of the earth as the stone splintered in her fist. At the shoreline, the water mages would be calling upon the bay to engulf the enemy. The Mangzarians were cut off from their ships and would not be able to fight the elements as well as the Gaffori. She could hear the roar of the water now and see the wall of frothing death as it swallowed warriors brandishing bloodied weapons. Their fighting skills would do them no good now.

She laughed. Victory was hers, and it only made it sweeter that every one of her advisors had told her she would be defeated. She could not wait to hear what they had to say now.

~ 4 ~

KEYRA

The sea, in its fickle way, has proven unkind. There is a distinct stillness pushed by intense heat that can only mean there has been a storm on the open ocean. The strangely quiet waves bring remnants of those unfortunate enough to get caught in the gale. Scraps of sails and ruined goods follow in numbers. The Elgir scramble among the beaches on the east side of the island around Harden, but it is Hardock that is hit the hardest. There are no sailors gathering in queues for barges, and no money to be made. Most people hide from the heatwave that beats mercilessly on rich and poor alike. The taverns remain full—now with locals instead of travelers.

Keyra and Isah are among them, drowning what little jewels they have left in ale and pastries. Ilyin sits across from them, muttering to herself as she fights with a cross stitch. "I swear I can't stop sweating long enough to see where my needle goes. Damn this island weather."

Keyra can feel the sweat herself, gathering in the round dimples of her plump body. Aching joints and a sedentary job followed by frequent tavern visits have not been kind to her. "At least the ale is cold."

"Until they run out of ice chips. No ships means no more

product. We'll be living off fish and strained seawater before the end of the week," Ilyin mourns.

"The ships will return," Isah says, lifting his mug in a salute. "They always do, no matter how bad the weather."

Keyra is constantly charmed by his upbeat nature. There is nothing bad in Isah's eyes, only potential for good. His people have called Elgireth home for generations and carry with them the native beliefs of good karma and strength. She is an immigrant and carries a heaviness that the sea breeze cannot lighten. She adds to Isah's optimistic outlook. "Whatever storm that caused this humidity could be headed this way. Then we'll get some welcome rain and whatever sailors were outrunning it will be trapped here for a few days. We'll make up the jewels we lost."

Ilyin, never satisfied, throws down her cross stitch with a sigh of frustration. "I should've gone to Harden like my mum always said I should. But no, I had to keep the family home on the bayside where the views are nicer. Little did I know the views in my shard purse should have been more important than the horizon."

Keyra can stand it no longer. She drains her ale in one long gulp and wipes the foam from her lips with a loose sleeve. Isah watches her in captivated silence. "That's enough of that, now. I'm going down to Oldeville, maybe Tika needs help around her hut."

"Sure, ask the witch if she has any manual labor to pay for. Mayhaps she'll set her magical broom down and give you a rush one." There will be no satisfying Ilyin; she is a bottomless pit of misery. Keyra can't say she blames her. The heat and lack of income are enough to drive any islander mad.

Isah senses the bristling in Keyra's shoulders and sets a few pieces of jewel on the table. "This one is on me, Ra. Go see what Tika is up to."

Keyra nods to him gratefully and leaves the tavern, Ilyin's

whining voice chasing her out over the bawdy patrons. Despite being surrounded by ocean on either side, Elgireth is often a claustrophobic nation, especially here on Veden. Keyra owns no boat so when she needs space, she is left to walk the length of the barely five-mile-long island.

She lets her mind wander as she passes the stone and driftwood huts clustered together at the docks. The dirt path turns to mud as she heads down the slope to the marshy Oldeville where water and land churned by countless feet combine and the poorest of Elgireth take up residence. Here, the huts are made of the abundant mud and marsh grass, with crude doorways covered by ragged scraps of old sails. Dogs chase mud crabs and children alike.

Somehow, she is grateful for Oldeville, even if for the sole purpose of getting away from Hardock.

"Excuse me, miss." A small voice prompts her to touch the purse on her hip.

"What?" she asks the chubby red-headed boy who stands uncomfortably close behind her. He stares at her with a vacant paleness common to the people of gray-skied Waheth. "Keep your hands to yourself, outlander. I've been having bad luck with young foreigners and I don't plan on being robbed today."

The boy scratches at lice and his sleeve falls to show his skin is several shades lighter than the bright pink of what is exposed to the sun. "Sorry, miss, you, uh, reminded me of my grandmum. I'm lost—"

"Grandmum, eh? Quite the charmer we have here. Unless you've got jewels to buy a flag for your skiff, be on your way."

"I'm lost and my friends are dead."

Keyra hates children. They never listen. This one is particularly needy and insistent. "Your name?"

"Tilsman."

"Odd name. You Wahelthian?" He nods his head. "Stop

crying, Tilsman. I can't help you if you can't help yourself. You came on a ship, right?"

"The *Straying Trout*, miss. Me and my mates overslept, and they shoved off without us. That was before this cursed heat set in and people stopped coming here. We thought they'd notice and come back by now. Then, I found them." He blubbers again and Keyra can't deny she feels chills at his words. Any manner of strange folk come through Hardock. Chances are there are bound to be one or two who mean harm.

"What happened to your friends? Quietly." She leans forward and waits for him to dry his eyes.

"They looked like they'd been eaten from the inside out. Their eyes were all rotted. I ran away. I couldn't look—" Keyra claps a hand over his mouth as he becomes hysterical. A disease of some sort, brought from a distant land? It has happened before. Such dangers, if left unchecked, could wipe out an island.

"Did you tell anyone else about this?" He shakes his head "no" through her silencing hand. She ponders her options. She could take him to the Maroon Men, the local authorities of Veden, and he would most likely be shipped back to wherever he came from and the dead gathered up. She could let him figure it out himself and be on her way. As much as she hates to admit it, neither are good choices. The Maroon Men are jaded and have little care for Elgir, much less foreigners. No, she will have to be responsible and investigate the extent of the danger for herself. If she leaves it to law enforcement, any potential danger to herself and her friends will be covered up in the name of protecting the peace. She'd rather know what she's facing, and whether she should flee the island. "Good. Take me to where you found them."

He obeys wordlessly and leads her down the street. "What were they doing when they died? Why did you get separated from them?"

"They wanted to go to the pub, and drink only makes me

sick. I saw them leave our room at the inn, and they never returned. I found them in the alley by the pub."

They are taking roads that lead deeper into the slums where the path refuses to release the feet of those passing through. Keyra's shoes make a distinct sucking sound with each step. "How long ago was this?"

"Just last night. I slept on a bench by the docks. I kept hoping a Maroon Man would ask me if I needed help, but no one came." They reach the pub and he takes a deep breath before pointing down a covered alley, the dark afternoon shadows making it impossible to determine what lay beyond.

Keyra puts her hand on her knife before proceeding alone. Had it been a Hardock boy, he would certainly be robbing her. Foreign lads aren't so clever.

Her eyes adjust slowly but she can smell the corpses long before she can see them. The humming of parasitic insects already gathering confirms the stench of death. Keyra holds her breath and the scene continues to come into focus. The boy is telling the truth. The adolescents appear as though their fluids have been sucked from their bodies, and their eye sockets are blackened as though they've been struck by lightning. Keyra's stomach lurches and she flees to the sunlight. She has experienced many troubling things in her life, but she has never felt this disturbed.

The boy tears up at the sight of her face. "No one's come to get them? I thought for certain someone would notice by now."

"Wahethians are nothing but trouble. I hear they take sheep as wives. Your friends marry sheep? Is that why their eyes are being eaten from their skull?" She has the urge to yank at his ear and remind him who is in charge here.

"Not Mocke and Runas, for sure. Do you think it's because they're not from here? Am I next?" He is terrified.

Keyra has decided she needs to get him to an authority who will take him far away. Her strides are long as she rushes back to the town where she can dump the kid. Hopefully, the Men in Maroon put him on the first boat to Gafforah; or better yet, a ship back to Waheth. She catches Isah's eyes as they pass through the marketplace. She looks away quickly. If this boy is carrying something, there is no sense in exposing her friend to it as well. "Why did you ask me for help?"

"In Waheth, men in uniform around the city are there to help people. Here, they are rude foreigners who—if they speak the same language as me—only curse me. This is a horrid place. I've been scared to talk to anyone. Like I said, you look like my grandmum and she would have helped me in this situation. Plus, I saw you use magic against those cabin boys. Are you a witch?"

"I'm a witch as much as you're Mangzarian. Just another reason to call this island horrid, I suppose. Crime doesn't get noticed here unless it's reported. Makes it easier to sell slaves while it's still illegal here. No Maroon Man is going to approach a sniveling little boy who looks like he ate the last person he talked to. You're lucky you weren't snatched up by slavers." It truly was luck. Any other time, snatchers would be drifting through the crowds. They had to be quick and discreet, but once someone is gone, there's a strong chance no one will come looking unless the kidnapped is a favorite among the island folk. For now, the gale and still winds have scared them off.

"No offense, but why would you ever want to live here, miss?"

"Stop calling me miss." She slaps him soundly on the ear. "It's an insult after calling me a grandmum. I'm Keyra. Not that it matters. I'm dropping you off at the station and then headed for the nearest skiff that'll take me down to Dunlin where I can pretend I'm a leemoah. Hardock's been nothing but trouble for me. And you, it seems." She wonders what it would be like to leave Elgireth forever, to embark on an adventure. She shoos the ridiculous notion from her mind. She is too old for all that.

They reach the stone building and Keyra leads them up the steps. Tilsman stops before they enter the flaps that let in the cool sea breeze during the summer. "They're going to deport me, aren't they? Back to Waheth?"

"I'm sure they'll ship you off to wherever you came from." She doesn't want to ask if he had family there. She doesn't want to care. She feels a headache coming on and is thinking fondly of her bed.

"Look, gran, I'll do whatever I need to for testing or whatnot so that you know I'm not just going to spread the virus somewhere else. Just don't send me back to that wasteland."

"And who is supposed to take care of you? Me? That will never happen. Now go inside and find an officer. I have to get back to work."

She walks away before he can respond. The sooner she is far away, the sooner she can forget this whole thing. She cannot explain how every inch of distance she puts between them makes her shoulders heavy and her head throb.

~ 5 ~

BETA
&
THE BOY

"The eel guts, as I'm sure you can tell, give a rather unique smell." The lecture hall is alive with exclamations of horror. Pairs of students hold up burning eel flesh for the professor to inspect. He squints through tiny spectacles, his own nose withdrawn with morphmage magic. The purple scar over his right eye glows faintly. "Now, now, it does the body good to be challenged occasionally. While the eel odor may be unbearable, its entrails are unique and should be recognized quickly on, say, a battlefield. Why is that?"

He points to a student in front. "Because eel entrails are a common ingredient for magical explosives. Catch a whiff in the woods and someone's most likely laid a trap nearby."

Beta knocks the pencil off her partner's nose where he'd managed to balance it after twenty minutes of failed attempts. She waves it in his face disapprovingly. "If you took notes with this for once, you might learn something," she hisses.

The professor's eyes flicker to her disapprovingly as he

drones on. "Correct, but what type of magic utilizes these ingredients for destructive purposes?"

"Red witch magic," Beta's partner answers while sticking out his tongue at her.

"Very good. The women of Lizaq can create magical compounds for explosives, healing potions, as well as sap abilities from other styles. Which of the five categories of magic do these methods fall into?"

Beta raises her hand before her partner can. "Power," she smirks at the distracting student.

The professor replaces the eel entrails into their jar and mercifully seals it. The smell fades but will linger on their clothes and hair for the rest of the day. "Very good, battlemage. As you all know, Elgir sorcerer magic is a subset of the Life category. While we are much more limited in the extent of our abilities, members of the Citadel can set themselves apart with their training to observe their natural surroundings and sense things like eel in spells. All of your assets are necessary to realize your full potential."

When the gong finally sounds for class dismissal, Beta's lecture partner blocks her exit. She's clearly touched a nerve by ruining his pencil-balancing career. "Beta, right? Vendar's apprentice? Are the rumors true that you like men with a little gray in their beard? I could dye mine, we learned how in Wahethian culture class."

Beta feels her face turn a bright shade of red. "That's none of your business." She knocks him in the shoulder as she pushes past.

"Another admirer?" Rolith tickles her neck with his breath as he sneaks up behind her. "Try not to break the poor boy's heart."

She shoves him playfully but doesn't push him away when he comes back. "You'd better get in line."

Rolith makes a noise of disgust. "Sounds like too much

work. You know I don't like waiting, especially in an orderly fashion."

"It's my loss then." Beta slings her bag over her shoulder and they move together out of the lecture hall.

Rolith checks his hair in the reflection of a door window as they walk. "We have a free day tomorrow. Feel like going to Hardock for a little drinking with foreigners?"

"We'll see if I survive today, first. Vendar's got it out for me."

"I've seen you practicing daily. It takes an incredible amount of concentration to maintain fighting stances as well as control of the elements; even for someone like you. You awe everyone you meet, my little battlemage." He touches the orange scar on her cheek fondly before melding into the crowd of other students.

"I'm no one's little battlemage," she grumbles before moving on. She pushes through the halls filled with students, lost in her own thoughts despite the many eyes that watch her pass. There are a good three hundred sorcerers and sorceresses in the Citadel, but Beta is the only student who bears the orange scar of a battlemage. She is used to being a constant source of curiosity and awe. If only they knew how much she was expected to master before being released into the world.

The grounds around the monolithic tower of the Citadel are no less crowded but at least here Beta can put up her hood and drift through the groups unnoticed. She heads across the lawn kept green by magicked weather and down the white-stoned path to the shore. At her back, the great tower cuts through the sky, its shadow ever present. Here there are only a handful of students lost in their studies as they hide from the chaos within. She walks parallel to the bay, her way lit by sand turned pink from the setting sun. While most sorcerers are headed to their bunks, Beta's training has just begun for the day.

She cannot say why it is imperative she train so hard. In the end it will not matter. Elgireth never goes to war. The last true battle was years ago when Vendar was still an apprentice and battlemages existed beyond Everlyn Island.

Vendar is meditating, legs crossed on the sand, when Beta arrives. His veins glow a soft sunset orange beneath his skin, showing the bones within. The trait is unique to battlemages. The threads of sunset light develop with use of their magic as the abilities are too strong for an average human to maintain. Beta wonders when hers will be noticeable. Ten more years? Five? It is impossible to say. She only knows that the more obvious the magic under her skin, the closer she is to death. It is the grim fate that accompanies the power of a battlemage.

A wall of wind as solid as stone whistles past Beta's ear. Her reflexes barely call the sand in a shield in time. Her feet skid backwards and dig into the wet ground by the surf. Beta kicks off her damp shoes and tosses her book bag to the side in the same motion. She can feel the energy of the earth and the strength of the ocean in a tingling wave through her bare feet. It reaches out to her, yearning for the power lingering under her skin. She is a conduit through which all life wishes to pass. She opens herself to the connection and releases it in her own wind barricade, mixed with the harsh sand grains of her shield.

Vendar is forced to exit his meditative state. He lands gracefully on his feet, as always. The crowd rustles with excitement. There is always a gathering when they train. It is the only time most civilians will see a battlemage in action. Beta turns back to the foamy water's edge where she digs her fingers greedily into the wet sand. Here, the motion of the waves supercharges her abilities. The most power is generated from natural movement. The wilder, the better. Darts of hardened sand propel towards Vendar, echoing the flicks of Beta's wrists. They freeze as the reach of her control collides with her mentor's. His demands of nature are stronger and more focused than hers. She uses the moment where he is focused on her spikes to drag a concentrated wave from the bay. It towers over Vendar, a churning pillar of roaring water. The battlemage keeps one hand extended to block the sand darts while throwing the other out towards the wave. With a throwing motion, he compels it to turn on Beta instead. The young sorceress has expected his action. Instead of blocking again, she clenches her fingers into a fist. The wave dissipates into a mist that fills the air with a salty fog. Vendar disperses her cover with a wind funnel she has yet to learn.

She allows herself a satisfied smile. He never uses advanced moves unless she is winning in a fair fight. She misses his front foot sliding to the right.

The ground beneath her feet is yanked to the side and she lands flat on her back. The crowd cheers as Vendar offers her a hand from above. "You never know your enemy, Beta, even if you think you do. Don't memorize patterns; predict changes."

Beta allows him to help her up and doesn't try to hide the fact that she's staring at the way the sunlight plays in his otherwise dark eyes. He is devilishly handsome for an older man. His skin is of a true waterman, tanned and weathered into a quality usually reserved for fine leather. His teeth are as white as whale bones and work magic on the female viewers. His hair is thick and brushes his shoulders, only his rough stubble showing gray among the black. The network of orange veins over his face from years of magic use lends him a mysterious aura. Only Beta knew the truth. The vein marks are the result of his blood being poisoned beyond repair by the magic he absorbs from the earth. Only she understands he will die suffering, a few short years from now. By choosing this path, she is accepting the same fate.

It is this knowledge that makes the claps and cheers of the spectators seem empty and frivolous compared to the trade she is forced to make.

Vendar grasps Beta around the shoulders and walks her away from the onlookers. They disperse as there won't be more of a show. "I was hoping we could have a more private session today. There's something I think you're finally ready to see."

Beta glances back with a smirk. "Want to give them one last performance?"

In unison, they pull the air around them like a cloak, bending the light with it. To the average eye, they vanish among exclamations of disbelief.

The rest of the walk down the beach is much more peaceful. Vendar motions Beta towards a small rocky outcrop that takes them to an overlook of the sea. The moon is rising in a cool sky of deep violet and indigo, melting like a dripping candle into the silver water below. Beta feels the ocean's breath in her ear and the salt spray tickling her face. Her shoulders relax as she slips into a half-meditation.

"Breathtaking, isn't it?"

"I wouldn't say that. More like breath-giving."

Vendar rolls his eyes. "There is nothing more embarrassing than a warrior who thinks they're a poet. Don't make things out to be more than they are. Tonight, you're going to be learning something entirely unique. This is a technique that must remain private to our kind. No publicity stunts, no fancy footwork for the entertainment of your adoring fans. This is between you and your individual connection with the world. Battlemages—"

"Connect with the life force of all living things, unlike other types who control individual aspects of physical magic. I know."

"Insolent wench," Vendar mutters. "Very well, since you are clearly the expert here . . ." He raises an eyebrow comically and Beta can't help a giggle. "Before this moment, you have learned to draw power from the earth and the air respectively. However, you can take it further. Focus on the moon if you will."

That is simple enough. Beta finds herself sucked into the crimson-soaked eye in the sky. It is a full moon, and she can feel the pull of the tides, interrupted by her demanding presence.

"Do you feel how the energy of the moon gives and takes with that of the ocean? Hold out your hands."

He guides her palms with his, so they are open to the sea. "There is no pulling of magic in this technique. You are not taking. You are simply accompanying. Your abilities are meant to be part of nature, not to control it. The only way to maintain this balance is to give it yourself."

The air leaves Beta's lungs in a long breath that moves of its own accord. She panics and her concentration slips. "Relax." Vendar's voice sounds muddled as though through water. "Does nature not trust you with its power?"

Beta ignores the reflex to pull away as her breathing begins a new pattern. The waves and her heartbeat become one. Her eyelids droop until they are nearly closed. Through her trance, she can hear Vendar still speaking. "Look."

She looks. The waves have abandoned the earth and risen to reach foamy fingers towards the sorceress. The wall of water is silent, but Beta can hear the pulse of magical energy charging it through her own hands; hands that are taking on a new orange tint in several places. Beta turns her eyes back to nature's song. This is why her short life is worth it. This is what makes her one of the most unique people in Andriel. This is her true purpose.

She is so powerful, the boy thinks as he watches her from his nearby island. He cannot see her clearly from the lighthouse, but her handiwork is easy enough to spot. She is going to become a powerful and well-respected sorceress. His fate is still undetermined. Either his father will finally die and he will inherit the shell of a lighthouse that hasn't been useful for decades, or his father will crack him over the head one too many times and defy all logic in surviving his son.

The demons themselves seem to hear the boy's thoughts. "Oi, pox face, where's all the food gone?" His father stumbles to the kitchen where the boy is watching out the window.

"We've had this conversation before. You spent all the

money on booze. No money, no food." He has no patience for his father tonight. Beta is not safe with that handsy mentor of hers. It is the boy's job to keep an eye on her. There are all manner of foul-minded perverts who find Beta's beauty and power intoxicating. It isn't anything she can help.

"Don't think I won't beat you senseless, whale spit. I work hard all day tending the light to save strangers' lives. The least my ungrateful son could do is provide food. If it's too expensive, start a garden."

"Start a garden?" His eyes are drawn to the window. Vendar is standing close behind Beta, his hands clasping her outstretched ones. "That's a great idea, Pop. Sorry I'm such a sack of whale spit. I didn't realize you were busy tending the lighthouse considering no one's been up there since I can remember. How *do* you fight the spiders every day?" He grabs his coat before pushing past the old lighthouse keeper to head for the door. He hesitates, then grabs the amulet he stole from the carpenter Baldur. Maybe the sea stone will bring him luck. His father's screams follow him as he takes the stairs two by two. Even in his best form, the lighthouse keeper cannot keep up with the boy's sober strides and is left to shake a fist and hurl empty threats. The boy still feels terror until he is safely down the stairs and across the first bridge.

His breath comes fast in his throat. Tonight, he is finally going to do something. Tonight, she will be in his debt.

He perches with purpose atop the rocky hill where the lighthouse stands. Today he is not going to let his fear control him. All it takes is a short walk to confront her would-be attacker.

"Did he see us?" A whispered voice fails to pull him out of his trance.

"Better safe than sorry."

He turns in time to see a rock barreling towards his head. He is hit and collapses to the stones without a scream.

"Heliendiel, he's still moving."

"Because you couldn't hit shore with the stern of a boat, you twat." The boy hears as he twitches on the ground, fighting the enveloping blackness.

"The stern's the backside, numbnuts. Haven't you been a pirate since you could stand? By Akai, pull him in. Maybe we'll get a few jewels for him back in Hardock."

"This is a slave nation?"

The keel grates across stone as the boy's attempted murderers drag their vessel ashore. "Don't think it's a nation at all. Just a bunch of rocks the sea forgot to swallow."

The two men approach their victim. While there are only two, the boy's vision saw four. "Gah, pirates!" His voice cracks as he screams. His brain struggles to send signals to his muscles. He drags himself away with one hand, but the pirates catch up to him at a leisurely walk. They tie his limbs with thick, salty rope. He can see them closely now. They appear Terralian but the saltiness of their skin and the lack of teeth suggest they are more pirate than citizens of any nation. He recognizes the symbol sewn poorly onto their vests as the Tower, the pests of the bay that pick off foreigners and locals alike to sell as slaves when they are not murdering for mercenary pay.

"Ugh, look at his face. Poor bugger. Should've finished him off as a mercy. That rock you lobbed didn't do him any favors, neither."

"Nah, I think it helped cover some of those pox scars. Not much left of his real skin to save."

"Beta . . ." he moans as the pirates haul him back to their rowboat, straining to spot his ward.

"Beta? You mean one of those magic folks on the next cliff? Bastards are the reason we was scared over here and ran into you, poxface. Nearly frightened me to death with that whole waves show. Water was rumbling beneath our boat."

"Ain't nothing wrong with a little magic. Me mum's got a touch herself. Uses it to tell animals what to do and such." The other pirate, who wears a greasy blue shirt and has only eight fingers, shudders and kisses his leemoah-forged talisman. Perhaps the boy is wrong, pegging him as a foreigner.

"I wouldn't trust no animal to do anything for me." They drop their captive with a hard *thunk* in the bottom of the rowboat amidst broken bottles and the stench of slimy rot.

"What d'ya think?" the superstitious one asks, changing the subject. "Should we keep looking for that cove or see what Captain Zai thinks of our little pox-faced friend?"

His friend shrugs. "You know I've been craving a foamy pint all night. Besides, there's sorcerers about. Terralian magic don't scare me, but this Eastern shit is different. They don't need prayers or paints to kill someone. The captain will understand."

The boy's feeling is returning to his tongue. "I've got to help Beta. Vendar—"

Eight-fingers lets out a low whistle. "I don't think your girl's in any trouble."

The boy sits up to see over the side of the boat. Beta and Vendar are on the rocks together, locked in a passionate embrace while water swirls around them, fueled by their fire. He falls back in the boat with a groan. He should have stopped it when he had the chance.

"Rough, scarface. Looks like you won't mind being our prisoner now."

He doesn't reply, but secretly hopes the boat will sink in a sudden storm, taking him with it.

~ 6 ~

WENDWYNN

"**Y**our Grace." The handmaiden stood with eyes politely averted at the doorway to the queen's private chambers.

The sorceress Frejith was donning a light robe that hugged her slim curves. It was on her that the queen's eyes remained as she addressed the handmaiden from her bed. "Yes, Levias?"

"The ambassador from Mangzar is here."

Frejith's lavender eyes darted to her wife. "Do you want me to come with you?"

"Perhaps, love," the queen sighed as she reluctantly reached for her slip on the floor. "Let me assess our friend from the great war nation first." She pecked Frejith on the cheek and retreated to the dressing room where handmaidens gathered to prepare her. "Be certain our guest is treated like royalty, Levias. I will be down shortly."

"I don't like it," Frejith said with a twisted frown. She sat on one of the chairs in front of the mirror, allowing a handmaiden to set her hair straight. "We defeated them just last week. They retreated to their black shores to lick their wounds. What other business do they have with you?"

"Politics are a headache, and I know you hate to waste

thought on such matters. I'll deal with our new friends to the west the way I always have." She gave Frej the wry smile that had won her over in the first place. "Swiftly, and with great style."

She turned, but still felt the eyeroll Frej gave her as she walked away. She hated being patronized, but the queen would not involve her more than necessary. This enemy was a unique one and she feared they hadn't seen the last of the bloodshed. Her audience today would determine how they would strike and how hard, without a doubt. She wanted nothing more than to have the sorceress by her side, but Frejith was exhausted from the magic she'd used during the battle at Uldin, both in her illusions against their leaders and reading the minds of the human enemies. Her role had without a doubt been the reason for Gafforah's victory and dragging her to a diplomatic meeting instead of allowing her a well-deserved day off seemed selfish.

The queen closed her eyes in thought as her handmaidens swarmed around her. They dressed her in a long black tunic striped with white. Loose sleeves gave some relief in the tropical summer heat. A purple-and-white cord cinched at her waist, above pantaloons commonly worn by both Gaffori men and women in a rich blue. Her dark curls were partly piled on her head and the rest left to cascade down her shoulders, threaded with chains so delicate they looked like glimmering spiderwebs in her locks. Charcoal streaked around her eyes to bring out the fierce gray blue that Frej always claimed was her strongest feature. Once her handmaidens stepped back and the short black cape and ropes of chain had been draped over her shoulders, the queen turned to the weapons hanging on the wall. One was Hearthslayer, massive and terrible, but far too large to carry even if it would be an effective intimidation tactic on the ambassador. She chose the dagger hanging on a red strap beside the war sword. With a kiss on the cheek for her wife and a nod to the handmaidens to release their services, Wen swept out of the chamber and down the hall.

"Wendwynn," a voice said as footsteps joined hers. The queen's oldest friend and advisor was one of two people who felt comfortable using her first name instead of her title. The slightly shorter man was from her own nation, where the people grew a head taller than the average Andreli. He had the same bronze skin and golden eyes of their people, but his hair had receded and gone white where hers was thick and black. He was closer to her father's age, and the time in Wight's Keep with her council had enlarged the belly that hung over a strained corded belt. He struggled to keep up with her pace, more from her tendency to walk quickly and with purpose, rather than his girth.

"Grevin."

"Before we go in there, you should know that I have found those books you requested. They have been sent to your chambers for your review."

Wen allowed herself a smile. Her streak of good luck continued. Supposedly, the books had been burned before her rule began. The two of them worked their way up through the windowless halls of Wight's Keep. She had done what she could to alleviate the darkness of her fortress, using bright paints and tapestries to decorate roughly hewn walls of ancient stone. Perhaps it was the ghosts of Gaffori long dead that still haunted the halls of their former catacombs, but she had yet to feel unwatched even in the brief moments she was alone. "Excellent. Is there anything I should know about this envoy?"

"He is frightening and rather gray, nothing you wouldn't expect. But Wen—" He paused at the door and gestured for her to stop with him. "Those books . . . is it wise? Considering everything we've been through?"

She respected his opinion, but often her reasons were hidden to him until her plans came to pass. He would have to trust that was the case then as well. "Knowledge either exists or it doesn't. Wisdom is how you *use* knowledge. Therefore, simply reading the books cannot be wisdom in itself."

She swept into the solar before he could ask more questions. He would just have to be patient with her for the time being. The room had an arched ceiling, and unlike the bulk of Wight's Keep, was open to the sea. Wen had seen to it that every effort was made to open the stuffy chambers upon her coronation. The salty breeze and sunshine were the only effective weapons against the keep's shades.

There were a handful of knights eyeing the black cloaked man at the table with wary trepidation. The Mangzaraian representative appeared oblivious to their distrust. He was helping himself to the fruit bowl in the center of the table, his cloak absorbing the light around him, twisting it into shadow. She would have to have one made for herself.

Wen recognized the sheen of marsh green in his skin instantly. She would have to be careful. Mangzarians were unpredictable, but their native vipr species were more feral.

He stood politely as she entered and wiped his hand on his tunic before extending it to the queen. Wen ignored his offer and took her place at the head of the table. A poured glass of wine was in her hand the moment she was settled. The Mangzarian sat slowly. "Good evening, Your Grace."

"Evening." She was aware of the imposing image she gave even as she sat across the table from the visitor. Besides her height and sharp eyes, the fresh scar on the side of her neck showed she had spilled her share of Mangzarian blood and led her people to victory. "Who are you?"

"Xyver, Your Grace. Ambassador to the sixth district of Mount Thoyax, on behalf of Warlord Halthax ky Dzaxar."

"And what is it your district wants?"

Wen didn't feel like wasting time. Luckily, neither did Xyver. "You and your army have made quite the impression back home. We have underestimated you and are ashamed of this fact. Mangzar is not accustomed to losing battles." Even saying the words clearly pained the vipr. Mangzarians took pride in two things—war and impossibly realistic artwork.

"I would like to point out that Gafforah is defending itself. We did not ask for this war, but if you insist on bringing it as close as Uldin, then we must do everything we can to fight. Perhaps you can tell your Warleader to remain in their accursed black land and leave my nation be."

Xyver must have been instructed to respond to this, as his words were monotone and practiced. "Gafforah is not and never will be your nation. Mangzar refuses to acknowledge you and will do everything it can to destroy your regime. Your very presence here is an abomination." His white-knuckled grip on the arm of his chair shook visibly. Wen wondered how long she would have to talk before he risked it all and lunged across the table at her.

In truth, they were both right. The reasons Mangzar and Gafforah had gone to war were lengthy and went back much farther than Wen's regime. But when it boiled down, her presence on the Gaffori throne had been the last straw. Not to mention Mangzarians were bloodthirsty and bored. They would have started a conquest of the world if the thirteen districts weren't constantly at each other's throats. "If it is Saltspire you want, I will send your head back to your Warlord as answer. The island belongs to Gafforah no matter how loudly you bang your fists against your shields." She knew as well as Xyver that Saltspire's sovereignty was not the only issue. Wen had insulted Mangzar, and specifically Mount Thoyax, by killing one of their own and disposing of the corpse in a disrespectful manner. A different time, but Mangzar had not forgotten.

"Mangzarians use no shields," he hissed reflexively. "Saltspire is sacred land, whether or not it belongs to you. Its history goes farther back than either of our nations have existed. If you stay your war ships from using it as a vantage point and a possible fortress, Mangzar's demands for Gafforah would lessen, and perhaps peace could be in our futures." Wen highly doubted this, but she was not about to continue the childish back and forth of accusations.

Tensions were building and those present held their breaths at the sharp tone this stranger was taking with their queen. Wen, however, did not hold her position for being short-tempered. "I would kindly remind you whose land you stand upon at this moment." Her calm tone and the sharp stares of the silent observers were enough to make the ambassador sit a little straighter in his chair. The queen continued. "Saltspire is mine to do with as I please. As you are aware, I come from a nation where religion holds no place. I fear not your spirits nor the wrath of the waves as, if they do exist, they have seen fit to grant me queenship over this land and victory over your soldiers. Now if we are done discussing the reason for this war, let us move on to the purpose of your presence."

"The captive," he said.

Wen pressed her hands together in interest. She hadn't expected an envoy for her prize. The sole prisoner of the battle of Uldin; Halthax ky Dzaxar the Younger, the Warlord's son and only child. His capture had not been accidental. Frejith's intrusion on his mind had allowed chaos in the enemy's ranks and given them time to take him hostage. Wen had chosen to make no demands to Mangzar nor kill the Warprince upon his capture. She wanted to know if the ash-hearted people cared for one of their own; especially one with a title. It held no real meaning as Mangzarians chose Warleaders by duels instead of lineage, but she was curious as to whether there would be effort made to rescue him. The presence of this unruly ambassador revealed more about their weaknesses than they realized.

"I would think that the Warlord himself would come to negotiate the release of a captive. Why you?"

"Warlord Halthax is busy at the moment, fighting a war. As

someone as well-read as you must know, Mangzarians put little to no value on those that are taken in battle—especially those with titles and reputations to uphold. The Warlord requests that you take his son's life so he may no longer know the suffering of captivity and failure. Let his soul join the spirits."

Wen did her best to keep her composure among this wealth of new information. "So, it is a demand. I see nothing in it for me. The young Halthax is a well of intelligence just waiting to be tapped. If he is pushed too far, perhaps then he may die, but it will not be intentional." The request was too close to asking for mercy. If the younger Halthax meant nothing more to his father, why beg for a mercy kill? She needed to get more out of Xyver.

"Perhaps the Ambassador would like to speak to Dzaxar so you can see for yourself how well we are treating him." Grevin's suggestion brought a smile to Wen's lips.

Xyver was taken aback by this suggestion. "It cannot be in your best interest for us to interact."

"But what about your Warlord's best interest? Would he not like to hear word of his son's health?" Wen played off Grevin's suggestion.

"He would like his son dead," Xyver said sharply.

Wen stood and walked to the massive map of Andriel on the wall. She pointed to a spot on the dark blotch of Mangzar, less than a mile from the bay that separated the two nations. "Mount Thoyax, the Fortress Blackfeather ruled by Warlord Dzaxar. It is a pivotal point in this war, isn't it? Especially considering I have yet to see another district involved in fighting Gafforah. Could it be that your views on our conflict do not align with those of the other districts? You are the closest capital to Saltspire and have the most to lose if I hold the island. I hear you can see it from Blackfeather's walls. I can't imagine what sort of information the warprince must know. He wore the armor of a general on the field, so there must be many war councils he sat in. Destroying such an important fountain of knowledge would be incredibly foolish on my part."

"Very well, Your Grace." He stood and moved to stand beside her at the map. Wendwynn felt the prickle on her neck that suggested she should be unsettled. There was a rustle of armor as the knights present touched hands to weapons and tensed. "It seems there will be no resolution here today."

"Is that not why we are at war?"

She saw the flash of metal before her knights. It was a collapsible blade; a common choice for assassins as it could be missed in searching. He was fast, but so was she. Training had been a part of her childhood that only increased during and after her rise to power. The blade plunged towards her heart, but she spun at the last moment, pinning his arm in her fist. The knife grazed her shoulder, and the queen snapped the vipr's wrist before he could make another attempt. The blade clattered to the ground as the knights descended upon him, suffocating him in a massive pile of heavily armored soldiers. Wen retrieved the blade and inspected it curiously. There was a switch that would conceal the blade within its handle, hiding it from even a practiced eye. She tossed it on the table in contempt. The ambassador was forced to his feet where he looked Wen in the eye fearlessly.

"Quite a bold move, to be sure, although I wouldn't expect any less from the warriors of Mangzar." She sniffed the blood on her palm from where she touched her wound. "Prayer's Wing if I'm correct? A rare enough poison, but not incurable." She nodded to a servant pressed against the wall in terror. "Fetch the apothecary and tell him I need sternblood." They ran off and the queen took her seat again. She had to stop moving to slow the flow through her bloodstream. She didn't show it, but it was affecting her already. Her fingers hummed with an odd numbness and her vision went blurry. She would be dead if she didn't learn from her experiences, no matter how long ago they happened. "Sir Edgar, if you please, take our guest down to the pits where he can reflect on his failure and my mercy."

Armor clanked as her bidding was carried out. The queen's vision went black as she waited for the cure. She chuckled inwardly. Just another day as a conqueror.

~ 7 ~

KEYRA

Today, the sailors come. They trek across Veden, carrying ragged remains of cargo on their backs and on wagons. They are tired and most are wearing little more than threads. The docks are a madhouse of frustrated sailors and the locals looking to make up for lost business. Keyra and the other women of the docks find renewed work in mending clothing and sewing new shirts and pants for those who are more salt than fabric. For the first time in days, she feels a warmth in her chest as her purse fills with jewels. She ignores the mutterings of those who claim they have lost everything at sea and the outrageous prices charged. Let them mutter; their shards sit heavy on her belt.

Through the chaos, Keyra catches a glimpse of a familiar head of red hair. She curses to herself and motions for Ilyin to keep an eye on her stall before shouldering through the crowds. Sure enough, it is the Wahethian boy, huddled on a bench with a sign advertising his usefulness on a boat. No one glances at him more than twice. He makes a sad picture, unwashed and dirty with a frightened look on his face that would scare away even the most desperate crew. She approaches him with hands on her hips. "What in the waves are you doing here?"

His eyes widen with fright at the sight of her. Clearly, he hadn't expected to see her again. "Granma! I did what you said, I promise. I went to the police but they were busy with something else so they shooed me away and wouldn't listen. I waited for hours but then I got hungry so I left and then I got lost and couldn't find my way back." He gulps for air as he has forgotten to breathe between excuses.

Keyra frowns in disapproval. She should walk away and leave him to the mercy of the dock workers and ship hands. She hates that he looks so small and pale. She bites her lip in frustration. "Veden in its entirety is five miles, boy, how did you manage to get yourself lost?"

Tears well in his eyes. He can't be older than twelve. "It was alright yesterday when the streets were empty, but now there's so many people and I can't even see over their heads—"

"Hush your blubbering," she snaps as his hysterics start to draw attention.

"Oi, what's going on here?" Isah has crossed the street from his own stall in curiosity. "Making little boys cry again, are we, Ra? I thought we'd talked about that."

"The kid's upset because no one wants to hire a blubbering Wahethian that could upend a boat by standing on one end. Back to your stall, Isah, I can see the vagabonds eyeing your wares already." The street children are doing just that, watching his pastries with gaunt eyes. The massive baker shakes his head.

"No one's dumb enough to take anything no matter how hard they may look, not after the example I set with Jilden. If you're looking for work, boy, I could use a sweeper in the kitchens."

Keyra pulls her friend aside with a white-knuckled grip on his arm. "He needs to be off Veden, not living here permanently. His shipmates died under mysterious circumstances, and I can't yet be sure of his innocence."

Isah eyes the doughy boy, who is wiping tears and snot

haphazardly on his tunic, leaving ugly streaks and spreading dirt onto his face. "Doesn't seem like the malicious sort, but I've been wrong before. What do you mean his shipmates are dead? I've heard nothing of the sort, and you know how tales fly around here."

It is true, she realizes with a sinking feeling. She should have heard whispers of the strange, dead boys by now. "Perhaps we should make a stop at the station again. This time I'll be sure we speak to an officer." She grabs Tilsman by the ear and drags him down the street. Isah becomes distracted by an overly bold street child and hurries back to his stall before his wares can disappear.

The crowds thin the farther they get from the docks, and soon they can speak without being overheard. Tilsman is quiet, still sniveling beneath Keyra's grip. She won't let him go in case he shows up again, unwanted, to ruin another day for her. "When we get there, let me do all the talking unless you're asked a direct question, you hear?"

He nods obediently. "I ain't trying to make no trouble—"

"'I'm not trying to make any trouble.' By Aryet, boy, do they teach you to communicate by grunting in Waheth?" Keyra gives a yank on his ear for good measure before they reach the precinct. It's as satisfying as she had imagined. It is her duty to ensure there is at least one child in the next generation that respects their elders. The headache that has plagued her since the day before ebbs as she focuses on the task at hand.

Beyond the wispy fabric doorway, the building is dark with no windows and individual candles at each of the four desks. The silence makes her uneasy. It feels like a tomb. "Excuse me," she says, waiting to be acknowledged with thinning patience. One of the Maroon Men looks up with a solemn expression.

"The precinct has been closed until further notice, miss. If you have grievances, you can take them up with mercenaries or the Citadel."

Keyra ignores his suggestion and sits in the chair across the desk from him. "What is this nonsense? Aren't the Maroon Men the enforcers here? Why should I have to go to the Tower for help?"

"I can't give that information out, miss, please just leave."

The man sitting at the head desk notices the disturbance and approaches. He has a magnificent moustache carefully pruned to turn up at the ends, and hair swept to one side to cover his balding scalp. "What's going on here?"

"What's going on here?" Keyra repeats in a shrill voice, "What's going on is that the peacekeepers of Elgireth have given up their duties without explanation. Are you the man in charge here?"

"I am the vice warden. Warden Erlan is currently at the Citadel on important matters."

"If the precinct is closed, then why are you here? Why is the warden at the Citadel?" She's asking too many questions, judging by the clouded annoyance in his eyes.

"This does not concern citizens. If you have a serious grievance, you can take it up with the sorcerers. They are handling things for the moment."

"I shouldn't have to go to Everlyn to have my complaints heard."

"I—hey! You there, stop!" The vice warden stands and points an accusing finger towards Tilsman, who has slipped unnoticed past the officers and is peering behind the curtain in the back of the front room. Keyra is baffled as to how he could have gotten so far without being noticed. "What do you think you're doing?" He drags Tilsman back by his collar but the expression on the boy's face shows he has already seen enough.

"They're back there, Grandma Ra. Belthen and Mocke and Runas, and others. Were there more people killed?"

The situation is growing dangerous. The other officers watch them carefully, awaiting a command. Their hands may be on papers and quill, but their chairs are pushed back, prepared for action. Keyra grabs Tilsman by the ear and drags him back to his seat. She hisses in his ear, "Be more careful, we're treading in dangerous waters here."

The vice warden's eyes are unblinking. "Perhaps you should leave. We cannot help you here. Officer Ilkar will escort you back to the docks."

Officer Ilkar is a massive man with shoulders that threaten the threads straining across his chest. Keyra clutches Tilsman's hand."We can find our own way back to the docks, thank you, vice warden. Seeing as the precinct is closed, I could not impose upon Officer Ilkar to take time out of his day to hold the hand of an old lady and a fat little boy."

There is a moment where he calculates them with his gold-flecked green eyes. Finally, he nods, and Officer Ilkar sits. "Very well. Enjoy the rest of your day. I hear the docks are overflowing with fresh meat."

They take their leave and turn down the path to the docks. Keyra can feel Ilkar's eyes following them until they are out of sight. Only then does she stop and face Tilsman. "Alright, boy, you may have just gotten us on the city watchlist, but you saw something. What was behind that curtain?"

The fear in his eyes is evident, as well as the poor attempt he makes to appear brave. "Bodies, probably a dozen. They were covered, but I could see my friends, their faces were out."

Why would they guard the dead so carefully? Why are there so many bodies yet no whisper or rumors in the streets? Her eyes are drawn to the south, where she knows Everlyn Island is separated from Veden by countless rocky islands. What could the sorcerers want on Veden? The magic users have always considered themselves above the Elgir natives. They never meddle with the locals as there are rarely enough jewels to make it worth their while. If they're available for work, it can't be a good sign for her or her people. Her skin prickles.

"Don't say any more about this, you hear? Now let's get some food and lie low for a bit. Then we'll pay a visit to my friend." Keyra fights the urge to show compassion to the boy. He's gotten her and himself into far too big of a mess to let him off easily.

"I thought you were trying to get rid of me?" He follows her with a new skip in his step. His face looks gaunt compared to the first time they met. He must be surviving off scraps. The prospect of a real meal is enough for him to risk the question.

"Whatever you brought to Elgireth, it's still here, so you're not going anywhere until it's been fixed." She says no more as they reach the crowded part of Hardock. She can no longer guarantee every eye is friendly. She and Tilsman have caught the attention of the Maroon Men and she's not about to wait to find out if they decide the duo is a liability. She leads Tilsman to a small cart with some tables and chairs laid out for customers overlooking the bay. She also has a clear view of the surrounding streets. She has never been one for adventure, but somehow the thought of possibly being watched is thrilling. She feels nerves she'd long thought dead singing with adrenaline. Her palm itches as though it is missing a weapon.

By the time their food arrives, Keyra's foot is tapping rapidly on the stone below the table. Tilsman tears off chunks of meat from his kebab and swallows them near whole. Keyra motions to the cook that they will need another round. They eat in silence. Keyra's mind is racing and she has little interest in holding a conversation with Tilsman, who cannot take a breath between bites much less answer questions. The tailor watches the chaos of Hardock as she eats. Jewels exchange hands at a staggering pace and disappear from belts as street children pass through. She should be down there, making up for the lost days. Why is she so interested in sticking her nose where it doesn't belong? Perhaps it's the strange warmth she gets in her chest from feeling separate from the collective mind of the islands.

Usually, there is nowhere to hide here. Every secret is known, every rumor changes the mood of the entire population. For a dozen deaths, there should be more weapons displayed, more shakes of heads and frowns as townsfolk give their opinions. There was a time when such small world views disgusted her, but she had come to Elgireth to seek out the peace and a good bay breeze. It has changed her. She is a small-town girl: the isolation of knowing a secret no one else does should frighten her. Why does she feel like a young woman again?

"Two shrimp kebabs, some mashed seapeas and a skin of wine." Keyra's attention is drawn to Isah, ordering with the cart keep. She is grateful for the familiar face. She waves him over and he pulls up a chair. There is something off in his face. He doesn't look her in the eye. "Good to run into you, Ra, I think we need to talk."

"Good to run into me? I just saw you not twenty minutes ago. Did you already sell out of inventory?" She knows him well enough to recognize that's not why he's searched her out.

"Something like that." He trails off and eats mechanically. His eyes drift to a figure in a burgundy cloak who is taking far too long to investigate the products at the food cart.

Isah and Keyra share their wineskin and allow the food they hadn't tasted to settle while Tilsman ate his third serving of kebabs. They only speak once they've made their way back into the thick of the crowded docks.

Isah keeps glancing at every face that passes. "Something happened earlier." Here it is, the infamous chain of information that came with living among a thousand. No rumor remains with its source for more than a day. "I saw something. That old drunk, Lod, he was in the gutter as he usually is. You know the one, came with a ship a month ago and never left. I always get him back on his feet since no one else'll get close for the stench. Well, I rolled him on his back, and Keyra, it . . ." He trails off and shudders. "His eyes looked like they'd been burned out of his head and his body was all limp and boneless like—like—"

"Like everything inside's been sucked out," Keyra finishes.

Isah twists the strings of his apron nervously as he nods. "I went to get the Men in Maroon, then decided to go back and hide him a bit so no one else had to see. I was only gone two minutes, but when I got back, he had vanished. No one noticed."

Keyra can't think about the new information too long. Her next step is the same, either way. "It's time to pay Tika a visit."

Isah shudders. "You know I can't stand that witch. She could be behind it, it looked like magic that'd done him in—"

"And nearly fifteen others? They are dead the same way, hidden at the precinct. This is bigger than us, and I don't mean to be stuck on an island that's infested with death." The red-cloaked figure she'd spotted at the food cart is trailing them several paces behind. "Also, she's a Seer, not a witch," Keyra mutters.

Isah glances at Tilsman, ignoring her correction. "Have you adopted this boy?"

"Sure seems that way, doesn't it? I don't have a choice in the matter. We need him for now. Tika can tell if he's carrying anything and whether it's a virus or something more sinister."

Neither of them said it, but they are both thinking it. A curse. If it is something that powerful and left unchecked, it could take out their entire nation. That would explain the Citadel's involvement and the shroud of secrecy.

They head down the muddied streets of Oldeville where the roofs are made of straw and the dogs outnumber the homeless on the street. One house stands out against the bleak land-scape of poverty and misery. A cottage nestled between two shacks, with stone walls painted a bright blue, surrounded by a rainbow of colorful flowers and a picket fence. It is through this vivid archway that the ragtag bunch marches. Within the boundaries of the oasis, the air smells of a summer bouquet of lilacs and daisies. Tilsman is thankfully silent as he admires the scenery. Keyra can't stand any inane questions at the moment.

A rapid knock on the door is answered by a surprised coughing noise and a crooning voice thick with a Terralian accent. "A moment, please!"

There are several sounds of clattering pans. Keyra is lost in thought. Tilsman scrunches his brow in concern. "What exactly are we doing here?"

"Undoing whatever you did with your Wahethian sheep magic. Now not another word or I'll have the good lady we're visiting turn you into a slug."

The good lady in question flings the door wide. She is nobre, with scales the color of sand and head spikes that mimic a crown. A cousin of the leemoah, nobres have small, slitted noses and hooves instead of webbed feet. Both species bear the thick tail, and in place of a fin, nobres have small spikes down their back. Her eyes are slanted and a brilliant ruby red. Silver chains weave through the bone circlet on the top of her head. Her scales are covered with pressed flowers of every variety and golden runes that shimmer when she moves. She beckons them inside warmly. "Ra! How are you? And you've brought friends. Are they joining us for tea?"

"Tea is on Midway day, which was yesterday. I apologize for missing our appointment, I've been distracted of late. I'm afraid I'm here for magical needs, not to enjoy your company." They join the hostess at a table designed for seances and other rituals.

The Seer's smile never wanes. "The two are not mutually exclusive. Very well, how can Tika help an old friend?" She glances to Keyra and then to Isah. "I've never worked with either of you, I should hope that we have been making wise decisions?" She taps her nose knowingly.

"No, not that kind of service." Keyra's cheeks burn red and

Isah looks to the ceiling awkwardly. "This whelp right here." Keyra plucks Tilsman's ear. "He was aboard a ship that may have brought a little unwanted magic from the grassy seas."

"Waheth?" Tika turns her star-bright smile on Tilsman. "Our people are neighbors. What was this nasty thing? A spelled ring? Perhaps a molestia?"

Tika's mask of joy falls when she notices one of her brews overboiling on the fire. "Sand snails! I forgot to add the scalum before it boiled. Keyra, be a dear and tell my patient his anti-poison will be a moment longer."

Keyra rolls her eyes and pulls back one of the many blankets covering the walls. "It'll be a few more minutes of itching that scratch, Sir Alder. For the wave's sake, start going to better brothels or go to your wife, though I know that's a foreign notion to you. Tika, dear, we think this may be serious." Her voice is strained enough to catch the Seer's attention.

"Mind your own business, Ra!" Sir Alder's muffled yells carry from beyond the blanket.

Tika sets down her ingredients and retakes the seat at the table. "How serious?"

"Like a virus. Or perhaps a beast." She does not mention the curse. Best not to frighten anyone if it is something curable.

"There was no beast on the ship." Tilsman shrivels under Keyra's glare. "Sorry to speak, lady, but all we carried were wools and dyes."

Tika moves to kneel at Tilsman's chair, covering his chubby hand with her caramel one. Her filed claws are painted a brilliant gold. "You are wise to speak up. This means either one of your men, or the goods you transported, are responsible for—what was it that happened again?"

"Tika, did you take your potion today? Sit back down and stay there." The Seer obeys. Keyra's matronly demanding voice is not to be ignored. "Something's killing off Elgir and the Citadel is covering it up. Sixteen at my count, including Lod today. Isah found him the same as the others—eyes burned out and body sucked dry till there's naught but skin and bone left."

Tika's mood shifts to business. She sips at the potion Keyra hands her as she mulls over her friend's words. "There have been whispers, although they are never louder than that. I had hoped it was like the stormcat rumors last year. But if you've seen it with your own eyes . . ."

"That's why we're here. I need you to look at the boy and see if he's got anything you can sense."

The Seer's eyes flutter to Tilsman and then back to her work. "I can tell he's special, even from here. I don't sense anything evil, though. More than likely it's some kind of rogue mage that takes out his frustrations on Elgir citizens. The world has no shortage of such thrill seekers. But if you like, I can try a few different spells and see what I can find." Tika is not a powerful Seer, but she is a quick study and curious. Seer magic is specific to her species and powerful when utilized correctly. Unlike sorcerer magic that draws from nature around it, Seers use words in ancient Var written with a variety of instruments and inks to conjure illusions, or shift reality itself. The vast array of possibilities forces most Seers to focus their studies on incredibly specific areas of expertise. Tika chooses to use her gifts to cure ailments of a sensitive nature. With the trust of discretion, she has become the one to see about certain diseases that are best kept from spouses or lovers; customers who are willing to spend quite a few more jewels for such service. Keyra can tell she is eager to use her abilities for something beside curing warts on shriveled men's parts.

"I'm grateful for our friendship, Tik." She feels relieved already. Her friend can handle anything and could be trusted unquestioningly. After all, her reputation depended on her confidentiality.

Tika offers her and her companions a cup of hot tea. "It will take a moment. I cannot guarantee the results."

Keyra sighs and reaches for a wine bottle on the counter beside her seat instead. "Get on with it, then."

"I don't like this," Isah mutters like the old man he is, unable to accept things he cannot understand. "Seer magic shouldn't even work this far east."

"Have a little faith." Keyra nudges him sharply. The baker shifts uneasily and keeps his eyes on his cup.

Tika winks wryly at Isah. "Should you have need of my services, perhaps I can convince you otherwise." She laughs at how red his face turns. Keyra rolls her eyes. Tika loves torturing men. She is convinced it's why the Seer got into her line of work in the first place. The nobre offers a hand to Tilsman. She leads him behind one of the curtains while Keyra simmers the potion for the afflicted Sir Alder.

"You shouldn't leave him alone with her. She's a snake, and there's no telling what she could do to him," he continues to protest. Perhaps the sole reason Keyra had never let a relationship blossom with Isah is his opinion of Tika. She could only guess that it was because of the Seer's chosen career path, or perhaps a distrust of her species, as nobres are foreign to Elgireth. Either way, she has little patience for small minds.

She pushes a glass of wine towards her friend. "Drink up. Tika's a good friend. She only does wrong to those who deserve it. Tilsman, as unpleasant as he is, has her interest. He's safest in her hands until we know he can't melt us all with his touch."

Isah shudders as Tika's monotone, whispered chant drifts through the blanket. "Magic has done nothing but evil during its existence, especially the foreign kind she uses. We were better off letting the Citadel do their work."

"I'm surprised you even care about Tilsman. You don't even know the lad. You could be profiting from this ship surplus the same as me. But you're here, in a Seer's house."

"Trust me, it's not because I care for your friend, Teesman. I care about you, and you've grown attached."

There is a flash of light from the room followed by a crackle of sparks. "At least we get a show," Keyra mutters. She takes a long drink of wine and turns back to Isah. "And his name is Tils—"

Isah falls forward on the table, blood dripping from his ear. Keyra rushes to his side and lifts his head. His eyes are black as though touched by lightning and his skin stretches unnaturally in her hand. She drops him in horror.

Keyra's scream cannot be contained by blanketed walls.

~ 8 ~

BETA
&
THE BOY

"So, there I am, toe to toe with this ham. He's as smelly as he is ugly, and his body is nothing but folds of fat. I tell him, 'I know you nicked it, you're the only bastard whose been dumb enough to bump into me tonight!' And he has the stones to lie through what's left of his teeth and tell me he'd not touched my jewels. Well, goes without saying, I used my magic to surround him with stones. He panics and tries to run, but no matter where he turns, he keeps knocking his head on walls of floating rocks." Malvin slaps his knee excitedly. "It was the funniest thing I've seen in a while, like throwing a ball at a wall over and over except this one started bleeding something fierce. There were some bystanders with their jaws all slack, couldn't believe their peasant eyes. Finally, when he'd had enough, he keeled over, and I took back my purse as well as the other jewels he had on him. Bloody bum would've spent it all on booze anyways."

"And what'd you spend it on?" Peynter encourages his comrade.

"Bought myself enough rounds to join him on the floor." Malvin clinks tankards with Peynter and they drink to the beggar's downfall.

Beta rolls her eyes. "They were afraid of you, you know."

Malvin wipes foam from his mouth. "What's that?"

"The people watching. They probably wanted to intervene but were too frightened that they'd have the same fate. You know, the people you took an oath to protect, and you've taken classes on how what we do affects people, same as me." Beta loves a good time as much as the rest of her crew, but there is something about Malvin that makes her want to put him in his place.

Malvin hates when his mood is altered for the worse. "Swim off. I was protecting them from people like that bum. Didn't you hear me? He lied about stealing my purse and had several others on him. He isn't worth wasting your breath to defend him."

"Enough." Rolith halts any further discussion. "We're here on vacation, not to discuss politics."

Beta takes in the tavern around them. It is decorated with dried coral formations and old fishing nets. The air stinks of fish and the sea. Outside, the dock is no more pleasant and the patrons are drifting home to their inns for the night. It seems business is booming for the natives of Hardock. Good, she hates coming here when there are no sailors. It's more depressing than relaxing. The tavern is filling at a steady rate with locals and weary foreigners alike. "Some holiday spot. A few hours' boat ride and we could have gone to Gafforah. It's arena season there."

"Damn, that sounds better," Malvin mutters to his tankard soft enough that he thinks Beta can't hear.

She also catches the twitch in Rolith's mouth. She leans back in her seat with a groan. "We're not here on vacation, are we? We have the best three Citadel students here, and our choice over Nahem was Hardock? Clearly this is a job."

Why else would they be here? Nahem is the capital of Gafforah, the largest island in Kaper's Bay. During the summer they have festivals and competitions, while Hardock remains a sad reminder of Elgireth's pitiful legacy—a dirty berth for passing foreigners.

"Damn!" Malvin curses. "Wait, three?"

"Yes, Rolith, Peynter and I. It's cute you think I'd include you in that classification."

Beta's reply prompts Malvin to steal a boiled sea carrot from her plate and chew it loudly in protest. "We'll see. When you're unconscious and Peynter's drowning cause he can't get the water to do what he wants, and Rolith's trapped by rocks, you'll see."

Rolith changes the subject before Malvin can antagonize Beta further. "Best four, actually. Vendar's here. He's keeping watch on the entrance." He can't resist getting one last shot in at Malvin. "Also, I'm a stone mage the same as you. When would I ever be trapped by rocks?"

Beta should have known her master would be here. Sorcerers have no vacations. She speaks before Malvin and Rolith can continue their bickering. "Alright, so are we keeping our eye out for someone in particular?"

"Keeping an eye on, more like. There, at the bar. The lee-moah with the cheek feathers. His name is El'rozai, or Captain Zai to his crew. He's a slave trader who sells his own people to landwalkers as exotic merchandise. While despicable, slavery is not illegal on the reef, and as we all know, slave selling is legal in Hardock. However, this fellow has pissed off some of his neighbors. Their Star Shepherd has gone missing, and they have reason to believe El'rozai is involved. They have no proof that he has taken her, however, and cannot pin him under lee-moah law until they can prove it. Our job is to find out if they have the right guy. Our employer requested no one, including Captain Zai, gets hurt."

"No guarantee there," Beta mutters. Her hand grips the wood table so hard she can feel the energy from it cling to her skin. "Haven't the leemoahs learned to handle their Shepherds better? History hasn't been too kind to them."

"It is true that the Shepherd is routinely kidnapped or needs protecting. But the leemoahs are a trusting people, especially when it comes to their own. Someone, we think El'rozai, released gallons of oil into the palace, forcing an evacuation. In the chaos, our quarry, the Star Shepherd, went missing. But that's beside the point. We're not supposed to judge the leemoahs or their rituals, just take their money and perform their requested tasks. We will also do our best to follow all the rules, including not hurting anyone." Rolith shoots Beta a warning look as she frowns into her drink. Her contempt for slavers is well known, as well as her tendency to lose control of her powers when faced with one.

"Star Shepherd?" Malvin pipes up.

"Do you use your books to wipe your ass and nothing else?" Rolith snaps.

"It was only that one time—"

"The leemoah's culture is centered around their star, Ashlikani. Once every thirty years, this star requires a new soul to continue existing. To replace it, the leemoahs call it from the heavens with a traditional dance. It descends beneath the ocean where a chosen leemoah filly must be given to it. She becomes the star's new fuel source and returns to the sky. Only then will the tides remain regular and the fish return to their sea." Peynter is quoting their textbook almost word for word. He sucks down the rest of his ale and belches loudly to drive his point home.

"Seems dumb," Malvin snorts.

Peynter winces as though his companion has struck him. "Come to think of it, a stone mage is the perfect magic ability for you. Takes a rock to understand other rocks."

"So, what is Vendar's part?" Beta often must change the conversation to stop the sorcerers from going at each other's throats. Besides, now that she knows this is work, she intends to take it seriously.

"Vendar is keeping an eye on El'rozai's friends. A high profile, notorious slaver like him needs lackeys to make him feel better about himself. We don't want them sneaking up on us if we have to confront El'rozai."

The slaver in question is deep in conversation with a Gaffori ship captain. Haggling prices could take hours. Malvin gestures over a serving boy and motions to their empty tankards. "Very well, more drinking it is. Got to fit in, you know."

The rest of the evening is a blur, and well into the night. Beta finds herself the last one standing, teetering on a bar stool with someone else's sick staining her tunic.

Old Elgir hymns play through her mind. Subconsciously she takes up a tune, tapping it out on the countertop with her mug's bottom and humming along. The bartender lifts a man's head to clean the bar beneath. "The Widow's Sparrow, eh? A southern lullaby. My mum used to sing it to me."

Beta squints at the stranger. He is oddly familiar. "Did you ever . . . attend the school?"

The man shakes his head. "I am friends with a friend of yours. One that would want you to know your leemoah acquaintance paid his bill and left about three minutes ago."

Beta giggles. "I don't know any leemoahs. They don't like sorcerers. They call our magic archaic. Can you believe that? I can control whatever I set my mind to, but my magic is archaic!"

The bartender rolls his eyes. "Damn mages, always mucking their work up with their drinking. Down Hearthash Lane, little sorceress, and quick, or you'll lose him for good."

Beta turns in her seat to point out Rolith. He is nodding over an empty tankard, a forgotten habalah roll turning to ash in his fingers. She curses to herself. There is no one left to be responsible except herself. She digs through her robe and drops a jewel purse on the counter. "Damn shame I can do whatever except sober myself quickly. Well, I could, but I don't even know where to begin with that spell—"

"Good to know my life and the lives of every Elgir are safe in your, er, steady hands. Run along now, quickly, and maybe choose to say less instead of more to strangers."

Beta is already out the door, engulfed instantly by a heavy humidity that plagues the island in the dead of summer.

Midtown is notably quiet in the gray hours of morning. Oldeville will still be alive with the heat of the night and the wild souls that fuel it. Beta has often escaped the pressure of her destiny among their dirty, uncaring mobs who prefer bonding over swampcrab hunting and drinking. No one and everyone exists in their streets.

Through her muddled senses, she draws from the power in the air and taps into the flow of energy within the air and the ground at her feet. From here, she can sense every citizen in their homes by the motion of their body through the otherwise undisturbed crackle of life. She is the spider in the center of an intricate web, and every breath, every twitch, sends a vibration back to her. It is the rustle of a cloak as its owner turns down an alley that catches her attention. She follows the tendril of magic energy to a flight of stairs. The form standing at a door at the bottom is recognizable by his embroidered clothing and the leemoah rudder that sticks out from beneath. She fumbles with her belt pouch for a flower petal. She blows it towards the target with a gust of magicked air, and it attaches to the hem of his cloak. A moment later, he disappears through the door.

Beta chuckles at her cleverness and turns to head back to the tavern. Vendar's heavily built chest blocks her way. "What's the first rule of being a sorceress in training?"

"I wasn't alone, you're right here." She pokes him in the stomach.

Vendar's cold disapproval cuts through Beta's drunken stupor. "Rolith is no longer in charge of this operation. Spending the first day on a bender not only guarantees failure, but it makes all of us look bad. I thought you four could be trusted to handle such a simple mission on your own. Clearly, you're not ready." Beta focuses on the faint pulsing in his orange veins to keep from crying. "Let me have the stem." He holds out his hand.

Beta reluctantly presses the rest of the flower in his palm. With it, he will be able to find the target wherever he goes on the island. "We were just blending in." She is quickly coming down from the buzz of the night.

"Then have the barkeep put water in the tankards. Irun is an ally. He should have known better than to keep serving you. Now, back to the inn. Sleep off the rest of this idiocy."

Beta slumps under his heavy tone. He stops her once more before walking away. "Don't be stupid, Beta. I can't afford to lose you. No one can."

The slave pit is everything the boy imagined it would be. He and twelve other miserable wretches are crammed into a shockingly small space with a grate just inches above their heads. One of the slaves is dead, or at least unconscious, suffocated by the circumstances and afflicted with some sort of foreign skin condition. The boy does the best he can to keep away from the sick one. The last thing he needs is something that will scar his face further.

His pirate captors have already moved on. There had been no jewels exchanged for his life; only a half-drank bottle of seabottom rum. The boy can't help but take offense.

He had done what he could to protest his capture. He is a native; he has a father who will be looking for him. The latter is half a lie, but they don't know that. He screamed himself hoarse until someone finally stuffed a rag in his mouth and threatened to take his tongue unless he shut up. There will be no pity here. Strangely, he feels only curious as to what this new future has for him. It can't be worse than being an unemployed, untalented, and ugly son of a drunkard.

"Lot 75's just gone out. You're next, Wilda, and then the main event."

"Last, eh? Let me have the block when all the pockets except the cheap bastards' have been emptied? I'm supposing you're still sore about the other night?"

The auctioneer stiffens. "You're lucky I let you sell on my block at all, after the rumors you've been screeching around Hardock about me."

"Twat," the slave trader spits. She turns her wrath on the miserable pile of flesh in the hole. "Alright, you mud pigs, arms up!"

The slaves obediently slide their hands through a slot on the side of the grate. Shackles are locked onto wrists and the grate is lifted. They emerge one at a time and stand in a line for inspection. Hair is sorted and placed strategically over bruises and gashes from former masters. The worst of the dirt is brushed off and the trader looks them up and down individually. When she reaches the boy, she comes to a halt. The corners of her mouth turn down in disdain, her gold tooth catching the sunlight. "By Akai, where did we scrape up this poor bastard? I don't remember him on the ship."

"Couple of pirates sold him to us for a bottle of booze. Figured we'd at least get that much for him at the block."

Wilda shot her associate a glare. "Next time, tell them to throw in a horse." She shakes her head at the boy. "If you're a new slave, you've found your calling. Keeping your head down while doing manual labor is your destiny, for certain."

The heir to the lighthouse keeps his eyes on the dirt at his feet. Hopefully, he will be bought by an especially cruel master and beaten to death within a few days. Nothing would please him more. "What is this?" She touches the amulet around the boy's neck—the only thing he has of his mother.

"That's mine!" He yells instinctively, snatching it away.

Wilda's eyes go hard and a whip unfurls from her waist. "That's seaforged, probably worth more than your sorry life, poxface. You can hand it over to me, or I can take it off your body."

A scuffle ensues as the boy screeches like a tortured piglet while Wilda struggles to rip the amulet from around his throat. The other slaves watch in bewilderment, unable to determine the cause of his mania. "Give it here, you sodden—" Wilda kicks the boy's feet from under him and they become entangled, both dropping to the dirt in a heap. The amulet's cord snaps, and the bauble hits the stone of the auction block's walls, shattering instantly.

Wilda is standing with the whip unfurled, looking rather disheveled. "I'm going to flay you alive for that!"

"Lot 76, to the block!"

She freezes with her whip arm back. The chain line shuffles towards the stairs that lead to the stage, taking the boy out of her range. She points an accusing finger at him. "I hope no one buys you so I can chop you up and sell you to the zarjens myself!"

She disappears behind the corner as the auction staff lines them up for the stage. The boy's eyes well with tears at the loss of the amulet. It was the only thing he had of himself, besides the stolen necklace still safe in his shoe. He is momentarily distracted by a slave standing alone to the side, flanked by two guards. How odd is it for one captive to be watched by two men? The slave's face is covered but he can see the silvery violet scales of a leemoah on her hands and on the tail tip that pokes from beneath the cloak. One of her guardians prods the boy with his spear butt hard enough to make him stumble. "Eyes on the ground, poxface."

He complies, but not before rolling his eyes at the unimaginative insult, and wonders if it's his imagination or a trick of the light that he feels her smile as he passes. It must be his mind. The same one that feeds him the obsession that one day Beta will fall in love with him and forsake her sorceress ways.

The harsh sun bakes away any further thoughts. There is a sea of prospective buyers hiding their own heads from the midsummer heat with colorfully painted canvas and fans. He takes a small pleasure in the fact that the rich he can see are still soaked in sweat through their golden silks. These are mostly Gaffori owners, who come across the bay for the first pick of the slaves before they reach the mother island. Among them are scattered captains passing through and looking for sailor replacements or a rower.

"Lot 76, good people of Elgireth and neighboring nations. Our last lot before the big-ticket purchase, we have an assortment for your selection." Numbers are hung around the slaves' necks.

The auction begins, buyers raising placards for their choice. Bids go up, but there is one number that never raised. The boy's number eight.

Money changes hands among the chatter of the market. Slaves are unchained until only the boy remains. The slave trader Wilda shakes her head yet again at the human. "I jested, but I must say I almost feel sorry for you, boy. I've never seen a slave just not be bought before."

"Everyone thinks he's got a disease," her lackey Nev admits meekly. They push the unwanted slave off the block. The leemoah in the cloak steps forward. She smells like salt and sun.

A leemoah stallion rushes in before she could go up the stairs. He whispers something in the block owner's ear. He speaks urgently and his body language suggests insistence. There are nodding heads and a jewel purse slips between hands. The newcomer takes the filly's chains to lead her away. The boy has nothing left to lose, and he can't deny he feels a connection to the slave. He lurches forward, calling out to the stallion that had taken her chain. "*Aiaari mend'ili*," 'I'm a woodworker,' he says in the leemoah e'likai language before he can stop himself. "I made this." He kicks off his shoe and hands the hidden necklace to the leemoah. Wilda watches with narrowed eyes. The male leemoah takes the amulet from the boy and inspects it.

"This is a mage pocket. It takes quite a skilled hand to get these tiny hinges right." It doesn't seem to be enough to convince him to take on the otherwise unimpressive slave.

"I know the Tower always has a need for woodworkers on their ships. Whether it's carving runes or even patching holes." His statement is a gamble, but he has nothing to lose. The leemoah wears no markings of the Tower but he carries their traditional scimitar and holds himself like a sailor. The mercenaries are everywhere around Kaper's Bay.

For a moment he believes all is lost. Then the leemoah tosses the pendant back to the boy. "If you are as good as this work, you will pay for yourself. If not, at least I get a mage's amulet out of the deal. Six jewel shards," the leemoah offers Wilda. The slave trader shrugs. There's no attempt to get more money for the scarred youth.

The leemoah tosses the payment to Wilda and grabs the boy's chains as well. "Number Eight, eh? A good enough name. How is it you came to speak the Reef's tongue?"

"I study when I can," Eight says.

The leemoah has already lost interest. They are approaching a barge on the docks. Eight's heart races in his throat. Is he finally going to escape the coffin of a rock he has spent his entire life on? Could he truly be more ecstatic to become a slave in a foreign land than to ever see his father again?

As they walk, Eight's hand brushes that of his fellow slave, giving him warmth he didn't know he needed. He doesn't glance once at the lighthouse in the distance as the ship's sails unfurl to catch the morning wind. As they board the slaver's skiff, more payment passes to the hands of a Maroon Man on the dock. It seems to the boy that the slave laws mean nothing on Elgireth when there are jewels to be had. He chooses to soak in the sensation of the sea breeze and the merciless sun before they are led into the darkness of the skiff's miniscule storage. There is no room for them to stand, and they share the underbelly of the ship with four barrels that take up the bulk of the space. The boy can't remember the last time he's been so close to someone that hadn't cringed at his existence. Then again, she could have not gotten a good look at him just yet. The hatch closes behind them and they are left in darkness and an oppressive heat settles on them. The only sound is the breathing of the leemoah filly. When they are alone, she speaks to him in musical e'likai. "Hello."

Could the mysterious angel truly have acknowledged his existence? "Hello." His voice cracks, but he doesn't care. For the first time in far too long, he smiles.

~ 9 ~

WENDWYNN

Gafforah's capital city, Nahem, is unique in many ways. Its docks open to the west side of the bay, accepting traders from around the world that have passed through Elgireth. The harbor is the only part of the city that is flat. The main road, the Street of Angels, carves a dramatic line from the boardwalk to the keep atop the mountain miles above. The way is near impossible to take without frequent rests or climbing equipment. While it is a bane for visitors, the citizens of Nahem embrace it as their greatest defense and a sort of test which only the toughest of natives can pass. The buildings are also a testament to the hardiness of the cliff dwellers. The Gaffori are said to have the blood of underpeople: a long-extinct race that prided themselves in their architecture and engineering. It is from this knowledge that they erected skyscrapers that jutted from the cliff sides like long fingers clawing through the ground to escape some underground tomb. To the sides of the Street of Angels, staircases wove between these towers, cut into the cliffside to ease passage and slow any army that looks for a way around the main road. At the very top, hidden by clouds, was Wight's Keep. The fortress was built straight into the mountain's heart where many black towers and windows cut into the mountain made it look like a great seacrab, escaping from the same tomb as the towers, spindly legs reaching for the open ocean.

Wen didn't care much for the keep. Her first visit almost made her rethink the choices that led her there. Hundreds of years ago, when it was still used for the dead, the leaders of the nation had lived among the *retyot*, the residents who wandered inland among Gafforah's grassy meadows, traveling on the backs of their horse-like creatures, staying connected with the many unique cultures that dotted their island. Wen could not say what happened for the king to decide to take up residence in the hall of the dead. Perhaps they had their first taste of war, or their open way of ruling had been taken advantage of, and they had closed themselves away ever since. Perhaps when the matter with Mangzar was over, she could renew this old tradition and spend her time under the sun instead of under massive ribs from some sea creature that held the roof like rafters.

It was because of her distaste for the dark that she held council on the great balcony overlooking Nahem and the bay. Here, the sun burned through the light silks used as shades relentlessly. Wen herself wore a cream shift and black robe of the same material, save the studs that lined her waist and the hems of the robe. It was a beautiful day and she intended to catch even the slightest breeze. She wore her hair up and off her face in hopes that the sun would brighten her skin and her mood. Around her neck she wore black pearls harvested from Kaper's Bay interwoven with the heavy silver chain links she wore as a reminder of her servitude. The previous emperor of Gafforah had left the people deeply scarred. She refused to let them down by taking advantage of her power.

To her right sat Frej, looking majestic in bright lace and silk, wearing the gold circlet of a master sorceress with pride. To her left was Grevin, sweating profusely in his thick sheep wool. He did his best to appear unbothered by the heat and his choice of clothing. His offices in the Keep were far cooler than here.

Further down the table was the leader of the *retyot*, Sir Nalag, sweat beading on his forehead. Beside Nalag sat Sir Edgar as the representation of her personal guard. The General of the leemoah army, Ip'akala sat across from the queen. Sir Embyr, the captain of the city guard, hovered to Wen's left like a constant shadow.

The council was silent for now, awkwardly fiddling with wine glasses or the arrangement of fruits in the center of the table. Finally, Ip'akala spoke. "Your Grace, you haven't introduced us to your friend." He motioned to the black-cloaked figure standing directly behind the queen.

Frejith glanced nervously at Wen but said nothing. The queen held out a hand for the man behind her and he took it as though accepting her offer for a dance. "My dear, if you would please remove your hood and show my council your face, perhaps they wouldn't be so frightened of you." She couldn't blame them. After all, her guest was special in many ways.

The vipr threw back his hood and Grevin growled. It was Xyver, the ambassador that had attempted her life. His eyes were glazed over strangely and he stood as stiffly as a suit of armor. Nalag swore under his breath. "What is this? Some sort of jest, Your Grace?"

"Far from a jest, Sir Nalag. Our friend Xyver has had a change of heart, so to speak. He will not be stabbing any more queens."

Frej stiffened. She would voice her true opinions later, when it was just the two of them and she could speak honestly. Wen hadn't told her of her intentions, or about the books she had studied fervently for the past week. The memory they would trigger was too raw for her wife. Wen could tell by the rigid way Frejith held herself that she did not approve. Grevin stood and inspected the vipr from inches away. The captive didn't so much as blink. "Incredible. Some kind of spell? I . . ." He trailed off as he began to realize the austerity of what he witnessed. "Your Grace, this vipr appears to be under a Puppetmaster spell."

Nalag, the boldest of the group, pressed his hands to the table and half stood from his seat. "Impossible! Your Grace, you ended the Verycheks when you conquered Gafforah. You cannot tell me that there is one of their undesirable kind still alive? Or is this some sort of twisted version of their ancient magic?"

Wen had been prepared for outrage. The Verycheks were the royal line before she had cut them all down not three years earlier. Their cruelty had been magnified by their incredible ability to control people in ways no one else could. After Wen slayed Haldeen Verychek, the last of his line, the curse over the island had been lifted and the throne all but thrust upon her.

It seemed they had all believed the Puppetmaster magic had died with Haldeen. Wen folded her hands calmly on the table. "Most people believe that magic is divided by species and geographic location. The Elgir have sorcerers, the nobres of Terrial have Seers, the Sidians have demons, and so on. But the Verychek magic was different and *is* different. It can be learned, and I have done just that," Wen replied. "Xyver is my first experiment with the Puppetmaster abilities, and you can see the results for yourself."

General Ip'akala shook his head in disapproval. "King Gar'ithol will not approve. The leemoahs worked with you to end the Verychek dynasty. Many deaths paved the way for that victory." His stern voice was unusual. Ip, as he preferred Wen to address him when possible, had always been a lighthearted soul. He had proven his worth in Wendwynn's rebellion, the leemoahs paramount in her success. His opinion weighed heavily on the queen. "I can't in good conscience stand by while you use the Puppetmaster magic."

Wendwynn bristled. She could not look weak in front of

the other leaders of her war efforts. She would have to stand her ground and beg his forgiveness later. "I'm sorry you feel that way, General. I have thought long and hard about the repercussions of learning magic and decided it is what's best for my people. As regent, I will abide by my decisions. But the leemoahs are ruled by their own king, and therefore you are free to choose your own path."

Ip'akala crossed his arms and looked to the other members of the council. "Are you all going to sit here and let this happen? You experienced the Verychek magic firsthand, more so than the leemoahs." His confidence was becoming brazen hostility.

"My subjects trust me," Wen snapped. "As should you. With my new knowledge, I can use the Halthax prince to our advantage. I plan to send him back to Mangzar with specific instructions and a little encouragement. He will be our spy among the enemy without risking one of our own. He can call them here, where I can use it against the leaders of our enemy and end this bloody war before it puts Gafforah into the sea. If they discover his restraints and kill him, then we will lose nothing. If you think I intend to use this ability on anyone other than our enemies, then I have failed you already." She risked the disapproval of her subjects, but they were scarred from their experiences. If they could see the magic used properly, in the hands of someone who had their best interests at heart, they would learn it was not the ability itself that was evil.

She herself hadn't expected it to work. Her natural connection to magic was nonexistent. It seemed too easy to learn the phrases and write them in blood in the empty pages, channeling her intentions and creating the specific environment outlined in the texts. But the words had been simple and effective. Xyver's dark magic had been useless against her.

Frejith's pale face and pressed lips suggested there would be a conversation after the council. "They'll notice immediately. Look at this one, there's nothing left inside his head."

Nalag seemed to be the only one recovered from the shock of Xyver enough to voice an opinion, especially one so sharp. "My queen, you were not here during the Verychek dynasty. The rest of us were. We saw how they used it to infiltrate their own people and turn those who whispered behind their backs into obedient dogs. It began to feel as though there were more shells than there were actual people. No one trusted anyone. The nation fell into disarray. To reveal that you not only have this ability, but taught it to yourself, would be more than they could stand."

Wen took a moment to compose herself. Frej's inner seething beside her was distracting. The sorceress knew first-hand the potential damage of the Verychek magic, having been a part of the enslaving of Gaffori minds herself. It cut Wen deeply to know Frejith saw the potential for such evil in the queen. She would use the power to save her people. It was their only chance. The Mangzarians outnumbered them and could outlast the Gaffori despite the recent victory in Uldin. She fervently hoped her wife trusted her more than she was suspicious of the magic she wielded. Wen took a sip of her wine. "It may seem odd given my past, but I do not care for war. It ends young lives needlessly and destroys history. I would like this war to be over as quickly as possible, and if that means using the incredibly rare knowledge the Verycheks left behind in their vaults, then so be it. The people can think what they want, but I crave peace."

"Then perhaps I can give some advice." Grevin had been quiet up until that moment. The eyes around the table turned to him. His counsel was always wise. "Keep this ability a secret, Your Grace. Do not let them worry needlessly over whether their future is the same as it would have been with Haldeen Verychek. Keep it a secret from the Mangzarians as well, until the time when it can change the course of war. Use it as a last resort instead of first. No one would expect you to learn the

Puppetmaster magic. If it is information you seek in Mangzar, we have one of our best sorcerers still out there. If you use it against the Warlord, do it in a way that does not draw attention to the magic."

"Ugden Lamaou has been compromised." Wen dropped the late sorcerer's bloody gauntlet on the table for all to see. "His partner sent it to us, which means the mission may still be intact, or he could have been captured and forced to send a message to us. Either way, we have a man in enemy territory who is missing. He needs to be found, and the mission in Mangzar continued."

Frej stared at her hands but said nothing. Ugden had been her friend while studying magic and had fought beside both of them in many battles. His loss had hit her hard. "If the team has been compromised, they will expect us to replace him," Captain Nalag said. "They'll be well prepared to intercept anyone we send."

"Your Grace, what reason is there for someone to be in Mangzar at all?" Ip asked, his eyes on the gauntlet. "I have heard you speak of it before, but no one will tell me the details."

Wen glanced at Grevin, who gave a small shake of his head. The queen turned to the leemoah. "Unfortunately, only myself and a handful of others may know the intention of our mission in Mangzar for the moment. But I can tell you they are pursuing a lead on a great power that can be weaponized to destroy the Mangzarians once and for all. It is both to find this power and connect the Puppetmaster magic with the warlord that I intend to send the lesser Halthax. I have been working with the magic, testing its limits. Xyver, please introduce yourself."

The vipr blinked for the first time and his body relaxed into a normal stance. "My—I, what? Where am I?"

The guards placed hands on their swords, but Wen motioned for them to hold. "Xyver, could you please tell my comrades a little about yourself?"

"My name is Xyver, I come from Mangzar. Well, I think. I don't quite remember." He looked at her strangely. "You're Queen Wendwynn of Gafforah?"

"I am."

He dropped to a knee; his face open with awe. "I am honored, Your Grace! I do not know what I did to deserve to be in your presence, but this is truly an honor—"

"Xyver, return." He snapped back to his feet and his eyes returned to blank lifelessness.

Jaws were slack around the table. Frej stood and excused herself without another word. Wen cursed the hot-headed woman. She would have gone after her if she didn't have business to attend to.

"Not even Haldeen Verychek could do something like that." Nalag made a sign across his chest to ward against magic.

Grevin seemed more interested in fiddling with his sleeve than commenting. Wen couldn't help swelling with confidence. "It would seem the Verycheks were not as ambitious as they would like you to think. These . . . puppets are so much more than shells to be manipulated. They can be retaught to become entirely different people. They can be trained to appear as in control of their minds as those of us at the table here." Her words fell on deaf ears. The council was still in shock. The queen could understand their reaction. "Very well, it seems our meeting has come to a pause. We will reconvene tomorrow and decide whether or not victory is sweeter at the hands of one casualty instead of thousands."

The advisors did as they were bid, and the council dissolved.

The queen knew exactly where she would find Frejith. She headed up the winding tower that started in the heart of the mountain. Here the walls were carved from the silver heartstone of Gafforah. As she climbed, the rock changed from onyx to layers of shale and sandstone, and finally stone blocks as it broke free of the mountain and towered over the entire island.

From here, everything was visible from Kaper's Bay stretching out to Elgireth, to the jagged cliffs surrounding Nahem, to the great forests and hills of west Gafforah. Beyond that, she knew the horizon stretched blue.

Frejith stood on the western side of the tower, leaning over the rails on tip toes like a child with their breath stolen by the breeze. The queen approached silently but nothing got past the sorceress. "That was some show you put on down there, Wen."

Wendwynn moved to stand beside her, letting the breeze cool her face. "I stand by my points. Why risk my people when I can risk one of theirs? We lose nothing if he is discovered."

"What if they discover him but allow him to continue reporting back? What if they give him bad information and then take us by surprise? What if they break the spell and find out what he knows about us? There's too much risk, Wen. It can't be him." She sighed with heavy shoulders. Wen could sense the concerns she had but would not voice. She had been used as a conduit before. "I thought you couldn't even do magic."

"As did I. But the books, in the Keep and elsewhere, they hold more power than I would have ever imagined."

The sorceress was skeptical. "From books? Magic is a power, and it requires sacrifice like any other achievement. There is a structure to who can use it and when. Knowledge may be a big part of that, but I've never heard of someone using knowledge alone to weave spells. Please, tell me you didn't do anything stupid."

Wen pulled away. "Anything stupid like support Emperor Haldeen even if you knew what he was doing?" She was tired of her wife dancing around the true reason for their fight.

There was a breath of tension. This was an argument which neither of them would win. Frej looked to the horizon. "I will be the first to admit that I was wrong in helping him amplify his power. You know that. But this all feels like it's happened before." Her amethyst eyes locked with Wen's blue ones. It was the only time the queen felt helpless. Frej continued, "Promise me, Wen, you'll never ask me to get involved. I don't agree with you using the Puppetmaster magic, and if I increase your abilities, two things will happen. One, I will be no better than the selfish sorceress I was a year ago. And two, you'll become consumed." She hesitated when Wen's expression went cold. "I know what you're thinking, you're different from Haldeen. Of course, you are. But you don't know what it does to you. While it's seeping into the minds of your enemies, it's also poisoning yours. I can't watch you become something you're not."

"If I borrowed it, I could destroy the Warleaders from a distance. I could end this war with no Gaffori lives lost and minimal Mangzarians. Isn't that worth the risk of my own health?"

Wendwynn hated when Frejith was the responsible one. It turned their dynamic on its head. "It's never that simple. Think about it. If you kill them, what happens next? New Warleaders rise in their place. Ones that will seek a vendetta against you. Right now, you are only at war with District Six. If you use the Puppetmaster magic against even one, then Mangzar will unite. You've said yourself that they are proud. They will not accept such a simple defeat. You would have to use it against every last Mangzarian."

Wen's mind cleared as Frej spoke. Her musical voice had a way of doing that. "If you will not help me become stronger in the Puppetmaster magic, then what do you have in mind?"

"You did have the right idea, to send another agent into Mangzar. We need to find out if Zavosh has been compromised as well and rescue him if he has. The mission must continue. There are too many lives at stake. It just can't be a Puppet."

"Then who?"

"I've been thinking, and it should be me."

Wen snaked an arm around her waist and pulled her close, chuckling at the idea. "You always have such big ideas, Frej.

It's endearing, but unnecessary. If you will not allow me to use it against the Warleaders, then trust me at least to use it on one person."

Frej turned in Wen's arms so their faces were inches apart. Her eyes were stormy with worry. "You don't know how it will affect you, even on a small scale. Magic is a power, Wen, and like any power, it corrupts, especially with someone who has never experienced it before. It's a constant battle, even for those as strong as me. You cannot invest yourself in something like this and expect it not to affect you. That's why I want to be the one to go to Mangzar. I can't risk *us* being consumed by it."

Wen didn't like that she had a taste of true magical power, and now she was being told it was too much for her. "You think too little of me, Frej. I have overcome worse obstacles than this, and I will continue to until my body becomes a fixture in the morbid fortress beneath our feet."

Frej reached in her tunic to pull out an amulet with a massive sea-stone center. "Do you remember when you gave this to me?" How could Wen forget?

She had taken the keep, bloodied and frightening. Frej had made her final choice, walking out on Haldeen instead of moving against Wen as she had been ordered. When the Emperor had been slain, Wen had found the sorceress in the hall outside, arms wrapped around herself as she stared at nothing, finally rid of Haldeen's influence and forced to face the reality that some of the choices had been made of her own free will. "Are you going to kill me?" she had asked, unafraid.

"I do not kill in cold blood, sorceress. Nor do I force those with no mind to lose their lives over a lost cause." She had offered Frej the amulet on an impulse. It was a part of her she didn't want to forget, but one that had to evolve just like the rest of her. She hoped Frej would be the one to help her accomplish that.

Frej stared at the amulet. "What is this?"

"A reminder that we are all mortals at heart, good or bad. I do not want to spill more blood here. The massacre stops with you. I was given this with the intention of killing someone who didn't deserve it, and I was able to use it to change the fate of Gafforah and Elgireth forever. I entrust it to you, as one of my new subjects, to hold and protect as I will hold and protect you."

They had been married under the stars in the sight of the waves not a month later.

"I remember," Wen said. She felt ashamed of letting the memory slip. Was she truly turning into someone else? Someone power hungry? She had been warned of the tendency in her family to become obsessed before. She had brushed it off, unable to think of herself as something sinister. Perhaps she needed a reminder.

"I fell in love with you that day, as did every Gaffori. You did the impossible and fought your way up the Street of Angels, with nothing more than a ragtag group of rebels. You offered us a kind of power we never had before. Wen, I cannot let you lose that part of you. The part that didn't need magic to be everything. I cannot let you use the Puppetmaster magic, even for a good purpose. I'm the only one who can go. I'm the only sorceress powerful enough to manipulate my appearance so even the strongest mage cannot sense me. I have been to Mangzar many times and know their culture and language. I can do this, Wen, you just have to trust me like you trusted me the day you conquered Gafforah."

The queen turned the amulet over and over in her palm, relishing the smooth surface. She knew it hummed with a magical energy, although she could not feel it herself. "You just want to have freedom to roam again, don't you?"

Frej shrugged but the light in her eyes was unmistakable. "I'm not made for sitting in the keep and in on council meetings. I need this as much as you do, but don't mistake that for selfishness entirely."

Wen sighed and her arms dropped to her sides. "Damn you, Frej, for insisting on being right. We'll discuss the details later, but you win again."

The smile on Frej's face suggested the win was hollow.

~ 10 ~
KEYRA

The world is a terrible whirlwind after Isah's death. Keyra can remember only flashes—Tika bursting into the room with hands clasped over her mouth. "Ra, I'm so sorry! Ra, I didn't know! I didn't think—"

Tilsman had come stumbling out next, looking dazed and even paler than before. Then the sorcerers had come. At some point Tika had fled, wailing that she could not be found by them. The next thing the tailor knew, she and Tilsman were sitting inside the same precinct they had been thrown out of not a few hours earlier. The Warden is there now, her head shaved to the skin where the sun had taken its toll in rolls of wrinkles. She is speaking in hushed tones to a man in a silver cloak. A sorcerer.

Keyra cannot remember getting here, but she knows she must get out. She grips Tilsman's hand tight and leans in as though resting her head on his shoulder. She whispers when she is close enough that their guards won't hear. "Say nothing. We saw nothing. Isah died and neither of us, especially you, had anything to do with it. Don't mention Tika. Do that and there'll be sweets in it for you, boy."

Tilsman pats her hand to show he understands. Good. Now it is a matter of ensuring he does not forget. "Ms. Anwave?"

Keyra perks up at her surname. "That's me." How did they know that?

The Warden motions for her to approach. "We're going to need to speak to you."

Keyra moves to the seat across the desk from the Warden. "What can I help you with?"

The Warden glances to the covered doorway in the back of the precinct where the sorcerer had disappeared. "This boy, how long has he been in your care?"

"Just today. I'm helping him find passage to Gafforah, or back to Waheth." She must tread carefully and not give too much away as to how they came together. As annoying as the child is, the last thing she wants is for him to be whisked away to the Citadel.

"Why were you in Oldeville if you're helping him find passage? Wouldn't you have better luck on the docks, or back in Harden?" Keyra doesn't like the Warden. Her movements are too jerky, too aggressive. It's as though she's going to fly into a rage at any moment.

"I was hoping to find someone to take him to Harden so I wouldn't have to make the journey myself. Old knees, you know."

"Someone like Tika the witch? You were traveling with another companion, weren't you? Isah La Flore. A friend of yours?"

His name sounds foreign on her lips. Keyra sits straighter in her chair. "The Seer that lives there is a local healer. She specializes in treatments for specific ailments, ones contracted through . . . intimate relations."

The Warden glances to one of her Maroons. He nods in confirmation. "I see. So, you and Isah sought treatment as well as passage to Harden for the boy, correct? Not addressing the fact that such places are not fit for children, and it is concerning that you thought it appropriate to drag him along, how is it that Isah ended up dead?"

"A boy like him needs to learn all aspects of life. Look at the poor bastard, he'll be buying whatever love he needs for the rest of his life. As for Isah's death, I am not familiar with methods of magic. Something must have gone horribly wrong."

"And where is Tika the Seer now?" Her cold eyes study Keyra levelly, searching for any cracks of weakness in the old woman's face. Keyra remains stoic but the heat is getting to her. She wants to be out of here as quickly as possible.

"I could not say. A fatal mistake like that, she must be halfway back to Nath'iki by now." She certainly hoped her old friend would be wise enough to flee Elgireth. She is tied to the strange deaths now, and there would be little mercy from the sorcerers if they caught her. She fights back the tears that well in her eyes as she remembers the inhuman husk Isah had become.

The Warden's eyes soften for a moment. "If you hear anything, be sure to let us or a sorcerer know."

She stands but Keyra remains sitting. "Are you going to find whoever did this? Whatever magic killed Isah . . ."

"I wouldn't fret about that too much, Madam Anwave. We know who is responsible and they will be punished to the full extent of the law. I would suggest going back to your daily life and be sure to remain on Veden."

Every word she says is a lie. Keyra does her best not to show that she smells the bullshit. "Remain on Veden?"

The Warden is helping her up, doing the best she can to get the questioning old lady out of her precinct. "Sometimes the Citadel likes to run tests on those that have been exposed to magic like this, to be sure there's no residue that could have adverse effects over time. It's routine, nothing to worry about, and you probably won't be called in."

Keyra would bet her favorite yellow thread she and Tilsman would be called in. That is all the proof she's going to get from the Warden. They shake hands and Keyra leads Tilsman out. He is significantly rounder from the goodies stuffed in his shirt.

Keyra smacks him on the ear soundly. "Stealing from Maroons? You never cease to disappoint me, boy."

Tilsman unashamedly reaches down his tunic and pulls out an almond cake which he tears into greedily. "Ahh, I haven't tasted almonds since those days we spent in Cath'iri. Would you like some, Granma Keyra?"

Keyra sighs and accepts the offered treat. "You're lucky I feel sorry for you," she says between mouthfuls.

"So where to now?"

Keyra doesn't want to think about the next decision that must be made, but there is no hiding from it any longer. She looks at his stupidly innocent face, and remembers the gaunt, hollow holes in the faces of the dead sailor boys. Her next step could not be clearer. "Nahem." Perhaps the Warden's words are valid, and she was genuinely worried about the future of the Elgir. But the rapid spread of the strange affliction has yet to be publicly acknowledged as a threat, and the citizens have been kept in the dark. Keyra will not allow herself to become another body in the precinct. In the capital city of Gafforah, they can find out if the happenings are localized, and if there is anything being done to stop it. If not, they will be but a short climb away from Wight's Keep and can bring the problem to a power that supersedes Elgir law.

Maybe she's wrong, Keyra thinks as she leads Tilsman towards the docks. Maybe they're going to spread it by leaving the islands, and the sorcerers really do have a plan in place that needs time and the public's cooperation to work. As she glances around the docks, she sees cloaked Maroon Men on every corner. At Isah's stall, there is a stranger holding out pastries to passersby, wearing her old friend's apron. The chills that crawl down her spine are undeniable. She needs to get out.

Finding a charter to Gafforah could prove difficult considering the silent ban on their evacuation. The barges and skiffs are overflowing and sit low in the water from the weight of sailors and goods. Keyra passes these in favor of the slave ferries down at the southern end of the docks. These boats never have jewel-paying patrons who want to ride with the scum below deck, and the prices will be significantly lower than the inflated demands that come with overcrowding on commercial vessels.

She approaches a ferry with the familiar emblem of the Tower. The organization is an empire in Kaper's Bay, owning most of the businesses in Elgireth and many in Gafforah. They are traditionally pirates, meaning her jewels may not be questioned as they would by a reputable merchant. It also gives them the benefit of ensuring their safety rather than meeting the pirates in the bay where she would most likely join the slaves below deck and Tilsman would end up skewered on a spit above a deck fire.

The captain is a hooded leemoah that takes her jewels without question and continues to prepare the vessel for the journey. The travelers settle with their meager belongings. Keyra has left behind her needles, thread, and most of her fabric, bringing only the bare necessities in a small sack. She hopes leaving all her things in the board house will buy them some time before the Maroon Men realize they're gone. Tilsman has nothing but himself and the snacks jutting out from his tunic. Their first order of business in Nahem will be to buy him new clothing. "Keyra, I—" Tilsman swallows the candied shrimp he is chewing and lets out a long sigh, "I'm sorry about your friend. I should have said something earlier."

She smiles wearily. Say what she will about the boy, he has yet to leave her side. "Thank you, Tilsman. Magic is unpredictable and uncaring. Remember that next time you're around it. It does no one any good."

"It wasn't anyone's fault, grandma Keyra. Like you said, magic is unpredictable. It is nature, after all. Sometimes nature kills and it ain't no one's fault."

"Not anyone's fault, Tilsman. Please don't speak like a Wahethian sheep boy when we arrive in Nahem." Her face becomes kind again. "And thank you for your sentiments." She moves closer to him to avoid any curious eyes. "What was it that Tika pulled from you? What kind of magic doesn't harm a boy but kills a man in an instant?"

"I don't know. I feel different since, though. Lighter. Even before I puked half my weight. It was evil, that much I can say. I'm glad to be rid of it and I hope Tika pulling it out of me means no one else will get hurt." It is hard for Keyra to imagine that the boy wiping jelly from his mouth could be the source of something so dark. Could this boy really be a dangerous magic user? To what purpose would it serve to murder dozens of people? No, she's being ridiculous. Tilsman starts to feel the effects of his bizarre diet and his face turns an odd shade of green as the ferry rocks in a small swell. Keyra is embarrassed she ever thought he could be something except what stands at her side. She turns her attention to the captain instead. He has taken a special interest in them. She has paid more than what they would get on the block for an old woman and a physically incompetent boy. Why does she feel like a hunk of fish in his eyes?

"What are you good at, Tilsman? We will need work. Tailors are always needed but you will have to find some sort of income as well."

"I'm good with a knife and wood. I used to carve little god talismans for the sailors."

"A woodworker, eh? Perhaps we can find you an apprenticeship. Unless you want to find a vessel to Waheth."

"You're stuck with me, grandma Keyra. Stop trying to ship me back to the damn grasslands."

Keyra refuses to let him see the warm glow his words give her. If he believed she had feelings for the child, it would bring back the excruciating pain she had worked so hard to repress for decades. Her heart cannot take losing another child.

"You're looking for work in Nahem?" The captain at the railing finally speaks. He is a leemoah with sharp purple eyes and scales the color of sea foam. Feathers line his forearms and cheekbones. "I have some propositions that may interest you."

"Merchant work may be my past, but I would prefer it not be my future," Keyra says flatly. In her experience, mysterious strangers rarely offer honest work, especially ones commanding slave ferries. There is something uncomfortably familiar about this one in particular.

"Jewels will get you only so far in Nahem. Only the dock stores accept them as tender. As a gesture of good will, I can exchange them for Gaffori caryns."

Keyra instinctively grabs Tilsman's shoulders to steer him away. "We will exchange our currency at a certified venue for the legal fee, thank you."

The leemoah bows graciously. "Of course. Should you change your mind, you can find me at my shop, Predaya's. Enjoy the rest of your trip. Under Akai."

Chills creep up Keyra's spine as he turns away. Where has she heard that phrase before?

~ 11 ~

BETA
&
THE BOY

"Here." Vendar's words nudge Beta awake. The darkness is heavy with the humidity of the night. Rolith slaps at a bug on his neck.

"I can see Nahem from here, can't we stay there for the night and sleep in actual beds?" Malvin's voice causes Beta's head to ache. Every word out of it embarrasses her.

Peynter simply rolls over and refuses to wake. Beta rubs the sleep from her eyes. They approach a grotto a mile south of Nahem. Thick fog obstructs the entrance, nestled beneath a hill overflowing with vines. Behind the cluster of twisted trees at the top of the hill is Bayside Road—the only way out of the city. In the distance, the buildings jutting from the mountain are dark shadows in a gray sky. Beta didn't anticipate the slavers trying to leave the capital city but if they left by land or sea, the sorcerers would spot them.

Vendar is staring out at the horizon, the bloodleaf stem hanging useless in one hand. Now that they are no longer in Elgireth, the tracker petal won't work as well. The boat nudges into the cove through the vines. The heat is twice as heavy here. "The gates will open soon. We have some time before they come down the road." If he's worried that they have been compromised, he doesn't let it show in his voice or face.

The group drags the boat onto the small shore, scattering crabs and trampling the otherwise pristine sand. "I call last watch," Malvin announces before flopping on the ground, not bothering to roll out a blanket first.

"First watch goes to Malvin," Vendar commands. "Beta, do a good sweep before getting some sleep. Rolith and Peynter, see if you can't get us something to eat." He brushes past the vines to exit the grotto. Beta senses his mind is heavy. Just how much are the older mages not telling the apprentices? She will confront him later. For now, she does as she is ordered. She searches the cave with magic first. She touches the damp stone, slick with sea growth from high tide. She feels the lazy pulse of life mostly unbothered by human interference. She reaches further, the energy embracing her like an old friend. There is a flutter, a sort of breath. A sleeping creature? No, it is far too deep within the cavern for her to sense cave life. Unless . . .

The breathing becomes irregular. It's waking up. She freezes and pulls back her probing mind. She becomes aware of just how loud the boys are. Their voices bounce across the walls and she hears splashing as Peynter attempts to catch fish in bubbles of water. He grumbles in frustration as the water fights his commands. He has been feeling especially powerless as he was ordered to leave his massive book bags behind on this mission. Rolith and Malvin compel rocks to pummel the fish, causing a disturbance in the stillness. Beta silences them with a wave of her arm and the command for their muscles to freeze, extending her abilities to their limits. Their muscles will fight her request, but even human bodies aren't immune to her battlemage dominance. The veins beneath her skin glow softly.

Once there is silence, her companions hear the sound as well and she releases them.

The stone formations hidden by darkness move. Beta becomes as still as one of them. The dripping liquid in the distance did not come from weeping rock, but from the jaws of some massive creature.

Beta flees. A clicking roar follows her back to the entrance where the sorcerers gather shields of rock and ice.

"Beta, what the hell did you do?" Peynter's dark eyes have equally black circles beneath them. Their rest is much needed but will have to wait.

"I may have woken something up," she admits. A tentacle thicker than most trees and slick with algae snakes out and latches around Beta's ankle. Her feet are yanked from beneath her as the creature drags her into the depths. The arm is severed in moments by the other warriors. From the blackness the creature gives a screech.

Vendar materializes from the night. "What have you done? That sound . . ." Beta wonders if the deep lines in his face are from battlemage magic or the stress of babysitting the sorcerers.

Six more tentacles lunge forward with frightening speed. Beta connects with the flame from the newly built fire and compels it to engulf the writhing nest of purple scales. Peynter dodges one of the tentacles and his cloak is stabbed through with a stinger as tall as he is. He squeals in terror and leaps away with an artful cartwheel.

"We've stumbled across a crucifer," Vendar says as he takes the full weight of one of the tree-like arms on a quick air shield above his head. His defense deteriorates in seconds but by then he is across the cave, using the wall as a springboard to give him the momentum to cut through the tentacle with an ice sword. "Avoid the stinger at all costs and aim for the tentacles first."

"We could have figured that out ourselves!" Malvin protests. His body is encased in stone, but it does little to save him from being drilled into the sand from the sheer weight of an appendage. More fire from Beta gives him the time to free himself. With renewed rage he screams as he calls the sand into a dense cudgel no human could wield with mortal strength alone. He waits for the stinger to whistle towards him and when it embeds in the ground, he hardens the sand around it so the crucifer cannot draw it back again. The cudgel comes down on the appendage with enough strength to shatter the bone within.

The crucifer screams and withdraws, giving them a heartbeat to catch their breaths.

Beta takes a step back to fully assess their adversary. Twenty eyes peer from a semi-shelled skull, attached to the stinger that hangs awkwardly to the side. It looks incapacitated but Beta cannot rule it out as a danger quite yet. Malvin is charging the crucifer with sharpened missiles in tow. He slings them at the eyes, and the stones shatter against impenetrable eyelids. "I said the tentacles first, you reef-breather!" Vendar says. "Its heart is in the middle of them!" He expands the flame available and releases it into the soft bed of tentacles. Beta joins forces, her yellow flame adding life to his red, the flares eagerly accepting the oxygen the battlemages offer it.

The creature shrieks in rage and swings at Peynter, who is trapping the tentacles in massive ice blocks while Malvin follows behind with sharpened stone.

Rolith draws from the rubble around them to block the crucifer's blow as best he can. The stones shatter as the tentacle smashes down, but by then Peynter has trapped the arm and has moved to safety.

There are only three tentacles left unchecked although it feels as though they have defeated dozens. She counts quickly. Twelve. They have destroyed nine.

The stinger strikes the dirt a miniscule distance from her

head. Ah yes, the stinger. The creature struggles to lift the appendage again but Vendar's faith in her has already been broken. He steps between her and the crucifer and burns away the tentacles with a combination of fire and wind that tears it to shreds, exposing a shriveled green heart. Malvin pierces it with a skillfully aimed rock before anyone else can take the honor.

The crucifer makes a horrible wheezing noise before dissolving into slime.

Peynter instantly begins scooping the goo into a bottle. Rolith raises an eyebrow in question. Peynter is giddy with excitement. "Crucifer blood is one of the rarest ingredients in Andriel. A Seer will pay a hefty price to use it as ink. You would all know this if you had read Chapter Twelve in our *Methods of Magic* text."

"I suppose that's why we keep you around, nerd." Malvin admires his handiwork in all its brutal glory, stones larger than him scattered across the cave. "It's certainly not for your fighting ability."

Vendar is sweating and the orange scars glow beneath his skin. He is in his mid-forties and Beta can't help wondering how much time he has left. "Do it quickly then, we're leaving. Someone must have heard the ruckus we were making and will be here to investigate. The city is our only choice now."

"Thank the waves," Malvin breathes. For once he is the first to gather his things and head to the boat to sit and wait for the others. Beta hangs back purposefully as Rolith and Peynter join Malvin in the boat.

"There's something you're not telling me," she says quietly enough that only Vendar can hear.

The elder battlemage speaks to Rolith. "Go ahead and scout for any curious guards or travelers. Beta and I will cover our tracks here."

The second in command nods curtly and Peynter pushes them forward by pulling the water alongside their vessel. Once they are through the remains of the vines, Vendar sags to the sand and places his head in his hands. Beta looks away from his show of weakness respectfully. If he is acting this way, it can only mean things are worse than originally thought. "How much time?" she asks.

"I can't say, but soon. Every spell burns my blood. I feel like glass, straining to hold, but eventually I will shatter. Come here." He motions her over and she sits beside him on the beach. "This is your future, little battlemage. Does my frailty frighten you? Is that something you can live with? It's not too late to extend what life you can."

She studies him carefully. He looks old, but not frail. His hair hangs limp, but it is from the sweat of the battle. His lungs struggle for breath not because of his life-sapping magic but from physical exertion. "I think you are an old man that can't keep up with his students. Even Peynter was running circles around you."

Vendar's eyes sparkle with life once more and he shoves Beta into the water with a gust of air. "Old now, am I? Not so old that I can still catch you off guard. If I remember correctly, you had to be rescued by Malvin near the end there."

Beta emerges from the water as dry as before, having protected herself in an air bubble at the last moment. She kicks up water at Vendar's face with her foot. "If I can't handle myself, then blame my master." Something is still troubling him. She returns to her seat. "Tell me what we're really doing in Gafforah. Rolith said we are rescuing the leemoah sacrifice— the star dancer. There's more to it than that, isn't there? There are secrets whispered where we apprentices can't hear."

"If they are told where you cannot hear, maybe they are not for your ears," he says, making her feel like a child once more.

She straightens her shoulders. No, she is not a child. She is a battlemage. She stands abruptly and walks across the water's surface to join the others outside. "You can choose what you tell me, but I can't be expected to perform my best work with only partial information."

"I know." Somehow his admission maddens her even more. He follows her into the dawn without another word.

The boy will never understand the appeal of foreign cities. Nahem is loud as well as filthy. The stench of stagnant water from their so-called innovative sewer lines overtakes the food being cooked over open flames, kicking up smoke into the faces of passersby. Over the elevated aqueducts and patch-worked towers, the boy can hear the shouts of the arena. The events last for weeks in the summer, one continuous battle royale where spectators come and go for their favorite fighters. There are posters announcing heroes of the pits, depicting fearsome faces and muscled warriors. Even the boy recognizes most of them. A loud cry from the crowds in the arena is deafening. Someone has died.

The boy turns his attention back to his own fate. Everyone that passes glances at the slaves. Most are calculating, sizing them up. These looks only hover on the boy for a moment before shifting to the leemoah filly. The worst, however, is the blank, dead gazes of other slaves. He has yet to see one with any spark of life in their eyes, or without the massive brand of their masters on their faces.

Their own master rides in the cart with them. He notices the boy's awe and smirks. "Do you like the arena, boy? I'd be careful what you show interest in. You could be fighting there soon. Don't worry, you'd be a filler fight, you'd probably die quickly. Just something for the reigning champ to tear to pieces as they clear the bodies away from the showcases."

The boy is sure to keep his eyes on the bottom of the cart

from then on. He may have a miserable life, but he doesn't plan on having it end before he can get out of this situation.

The sounds of the arena fade as they travel farther up the treacherous Street of Angels, named for the way enemies would fly off the mountainside when rained on from above with debris and arrows. The boy feels his stomach lurch as he looks up the steep street and then down the way they had come. The donkey pulling the cart seems sure enough of its steps; but the boy cannot say the same. The jutting buildings lean strangely to either side and do nothing to ease his queasy stomach. How can people live knowing that with one misstep they could tumble to the ocean?

To his relief, they turn left. Perpendicular to the Street of Angels, the roads are leveled with packed gravel and the drop is hidden by buildings. He can pretend he is safe on steady ground here. They travel down a small set of stairs and stop in front of a black building with letters spelling out *Predaya's* in a brilliant shade of green over the doorway. Three mercenaries meet them there, clad in earthy colors and wearing the Tower sigil. They help the leemoah girl out of the cart and eye the boy unpleasantly. "Under Akai, Captain. Who is this?" The speaker wears a beard and the sharp stench of the ocean.

"Under Akai. The boy is a woodworker and e'likai speaker. Our new friend seems to have taken a liking to him, so I bought him for less than I paid for my meal. If he proves too much trouble, we will sell him to the arena."

The woman mercenary pinches the boy's arm painfully. "Not much in the way of muscle, are you boy? More than likely, they'll buy him just so the Matcher can use him as a cudgel." She laughs at her own joke and slaps the boy on the ass before losing interest. "How was the journey?" she asks the leemoah.

"We were not followed, if that's what you mean. Your lack of faith in me never wavers, does it, Ayrek?"

"I always assume that salt water you come from has shrunk

your brain. Murdon, why don't you do a sweep for us before we relax?"

The youngest of the mercenaries hops into action, saluting several times before tearing down the street. El'rozai shakes his head. "That damned boy will be dead before the end of the week if he keeps rushing into things so eagerly. Best you sent him away, though, now we can speak candidly."

The slaves are herded through the doorway and into a cloud of thick incense that stings the boy's eyes. Candles line shelves on the walls, each flame burning a different color. The boy sees black, red, green, gold, and one that changes with each flicker. Against the back wall behind a counter, skulls leer at him from rows of shelves. Most are human but there are the jutting nasal bones of leemoah skulls and others he cannot identify. There are some with spikes and horns curling from scalps, and some with ridges and extra eye sockets. Just how many different creatures are there in the world that he has yet to see?

"How much time do we have?" the bearded mercenary asks as the slaves shuffle through the shop to the back, where a bookcase has been shoved aside behind the cluttered desk to reveal a staircase. They are marched down the stairs into a cold basement that looks like something out of a nightmare. Vials and jars of every size line the walls and shelves, some holding mysterious liquids and others containing body parts in preserving juice. Eyes bulging from absorbed oils stare back at the boy as they sit on the floor as instructed. Their shackles are clipped to long chains drilled into the stone floor as the mercenaries reach inside a shallow bowl of ice for chilled bottles of booze.

"Three weeks," Captain Zai responds as he pours his drink into a glass. The slave girl stiffens but remains silent as always. The slaver glances to his charges. "We'll speak of the details later. Obtaining the gem has proven difficult. As usual, the sorcerers are reluctant to cooperate."

Ayrek drinks straight out of her bottle. "You know how I feel about working with them. They'll never adhere to any deal we make." She spits on the floor.

Zai remains cool but the boy can see his tail flick beneath his cloak in annoyance. "We do not always have the pleasure of remaining separate from our . . . comrades. Try to keep an open mind, and remember you are not in charge here. They will cooperate. With the girl as collateral, they will give us what we want and both sides will prosper."

Ayrek wrinkles her nose in disgust. "We have to be better than them if we can help it, Captain. They'll use us and toss us aside like they always have. At the very least, you'll have to tell them what we're planning. Some caryns won't buy their satisfaction."

The leemoah slaver clenches his webbed fingers into a fist. "Let me handle the Citadel, agent. I respect your seniority here, but we will not refuse a guaranteed successful mission because of your personal opinion. Do you understand?"

Ayrek stands stiffly to attention. "Under Akai."

"Under Akai," the Captain mutters under his breath.

Ayrek turns to leave but hesitates, staring at the corner of El'rozai's cloak. She plucks a flower petal from the hem. "You may not need to negotiate with them to find out where they stand. This is a bloodleaf petal, the choice of the Citadel for tracking."

The dark pink leaf flutters to the top of the desk. Ayrek jerks her head towards the slave girl. "You, you know magic, right? See if that petal is spelled."

"You can call me Star," she says, obeying her command all the same. She holds a hand over the petal for only a moment and then nods. "Sorcerer magic."

Ayrek strikes a match and touches it to the tracker petal. "I didn't take you for an amateur, El'rozai, or someone who wouldn't change their cloak for three days."

"I've been travelling," he hisses, "and don't think this proves your point. We don't trust them, either."

Ayrek rolls her eyes. "But you'd just as soon take their money." Her attention turns to the boy with eyes that are not devoid of empathy. It is an expression he is unused to. "What do you plan to do with this one?"

The bearded mercenary, who has been silent until now, strokes his facial hair. "I'll take him."

Ayrek shakes her head solemnly but does not come to the boy's aid. "You're a cruel one, Reyder. He'll be dead within the week. Perhaps it's a mercy."

She heads up the stairs, followed by El'rozai. Reyder looks over the boy with a grin that reveals mostly metal-plated teeth. "Ever wanted to be a gladiator, boy? I'd start getting excited if I were you." He slaps him playfully on the shoulder before trotting off after his companions. The bookcase slides shut with a heavy definity, leaving Star and the boy in the dark.

"Are you alright?" the boy asks in e'likai.

"For now," Star says. "It is not my life I fear for. My people need me alive and well in three weeks. I fear the Tower means to either ransom me or leverage me for some other dark purpose. If my people cannot pay the price, our magic will be lost, and they will be scattered to the seas. If they can't pay it, they will be destitute and vulnerable."

It is the most he has ever heard her say at once. The boy scoots closer in the dark to reach for her hand. The scales on her palm are dry and cold as happens to most leemoahs who remain out of the sea for too long. The boy has seen some on Denali with scales flaking off, revealing sharply pink skin beneath. It is a distinct reminder that they do not belong in the world of the landwalkers. "If you're so important, why weren't you protected?" the boy blurts out before he can think of how it might be a sensitive subject.

Star doesn't seem to mind answering. "I was. The ceremony

happens every thirty years, and halfway through the cycle, the next Star Shepherd is born. We are revealed by Ashlikani herself a month before the next ceremony. I was taken in by the king, Gar'ithol, as his own. In his palace I was protected and kept hidden from the rest of Utali'hali. It used to be that there was a great feast in honor of the Shepherd, but one of my predecessors was kidnapped during that feast, so even that tradition has been abandoned in the name of protecting the Shepherd. Unfortunately, there are rules prohibiting leemoah kings from closing cities to their own even in grave times. The leemoah slaver, El'rozai, was able to enter Utali'hali and flush me out of the palace with oil in the water. It will take them some time to fully recover the ocean quality, but I fear my capture bodes worse for my people. To avoid being discovered, he handed me over to the slaver Wilda and had her sell me back to him through the proper channels. Now, he legally owns me, and my people will be forced to either buy my freedom at whatever price he demands or regain it through lengthy petitions and bureaucratic processes."

The boy burns with anger. "The system shouldn't be like that."

He may be imagining things, but he swears he can hear her smile in her words. "No, it certainly shouldn't. Slave flipping is a common practice, however. Slavers often enter unofficial contracts with others in their profession to buy back the people they have kidnapped to officially stake their claim. Once the papers have been signed, it is too much trouble for an inspector to search out the previous owner and ask for their documents, which would have been forged or conveniently filed away by then."

The boy has been keeping his head under a rock in his lighthouse for too long. "What was it they were saying? Under Akai?"

"It is the traditional greeting of the Tower. Aren't you Elgir? I thought everyone knew it."

"I'm Elgir, but I'm . . . well, I didn't exactly get out much." He's glad she can't see the burning red in his cheeks. Then he remembers leemoahs are supposed to see far better in the dark than humans. He turns his face away from her.

She is patient enough not to press further. "The moon has two faces. The goddess Aryet is the glowing white face, giving light and power to those of the ocean. Akai is the new moon, or when it is clouded. Under Akai, the darkness reigns and evil deeds can be done among the waves before Aryet turns her face back to Andriel. I'm sure you can imagine why the Tower chooses to worship Akai instead of Aryet."

"I thought you drew your power from Ashlikani? Isn't she a star?" He is growing bold now and intends to get as much information as he can before she grows tired of his ceaseless questions.

"Ashlikani is a steady source of magic in the form of a star. She guides only the leemoahs, unlike fickle Aryet whose power waxes and wanes. I thank you for your companionship, friend, but I fear I grow weary. If you don't mind, I am going to try to get some sleep."

"Oh, sorry," the boy says quickly. "Good night. Under Aryet."

"Under Ashlikani," the leemoah replies in musical e'likai.

~ 12 ~

WENDWYNN
&
ZAVOSH

I t was from the balcony of the Keep that Wen watched the boats. The ships with the green sails were bringing slaves. It was a practice she intended to put a stop to once she had time to rule after Mangzar's war. For now, her rule had been too short and her list of duties too long. She chose to focus on the more positive aspects of the economy. Ferries darted through the channels, bringing fabrics and jewels directly to factories to be refined and resold as clothing and jewelry. A vessel from Terrial was stuck on a reef. Foreigners always believed they were skilled enough to maneuver the dangerous waters because they were used to bad weather in the open sea. The bay, however, was not open water. The dangers lay beneath the surface, and in many places was rocky enough that even the most experienced captain could not get through.

One boat drew her attention. It was hardly big enough to be considered seaworthy, with a single sail and a small hull. Beyond the trapdoors on deck, Frejith waited to reach Mangzarian shores. Wendwynn was weary from the lengthy conversations they had before her departure. They had lasted the better part of the night and had been draining both emotionally and mentally for the queen. The conclusion they had reached could very well mean she would never see her wife again.

The trembles Wen had every so often from the poison were a sobering reminder that Mangzar was not ready to surrender just yet. There had been no attempt to hide the nationality or intent of the assassin. They had sent a vipr, as an ambassador, to make a wild attempt on her life in front of several important witnesses.

The war was just beginning, spy or no.

"Your Grace?" She hadn't heard what Yo'aro said. The Admiral of the Gaffori Navy stood with arms behind her back, watching the queen curiously. She was tall for an Andreli woman, with skin darker than Wen's and thick braids plaited in gold. She wore leather armor and a cloak that wafted scents of the sea when she moved. Her golden stripe tattoos glittered on exposed arms as they caught every flicker of the candles on the balcony, matching her plated canine teeth and sharpened fingernails.

"I apologize, Admiral. Do you mind repeating yourself?"

Yo'aro was a Tigress, one of the elite female assassins of Nath'iki. More recently, she had been a key part of Wendwynn's assault on Nahem, and one of the very few who had taken on a vipr in single combat and survived. "The colonies. They are between us and the northern peninsula of Mangzar. I suggested that we bolster our defenses there as the people are farmers, not fighters."

"We are not at war with District Two." Wendwynn wanted to rub the weariness from her eyes like a child but refrained. "Why would District Six go through the colonies when they are to the north? It doesn't make sense from a militaristic standpoint."

"With all due respect, Your Grace." Yo'aro's dark eyes flashed. "Assuming they will not be attacked is not a genuine strategy. You are sworn to protect them as well as the people of Gafforah and Elgireth. If Mangzar were to take them, they could move in from two sides." She pointed to the crescent shape Mangzar made around the north side of Kaper's Bay and the speckling of tiny islands between it and Gafforah.

Wen's eyes blurred as she stared intensely at the map. "Even if they do take the islands, there is no space for armies to gather. They would be spread out and easy to pick off by our own navy. As you said, these people are farmers. Mangzarians only find honor in fighting warriors. I need your ships here, where we know they have attacked, and where we can rebuild what was lost in the Ulden assault. You're supposed to be there as it is, overseeing the restoration." She knew her tone was sharp, but she had little interest in tempering her frustration.

Yo'aro stood rigid. "I thought you would want to know about the scouting vessels scoping out the colonies seeing as we are at war. I apologize if I have overstepped my bounds." Her tone suggested she was far from sorry.

Wendwynn had always surrounded herself with strong personalities. She wanted advisors that would be honest with her if she was making an unwise decision. But now she was seeing the downside of her strategy. "I will defend the colonies by defeating my enemy, Admiral. If you fear for their safety, send your own sentinels to take out the scouts and send a clear message that we know they are there. They could be trying to lure the navy there and weaken the frontline for another assault. They reached Ulden because they used the same strategy with Elgireth. As for you, return to your command post and send a messenger next time you feel I need to know something. Am I understood?"

Yo'aro kept her lips tightly closed as she bowed and took her leave. Wendwynn's heart was pounding with pent-up frustration and stress. She should speak to Grevin. He was always her source of sound wisdom when Frejith was gone. Instead, she decided to wrap up another loose end.

Her confident steps took her down flights of stairs deep into the mountain's core. The warden at the gate to the dungeon stood as she approached. "Your Grace. Do you require me to show you to a cell?"

"Just open the gate, Uchfer. I can find my own way."

He bowed and complied. Wen passed through into a cavern lit an eerie orange by the channels of lava to either side of the walkway. While Gaffori's fire mountain was dormant, the architects of Wight's Keep had engineered pumps to channel lava from deep beneath the earth, channeling it across the dungeon's floors. Small bridges connected the path to stone blocks with barred trapdoors. Beyond the bars, inmates of varying severity awaited her command as to their fate. They would have to wait a while longer.

She found her quarry and peered into the pit below. The vipr was meditating, arms and legs crossed. Sweat beaded on his forehead from the proximity of the cells to the fire river. "I thought your kind was molded by lava. I didn't expect it to be unpleasant for you," the queen said.

The vipr didn't move or open his eyes. "It is our magic that protects us from the heat. Your collars cut off any connection I may have had to that." He tugged at the glowing metal circlet around his neck.

"Good," she said.

"What is it you wish to ask me, Your Grace? You did not come here solely to ensure I am uncomfortable."

"You have been a guest with me for some time now, Prince Halthax. I thought it rude that I had yet to properly introduce myself as your host."

The Prince was intimidating outside of her walls, but here in the belly of Wight's Keep he looked small and shriveled. The dark circles under his eyes were not from war paint or magic use, but from exhaustion and malnutrition. "Wendwynn the Usurper, I presume? Regards. Now let's get down to business." His tone confirmed his weariness.

Wen maintained eye contact with him, unblinking. She knew her eyes made even the strongest second guess their confidence. The warprince was no different. He looked away long before she did. "I don't have much business to deal with you, or I would have invited you to a more appropriate meeting place. From what your ambassador has told me, I won't get much, if any, information from you. I believe he said your father would rather us just kill you."

Halthax wasn't shocked. "That would be preferable to sitting in a lake of fire, yes. You can't use me as collateral or bait of any kind, so why keep me alive? I'm just a liability at this point."

"How much do you know of Gaffori magic?" she asked. "I have extensively studied Mangzarian black magic. It is rather incredible. It is a powerful connection between those who have the blood of your fire mountains. It revolves around death and bone and passion. The magic of the islands is different. Those touched with the abilities pull from the world around them, to control certain elements up to time itself. The royal family has their own abilities, as I'm certain you've heard the tales."

There was a falter in his expression. "Of course. The Verychek curse. But you are no Verychek. You are not even Andreli. Our magics will always be locked to you."

Yet again, the Mangzarians had underestimated her. She knelt to be closer to the captive. He was squirming in his chains. "I was hoping you hadn't heard so I could tell you the tale myself. I think I will anyway. The Verycheks ruled Gafforah for generations, ensuring their throne with a magic unique to their family. They drew power not from raw sources but reached inside the minds of fellow humans. They used these powers to manipulate human subjects by creating false memories and thoughts into the minds of those around them. No one knew if they were in control of their own minds while lacking proof to the contrary.

"There were six generations of Verychek dictators, all with the same mysterious ability. Who could hope to challenge them? It was only thirty years ago that the infamous Prince Haldeen Verychek decided his powers were not good enough. He didn't just want to manipulate parts of the mind, but the whole thing. He traveled to the heart of Gafforah, deep within Iradan's Forest where he vanished.

"Years went by and Haldeen did not return. The nation thought him dead, a victim of his own greed. Then one day, people started going missing. First, it was a village child or a drunken commoner. No one paid heed until nobles began disappearing without a trace. The people panicked, and the disappearances continued. The rest of the royal Verycheks were helpless as their ruse of invincibility faded with each failed search party led by mind-controlled hounds.

"Then, exactly ten years after the prince's disappearance, the emperor himself vanished. In his place, Haldeen sat on the throne. His court was made up of those who had disappeared, except they were not the same. They were shells of humans. Their minds had been broken and melted until they were nothing but vessels to hold magic that he could draw on as needed to feed his spells, leaving them gaunt and rotting. Their eyes hollowed, their teeth and hair fell out." She leaned closer to the bars. She was a snake and the vipr was a mouse caught in her hypnosis. "The citizens were terrified into submission. Anyone who spoke out against him was found in his court the next day, praising his name with a smile. Gafforah was nothing more than a man and his tools. Those under the spell were conscious of their actions, aware of their bodies rotting slowly, but could do nothing except smile and thank their ruler for his kind charity."

"And then you came straight up the Street of Angels and cast down the Verychek dynasty with no more than two hundred soldiers," Halthax breathed rapturously. Wen found his change of tone fascinating. He knew exactly who she was, and he feared her. It was too late for him to save himself. She left out Frejith's part in the hypnosis. Let him think she could control all his people on her own.

"The people were ripe to be led by someone new. *Anyone* but a Verychek. I did not cast Haldeen down; he was brought to me by the Gaffori commoners. In gratitude, I burned everything that whispered the Verychek name. Well, not everything. Haldeen learned this mind-controlling ability and recorded everything for the children he never had. All I had to do was dedicate time to learn what he had to say."

"You're a Puppetmaster." He was breathless.

"I am a queen that has proved herself several times yet is still tested by those who doubt me. Perhaps my people and the people of Andriel need a reminder that I, myself, forged the path that led me here. I alone will ensure that my legacy is solidified."

She stood and the vipr moved to sit as far away from her as he could. Nothing could save him now. "You are no better than the Verycheks yourself if you turn me into a puppet. I thought you were a liberator, a warrior queen that protects people."

"I protect *my* people," she reminded him. "Warden Uchfer, if you would be so kind, I would like to perform a little surgery on our friend Halthax ky Dzaxar." Frejith's exit had left her feeling vulnerable and abandoned. She should wait to try the Puppetmaster magic on Dzaxar. He could be of more use with his mind intact. Perhaps it was the feeling that she was losing control, or it was the desire to end the war to truly begin her time as queen of Gafforah, but there would be no waiting. Let them see her power now. Let Mangzar send more envoys, more princes, and she would turn them all.

Uchfer obeyed, Halthax screaming and struggling against his chains. Wen did not miss the expression of disappointment on the old Gaffori's face.

District Six of Mangzar was surrounded by black mountains where liquid fire stirred and rumbled the earth. One of the peaks oozed liquid flame, penetrating the otherwise unbroken clouds of ash with an eerie light. There was no sun here. The houses of Mount Thoyax, the sixth district, were their own eerie display. The Mangzarians set their cities in perfect rows, each building the same size and shape as the one beside it. Looking straight on down the main road was dizzying. There were hundreds if not thousands of black boxes all the same size, all in the same position. The streets crisscrossed among them like cutting a cake. Towering above it all was Fortress Blackfeather. It was its own mountain, monolithic in its stature and built entirely for war. A moat filled with spikes surrounded the walls and lined the tops of the battlements. There were no windows, but if the stories were true, those inside the fortress could still see through the walls thanks to spells only the Warleaders understood. On the highest battlement overlooking the city was a statue of Halthax ky Dzaxar the Elder, carved in the startling lifelikeness that Mangzarians were renowned for. The statue must have been twenty feet tall with eyes made of rubies, a stone sword clasped in his hands.

Before Wendwynn's reign, Zavosh had been living in Gafforah, defying his vipr blood. There hadn't been anything left for him in his homeland when his sister married a human, bringing disgrace upon their family. That had been Thu'kal isilth Zavosh. As Versenai ky Akern, the spy, he found life much kinder among the ash mountains. Knowing he was assisting in the demise of those who had shunned him and belittled him for a choice that hadn't been his was a bonus. That is, until Ugden had exposed himself by trusting someone he shouldn't have. The spy had been beaten to death in the streets while Zavosh listened from the next block over. He couldn't come to his rescue, and he couldn't come any closer without being expected to join in the murder. It had been a big enough risk to get Ugden's gauntlet back to Gafforah as a signal that his cover had been blown.

All the vipr had left was to wait. He couldn't sail back to Gafforah without raising suspicion, and even if he could, there would be no returning. The queen needed someone looking for the prize, the great mysterious secret that Mangzar was said to hold. Instead, he pushed forward until the next opportunity presented itself. He trusted no one—watching every soldier, every citizen, with wariness. Ugden had been set up by one of their informants. Who was to say that Zavosh hadn't been exposed as well? They could be waiting for him to slip up. He kept his head down, training with the community army as required of every citizen from the age they could hold a weapon to the day they died. His work continued at the shipyard where he repaired vessels that had been used against his own nation. Gafforah was not visible from Mangzar's shores, but he could imagine the island looming in the distance.

"Versenai ky Akern." The voice startled him. The vipr woman that approached him looked strangely familiar. Her skin was more gray than green and traced with fewer tattoos than most her age. Her eyes were a deep red and she wore her hair in a long braid. When she smiled, he saw through the illusion.

"Frejith?" he whispered, aware of the Mangzarians working in the yard around them.

"Ore'xi ky Maryin. Your new assistant."

Zavosh noticed a worker watching them with interest that

was more than mere curiosity. "I'm not looking for an assistant, especially one that doesn't look like they could use a hammer. Look for work at the market. I hear the local bar is looking for a brew assistant." He turned his back to her, his mind racing. Why would the queen send her wife here? She had minimal experience with Mangzarians, and her Var was choppy at best. She could become a liability, and he couldn't stand by and watch if the great mind mage of Gafforah was discovered. The queen had to know what kind of pressure she was putting on him, asking him to keep her wife alive and untortured.

He spent the rest of the day distracted and when it came time for the red smudge of a sun to set behind a sky choked with black clouds, he had to stop himself from jogging towards the market. Already, he was stressed that she hadn't lasted the day. If he let the queen's wife die in this forsaken land, he would be down another homeland.

He found her sitting at a table at the brewers in question. The market was open air as the temperature in Mangzar was never cold enough to warrant hiding from the elements. There was no rain, as the sky was always filled with volcanic ash. Yet another worry for Zavosh. Viprs and native Mangzarian humans were impervious to the effects of the poisonous gasses. The ash would slowly kill a girl from a tropical island.

Frejith was surrounded by Mangzarians who were hanging on her every word when Zavosh found her with a mug of ale in hand. They were laughing and nodding to her tales. Zavosh went to the bar to get himself a drink and sat at the table on the other side of the roped-off tavern area. He watched curiously as she told tales of raiding and travels that had the spectators hanging on her every word. Zavosh drank alone as one by one, they dispersed and said their goodbyes to Frejith as though she were an old friend. Finally, she was alone and able to make her way to the vipr at the other table. Her relaxed demeanor shifted to business. She half smiled at Zavosh's questioning expression. "Water in the tankard. Every good sorceress knows that."

Zavosh had always known Frejith was a powerful sorceress, a mind mage by birth and trained in advanced techniques. She used these powers to hide her yellow scars in public to keep her abilities a mystery. In Mangzar, she had taken it a step further. Zavosh could tell she had an additional layer of spells beyond the basic illusion that made her appear a vipr to the untrained eye. She had also hidden her magical ability from any third eye until the illusion was more truth than trick.

"Are we safe here?" she asked as she finished her drink.

"As safe as we can be. If we speak lightly, we shouldn't draw attention. That applies to your admirers, as well." He frowned.

"I'm making connections, something that is important for gathering information. I think I may have met some people that will get us positions within the fortress at some point. It's better than repairing their ships where you have no access to anything."

He didn't like the confidence that radiated from her. It would get her killed. "What are you thinking? You've been here less than a day. You don't know the culture, and you barely speak the language. You can't trust anyone, not even yourself yet. Besides, I work on ships because we were *compromised* not two weeks ago. Remember that? Ugden was murdered and I had to lie low."

Her orange eyes flashed darkly. "Don't think I'm writing off Ugden's death. It was horrible, and he was my friend as well as your partner. The fact is, whatever you've been doing for the past six months, it's clearly not working. Your partner is dead, and you are no closer to finding our quarry, especially wasting your time in the shipyard. The queen is impatient and will not stand anymore blood loss. You were just a customs officer when Emperor Verychek ruled, but I was busy doing exactly this. Making connections, shutting down insurgents. I was good at it. You've taken so long to do nothing that it makes me wonder if you are really as supportive of our queen as you say you are." She studied him closely. It was true that Zavosh had not always been a friend to Wendwynn. He had tried to kill her once and allowed her to be taken as a slave before that. But much like Frejith, he had been seduced by the conqueror and her strength. He had found himself among her advisors in a position of power as she was known for supporting her ex-enemies. She had a talent for building up loyalty.

"Let's not point fingers about the past." He needed to defuse their animosity before it increased. She was still his only friend here, and his superior, whether he agreed with her or not. "What's your big plan? You intend to take on the risk of interacting with the highest levels of Mangzarian society with no experience, and then what? You were never the studious researcher if I remember correctly."

"No, but that's why I have you. You will work in the archives, where there must be something recorded about the source. I will work in the soldiers' barracks, doing what I do best. Between the two of us, we will find something. And then we will go home victorious to end this war. Do we have an understanding?"

Zavosh didn't realize he was grinding his teeth until his jaw began to throb. "Is this punishment for letting Ugden die? It wasn't my fault. I don't deserve being babysat by the likes of you."

Frejith was already losing interest in their conversation. She gathered her cloak about her shoulders, unbothered by the look of rage on her partner's face. "Where are you boarding? It's too late in the day to start a fight. I've been sailing for the past two days and could use a bed."

"Nowhere you're allowed. If you're so good at making connections, why don't you ask someone to give you a bunk? Bat your eyelashes and flash them that winning smile?" He didn't care that he could be bordering on insubordination. He had been on the mission far longer than her and had little patience for her arrogance.

Frejith lifted an eyebrow at Zavosh. "Are you forgetting I'm a mind mage? While I may have my powers hidden and unusable right now, I've been in the minds of Mangzarians before. Some of us have been fighting battles while you were here wasting time."

Zavosh wondered why he was more frustrated: because Frejith was barreling over the time he'd spent here, or because she was starting to make sense. "Fine. I can take you to the female barracks if you promise to meet me at the docks at dawn. I think we can both agree that we should take the path that requires us to spend the least amount of time together."

Frejith gave a mock salute as she walked with him down the road. Zavosh would have to remember to demand a raise from the queen if they survived their time in Mangzar.

~13 ~

KEYRA
&
TILSMAN

Nahem may be the thriving epicenter of Gafforah's eastern shore, but its steep incline makes building large factories and storage facilities impossible. The sprawling buildings are erected on the surrounding beaches and pockets of valleys, allowing small villages to sprout from their employment opportunities. In these settlements, even the richest cannot afford slaves. Instead, they hire the desperate and abandoned for pennies, charging them for room and board until there is nothing left in their pockets except debt to their employers. They are the option for those who have no options, with the guarantee of dangerous work and an early grave.

Keyra had signed a weeklong contract with the option to extend, hoping there would be no need to. Tilsman had muttered about finding somewhere he could do woodworking and avoided the piece of paper that had been waved in his face by the factory manager. Keyra has no intention of pressuring him into a contract even if he does nothing while she works. The younger they start, the less likely they are to be able to get out.

Besides, Keyra is at this particular dye factory for a reason. *He* is here, somewhere, and with the world coming to a strange and horrid end around her, she needs to make things right.

She has yet to see him as she squeezes excess liquid from brilliant pink and yellow fabrics and hangs them to dry. She imagines he has worked his way up to foreman, or even an office employee left to do paperwork, never to be seen on the floor. Her eyes dart to the face of every passerby as she works. Tilsman stays with her, helping as he can. The supervisors don't seem to mind as he is entitled to no compensation. Days pass with each the same as the last. Keyra feels her joints complaining at every bend of her knees, every twist of her wrists. She can't keep this up long.

Even Tilsman notices the wear on the old woman's face. He does what he can to lift the bolts, heavy with water, ignoring the pinch in his stomach that starts before midday and continues through the night. Despite her name calling and ear twisting, he has come to rely on her steady presence. He wishes he truly were a woodworker so he could contribute in other ways. Then his legs begin to ache, and he is grateful for the ability to sit and rest when it becomes too much. By the fifth day, his pants have become looser, and his shirt isn't as tight as it used to be.

The bell rings to signal the end of the shift and the pair wearily work their way to their feet. Tilsman rubs his shoulders with a grimace. "Finally. I swear they wait longer each day to ring the bell. When your week is up, we should find that leemoah that offered us work on the way over here. It has to be better than this."

Keyra shakes her head disapprovingly at him as they head for the exit where the foreman hands each of the workers a coupon for their meal in lieu of caryns. "It's more important to have honest work than be paid well doing illegal things. People like him are never worth selling your soul to. You would do well to learn how to discern between those who mean well and those who wish to use you."

Tilsman squints at her suspiciously as they make their way back to the dormitories. "Are you using me?"

"For what?" She laughs at the notion. "You eat more than I do, do half the work, and snore louder than a craykrat. I'd be more likely to think you're using me."

"It's just that you haven't tried to send me away. You could have put me on a ship back to Waheth, or even left me on Elgireth. There's plenty of ships that could use a cabin boy and I'd be out of your hair, but I'm still here, being dragged along even though you're not making enough to take care of yourself and you don't even know if the deaths will follow me." His eyes well with tears.

"I ought to smack you for being so ungrateful," Keyra growls, not unkindly. "Don't think I'm not going to put you on a boat away from my little world. But you caused this upheaval, and by Aryet, you're going to see it put back together. Every crust of bread I give you is going into the count of what you owe me."

Tilsman began to think of all the food Keyra had given him, and the new shoes and clothing when they had landed. His head begins to hurt, and he has to stop. He can't imagine he'll ever be in a position where he can repay her fully. If he owes her a debt, he may as well get something out of it. "Fine, but if I'm paying my half then I should get a say. I want to go into Nahem and see if there are any real opportunities, not being a glorified slave kept under worse conditions."

"We can go into the city for dinner, so you'll shut up about it, but that's it. A soft child and a fat old woman will be prime for snatching, then you'll see how much better we truly have it than a slave. We have to be back before moonrise, or they'll lock us out of the dormitories."

Tilsman's heart leaps and he claps his hands in excitement.

"Thank you, oh thank you! I'm going to try a kaper wrap with real crain sauce, not the cheap knock off they have in Elgireth."

"Some people prefer the cheap knock off," Keyra huffs to herself as Tilsman jogs on ahead, somehow finding energy that had been nonexistent all day.

They walk down the waterside road that hugs both the bottom of the cliffs on one side and the ocean on the other. They trek half a mile in silence, absorbing the dramatic peace between New Nahem and its namesake. There is no evidence of civilization here. There is nothing except the grating of waves on rocks and the cry of a passing seabird. The cliff curves inland, taking the road with it. Another quarter mile around, and Nahem opens up before them, a nearly vertical megalopolitan that defies all logic and physics—as well as the island's very shape—with its mere existence. Tilsman catches the scent of fried fish on the wind and shuffles towards it. Keyra sits wearily on a bench at the base of a staircase. She rubs her hips with a wince. "Go and find yourself something delicious, Tilsman, and bring me back something. My bones are too old to be climbing Nahem's steps. Be here before dark or I'm selling your blankets!" Keyra's voice chases him away as he takes the stairs with a rush of adrenaline. The boy is tired of Keyra's harsh words and inability to understand how hard their situation is for him. Who is she to tell him how to live? He is practically a man himself—he should decide his own fate.

Tilsman travels up the stairs, as the scent of fish has been replaced by a new trail that he hopes is a hearty meat stew a few streets higher. He stops at the landing where the sensation is the strongest and turns down the street, alone among mostly empty storefronts. There aren't even beggars here. The seller at the source of the smell offers chunks of dark meat and onion in bowls of broth from the doorway of one of the leaning towers. Tilsman buys two and tears into the food with renewed strength.

As he eats, he notices the name of the store across the street. *Predaya's*. Where has he heard that before? Ah yes, the captain on the ship that had taken them from Elgireth.

"It's true! My cousin is a knight, they're not allowed to lie." Two pirates exit the shop.

"You're full of fish guts, Rydar, always have been. Just because the people of Hardock are hicks doesn't mean they're dead men."

They stop at Tilsman's meat shop, ignoring the red headed boy with juice running down his chin. "Excuse me," he pipes up timidly, "what were you saying about Hardock?"

The older pirate tears into his own meal and seems all too eager to share his gossip. "Dead men! My cousin, Nilfin the Sure Shot, told me mum he saw rows on rows of dead men on the shore, all their eyes burnt out like they'd been struck by lightning and their skin flat and lifeless."

His companion rolls his eyes. "Don't mind him. The sun's got to his brain, at least the parts that aren't soaked in rum."

"Nilfin the Sure Shot? Came from a poor Nahem family. When he got famous for his archery tricks, he took off and never looked back. He very well could be related." Tilsman's stroke of intelligence triggers surprise from the listeners. The boy shrugs. "I read a lot back home."

The younger pirate reluctantly concedes his point. "Alright, so even if it's true, what's to say they didn't have some sort of disease there? A small, isolated island like that that sees a lot of traffic is always picking things up. They could be mummifying them like some traditions."

The elder pirate is missing the teeth on one side of his mouth. He chews his food on the other side awkwardly, saliva dribbling from the corner of his lips. "Mummifying? Elgir don't mummify. They bury at sea like any good island community. I'm telling you, Nilfin was pale as a ghost talking about it. Maybe there was a curse." They make a sign to ward against evil magic across their chests as they go back to their meals silently.

Tilsman has lost his appetite for the first time in his life. "How long ago was this?"

The pirates jump, having forgotten he was there. The younger eyes him with a new suspicion. "About a week ago. Who is this little butterball anyways?"

Tilsman has the urge to throw his leftovers on the dirt and run, but he holds his ground. "Til—Calven. I'm a dyer but I'm looking for better work, maybe carpentry related. I heard Predaya's is hiring from a leemoah fellow. Know anything about that?"

The pirates are losing interest in the strange child. "They're always hiring," the younger one shrugs, "just not carpenters. That's the most sought-after line of work around here. I don't think you can compete with some of the local master wood-workers. Predaya's is more for people who aren't afraid of odd work."

The older one laughs although the joke is lost on Tilsman. They make their way back down the street and the boy is left staring at the black storefront. He knows he should head back to Keyra and bug-ridden dormitories that wait for them back in their village of New Nahem. Nothing about this place is friendly. Before he can lose his nerve and scamper away, the leemoah from the ferry exits the building. He smiles when he sees Tilsman. "Ah, the Wahethian. Good afternoon. Are you here to discuss employment?"

Tilsman has been taught not to say no to an elder, so he nods and shuffles forward. The leemoah leads him into the store, which is cloudy with incense that makes the boy's eyes water. "What kind of work are you offering?" he asks to settle his nerves.

"All business, eh? I took you for a hard negotiator. Let us start with the pleasantries, shall we? My name is El'rozai, but you can call me Captain Zai. I'm an officer of the Tower and a powerful ally to have in Kaper's Bay."

"My name is Calven. Are you a pirate?"

El'rozai motions for him to sit in a chair in the corner between two stuffed creatures with multiple eyes while he puts on tea.

"Not for quite some time, although I have done my share of plundering in the bay. No, my talents are reserved for specific projects these days. Enough about me, let's talk about you. Calven is a Terralian name, yet your appearance is Wahethian through and through. Where is it you hail from?"

Keyra has spent much time drilling Tilsman on what to say and what not to say. Surely, she meant people that are evil. This leemoah is offering him employment and tea. "I'm from Waheth, yes, but I've traveled the world with a crew that led me to Elgireth. My grandma and I came here looking for better money."

Captain Zai nods in agreement as he stirs the flavors into the hot water. "As many do."

Tilsman glances around the shop. There are strange skulls and elixirs and creatures in cages that give him chills. "I heard from someone that Elgireth is under some sort of plague. Do you know anything about that?"

The leemoah pours liquid into cups and hands one to the boy. "I have not been to Elgireth myself since we came here together, so I cannot say for the truth of the rumors, but there are certainly whispers that are concerning."

Tilsman sips at the tea and his face scrunches at the sour taste. The leemoah shows a fang in a half smile. "The tea of my people is an acquired taste. You won't have any trouble breathing for the next few days, though."

The boy sets the cup on the table beside the chair. "I have to be getting home soon, can we talk about what kind of work you're offering?"

Captain Zai perches on the countertop thoughtfully. "To understand that, you must get some back story. The Tower, and myself specifically, are involved in a project that has been many years in the making. You see, all magic comes from a single source—a well gifted to mortals by the gods that holds drops of their blood. Each god's blood holds a different type of magic meant as a gift for their devout followers. Unfortunately, even gods are not all powerful. Once they had created this separate entity with god essence, they had no power over who was chosen to bear these gifts. While the blood gave abilities to those who worshipped the god of the same, it had no discretion as to who deserved it. This is where my companions and I come in. We have been searching for this well for many years to secure it and ensure it is used for good instead of by evil people. We have been thwarted in the past but with the help of intelligent young men like you, we are finally close to success." His reptilian eyes glint strangely in the darkness as they rake over Tilsman, making the boy feel exposed and vulnerable.

Tilsman has never considered something this serious. His job at the dye factory seems a happy dream now. "I am no hero, Sir Captain Zai. I couldn't tell you how to find a magic well."

The leemoah finishes his tea. "I am no sir, good Calven, but before you turn me down, you must remember, heroes take many forms. I have highly qualified sorcerers doing the searching thanks to some fluid alliances with the Citadel. I wouldn't dare to put you in a position you're not ready for. Someone like you is blessed with different talents."

"What kind of talents?" Tilsman has never been called talented before. He cannot remember the last time someone commented on his work in a positive way.

"Being yourself. I don't ask anything of you except to take this and give it a good squeeze once a day." He hands Tilsman a smooth pebble the color of steel laced with pink veins. It is warm to the touch.

"What is it?"

The leemoah offers more tea but Tilsman shakes his head. El'rozai shrugs and drinks directly from the pot. "A gift from a friend. You seem like a wise boy, Tilsman, so I'm going to let you in on a massive secret." He moves closer and Tilsman holds his breath in anticipation. "Your friend, the old lady? Who, by the way, is the same size as you so it seems incredibly unfair that she calls you fat." Tilsman nods, so enthralled that his feelings are validated that he doesn't question how the lee-moah knows this detail of his and Keyra's lives. "She used to be a murderer. She's destroyed entire villages with a group of bandits that roam Gafforah. She came back here hoping to find work with them again."

Tilsman wrinkles his nose. He has believed El'rozai so far, but this is too much to be true. "Grandma Keyra? She wouldn't hurt a fly. In fact, I'm here because she took the most boring job in Gafforah and refuses to do anything else."

"The dye factory in New Nahem?"

"How did you know that?" He is oblivious to the stains of colors up his arms.

"Because that's the cover for the old organization. She's working there hoping to see a familiar face or find out if it's still their base. What we are unsure of is just how far gone she is. So here comes the most important part, Sir Tilsman. You cannot breathe a word of what we spoke of here to her. Don't let her know about the pebble I gifted you. There is a chance she has forgotten everything, and if that is true, we don't want to trigger any old memories. Does that make sense?"

Of course, it did, he was no simpleton. "How do you know all this about Grandma Keyra? I've never seen you before until the ferry."

El'rozai begins clearing the cups. "Her reputation precedes her. Ask anyone about the Reaver. You'd best be getting home, boy, the sun is setting. Here, have some coin. Say you were off making some extra to support your little family. Think of it as a bonus for the caryns you're going to be making." He offers a purse to Tilsman but holds it firm when the boy goes to grab it, to make eye contact one last time. Up this close, the leemoah's scales shimmer. "I hope this will be enough to ensure you remember our conversation."

Tilsman breathes a "yes" before tearing out of the store. He is glad he won't be required to come back there. El'rozai frightens him more than the menagerie of dead things. His back crawls with goosebumps as he takes the stairs that wind through the side streets two at a time.

While Tilsman follows his nose and, Keyra assumes, inexplicably gets himself into a life-threatening plight, she turns her face back down the road they had come. She has seen him, following her. She will give him time to approach her himself. Then she will chide him for being so obvious.

"You should be more careful," a familiar if not much older voice sounds behind her. Keyra jumps. It seems he isn't as inadequate at espionage as she thought. "Little old lady like you stands out like a sore thumb to a desperate slave looking for enough caryns to buy his freedom or a pair of shoes."

She fights the urge to embrace him but fails to hide the tears that threaten to fall. Her arms ache to embrace him. She's imagined it a thousand times over the years. "You've gotten shorter."

In truth he is no longer a lanky youth but has filled out into a full-grown man with the shadow of a beard and broad shoulders. He still carries her dark eyes and chestnut hair. "Erey," she whispers.

"Hello, Mother. I can't say this is a total surprise, although you took your sweet time looking for me." He sits on the bench beside her and hugs her warmly. Keyra allows a couple of tears to fall and wipes them away quickly before they pull away. He smells strange, of paper and the dyes and clothes washed with sweet-smelling herbs. But there is no doubt it is her son beneath the years apart. He smells of salt and sun. She hopes to carry the tingling essence of his embrace for the rest of her days.

"There were so many times I wanted to and so many excuses not to. Whether it was my health, or the weather, or there were no boats. Then I would get the chance and grow too frightened to get off the damn island. I didn't think you'd want to see me again." Every word is a painful sword in her throat. She wonders if that's the real reason she'd never looked for Erey—she hadn't wanted to face her own repentance.

"It's true I was angry for quite some time." Even now, his stature is stiff, and his eyes lack spark. "But I learned to accept it as best I could. I've moved up at the factory, that's how I knew you were here. I stamped your contract myself."

Keyra eyes his professionally sewn clothing and soft leather finery. "Upper management, eh? It suits you. I'm glad you're thriving here."

There is a flash of suppressed frustration in his face. There is much he wants to tell her but is refraining. "It was only a matter of time. I signed up a month or so after you left, and I realized I'd have to sell myself to survive. It was better than becoming a slave."

"I left you funds," Keyra snaps back, unable to stop herself. "Enough to last four months, with monthly payments. I did everything I could to ensure you were safe and comfortable."

"Everything except vet the Tower pirate you sent to take care of those funds." He grinds his jaw. It's a bad habit he must have picked up after the last time Keyra saw him.

She is silenced. She tries not to think of the past, preferring to keep it a gray blur during which time she was a different person. A worse person. It is true she had been somewhat dismissive, trusting her colleague to support her child in her absence. "I'll never live down that mistake. I'll never live down a lot. But I'm hoping while I'm here, I can set things right with you."

"I was ten, mother. I was ten when your so-called friend robbed me of everything except the clothes on my back and then left me in the street. You never thought to check on me once in *thirty years*. I think that has to be worse than whatever else you did during your illustrious career."

Keyra has a flash headache as memories are pushed to the surface. She shoves them down and her head clears. "I—I—" She can't find words. He's right, she knows that, but she also knows that she belonged on Veden during that time. It was where she needed to be.

Before she can analyze her decisions further, she sees Tilsman coming down the stairs looking flustered and out of breath. Erey catches that they recognize each other and scoffs. "You're not even here alone, are you? I've heard the rumors about Elgireth. How they've cut off transport and something is happening to the people there. You're fleeing the plague, or whatever it is. You decided to come by just because you were already here." He stands suddenly and stares down at Keyra coldly. "Your contract expires in two days. I recommend you find employment somewhere else."

Keyra can only watch him walk away, wondering why he has taken her voice with him.

~ 14 ~

BETA
&
THE BOY

It feels like days that the boy and Star are kept in the basement of Predaya's. There are no windows with which to gauge the time, so he measures it by sleeps. Two, by his count. He and the leemoah are chained to the floor by restraints short enough that the farthest he can reach are his pants to use the bedpan the captors had left them. The boy holds it as long as he can, but when the urge becomes too much he sits to use the pan, informing Star it is to spare his decency, while knowing in truth he could not stand if he was alone.

Besides the odd embarrassing moment, the boy is grateful for Star's company. She tells him tales of the underwater villages of her people and teaches him different dialects of e'likai. Their second sleep had been after a long conversation, which resulted in them drifting off on each other's shoulders.

On what must be the third day, El'rozai enters the back room with two other leemoahs. One boasts impressive muscles shown off by a tunic with the sleeves ripped off. He carries an array of weapons in his belt and a pike across his back.

The woman from before, Ayrek, follows behind the group, a sack over one shoulder with a large lump visible within. She boasts a fresh slash across one shoulder and a sour expression. "I deserve a raise," she grumbles to El'rozai.

The slaver is stressed. He growls and hurls an empty bottle against the far wall. It shatters instantly. "If they want to ignore the terms of our supposed collaboration and enter a competing contract, then so be it. We will go through with it on our own. We must move the filly. See to it, Ayrek, and try not to cause anymore chaos. They're not going to forget that you killed three of their own and stole one of their most prized artifacts from under their noses. Now they *know* that we have bigger plans than a kidnapping. Don't draw any more attention to yourself, do I make myself clear?"

The female agent is stiff but keeps her mouth closed as she nods her understanding. Her eyes turn to the boy with that strange softness again. It makes him uneasy. "What about him? Am I taking him with me, too?"

El'rozai seems to have forgotten the boy. His face wrinkles with annoyance. "No, he's just another potential liability. Reyder, weren't you going to use him in the arenas?"

The bearded agent squints as though trying to recall. "Did I? I must have been drunk. Honestly, I have no memory of saying that. But sure, I can take him off your hands. All I have for payment is some old tack though." He fishes a crumbling cracker from his pouch and offers it to the leemoah.

"I'll take it." El'rozai claps hands with Reyder.

The boy is unchained as the Tower agents laugh at his expense. No one has paid more than the price of a loaf of bread for him in his short life as a slave. He burns with rage, frustrated with the calloused nature of mortals, and the disregard for lives that mean so little to them. He sees red, and charges El'rozai.

The boy has never been a strong fighter or physically fit, but he has one trait his father had never let him forget. His skull is as thick as a cudgel, and just as hard. He rams El'rozai's gut, his stance strong and his head down. The leemoah goes flying back with a *whoosh* as the breath is knocked from his lungs. He hits the far wall and slumps to the ground, stunned and gasping for air.

Reyder roars with laughter. "Looks like I'll get my money's worth, eh?" He is too busy mocking his companion to see the second head butt from the slave boy. It hits him in the side, and the boy can hear the crack of ribs beneath his skull. Reyder howls and hits the boy squarely in the jaw. He slams the corner of the desk and feels warm blood pooling in his hair. Nausea hits him suddenly and he vomits.

Ayrek pulls him up, having watched during the entire incident. She leans forward and shakes him roughly as though to whisper some threat in his ear. Instead, she gives him information that his fuzzy brain struggles to comprehend. "Barten's Street, the red house, yellow door. That's where she'll be." She tosses him to the floor where Reyder grabs his hair and pulls him up to look him in the eye.

"That was dumb, boy, but impressive. You broke a rib or two, I can feel it. No one's done that before." His eyes are black slits in a scarred face. "Ironhead. Yes, you are Ironhead, boy, and you may be proud of that title now, but you will die in the arena, and I will laugh louder than anyone."

The boy's concussion causes him to lose his sight, unable to stop El'rozai as he and Ayrek drag Star away.

Beta has been to Nahem on more than a few occasions, but this time of year is her favorite. The perfumes of the city are heightened by the intense heat from the summer sun, as well as the scents of cooking street food. The arena's noise can be heard through most of the city and lends an air of excitement to even the most mundane days. If there is one thing that can ruin a summer day in Nahem, it is being on a mission. Vendar watched the gate while Peytner took the docks. That left Mavlin, Rolith, and Beta to spread out across the city in search of the leemoah. Malvin had been quick to take the entertainment sector where women wearing clothes smaller than most linens gestured to those with heavy coin purses and escorted them into the arenas. Rolith had taken the Sky District where at least there would be a breeze.

Beta has been stuck with the lower city where the humidity settles like a cloud and the streets stink of shit and the poor. While unenjoyable, her sector is most likely where they'll find their quarry. Here is where the slaves are sorted and exchange hands before sale. She sees countless gaunt-faced skeletons shuffling as the clang of metal announces their presence. There are branders for new captives and women bathing those about to go to the block. Beta feels a knot in her stomach as she looks at each of their empty eyes. These people are no different than the baker woman she buys bread from, or the blacksmith forging new chains. Shouldn't there be outrage over the enslavement of brothers and sisters? The Citadel works towards many goals but freeing the slaves has never been a priority. Perhaps she is reading too much into it, or perhaps the mages allow themselves to be swayed by jewels more than they care to admit.

Either way, she is not paid to save these slaves, but one in particular. In hours of searching, however, the only leemoah Beta sees is an old stallion with flaking gray scales.

Her stomach complains and she sighs wearily. She needs a break, and to get out of this heat. There is no edible food suitable for her sorceress palette in this area, so she heads up the Street of Angels. She smells garlic sea turtle from the entertainment district and follows her nose to a street stand. An old woman stirs a massive pot of soup that must be the source of the scent.

"Apprentice! You are out of your zone." The sharp voice startles Beta into standing straighter, prepared for a rebuke from Vendar. Instead, she sees Rolith, strolling towards her with a kebab in one hand and a mug of ale in the other. He is grinning ear to ear. "I scared the piss out of you, didn't I? I've been practicing my Vendar voice. It keeps the first years in line."

Beta rolls her eyes at him as she pays for her bowl of food. "Last time I checked this wasn't Sky District, either. Are you drinking on the job? You've got balls. I wouldn't dare after the lecture I got last time."

"Vendar's on the other side of the city, probably hunched in some shadows waiting for a dangerous attack that will never come. We're in Nahem in the summer, live a little! Come on, I hear the Gruesome Goblin is next in the Red Arena."

Beta gasps despite herself. "The Gruesome Goblin? Well I guess one fight couldn't hurt. I need to sit and eat somewhere."

"And stay hydrated." Rolith winks as he hands her his ale. He pulls a flask from his belt in its stead. Beta doesn't refuse it and they head deeper into the chaotic celebrations. The mission takes a back burner to the sights and smells of arena season.

There are five arenas in total, forming a line between two roads, the Brother and the Sister. The center arena is the Red Arena, reserved for reigning champions and final battles. To either side are the medium arenas, or Yellow and Orange. The outside arenas are Blue and Green, for the new fighters and criminals with death sentences.

While all five arenas are full at any given time, the Brother and Sister are their own sort of excitement. The Sister is for the women, scented with exotic spices and incense, the stalls and sitting areas covered with bright silks and flanked by palm trees alive with local birds. There are merchants who sell dresses in the most current fashions, face paint for the nobles to set themselves apart as financially superior, and countless places to find food and drink as well as spas for pampering skin beaten by the merciless sun of the dry season.

The Brother is an area for those who wish to test their skills without the risk of death in the arenas. Mostly there are nobles participating in contests such as archery, sword fighting, and comparing hunting trophies. There are also women here, although not for the same purposes as those who spend their time in the Sister. The Brother ends at a drop off that plunges forty stories into the bay below. Walls have been put in place to cut down on drunken accidents, but the view remains breathtaking.

Beta's favorite part of the arenas is the people. There are foreigners from all over the world, Lizaqese witches in their gilded red and gold robes, faces streaked with the crimson dirt of their homeland. There are Terralian nobles draped in jewels, both nobre and human alike. The nobres tower over their human neighbors, standing a good seven feet tall on hooved feet. They have red eyes that judge all equally and spikes of bone sprouting from their sand-colored scales.

Nath'iki in their golden tattoos and teeth whisper in their rapid language with the winged destriers of Loiyed. Magic-dealing demons of Sidia peer from beneath smoke-filled hoods, hoping to barter with Ankarthin bankers who wear fur-lined vests and elegant hats despite the heat. Almost all have pets of some sort or shape, from docile predators on leashes to their caged counterparts frothing at the bars. There is even a Qan man wearing leaves as clothing, followed closely by a loyal flock of white birds.

The battlemage can hardly process everything. Somehow the ale has disappeared before they can reach the Red Arena and has been replaced by a second and then a third. She and Rolith are waved in as honored guests and shown to boxes saved for highborn and retired champions of the arenas. Their scars of gray and orange work better than caryns for seats. More wine and ale are brought as well as platters of smoked fish, cheese, and bread brushed with spices and butter. A pitcher is left on their table and the sorcerers joke that their reputation precedes them.

Below, the announcer steps into the center of the massive dirt arena as slaves scamper to scrape blood and entrails from the sand. The man with the drooping moustache uses magic to expand his voice. "Ladies and gentlemen of Nahem and beyond! We have a volunteer to fight your reigning champion, the Gruesome Goblin! Hailing from Elgireth, join me in welcoming, *Ironhead!*"

There are scattered cheers from the crowd, but most are using the time to relieve themselves or gather more food. The gladiator in question enters, wearing a spiked helm that is a good three sizes too large and wobbles with every step he takes. He has a rusted flail in one hand and a splintered wooden shield in the other. He looks about Beta's age.

The announcer clears his throat for silence once more as Ironhead enters the center of the ring. "And now, the moment you've been waiting so patiently for! He hails from the mountains of Sidia where men grow as large as the rocks they carve their homes from. He has been a gladiator in these arenas for over a decade and has yet to be defeated. Known as the Smasher, the Basher, the Skull Crasher, *pleaaseeee* join me in welcoming, *The Gruesome Goblin!*"

The roar that goes up from the Red Arena startles birds from their nests on the nearby cliff sides. The man that enters is taller than any nobre and as thick as six of them together. He wears glittering armor bearing his own insignia—a rare honor for a gladiator. The red sun on his chest glows, bathing the dirt the color of blood. He wields a tree trunk as his weapon and nothing else. He beats his chest plate with it as the crowd continues to scream. He circles twice before coming back to the center of the ring, dwarfing the poor slave with the oversized helm. The announcer starts to back out of the ring but Ironhead tugs on his sleeve before he can exit. The boy whispers something into the announcer's ear and the man laughs.

"Ladies and gentlemen, our brave Ironhead has just told me he wishes to yield!" The cheers are replaced with laughter and the young gladiator hangs his head in shame. The announcer shakes him on the shoulder. "There, there, little slave, it will all be over soon!"

"Goblin came here to draw blood, little man, and I will have yours!" He bangs his chest again and the crowd loses it.

"There you have it, Ironhead, best say your prayers to whatever spirit or god you think can save you now!" The announcer gives him one last pat on the back before sprinting out of the arena. The Gruesome Goblin has a habit of starting fights before he and his opponent are the only ones in the ring.

Beta dips bread in her wine and sucks on it eagerly. She has hoped for a fair fight, but it may be the only one she watches before Vendar discovers their betrayal yet again.

"Whoo! Beta, Rolith!" Malvin waves to them from a few boxes below, his bench full of fawning escorts. He is several pitchers in judging by the sway of his body and the red in his eyes.

Rolith salutes the stone mage with his own chalice and shakes his head. "I don't know what we expected, sending him here for recon."

"Speak for yourself, I expected just that. I also expected we wouldn't see Peynter here."

Rolith smirks. "He is either reporting us missing to Vendar at the moment or ended up falling into the bay because he saw something suspicious in the waves."

They are distracted from further conversation when the fight starts with the Goblin rushing Ironhead. The tree trunk slams into the dirt hard enough to send up a massive cloud of dust. The smaller boy comes dashing out of the cloud as though Heliendiel is on his heels. His shield and weapon have been discarded as he gives way fully to cowardice and makes for the nearest entrance. The crowd boos as he pulls at the bars to no avail. The Goblin becomes frustrated. "You are scared little man. You do not deserve to fight the Gruesome Goblin!" He throws the trunk like a javelin with impressive accuracy. The boy barely dodges the blow by ducking but cannot get out of the way of the weapon as it bounces off the bars and hits him squarely in the chest. Beta sucks in a sharp breath as she recognizes the sound of air jarringly smacked from his lungs. He lies there, moaning, his helmet thrown to the side so the pain in his face is clearer than ever. There is more booing from unsatisfied spectators. They came here to watch a battle, not a hunt.

The Goblin raises a fist the size of an adult skull. Ironhead reaches for his helmet, face red from the effort of breathing. He pulls it over his head just as the Goblin slams down. The Goblin howls in pain and draws back before he can follow through. The spike has pierced straight through his palm, embedded there even as he pulls back, spraying blood. The giant plucks the weapon from his fist like a splinter and tosses it to the side.

"That's it! I will squash you, bug!"

Ironhead is sprinting for his weapon and shield now that he understands escape is not an option. As he runs, Beta squints curiously. She recognizes him, but from where?

The crowd cheers as the Goblin rips off his armor, revealing massive wings on his back in a dramatic display. Beta is on her feet with the rest of the spectators as the Goblin is airborne with three solid pumps of feathers as long as a ship's mast. He hovers over the boy at eye level with the stands, dropping on him and gripping him in a bear hug. He carries Ironhead above the ground as he squeezes, the boy's legs flailing wildly. A lucky back kick catches the Goblin in the groin, and he is dropped.

He scrabbles at the air desperately, giving a shriek that would embarrass a child, before he lands heavily on the ground. There is a collective sharp breath from those watching when he doesn't move right away. At best, the wind is knocked from his lungs for a second time. His stillness suggests that if he is not dead, he has accepted that it will happen soon. "Kill him!"

"Die, already!"

"Now's your chance, Gruesome Goblin!" The jeers come from those who are here for blood.

Beta does not care to see the boy's skull squashed like a fruit. While the bloody show is satisfying in the moment, seeing strategy on display keeps the arenas from becoming dull to her.

Goblin groans as he recovers from the well-placed heel kick, crumpled unceremoniously on the ground where his great wings trail in the dust. It gives Ironhead time to gather his breath and pop back up to mixed reactions. No one appears more surprised than he is. Beta is almost impressed. He may not be a warrior, but he can take a hit. He retrieves his spiked helm, which is now dented enough that it fits. He adjusts it squarely and charges Goblin with his head lowered and a scream of terror on his lips. The yell is high pitched and carries over the arena to the tittering of the spectators. This combatant is certainly an odd one. He catches the Gruesome Goblin in the thigh as the bigger man rolls to his feet. The champion howls in pain and swings wildly with both fists. One catches Ironhead in the temple and he goes sprawling in the dirt, unmoving. The crowd stills as they sense the match is coming to a bloody end. The Goblin tears the spike from his thigh and limps over to his victim. With his face open to the sky, Beta remembers where she knows him from.

"Let's see how you like getting poked with this thing!" He stabs down hard enough for every person to wince and hold their breath. The spike hovers a millimeter from the boy's heart, stopped by an invisible shield. The boy jumps out of the way before the weapon embeds in the dirt up to the broken hilt. "*Sorcerer!*" Goblin howls and points an accusing finger at Ironhead. The boy has gathered his flail and shield and is standing in a defensive position. The crowd is renewed with fire. There has never been a magic user in the arena before. Those with gifts do not become slaves. There are shouts from the gambler's boxes as betters call "foul" and "cheat." They mutter that the arena owners brought in a ringer knowing there is no other way to defeat the great Gruesome Goblin.

Rolith glances curiously at Beta and her slightly glowing skin but says nothing. Beta is as still as a stone. She cannot interfere anymore, or she will start a mob.

The second chance has accomplished its goal, however, and the boy is more engaged than ever before. He recognizes his luck has run out and the next blow will find its mark.

He dances around the giant for a few moments, calculating his next move and wearing down the bigger man. The Goblin's wings hang limply, and his breaths are labored. He spins to face Ironhead again and lands heavily on his wounded leg. This is the chance the boy's been waiting for. He jumps from behind Goblin, using his wings as a ladder to get where he can wrap his flail around his neck and yank him to the dirt.

The spectators go wild. Beta notices the benches are full now and commoners flood the entrances, straining for a peek at the historic fight.

Ironhead scrambles up from beneath Goblin and pulls his flail free. The Gruesome Goblin has landed the back of his head directly on the spiked ball and whimpers as blood pools beneath his skull. Here is the part that gives Beta chills. The crowd begins a chant, barely above a whisper at first. "Kill him, kill him, kill him." It grows louder and louder as Ironhead hesitates, his defeated foe breathing shallowly on the ground. "Kill him, kill him." The chant is now a shout and then a scream. The boy looks once more at the Goblin, then shakes his head and drops his flail.

"I don't want to be the champion! These arena fights are fish guts," she can see him mouth, his actual voice drowned out by the spectators. He gives them a rude gesture and makes for the exit. The crowd falls silent. Denying a death means the fate of the victor is in the hands of the arena king, a mock royal figure whose sole purpose is to sit and watch fights, occasionally making a call such as this one. The rotund man is draped in false jewels with a crown tipped sideways on his head. He stands and lifts his arms. With a brief nod, his judgement has been made. The boy lives.

Beta cheers along with Rolith, downing the last of the pitcher in victory.

Their celebration is short-lived as Vendar's gloved hands come to rest on their shoulders.

~ 15 ~

WENDWYNN
&
ZAVOSH

Warprince Dzaxar was handsome by Mangzarian standards. His eyes were a deep orange, and he had the signature widow's peak of his family. He rivaled Wen in height but not in stature. He had a lithe build that would do him no good in hand-to-hand combat. Not that his physical attributes mattered anymore.

The warprince sat beside the queen as she worked in her solar, studying maps and running her finger down pages of books that explained the lore and culture of the many districts of Mangzar. She would need every weapon she could find against them, including superstitions and religion. Dzaxar answered any question she had to the best of his ability. She liked this version of him. He was open, friendly, and utterly devoted to her. She kept him with her everywhere she went, from holding court to travelling to different military posts. He was crucial to the next step in her plan. She needed to buy herself some time. With Dzaxar's knowledge of his father's military movements and strengths, she could stage low-risk raids and sabotage to distract them and slow them down. Having him seen often by her people and anyone that may leak information back to Mount Thoyax enabled her to simultaneously inspire her followers and demoralize Warlord Halthax by openly defying his request for the war-prince's death. The Gaffori saw a Mangzarian that had taken to the queen and stood on her side of the war. Recruitment was up, and general morale was high. If Wen could speak sense to the Mangzarians, then there was a chance for peace. They no longer saw her as a struggling queen in a land she was unfamiliar with, but as a savior. Nobles and commoners alike whispered to each other. Good, Wen wanted the word to get back to Mangzar. She wanted to antagonize Halthax into attacking blindly. She would love to see him fly off the Street of Angels.

Those that recognized the prince were wary. The generals who had captured the prince during the Ulden invasion kept their mouths pressed shut but did little else to hide their disapproval. They would remain loyal to her for now, but at the first sign of her abusing the Puppetmaster power, she had no doubt they would turn on her. She would expect no different.

"And what about the family of a Warlord? Do they live in the fortress?" She had learned to focus on both the page and Dzaxar's answers to her incessant questions at the same time.

"No. A true Warleader can be usurped at any time, and that includes direct family. The spouse and children will remain in their previous home, although most Warleaders see it as a liability and choose to refrain from procreation."

"You really do think of little else than killing, don't you?"

Her faithful shadow laughed. "We are the warriors of the fire mountains, Your Grace. Do the volcanoes stop spewing molten fire and death? No, they must continue if they are to survive. The largest are the strongest because they feed off their own flames. The weak cool and harden until they become a field for planting. You have seen Mangzarian artwork, correct? The intricate details are more lifelike than any other."

"I have," Wen admitted.

"We perfected it through generations of hard work, as we have weapons forging and the art of taking life. Viprs more so than the human integrations, but their blood is still that of lava."

"I have seen viprs taking souls, it is easy to see how your people believe you are meant to kill." The memory was not a pleasant one.

"Your Grace," Grevin said as he bowed from the doorway. He never called her by her title unless there was grave news. "High Priest Lekala, of Saltspire."

Wen closed the book in front of her. It was strange for the religious island community to get involved in matters of conflict. She feared there was grave news. The priest that entered was a small man in orange and silver robes who wasted no time in throwing back his hood and bowing. "Your Grace."

"High Priest. It is an honor to finally meet someone from Saltspire Temple. What can I do for you in this time of war?"

The High Priest looked no more than a child, with a shaved head and face. His black eyes were emotionless as he looked up at the queen. "You were never known for small talk. I appreciate that. It is the war that brings me here, Your Grace, although not for the sake of Saltspire. I have spoken to Admiral Yo'aro, who is currently engaged in combat and instructed me to bring tidings to you. The colonies have been attacked in force. The sky blackened overnight. Your ships have been engaged in combat with them since this morning. Saltspire has opened its beaches to Gafforah's own to do repairs and take on the wounded. Your Admiral attempted to send word through scouting ships, but none made it through. She feared the Mangzarians would encircle her forces if she broke off any to warn Nahem, so she sent me as an envoy."

"Mangzarians are not sailors by nature, but their engineering makes swift ships. It was lucky you made it through, and unlikely that anyone else will," Dzaxar stated soberly.

Lekala glanced at him in confusion, but Wen spoke before he could question the vipr's presence at the queen's side. "This is deeply disturbing news. My studies suggested that they would not attack non-military targets as there will be no altercation worth their time. What would they have to gain from killing farmers?" she wondered aloud, but Dzaxar answered eagerly.

"You are correct in assuming the honor system of the Mangzarians. It is not their nature to attack people that are not warriors. My deduction is that Warlord Halthax intends to enrage you to the point of a misstep. You have outwitted him more than once now, and he's attempting to level the playing field."

"The captains I spoke to feared that as well." Lekala bowed to Dzaxar, accepting him for the moment. "Saltspire Island will not engage in warfare, but it goes against our values to sit back and watch people die. I came at once, but even my sloop could not slip past them. They captured me and told me to bring a message to you. Warlord Halthax ky Dzaxar the Greater seeks an audience with your grace, on my island where there is still some neutral ground."

The burning of the colonies was a hard blow to Gafforah. The tiny islands were often the most fertile and supplied many different products to Gafforah and Saltspire alike. There would be shortages in the city now, and they would have to import more. Relations were good with Nath'iki, but the other nations were not so welcoming of Gafforah's new queen. Wendwynn could swear she heard Yo'aro screaming "I told you so" from her position nearly a hundred miles away.

The High Priest pulled a scroll from his sleeve and handed it to Grevin, who passed it to Wendwynn. The seal was a black skull, a feather clenched between its teeth. There was no doubt it came from Dzaxar. Instead of opening it, she handed it to the warprince. "Halthax ky Dzaxar, what do you make of this?"

The Priest, realizing who she was addressing, finally showed emotion on his face in the expression of confusion. The warprince was unconcerned with the opinions of the people and nodded as he inspected the scroll. "This is my father's seal, Your Grace. I have seen it only a few times before. He prefers to send messages on the end of his sword."

"He has already done that in the colonies, it would seem. In your opinion, why would he send me a message in writing?"

"He would only do so if he felt threatened, Your Grace. He is playing by civilized rules because traditional Mangzarian methods of aggression aren't working."

"And the burning of the colonies? Is that civilized?"

The warprince smiled, his eyes open and honest. Wen could sense Grevin watching him with intent concentration. "While he may intend to take hold on the islands, the more likely reason is he is angry, and acting irrationally. It is a blow to his honor that he has not defeated you yet, and the longer the war drags on, the more incompetent he appears as a leader."

Wen gritted her teeth. "Therefore, if I cannot win the war quickly, he will continue to push harder. Read the scroll," Wen commanded.

Dzaxar's voice boomed through the solar. He read it first in Var, then in translation to Andreli. "Foreign thief, we have stolen enough from each other. Let us face each other as equals and determine the future of this war."

"What does that mean to you, Dzaxar?"

"It sounds like a trap, Your Grace. What would my father have to discuss? He will not treat for peace, and he will not negotiate for my release. I can think of no reason he would want to speak under treaty."

Dzaxar must not have known about Wen's spies, or their mission in Mangzar. Warlord Halthax had known about Ugden, and she was willing to bet he knew what they were looking for there. Did his message have a deeper, hidden meaning?

"I will discuss this amongst my leaders and seek action against Mangzar for the colonies right away, High Priest. You may rest here as my honored guest until it is time to return the message."

The priest bowed low, understanding he was dismissed. "I thank you for your time, Your Grace. The priests mourn for your dead and pray for the war's swift end. Should you seek the solace of the spirits or agree to treat with the Warlord, our gates will always be open to peace."

He turned to leave, and the queen smirked to herself. She was wise enough to catch the undertones. The priest feared the war would come to Saltspire, and he would do anything to stop it. She hoped it would not come to that but there were no guarantees in battle.

Grevin sat across from the queen, stiff and uncomfortable in the warprince's presence. "I may not like your new friend, but he does have a point. If you go to Saltspire, you'll certainly be walking into a trap."

"One crisis at a time. We need to send reinforcements to the colonies. Have Nalag send word to the northern fleet, at Gerildd. We will evacuate the colonists to Ulden until the war is over. Those that are willing to work with the *retyot* can till the land until the colonies are restored."

Dzaxar seemed surprised through his spelled features. "They won't be there by the time reinforcements arrive, Your Grace. They have accomplished their task. Not only have they struck a blow against your economy and morale, but your arrival after they have dissipated will make you appear weak to the farmers as opposed to engaging the enemy."

Wen drummed her fingers thoughtfully on the table. Warlord Halthax was leaving her with damage control in a land where she was yet to be completely accepted. Perhaps he wasn't all bloodthirst and aggression after all. "Then we shall press harder. If they don't view this as a battle, and therefore there is no loss of honor if they retreat once they have done a significant amount of damage, then we will use it against them. We will have Yo'aro chase them back into their own waters. If they defend themselves, we will decimate them. After all, they aren't sailors. If they continue the retreat, we will have shamed them."

Grevin gave her an empathetic glance. "I agree that aggression is a wise course of action against Mangzar. However, we must also consider the people that have been affected. I think you should go there yourself. They will need to see that the queen is engaged on a personal level with the victims."

Her shoulders drooped wearily. Apologizing and swallowing criticism had never been her strong point. She was already dreading the next conversation she would have with her Admiral. "After the summit with Halthax. I need to have something to show for them besides empty regrets and the promise to defend the ashes of their lives." Just a little more time. If Halthax had found her prize before she had, then all was lost. She dared not mention Frejith's mission in the presence of Dzaxar, even in his state. There was always the minute chance that it could leak back to Mount Thoyax. She and Grevin exchanged knowing looks confirming they had come to the same conclusion. "Dzaxar, that will be all. You may return to your chamber and sleep until you are needed again."

The warprince bowed deeply. "Many thanks for the honor of being in your presence, Your Grace. I think I will retire for the moment, until your next summons."

Once the queen and her advisor were alone, Wen allowed her royal mask to slip ever so slightly. "If he found it, he wouldn't be raiding the colonies. It's almost as concerning as the fact they were able to burn them to the ground overnight and I'm just hearing of it now."

"The colonies are far to the northwest, Wendwynn, closer to Mangzar than to Gafforah. They are not visible to any other Gaffori outpost, and they have no army to speak of. It isn't as large of a mistake as you may think."

The queen stood and lifted an eyebrow wryly at Grevin as she unfurled the map. "The fact is, Yo'aro was right, and I was wrong. I was too swept up in my own personal issues to consider a move that could have saved hundreds of lives." She stared calculatingly at Grevin. "And what is the truth that you are so eloquently attempting to hide from me?"

He leaned back, comfortable with revealing all his cards. "You and I are strangers here in Andriel. You have never been to the colonies, and I daresay I've forgotten about them more than once, which means they have to have slipped your mind on occasion. They aren't clear on any maps, so they aren't readily obvious to the distracted eye. They provide only a fraction of the food in Gafforah, remaining mostly self-sufficient and travelling to the mother island only when necessary. They have no military presence because they have never needed it. Mangzar has until now, never had a desire or need for the speckling of tiny islands in the bay. They aren't large enough to house troops, or strategic enough to prove useful in war. The ugly truth, Your Grace, is that you made a mistake that should have been small but was used against you in a major way."

Wen stared out at Kaper's Bay, wishing she could jump from the window into the enticingly cool waves far below. "And now I must eat crow," she muttered more to herself than to Grevin.

"It's what a good queen would do."

"Thank you, Grevin. Please see to it that we have a military presence in the colonies from now on. I will inform the High Priest in the next couple of days what my reply to Warlord Halthax is." She couldn't seem too eager, or available to come at his beck and call. "I need a moment."

The queen made her way with heavy steps to her chambers.

She rarely spent time there, preferring the comfort of the library or parts of the Keep that opened to the sun. The royal chambers were in the heart of the mountain. Its position was meant to be strategically safe, but it felt more like one of the tombs that riddled the Keep. The lack of sound was more oppressive than the clanging of the arena, closing in on the queen as though she was already one of the dead. She hated being alone. It terrified her.

As they always did when she was away from Frejith and matters were becoming overwhelming, the queen's thoughts strayed to her wife. She had heard nothing since her departure from Nahem. She had to hope that meant the sorceress had vanished into the Mangzarian populace as she had promised she could. It could also mean that she had been captured and Wen would watch her die on Saltspire. Perhaps they would all die on Saltspire, and her troubles would come to a sudden, if not welcome, end.

Zavosh ensured he was awake long before the rest of the barracks was. He intended to confront Frejith again before there were too many prying eyes. He knew he should trust the sorceress, as well as his queen, but he couldn't shake the heavy feeling in his gut that her headlong rush into their mission would end horribly. Memories of Ugden's brutal screams as he was ripped apart kept playing through the vipr's mind. Mangzar did not offer trials or jailtime as punishment. Every citizen was judge, jury, and executioner when they deemed someone a threat to their way of life. It was a sobering reminder of how dangerous their position was.

He found her sitting on a barrel near the ship he'd been working on for the past month, dashing spice sauce on the traditional meat wraps of Mangzarian breakfast. She offered him one with a smile. "I think we got off on the wrong foot yesterday. The last thing I want is for you and me to be fighting when we should be devoting every second to completing our search."

Zavosh accepted the wrap and dipped it in the sauce rather than sprinkling it on. He gave her a knowing look that suggested she should do the same. No self-respecting Mangzarian would be so frugal with the spice sauce. "I agree. However, we seem to disagree on the methods to continuing our search. It will be nearly impossible to get into the keep, much less be allowed there for long increments of time. It could be months or years before we make any progress."

Frejith was doing her best to eat the spiced wraps, her face muscles twitching with the effort of concealing how uncomfortable she was with the intense flavor. She cleared her throat inconspicuously before speaking. "We don't have that much time to spare. I don't know how much you've heard about the war, but we're incredibly lucky to have made it as far as we have. You need to understand that there's a reason Wen sent me. She can't afford to play it safe any longer. None of us can. It's time to take risks." There was urgency in her face, even disguised beneath her spells. Frejith had always shown the most expression in her eyes.

"Maybe you're right. Maybe we need to think more about reaching our goals than protecting our own skins. But if we die, the mission will probably never be completed. They will lock down the borders even more and any progress will be lost. It could be months before the Queen even knows we're gone."

They paused their conversation as the rest of the shipwrights filed in for their own jobs. There were a surprising number of ships to be repaired, suggesting there had been a battle recently. "Do you trust me?" Frejith asked, catching Zavosh off guard.

"I—well, I don't know." How could he lie to the mind mage? "I don't know you."

"The hard truth of it is we've tried it your way, and one of my friends died." The spark of humor that always crackled in her hair and skin was gone. "Ugden liked to take things slowly, too. Now it's time to do things my way, and I need to be sure you're on board, or we're unquestionably doomed. Do we have an understanding?"

"Yes." Zavosh swallowed around the lump in his throat. It seemed he was outranked and outvoted. "*Rath Noki Saryn.*" 'I will hold them down for you'; a traditional Mangzarian acknowledgement of comradery and unquestionable support.

"*Mo'al thran ketar sa,*" Frejith responded in perfect Var. 'And there will be blood.'

They didn't have time to discuss their plans further as a long, low blast cut through the silence of the morning. The Warlord was on the move. Zavosh and Frejith moved with the rest of the viprs to the main road, answering the horn call. The street cut from Fortress Blackfeather's steps all the way east to the shoreline where the Warlord's wavecutter swayed in the breeze in the nearby harbor. The vessel was painted black with maroon sails and a flag that bore a skull pierced by a feather. Four smaller vessels clustered in its shadow. The crowds that gathered were small. Every able-bodied person was off training or already raiding. Those that lined the street were hunched with age or a child. Babes hung from most backs, left to be tended by the grandparents while the parents fought and died together. Zavosh had been one of those children the last time he was here.

The marching steps of the warriors signaled their approach. There were three hundred of them—men and women of varying heights. They wore the spirit masks of Mangzarian warriors, each one more terrible than the last. Fangs leered through bloodstained mouths and striped masks framed striped eyes. The warriors walked not in unison by rank, but as one, pouring towards the ocean like a waterfall alive with fish. They greeted the spectators, hugging a child here and shaking an old man's hand there. There was laughter and conversation as they made their way to the docks. They may as well have been headed off for a day of fishing.

Zavosh's eyes were drawn to a man wearing studded black leather of a finer quality than the average foot soldier. His mask hung from his neck, leaving his tattooed face exposed.

"Who is that?" Frejith whispered.

"Kovay. A lieutenant. He is renowned around here. You would do well to know the war heroes."

"The magic around him is strong," she commented. Zavosh was pleased to hear there was a sober tone to her otherwise carefree voice.

As they watched, Kovay took notice of the couple and locked them in his striped gaze. He was frightening with a shaved head and countless tattoos, but his voice was friendly enough. "You look too young to be among the *inthaie.*"

Zavosh spoke quickly as he assumed Frejith wouldn't know the Var word for elderly. "She was wounded in a previous raid. I repair ships and tend to her."

Kovay was unimpressed. "Mangzar is at war. Only the *isilth* cower on our lands."

"I am strong enough to fight. We are going to the Fortress for *xari'kai.*" Frejith's statement caught Zavosh off guard. *Xari'kai* was rehabilitation in the form of training with specialized warriors. It was precisely what someone in her condition would do as a true Mangzarian.

Kavoy nodded his approval. "*Rath Noki Saryn.*"

He waved and was gone among the soldiers as Frejith answered, "*Mo'al thran ketar sa.*"

"Impressive," Zavosh murmured.

"Just because I don't read doesn't mean I don't listen when

my wife does. Maybe you shouldn't assume I'm as simple as you told the dockworkers." She smiled wryly.

There were five warriors bringing up the rear. Their armor had spikes and studs and were made of ash steel instead of leather. The specialized Mangzarian metal did not glow or reflect light. In the center of the group was a vipr with skin the color of olives and long hair that came to a point in the center of his forehead. It was white, as were his heavy brows and the shadow of hair along his jaw. The aura of magic he gave off must have been felt by Frejith because she clutched his arm tight. Zavosh didn't have to be a sorcerer to know who and what this man was. It was Warlord Halthax ky Dzaxar. He wore only two tattoos, a skull on the back of each hand. He wore no armor or visible weapons, only a light gray tunic and black breeches tucked into rough boots. Just like the legends.

He passed without a word to anyone on the streets, but his eyes lingered on every face. Zavosh felt chills when they touched him. Was it his imagination or did he pause a moment longer on Frejith? She was frozen; breathless. Then his red-and-orange striped eyes moved on and she could breathe again.

"Kovay won't just forget us, you know. He'll come looking for you at the fortress when he returns," Zavosh told Frejith, the roiling fear in his gut renewed by their brush with the Warlord.

"We'll be there when he returns. We'll say my *xari'kai* was unsuccessful, but I'm determined to help the district by working as a servant there. I'm one good drinking session away from being offered a position with one of my connections."

Zavosh cringed at her cursory thought process. One misstep, one hole in her story, and they would meet the same doom as Ugden. He forced his jaw to unclench. Maybe she was right—he needed to trust her. He'd blown his chance. "It's going to be incredibly dangerous, Maryin. You already reek of an *isilth* without adding the fact that you're actually a Gaffori."

Frejith patted his cheek reassuringly as though she was comforting a frightened child. "Overthinking is just as dangerous as underthinking, if not more. Trust me. I've gotten us this far."

"And where exactly have you gotten us? Under the watchful eye of Mount Thoyax's most powerful?"

"You mean *closer* to Mount Thoyax's most powerful."

Zavosh felt a churning in his stomach at the frenzied light in his partner's eye.

~ 16 ~
KEYRA

It is nearly light when Keyra gives up on sleep. The tossing and turning she's done all night have left her feeling stiff and aching. She decides to stretch her legs and give her creaking bones a chance to warm up before her last day of work at the dye factory. She has glimpsed Erey in his office above the floor, but any efforts to make eye contact have been blatantly ignored. She knows she deserves it, and that there is little chance of reconciling with her son, but it hurts deeper than any sword all the same. She glances at Tilsman to ensure he is snoring peacefully before exiting the barracks. Unlike her, he has no trouble finding comfort on the straw-strewn floor.

Keyra shuffles down the street in the predawn gray, relishing the peace before the fires of the factories start up and the air is clogged with the scent of smoke and burnt leather. She heads for the nearby docks where fisherfolk are gathering their nets for the upcoming day. They pay her no mind, having no time to waste when it comes to their profits. Seagulls gather hungrily, awaiting the feast that comes with the small fleet. It makes her miss Hardock and the familiar scents that are as much a part of her as they are the sea. She wonders if she will ever see her home again, and her heart hurts at the question.

A small sloop catches her eye farther down the boardwalk. The flag bears the symbol of the Tower, a ship with a stone column for a mast on a blue background. It was meant to symbolize the organization's ability to adapt to matters of land and sea, to show they were always moving, yet always the same. It seems ridiculous to Keyra now, years later. What kind of ship can float with a stone tower for a mast?

The former seamstress approaches the vessel to find a single courier loading bundles of papers on board. The Tower has thousands of contracts shuffling hands at any given time, for trading, pardoning members, processing warrants for unruly crew, and the ever-lucrative slave business. "Under Akai," she nods to the cloaked figure.

The messenger looks young enough to be a child and jumps at Keyra's greeting. "Under Akai." He clutches the bundle in his hands close to his chest as though she will try to snatch it from him. "Did someone send you? I know I was supposed to head out last night, but someone was late for their delivery to me."

"I'm not with the Tower. Not anymore." Are those memories trying to push their way back to her conscious self? They make her head pound. She mentally shoves them away. "I'm wondering if you have any news of Elgireth? I hear there was some trouble there."

The courier's eyes dart around the docks nervously. "I shouldn't be talking to anyone about that. Very few people know so as not to start a panic."

"Well, I know because I fled from there," Keyra snaps impatiently. Since when are Tower members so fidgety? "Tell me what you know."

He shakes his head definitively and finishes loading the bundles onto the vessel. "I won't say a word. You won't hear it from me, no."

Keyra grumbles to herself as she steps onto the sloop and slams an elbow into the boy's throat with accuracy she didn't know she possessed. He gasps for air and loses his balance, falling back onto the deck. Keyra stands over him, rolling up her sleeves, unsure as to what it is she's threatening to do to the boy if he doesn't talk. "Listen here, whelp, I'm sure you've heard that once you've taken your oaths, you're a member of the Tower for life. Respect your elders and your seniors and tell me what in the waves is happening in Elgireth."

The boy flounders for breath, rubbing his neck and wincing. "Okay, okay, I'll tell you. They've shut down the docks and are turning vessels away. That's about it. They don't tell me much, but I have been bringing messages to and from the Citadel, so I'm sure they know what's going on."

Keyra doesn't bring up the tales of the hollow-eyed Elgir. The boy has been frightened enough for the time being. "There's a good lad." She pats his cheek comfortingly. "You'd better shove off before you get further behind schedule."

He scrambles to obey as she disembarks and nods curtly to the curious few that witnessed her assault on the courier. His information is troubling for how little there is to tell. Certainly, there should be emergency action taken to save the people of Elgireth. Keyra has always known there is prejudice from Gafforah to the smallfolk of their neighboring colony islands, but she can't imagine they would be left to die. She won't ignore the itch in the back of her head that the best place for her to be is at the Citadel. It seems foolish and dangerous, and she knows they cannot be trusted, so why does she want to take Tilsman and go back to Elgireth?

The damned headache returns and Keyra empties her mind to be rid of it. She can't go to the Citadel. Leaving Erey again would cement her reputation as a horrible mother in his mind. This is her last chance to make things right.

The sky is a gentle pink that warns the summer sun in all its brutal glory is not long in coming. Keyra heads back for the barracks where her colleagues are just waking up for the day.

She nudges Tilsman awake with a foot. "Come on now, boy, it's our last day of work, which means we should enjoy eating while we can."

Tilsman groans at the thought and shakes fleas from his shaggy red hair. "No need, Granma Keyra, I found some caryns yesterday." He pulls out a heavy purse with coins spilling out the top. Every eye in the barracks snaps to the boy and the treasure waving in his hand. Keyra slaps it down quickly.

"What are you doing?" she hisses, nearly dragging him outside where she feels less exposed to hungry, desperate faces. "Where did you get that?"

"I did some woodworking," Tilsman lies quickly. He is unconvincing and gets his ear twisted for his fib.

"Try again." The factory workers start dragging their feet to work but Keyra hangs back with her charge. "Did you steal it?"

"I got it honestly, Granma Keyra, honestly." She can tell he is holding something back, his cheeks puffing up comically with the physical effort. He should spill his secrets with a good squeeze. Keyra twists his ear harder, and he does a little jig trying to get away.

"Hey, you! You can't torture that kid." One of the local law enforcement officers jogs up to the two of them, whip in hand. He pulls Keyra away from Tilsman and the seamstress curses her luck.

"Apologies, officer, my grandson was giving me lip. I'm sure you don't tolerate the disrespect of elders."

He narrows his eyes suspiciously at her. "You have an Elgir accent. What are you doing in Gafforah?"

"Working, same as yourself, sir. My grandson and I would like to finish up our last day of work at the factory if you don't mind. We're not here to make trouble."

She looks to Tilsman for support, but the child has had enough. His cheeks have reddened to match his hair. His hands are balled into fists as he stamps a foot. "I'm not your grandson, as you've made clear many times." He crosses his arms defiantly, blatantly ignoring the fact that he has called her "Granma" multiple times. "I'm tired of you twisting my ear and calling me fat and treating me like I'm an idiot."

Keyra is taken aback by his forwardness, yet internally proud that he's sticking up for himself. The officer looks again to Keyra with a disappointed shake of his head. "Not only do you physically assault this child, who is unrelated to you, on a regular basis, but you also verbally abuse him? I think it's best if both of you come down to the station to answer a few questions."

"I don't think that's necessary—" Keyra is cut off as two more officers arrive as reinforcements. Keyra and Tilsman are marched sternly away from the factory towards the local station, firm grips on their arms. She turns to Tilsman with a growl. "What do you think you're doing, boy? They could put me in jail or ship me back to Elgireth. What do you think will happen then? You'll be snatched up and sold as a slave within the day!"

Tilsman's defiant expression falters but he pushes through and squares his shoulders. "That's my problem, not yours, now. You don't even believe me when I say I'm making an honest living. You assumed I stole the money, and then punished me when you didn't believe me."

"Quiet," one of their escorts says gruffly. Keyra keeps her mouth closed until she and the boy are sat on a bench in the station's foyer.

When they are alone, tears brim in Tilsman's eyes. He's frightened despite his stubbornness. Keyra sighs as her heart softens. "I'm sorry, boy—Tilsman. I'm a grumpy old woman and I've lived a hard life. Tough love and putting people I'm in charge of in their place is the only thing I know. I forget how it can hurt a soft kid like you."

Tilsman sticks his nose up in the air in indignation. "I'm not soft, I just don't like to yell at my elders because I am respectful. If you'd stop criticizing me for a moment, you'd see that."

Their arresting officers are speaking to the uniform at the desk across the room. Keyra leans close to the boy. "You're right, you've survived some of the most horrible things I've witnessed in this life, and I often forget how young you are. I understand you wanting to act out, but this isn't the place or the way to do it. There could be serious repercussions if they decide I'm unfit to watch you."

She sees a twinkle of understanding in his face, but it is gone when he touches the redness of his ear. "Repercussions like what? I bet they'll give me to someone that will be able to take care of me properly, not force me to work in a factory for table scraps! Or they'll get me back home to Waheth where at least people won't insult me for my red hair and freckled skin, even if it is a craphole of a country. I could even find that nice leemoah and start up with the Tower. It was good enough for you, wasn't it?"

That strikes a chord Keyra can't ignore. "You *stupid* little brat! You were wandering the streets alone, starving and moments from being enslaved or worse when I found you." Her voice raises enough to draw attention from the officers, but she doesn't notice. "I brought you with me to Gafforah when I could have left you to die and saved my own skin. Isah died because I thought I could help you and did what I could to save you from whatever *curse* you brought on Elgireth!"

The silence that follows her statement only makes her statement echo the louder. Every eye in the station, from the officers at the desk to the criminals in the holding cells, their faces pressed to the bars to see the speaker, are on her. Keyra stammers as the flame inside her belly subsides. "I—I didn't mean that. He didn't—he's not—"

One of the enforcers that brought them in pulls them to their feet and shoves them apart from each other. "I don't know how they handle things in your backwater village, madam, but in Gafforah we don't use that word lightly. Since there were witnesses to your claim, we will have to process you two as a serious threat to national security. Yirgrim, put them in separate holding cells and lock down the precinct. Lieutenant Cole, send word to the Citadel for a thorough investigation."

Keyra hangs her head dejectedly as she is shoved roughly into a cell and a flurry of activity commences as officers remove suspects and gather things from their desks. She cannot blame them. She used the word "curse." Andriel is full of magic, each region with their own specialties and types. Most can be used for good. Other kinds are notorious as they have potential for personal gain or malintent. But there is one universal term that transcends all others. Whenever there is a horrible disaster that claims thousands of lives, or an unexplainable tragedy of massive proportions that can never be remedied, it is a curse that comes to mind. It is more of a legend than a fact, a whisper in the shadows of the worst possible scenario. There has never been proof that casting a curse is possible through mortal means. It is supposed to be a word from the gods that mortals have passed the point of saving. It is a cleansing—a terrible redemption through fire and blood.

A *curse* is not a type of magic that can be learned and controlled. It is an apocalypse, and Keyra has yelled Tilsman may be responsible for one for all to hear. She stares at her shaking hands as her world crumbles into chaos around her.

~ 17 ~
THE BOY

"**I**ronhead! Ironhead!" The chant is like something out of a dream to the boy. He is lifted above the heads of his new and adoring fans while the Goblin is surrounded by medical mages. These people are looking at him not with disgust or indifference, but with love and respect. The sensation makes him lightheaded, and he trembles with adrenaline. Is this what it feels like to be a king? It must be. He is untouchable.

Reyder follows along beside the procession, receiving congratulations and accepting money from those who bet against his slave. He has forgotten Ironhead was supposed to die in the fight and is basking in the praise just as much as his gladiator. He calls over three women who drape themselves over him and pour wine down his throat. Ironhead wonders if he will receive such a prize as well.

The procession comes to a halt at the victor's tent, a permanent fixture on the cliffside. It is a massive fabric roof covering a table long enough to fit every noble in Nahem. It has already been laid with every kind of food imaginable, from cheese and bread to fruits, vegetables, and entire roasted animals. The head of the table boasts the best delicacies, rare seabird flank broiled with Nath'iki spices and sharks cooked whole with onions stuffed in their mouths. It is at the raised chair that the crowd sets Ironhead, with a twisted iron circlet made just for this occasion set on his brow. The chant dies down as the celebrators take their seats.

The boy eats as he has never eaten before, having first choice of everything at the table. He cannot hope to remember how many people congratulated him, or their titles. There arc women aplenty who offer themselves to the champion, but Reyder turns them away before Ironhead can accept their affections. "They'll make you soft, boy, and someone with a head of iron cannot afford to get soft." The man's excuse seems poor to the boy, but he has no say in the matter.

He believes things cannot possibly get better, and then they do. He sees her across the many heads surrounding him, looking at him with narrowed eyes. His breath catches in his throat. She is escorted by the invalid Rolith and her handsy mentor Vendar. She says something to them and points at Ironhead. He chokes on the rice in his throat.

The sorcerers approach and the crowd parts ahead of them like a sea. Vendar eyes Ironhead with the familiar disdain he is accustomed to. "My apprentice says you are the lighthouse keeper's boy from Elgireth." Beta stands behind Vendar. Is she afraid of him? No, disgusted by him. He knows that look.

"Yes," he chokes.

"And you came here as a slave?"

"Yes."

"Can we speak to you in private?"

Reyder steps up, reeking of wine. "Hold up there, sorcerer, this slave is mine and I say where he goes."

Vendar's eyes are cold as ice. "I'm afraid this is out of your hands, pirate. We need to speak to the gladiator." Reyder does nothing to stop the sorcerer from grabbing Ironhead's arm and dragging him from the party. The boy hangs limp, petrified. The revelers pay no heed to the disappearance of their guest of honor. They are either too far into their drinks or have no interest in his life further than it can get them a feast.

The sorcerers toss him into an alley where they corner him, their cloaks and colored scars adding to their intimidating presence. Vendar is clearly in a foul mood, and Ironhead can smell wine on the other two. "Where are Peynter and Malvin? Already unconscious in a ditch, I presume?"

"They weren't here. Peynter's probably still scouting, and Malvin—"

"Malvin's piss drunk around here, probably in a brothel or cheating at strength competitions in the Brother." Beta is quick to sell out their companion, unlike Rolith. She sways slightly.

"Incredible," Vendar growls. "Think of the work sorcerers could get done if they weren't sniffing out wine whenever they could. Beta, tell me why we need to interrogate this slave."

She shrugs, giving no effort to the thought. "Because he's a little creep that's been stalking me as long as I've been at the Citadel."

Ironhead winces but does not protest. She has a point. Vendar's grip tightens on the boy's shoulder the more frustrated he becomes. "Because slave barges leave from Elgireth on specific schedules, and in large amounts. The chances that he was on the same boat as our leemoah are high."

"You mean Star?"

"You will speak when spoken to," Vendar says. "Now, tell me why this boy is helpful."

"Because he would be included in slave ledgers while she wouldn't. We could tell what boat they came on and the captain. The captain could tell us who owned a leemoah filly." Her words are droning and slurred. The dark circles under her eyes show all she wants is a warm bed and fried food.

"Rolith, what is wrong with Beta's statement?"

The stone mage jumps at the mention of his name and he stands straighter. "Captains can be bribed to lie."

"Very good." Beta rolls her eyes at Vendar's praise.

"I know the leemoah you're looking for, and I know who owns her." The boy speaks up louder. Vendar moves to cuff him for opening his mouth and then pauses curiously.

"Describe her."

It is all too easy to picture her in his mind. "Violet scales, about six inches taller than me, blue eyes, and small green jaw feathers. There were some gold scales dotting her nose as well."

Vendar releases him. "Tell me everything you know."

The boy sees his chance and jerks his head towards the revelers. "If I tell you what I know, I want something in return. Buy me and don't make me fight in those arenas anymore."

Rolith wrinkles his nose in disappointment. "Even the greatest warrior is a coward here."

Vendar is still in no mood for jests. "You will tell me everything about the leemoah or I will slit your throat here and now. Then the arenas will be the least of your troubles."

Ironhead panics slightly. The battlemage is much bigger than him both in stature and height and intimidating with his piercing eyes and streaks of orange. "Reyder, my master, he's one of the Tower. His friend El'rozai owns Star. She's been taken somewhere by an agent by the name of Ayrek. I don't remember where." He wracks his brain for the information the woman had given him before he was taken to the arena. Berthil Street? Bordin? Something like that.

"Leave, boy, before I tell all of your adoring fans what a sniveling coward you are." Vendar shoves Ironhead roughly back into the streets with a gust of wind. The boy staggers to keep his balance and spits in the dirt. So much for the heroics of sorcerers. Still, he had spent a moment with Beta and that was more than he could have ever asked for. He would hold the memory of her flushed, drunken face until the inevitable day he is cut down in the arena to the cheers of strangers.

The last thing he expects is for Beta to run after him. "Hey, I want to talk to you before you leave!" She approaches him and he freezes. He is afraid that if he moves, she will disappear. Her green eyes catch the sunlight like glazed emeralds.

His shock melts into terror. He fades in her presence. "B—Betallia—"

Her hand is around his throat before he can choke out anymore. "How do you know that name? No one knows me by that name except my parents and they're dead. Who in Heliendiel are you?"

"Oi! Hands off my slave!" Reyder approaches with a whip coiled around his hand.

"I'm a fucking battlemage, you pig. Do you think you can touch me with that thing?" she growls at the slaver before turning her attention back to her stalker. "If you're messing with us, I'm going to pull the blood from your veins through your massive pores. Do you have any idea how unpleasant that would be?"

The boy snaps out of his stupor. "I'm not lying! Star is my friend. I don't want her to die."

"Vendar may think your use has run its course, but I don't think we're that lucky quite yet. I can't have you dying in the arena before we can question you again when something goes wrong." She jerks her head towards Reyder. "Is that the man that knows Captain Zai?"

The slaver has yet to put away his whip. He is eyeing the interrogators suspiciously. "I think you and your friends should leave."

"I think you should consider my friends and I could destroy every person here without so much as breaking a sweat. Now, both of you should come with us. Somewhere more private." Their discussions draw curious eyes and whispers from civilians. Ironhead is uncomfortably aware that they are all armed, and probably have investments in him and the arenas. Beta remains oblivious, the wine still pounding through her veins.

It is a street boy sneaking food from the celebration tent that points first. "Those are battlemages!"

There is renewed interest in the sorcerers and the crowd begins to press forward to get a better look. If they're lucky, maybe they'll be able to touch one of their cloaks. Reyder draws confidence from the knowledge that the sorcerers are no longer incognito. "There is business being conducted around here. Whatever work you mean to do in Nahem, you should tend to it away from the arenas. Tower agents have rights when it comes to Oscil interference."

From behind Beta, there is a weapon drawn. She spins on the guard, a warrior wearing a red plume from his helmet. He probably belongs to one of the nobles sitting at the table. The alcohol in the battlemage's system causes her to react before common sense can have a say. Stone spikes arc as they follow her motion and launch at the would-be attacker. He falls with a scream as his body is impaled in six places in a neat row down the front of his chest. Vendar curses and chaos ensues.

Nobles scream for their guards and slaves are pushed towards the warriors as they scramble to get out of the way. Ironhead notices a symbol in the soldiers' clothing. There are Towers stitched onto breasts that he hadn't noticed before. Had there been this many warriors a moment ago? Where had they come from? Reyder throws him a knife and points towards the battlemages. "Well, champion? Fight!"

Ironhead fumbles the weapon, dropping it in the dust. He scrambles to retrieve it. Beta pushes him out of the way and approaches Reyder. "You're under arrest!" She rips the weapons from his hands and clasps his wrists behind his back with stones warped by her magic.

"You can't arrest me, you're a mercenary!" He laughs and runs. Beta rolls her eyes and yanks his feet out from under him, wrapping the street around him like a blanket until only his feet can be seen flailing wildly. Ironhead can't help smirking.

The sorcerers are everywhere at once, only visible from a flash of fire or gust of air. Screams echo and Ironhead finds himself lost in the chaos. He grips his knife as though it will grant him courage but makes no move to step towards the fighting. There are so many soldiers now, and more coming from either side of the street. Beta is forced to jump back on a rooftop to avoid being surrounded. Vendar and Rolith join her a moment later. They look otherworldly with their glowing skin and professionally cut leather armor. Vendar is breathing heavily. Captain Zai is there, from where Ironhead could not say. He must have been nearby. Now he opens his arms wide to the battlemages, the dozens of Tower warriors surrounding him. The rest of the street is deserted. A hush falls at his presence and the battle pauses to let him speak. "You are not welcome here, Citadel. These matters do not concern you as they do not violate our pact."

"They *do* violate our pact!" Vendar spits. "You have kidnapped a vital member of the Elgir community without consulting us. We cannot let that happen. You will give us the sacrifice and we will allow you and your pirates to continue your work in Kaper's Bay."

The leemoah leers. "You do not frighten me, battlemage. I know you, and I know your superiors. I will tell you once more, go home to your island rock and tell your employer the girl is dead."

As they discuss, Ironhead can see archers gathering on the buildings behind the sorcerers. "Look out!" he calls.

His heroic moment passes when he is hit over the head by someone from behind. He turns, swinging his knife. His skull throbs but he is not known as Ironhead for nothing. Captain

Zai has disappeared, and the fighting resumes. Rolith keeps the archers at bay by controlling the metal in the arrow tips, knocking them to the side harmlessly or sending them back to their owners. Beta and Vendar are back on the streets, but their movements are slower. Vendar's orange veins are multiplying by the second and he glows darker as though he is overheating. Beta does her best to protect him as well as put herself on the offensive, but she is strung too thin. An arrow grazes her shoulder, and she hisses in pain. Vendar notices and grabs her by the arm. He holds her close and protects them with a miniature whirlwind, whispering something into her ear. She nods and steps away. She spins, a brisk wind tickling her outstretched palms. Ironhead hits the ground just as the air crackles with an explosion of heat and power, slicing through anyone dumb enough to still be standing.

She wraps her arms around Vendar's waist, and he lifts his hands high above his head. Wind tears around them in a tornado. Beta holds out her hand, allowing the air current to run through her fingers like sand. She summons flames from the cooking fires dotting the streets, threading them into the wind. The whirlwind quickly becomes an airborne inferno, strong enough that Ironhead can feel the heat from half a block away. Within the fire tornado, they lift off the ground and away from the warriors below. Rolith sees their movements and leaps from the roof. He joins the sorcerers in the wind tunnel just as it slings them off the cliffside. They are dots on the horizon in moments. Ironhead's hair is mussed from the high winds and he is sure his face is covered in ash, but he feels more alive than he ever has.

~ 18 ~

WENDWYNN
&
ZAVOSH

The queen chose simple gowns for the meeting. Light gray with black patterns, silver chains at her wrists and neck. It was hubris to wear gaudy clothing to a holy place, as every good worshipper knew. She covered her hands with soft black gloves adorned with red shells in homage to the Sea Goddess Desanwa. The juicefruit on top of the cake was the wispy veil she used to cover the bottom half of her face. Not only would it show her piety to her potential allies on Saltspire, but it drew attention to eyes the color of an icy sea storm in which she hoped the Warlord would drown. With her were Grevin, Sir Nalag, Prince Halthax, and her leemoah handmaiden, H'iltha. They had boarded the tiny, unmarked skiff hours after the city had gone to sleep. Wen was grateful they were finally leaving. She could not have taken another moment alone in her chambers, dissecting what they were about to do. She trusted Dzaxar's information, but she didn't trust that the vipr knew his father as well as he might believe. His memories, while truth, were skewed as every memory was. Once away from Gafforah there were no guarantees.

That was a risk she was willing to take. Grevin, who had disagreed with the plan at first, was only placated knowing he had authority to evacuate her at the first sign of danger. He nodded to her when they were settled. "On your command, Your Grace."

She gave the signal for them to disembark. Wen had chosen to meet Warlord Halthax under the cover of night for several reasons she kept to herself. He had complained that she was acting suspiciously but ultimately agreed. The question now was whether there was a trap waiting for them. The Mangzarians would expect an impressive escort and a royal barge. Going in silently would give them the element of surprise and allow them to assess their enemies before engaging.

The skiff caught the night breeze playfully and skipped across the waves as it headed south. Grevin had insisted they go by land across the island and depart from the small port town of Tamilah, but the queen knew they would be expecting that as well. While this route was much longer, they would see any enemy ships meant to be hidden from those approaching from due east of the island instead of south, as they had. She fully expected there would be ships. If Frej was not kidnapped, the only reason the Warlord would set up this meeting was to ambush her. Perhaps he thought she was compassionate, as she hadn't killed his son yet.

The night was cold for summer. Wen wished she had worn her furs, but she knew once the sun rose the heat would cook her in her clothes. She studied the lesser Halthax as they rode. He was staring at nothing as he did when awaiting a command. No matter how many books she read or spells she tried, there was always a slight tell that he was not completely present. She would just have to do what she had to do quickly.

It wouldn't be long now. The temple that gave Saltspire its

name cut through the gray sky in the distance. Sir Nalag held a seeing glass to his eye and shook his head in disappointment. "I can see at least six war boats, behind the cliffs just like you said, Your Grace."

Wen nodded. "Alright, H'iltha, your turn." The leemoah nodded to the queen and leapt gracefully into the water.

The temple took shape as they neared. The walls were impressively fortress-like. There were slits for archers, narrow windows in spiked towers, and fires burning behind the iconic sandstone. Blank faces of carved deities took form from the ramparts. Wen recognized Mangzarian spirits as well as leemoah godheads and the two faces of the moon, Aryet and Akai, entwined in their circle over the main gate.

"These three nations appear to be connected more than they will admit," she noted

"Legend tells that Kaper's Bay used to be part of the Mangzarian mountains," Nalag confirmed. "Gafforah is supposedly the peak of the greatest volcano under which the only dynasty that has ever united all the districts thrived. Then the mountain erupted, burying civilization, and creating the bay and the islands within. Ever since, Mangzar has been cursed to be scattered and broken."

Wen's thoughts fluttered unbidden to what it would be like to fuse all the districts into one coherent nation, with her as their queen. She didn't allow herself to daydream too long before pulling herself back to the present. She must survive Mangzar and heal Gafforah before she could think about other conquests.

H'iltha emerged from the water and pulled herself onto the boat with a shake of her scales. "You were right, Your Grace. There's at least a dozen of them."

Wendwynn had expected the Warlord to bring along reinforcements, but twelve seemed extreme. It bordered on breaking their truce, showing a Mangzarian's word may not be as binding as they would lead the world to believe. "And were you able to pass on the message?" She nodded in affirmation. Wen continued, "Thank you, H'iltha. You know what to do from here." The boat reached the shore where priests waited to accept the newcomers. They were strangely still in the pre-dawn mist. Wendwynn stepped into the shallows, followed by Warprince Dzaxar. The rest of her party pushed off, back into the open water. They would have only a short time to get as far from Saltspire as possible. High Priest Lekala bowed to the queen as she sloshed to the sand. He had gone on ahead of the queen's party the day before to arrange the meeting. "Your Grace, I was not expecting you to come alone—well, mostly alone." His eyes darted to the vipr at her side.

"I want it to be clear to the Warlord that I can defeat him without an army, and without violence. I want you to know that I am going to do everything in my power to keep the peace while we are here on your holy island. I assume the Mangzarian will keep his word on the matter, as well." Her hands were folded neatly in front of her, showing grace and submission.

The High Priest was tentative but nodded his agreement. "My fellow priests are nervous. We have avoided war on our shores for so many generations, knowing it couldn't last forever. But we take faith knowing the two sides in question have an equally strong connection to Saltspire."

"Your island is beautiful," Dzaxar commented with a broad smile. The facial expression looked awkward and unnatural.

"Thank you," Lekala muttered. "The Warlord is already here, along with twelve warbarges, catapults on deck." Wen could sense the tension in the priest's words. His shoulders were stiff. He regretted hosting their meeting.

They walked inland to a small patio on the sand where Warlord Halthax ky Dzaxar stood, hands behind his back, staring up at Saltspire Temple with a calculating gaze. He wore no armor and no weapons, long white hair loose on his shoulders.

He turned when the queen approached. "Queen Wendwynn. I am glad to see you answered my summons."

"It's not often a leader gets to speak to their enemy directly after a backhanded attack like what you pulled on the colonies. Now I get to look you in the eye and tell you how despicable you are." She didn't allow him to break their gaze. His eyes were orange-and-red striped with jagged black around his pupils.

"Bold words from a woman who dresses so piously." He motioned to the veil across her face. "I must admit I hadn't pictured you dressing so modestly. You have said your piece, but we are not here to discuss the colonies."

"Of course. Warprince Dzaxar, say hello to your father."

Her thrall bowed deeply to the Warlord. "Father, it is good to see you again."

"Dzaxar, you wear the garb of Gaffori." Wen could hear the tones of worry behind the Warlord's simple statement. He was afraid of showing too much affection.

"Father, I have been a prisoner. I must wear what I am given."

The Warlord wrinkled his pointed nose in disgust. "He reeks of spells. He is no longer my son."

Warprince Halthax's face fell. "They are spells of binding, Father. To ensure I cannot take my own life. I live every day waiting for the right moment to kill my captors or end my shame."

Warlord Halthax turned back to the queen. "Since you have not killed him, I ask that you let me do it myself. Hand over my son and we can return to the war."

Wendwynn glanced towards Lekala to ensure he was out of earshot. The High Priest stood a respectful distance away, watching the regents carefully. "Your son and I have become close during our time together. He has helped me in ways only a Mangzarian can. I wondered if the spell would work at first, given viprs' connection to black magic."

Warprince Dzaxar's face twisted as though he was trying to escape invisible ropes. The Warlord narrowed his eyes with a leer. "You cannot use magic. I know this, everyone knows it. So, how—" He trailed off. "There's only one kind of magic that people like you can use. But are you truly that stupid? To wield the Puppetmaster magic after the former dynasty crumbled because of it?"

The lesser Halthax grunted and collapsed to his knees. He sucked in a sharp breath and threw his head back. "It's a trap! Father, it's a trap! The priests have joined her and turned the temple into a fortress. They're gathering in the towers to destroy you and your ships!" He crumbled on the ground from the effort. Wendwynn cursed.

Halthax sneered and took up a defensive stance. "I knew it. I knew you cared nothing for piety or treaties. You're a conniving foreigner, and you'll never be anything more. Unfortunately for you, I planned on your betrayal." He reached in the top of his boot and squeezed a smooth rock found within. While he feigned shock at her betrayal, his face opened in glee. Now he had permission for violence. "My soldiers are going to demolish this temple before you can desecrate it. You're not going to get away with such treachery."

From where the Mangzarian ships were hidden on the western side of the island, there was the snap and creak of trebuchets launching their loads towards Saltspire. The first wave hit their marks, tearing into towers and shattering statues. Wen watched with mild interest. Dzaxar forced himself back to his feet as Lekala came running back to them. "What have you done?" the High Priest screamed. "Who is responsible for this?"

Warlord Halthax pointed an accusatory finger at Lekala. "You brought the end of Saltspire upon yourselves, priest! You chose poorly when you stood beside the foreign queen." The vipr spat into the sand.

Wendwynn held out her hands for peace as chunks of

granite rained above and Lekala tensed as though to attack Halthax. Several other priests rushed to surround the leaders of Gafforah and Mount Thoyax. They stayed at a distance at Wen's insistence. "Wait! I can fix this. High Priest, I would never act aggressively without your permission. Do I have authority to retaliate against the offensive actions taken by Mangzar?"

"Yes," Lekala hissed. "Do what you must to salvage our island."

Wendwynn was glad for the veil to hide her smile. "Thank you. Know that I take no pleasure in involving Gafforah in the violence here today." She held up a fist, knowing the party in the rowboat would see. "While warships were specifically prohibited from our meeting, meaning you were the first to break the truce, Warlord, leemoahs are residents of Kaper's Bay and a natural occurrence. They will see to it that the ships are destroyed and no longer a threat to Saltspire." Ip'akala would be commanding his troops to tear at the hulls of the vessels, sinking anything that floated. She turned her attention to the Warprince as the ground shook with the Mangzarian assault around her. "You have directly caused the conflict today by lying through your teeth. As a result, I sentence you to die. Swallow your tongue, warprince, and perish in a way that does not draw blood."

Warlord Halthax screamed. "No!" But he was too late. Dzaxar did as Wen bid him, and his eyes rolled back in his head as he choked. Lekala watched with grim satisfaction.

"Look to your ships, Warlord. Or what is left of them." The last Halthax turned his eyes to the horizon. The sounds of splintering wood and churning waters as they swallowed the ships were dwarfed by the screams and shouts of both priests and Mangzarians alike. Wendwynn stood calm amid the chaos.

The Warlord had no weapons with which to challenge the queen. She doubted he would if given the chance. Attacking from off Saltspire was a gray area, but inciting bloodshed on the beach was blatant disregard for the spirits. Instead, he fell to his knees. "The spirits have spoken. They have taken my son, my ships, and my dignity. Kill me."

Wendwynn stared down at the fallen warlord. She wondered what drove him to give up. It was unlike anything she had studied about their culture. She could think of only two reasons. One, that the fate that awaited him in Mount Thoyax would be far worse than death at her hands on Saltspire. What sort of horrors would his people unleash on him after yet another defeat at the hands of a human? The second reason was that he wanted to be with his son. For all the culture, the distance, the coldness, Halthax had loved his son, and the loss was enough for him to see no further purpose for the war efforts. She had to admit the reason was far from important. He was a cold-blooded murderer, and he would meet justice that day. "Are you begging, Warlord? Did my colonists beg on their knees as well? Did they hold their children close as they cried for mercy? Perhaps we are not so different, after all. I will also choose to ignore your pleas." She nodded to Lekala. "Have your priests bind him and give him a rowboat. Let the sea reclaim him, or have him continue to suffer, as the gods see fit."

"As the gods see fit," Lekala nodded. The priests bound Halthax hand and foot and dragged him away.

Wendwynn bowed to the High Priest as he watched the temple burn. "I cannot change the course of events today, but I can make them right. Let me rebuild Saltspire. Let me end the war from your shores and return peace to the bay."

Lekala ground his teeth. "You would turn our temple into a fortress." His eyes were clouded with pain. It would guide his decision. "But we have no choice. The war has come to us. Very well, Your Grace. Destroy these desecrators of peace. Saltspire is yours." He turned back to the temple wearily. Wen watched him go, alone with the body of Warprince Halthax on the beach. Even she had been impressed with the prince's show, carefully placed inside his head with the Puppetmaster magic. While her people had not been in the temple as he claimed, they would be now.

The satisfaction of victory felt small in her hollow chest. Was this the sensation Frejith had warned her about? The emptiness that could only be filled by using more magic? By becoming stronger. Her heart ached. She was glad Frejith hadn't been brought as a captive to the summit, but more than a small part of her had selfishly wanted to see her again. She could hear her wife's words in her head, warning her to fight the urge. The magic would consume her. Wen allowed her clenched fists to release, hanging loose at her side. She hated that Frejith had been right. She felt nothing but empty and hungry for more. "Fine," Wen whispered to the wind, hoping Frejith could sense her change of heart. She would no longer use the Puppetmaster magic.

Her heart weighed heavy as she watched the bay swallow the Mangzarian ships one by one. Only when the bay had become still again did General Ip'akala emerge from the water. While he had always seemed young to Wen, his face suggested he had aged decades in the past weeks. The playfulness that was ever present had vanished. "Your Grace, your enemies have been defeated. Is the Warlord dead?"

"Worse," Wen whispered. "He is no longer a threat."

Ip'akala moved to stand in front of the queen, examining her face with a new clarity. "Is the war over, then?"

"I don't know," she answered honestly.

The General touched a wound on his arm and stared at the blue blood on his fingertips. "You may be accustomed to violence, Your Grace, but my people are not. We can no longer take part in your war, whether it is over or not. We have lost too many and stretched ourselves thin to follow your commands. I would ask that you release the leemoahs of Uta'lihali from your army."

Wendwynn knew it was coming. "I'm surprised you didn't say so when you knew I was using the Puppetmaster magic. You are right, of course. Your people are not warriors and you have done more for me than you would any other ruler, I like to think. You are free, Ip. Thank you."

She didn't watch as the leemoah left without a sound.

Fortress Blackfeather stood as the symbol for a powerful district, named for the active volcano that carved a dark silhouette against the gray skies. In stark contrast to the dark architecture, the fortress was carved from white stone. Each of the six pillars that held the ramparts above the walkway into the monolith were carved into the shapes of spirits and equalled the district's number. Zavosh had known the spirits as a child but becoming an isilth had meant there was no point for him to study the deities that had abandoned him. Their contorted, leering faces on twisted bodies of muscle and bone brought back memories of growing up in Mount Thoyax. He tried to push these down as he helped Frejith up the road.

A fortress anywhere else would have guards standing at the ready, watching the milling crowds entering and exiting on various missions. Mangzar held strong in its belief that if a Warleader could not hold a fortress on their own, they were undeserving of their title. Those who wished to lead a district were required to kill the champion by any means necessary—if it was in the daytime. Historically, even a sleeping Warleader was a potential target, until sleep deprivation drove them to madness.

"Where did your contact say he would be?" Zavosh asked Frejith warily. She claimed to have found someone who would help them as he finished his last day as a dockworker.

The careful part of him screamed that he should have met her new friend before they agreed to march into their enemy's fortress.

The sorceress studied each face carefully as they passed. "All you viprs look the same to me. Even the humans have gray skin. At least us non-Mangzarians come in unique shades."

"Perhaps you should be mute as part of your character," Zavosh growled.

The courtyard beyond the pillared entrance was full of armored warriors honing weapons or sparring on the ashy dirt. Zavosh overheard whispered conversations between anxious combatants. The Warlord was missing. No ships had returned and charred pieces of Mangzarian vessels had washed ashore. The crowd was here in preparation for a *milta*. Usually, the battle for a Warleader position would be between a challenger and the incumbent. With no reigning champion, the battle could become an all-out war within the city. Could Wen have planned such unrest? It would leave Mount Thoyax exposed.

"There," Frejith pointed.

"A human?" Zavosh spat.

"Now who's being ignorant?" She motioned to the man in question. He was not Mangzarian, that much was obvious from his pale skin and unkempt silvery hair. He reeked of manure and dust as he approached.

"If it isn't the wounded warrior. Welcome to Fortress Blackfeather. Who is your friend?" He nodded to Zavosh, his weapon hanging carelessly from his hand.

"Someone who owes an outsider no introduction." Zavosh would scold the sorceress later. Of all the friends she could make in Mangzar, it had to be someone that wasn't even a native.

"Come now, I work here, so I cannot be so bad. I've lived in Mangzar long enough to make a name for myself."

"And what is it you do here in the fortress?" Zavosh could

feel Frejith's nails digging into his arm at the continued interrogation, but he didn't care.

"I tend to the animals in the stables. I'm also probably the only one that is willing to help your . . . sister, is it? Instead of putting a blade through her skull and calling it a day."

As much as he hated the idea of working with a foreign human, Zavosh knew he was right. Only the greatest warriors were given the honor of *xari'kai*. He doubted Frejith the mind mage had ever picked up a weapon to be proficient with one.

The stable boy took his silence as an answer. "Greysen Cordova, at your service. But you can call me Grey." He looked straight at Frejith with a smile Zavosh knew too well. Their savior hadn't offered to help her because she was a warrior, or because he was sympathetic. He was attracted to her.

As Grey led them to the stables, Zavosh cursed his luck and the queen for unknowingly making him responsible for protecting the sanctity of her marriage.

~ 19 ~
KEYRA

Keyra finds herself fighting an inner battle as the station around her changes. Once the suspects from other cases had been removed, the officers and the contents of their desks had followed. Magic users warded the walls with Seer symbols and incantations in dead languages. She can make out little of the whisperings of those who come and go, but what she does hear is dire.

". . . No answer from the Citadel. You think they'd care about something like this."

"Unless they're already dead . . ."

". . . Should kill them before it spreads to us . . ."

The seamstress struggles to focus on reality as her mind swims in and out of the present. Her headaches are growing in intensity and harder to ignore. When she sleeps, she has fitful dreams of committing atrocious acts that are far too realistic for comfort. She knows she was a member of the Tower in her youth. Why can't she remember the things she did? Why is she incapable of focusing on her own past without triggering intense pain? The only thing she worries about is Tilsman, alone in his cell, watched distrustfully by guards with hands on their weapons. What do they think the child will do to them? He's half their height and twice their girth. He would get one feeble kick in before they overpowered him.

They bring food to the captives, but Keyra finds her appetite has vanished along with her grip on the situation. She drinks some of the water they bring but otherwise spends her time fighting the shadows in her head. She must get out. She must protect Tilsman and find help for herself.

"Under what authority? Do you have any proof?" Erey's voice snaps her back to existence. He stands in a newly gilded cloak, snarling at the guard blocking his way.

"I'm sorry, sir, I'm going to have to ask you to leave. It's not safe here." The officer places a hand on Erey's chest which Keyra's son slaps away contemptuously.

"Do not presume to touch me, officer. From what I can tell, you are illegally detaining my mother and her ward based on wild and unconfirmed accusations."

"Sir, we don't want to start a panic, but we have reason to believe that these two are responsible for a potential . . ." He trails off, afraid of hexing himself, and leans forward to whisper the word into Erey's ear.

Keyra's son scoffs. "You and I both know there's no such thing as a curse. And if there were one, it wouldn't come from an old, non-magical woman and a Wahethian sheep boy. Have you seen those two? They're not exactly the picture of powerful sorcerers. Now are you going to release them and continue your asinine investigation, or do I need to summon my legal counsel to convince you for me?"

The officer is not high ranking and shrinks before Erey's onslaught. "That won't be necessary, sir, I'm just trying to do my job. If you wait here, I can get my supervisor and he can release—"

"I would suggest releasing them *now*." The ice in his voice is enough to make a mother proud.

The officer fumbles with the keys, unlocking Keyra's cell

followed by Tilsman's. Erey barely glances at Keyra as he leads them out of the precinct. "Thank you," Keyra says as she struggles to keep up with his long strides. When he says nothing, she ventures to speak again. "You didn't have to do that. How did you even know we were there?"

Erey stops and pulls her to the side of the street cautiously. Tilsman huffs and puffs to catch up to them with his significantly smaller strides. "There are people here watching you, mother. Following you. Very powerful people. I don't know what you did to gain their attention, but they came to me to have you released. I'd wager it's something to do with your time in the Tower, isn't it?"

Keyra's heart aches to see the distrust and skepticism in her son's hardened eyes. She cannot deny it was her that made him that way. "I don't know. I truly don't." Her mind races. Who could be following them? The Citadel? The Tower? Someone else?

Erey sighs. "You two can come to my home for now. It's not an invitation back into my life, and it's not permanent. But until things calm down and I can get you out, I feel obligated to show you that much clemency."

Keyra gives him a wavering smile. "I don't know how you ended up as good as you did. It certainly wasn't because of me."

"On that, we can agree." Erey turns to lead them farther down the street. He takes them up the hill from the factory, where the air is clearer, and the population cleaner. His home is a stately multilevel made of whitewashed stone and a slate roof. It's far nicer than anything Keyra can remember living in. Through the door, an elderly man wrinkles his nose at the newcomers.

Erey wastes no time in giving orders. "Have a bath drawn up and see if we have some fresh clothing that will fit them. Have Ursla make enough for two extra tonight and send up some fruit to snack on." The man bows and rushes to do as he is bid.

"Do you own slaves?" Keyra asks carefully.

Erey's eyes flash hotly. "No, they are not slaves. I pay them well, and they are free to leave my employment when they see fit. I am not you, mother, dragging people from their homes into forced bondage. Although, it is because of you that I swore never to own slaves."

Keyra regrets speaking and looks at the floor as Erey leads her and Tilsman up the stairs. Keyra's ward has been uncharacteristically quiet since their imprisonment and release. He hasn't whined about hunger once or complained of his feet. She wonders if he is feeling as odd as she is.

The seamstress is distracted when she sees the steaming bath in a chamber open to the warm breeze. There are plants everywhere, long green vines hanging from ceilings and large-leafed varieties with red stripes. Most are unfamiliar and some appear exotic in nature. She hadn't realized her son had risen so far in her absence.

Keyra starts to tear up as she lowers herself into the bath. She can't remember the last time she's experienced something so luxurious. Most baths for her have been a quick scrub with a rag or sponge, or a dip in the sea. There is a tray beside the tub with a comb, bath salts, a bath brush, and three lotions in different scents. By the time she is done, the water is nearly black with dirt. The clothing laid out for her is tight around the chest and drags on the floor behind her, but it is clean and lacks sea salt in the stitching.

Tilsman has finished his own bath and is in the kitchens scarfing down food as fast as the cook can place it in front of him. His hair glows like a bronze coin and his curls have bounced into ringlets. He will need a haircut before too long. Keyra joins them at the table and selects grilled fish and fried tomatoes for her meal. Erey is there, whispering in urgent tones with the butler of the house. He turns to them as his man leaves to attend to some business or another. "You two look nearly presentable now." He allows a small smile. Keyra's heart skips a beat. It is the first time she's seen her son smile in three decades.

"That bath was something nice," Tilsman says between chews. "I don't think I've ever smelled this good. And no offense Granma Keyra, but the food here is better than anything I tasted on Veden."

Erey flinches at Tilsman's statement. "Granma Keyra, eh? At least we were both eventually able to move on. Me with my new life, and you with a new descendant."

Keyra pushes away the plate, her appetite gone. "I don't know what else to do, son. I really don't. I've made countless mistakes in the past and continue to make them now. I understand you're upset, and you have every right to be. But isn't there some way we can lessen the guilt trip? I promise you; you can't make me feel any worse than I already do."

There is a tense silence during which even Tilsman pauses with cheese halfway to his mouth. His eyes dart between mother and son nervously as though expecting a fist fight. "You're right, mother, of course. You were never around for me to gauge how difficult it was for you to abandon me. I only had my imagination to keep me company. In it, I always assumed you were happier on your own." His words drip with sarcasm through gritted teeth.

Keyra fights back hot tears. She will not let him drag her down into the bitter pit she dug for him. "Tilsman and I will be on our way now. I think we have intruded on your hospitality long enough." She pushes away from the table and stands. Tilsman whimpers at the food left on the table and stuffs pastries into his pockets before following Keyra's example.

"Very delicious," he praises the cook through a mouthful. "Excellent. Just marvelous." He bows deeply to the surprised woman before Keyra tugs gently on his ear to signal it is time to leave.

Erey's eyes soften for a quick moment. "I'm sorry I can't offer you more. I really am. I fear the part of me that would have been glad to see you return died when I was about fifteen. I can't force myself to be glad to see you. Not yet."

"Thank you for your honesty." At least he had inherited that much from her. "This was too much all at once. If you're willing, I'd like to visit again soon. I can't make up for what I did to you in the past, but I can build toward a better future."

"I would like that. Whatever you've gotten yourself into, I hope it works out." On that much, they can agree.

Before Keyra and Tilsman can take their leave, the butler enters the kitchen looking flustered. "Sir, there are people here looking for Mistress Keyra and her ward. A leemoah and two men."

The way he says the word 'leemoah' suggests he thinks little of the species. Keyra feels a lump in her throat. Could it be the Tower captain? How and why had he found them? She has just found some sort of peace with her son. The last thing she needs is a pirate bringing turmoil into his house because of her. "I will speak to them," Keyra says quickly. "Tilsman, you stay in here with Erey."

Erey says nothing but she can tell the ground she has gained with him is in jeopardy. The seamstress moves into the foyer where the purple-scaled leemoah stands flanked by pirates. He has shed his cloak in favor of leather armor and exposed cutlasses. He is here to intimidate. "Under Akai." He bows slightly.

"I thought I told you I wasn't interested in anything you had to offer. Following me here was overstepping your bounds. I'm going to have to ask you to leave and remain out of my life and the lives of everyone in this house."

There is something familiar about the leemoah that she cannot place. "I'm afraid that's not possible. Technically, I outrank you. I'm afraid that your son has become something of a distraction from your mission."

"What mission?" By the waves, why wouldn't the Tower just leave her be? She is far too old to be a mercenary. "I owe you nothing."

Erey moves to stand behind Keyra. "If my mother doesn't want you here, then I'm going to have to insist on your compliance. If you refuse, I will not hesitate to summon the authorities."

Keyra realizes in a moment of horror that Erey is unarmed. She hadn't seen a single weapon since her arrival. Had he never learned to defend himself? She glimpses his hands, soft from learning the pen as his sword of choice. Her face goes numb. Failing to teach him self-defense is by far her greatest downfall as a mother. Erey's threat amuses the leemoah. "The authorities? I'm afraid you've miscalculated the situation here, young man. Out of respect for the fine work you do in New Nahem, I'm going to give you a chance to back away and allow me and your mother to speak business."

Erey balls his fists and straightens his shoulders. "This is *my* house, leemoah, and I will not have you speak to me in that manner. Grendall, please go to the nearest precinct and tell the officers that we have armed intruders threatening us."

Keyra wishes she could close her eyes and open them to find she has been experiencing a nightmare. One of the Tower agents strides with easy purpose to slide a blade between Grendall's shoulders as the butler turns to do his master's bidding. Keyra spins and grabs Erey by the sleeve. "You have to run! Run, now!"

Erey is frozen in place, unable to process the unfolding scene. The leemoah makes no move to draw his own weapons. "So sorry for you to have to see that, good sir. The authorities will not be necessary at this time. Now, I could kill you as easily as my accomplice has skewered your houseman, but that would be poor poetry, don't you think?"

He locks eyes with Keyra, and her head begins pounding

with a pain so intense her vision fails her and her muscles crumble beneath the pressure. She cries out, unable to push through the agony. She's falling, falling, and there is no ground to catch her. "Don't forget the *mission*," he hisses, eyes refusing to release her.

When she regains control of her senses, she is slumped against the wall with a bread knife from the kitchen in her hand. The white marble on the floors and walls have been christened with black droplets of blood in patterns that tell a gory story. The blade in her grip is darkened with the same ill tidings. Keyra scrambles to her feet and sees the body of the cook in the hallway. She rushes past, following the trail she has left for herself.

Tilsman is curled in the corner of the kitchen, crying and shaking. He cringes when he sees Keyra, pointing towards the opposite side of the room.

Keyra has felt pain before. She has felt loss, felt failure, felt human. But what she experiences in this moment is something deeper, something primal layered with acute agony. Erey lies dead with several stab wounds in his chest. The knife clatters from Keyra's grip as she sinks to her knees beside him. The energy to cry is sucked into the empty void in her chest left by the knowledge that she had returned to her son after decades, only to fail him again in the most horrendous way possible.

~ 20 ~
BETA
&
THE BOY

Beta and Peynter watch the boat as it launches into the bay. Aboard is Vendar, barely clinging to life; Rolith, tasked to bring back a detailed report as team leader; and Malvin, wrapped in a sheet to be sent to his family. They should have ensured he was safe before they engaged, but they hadn't—and his throat had been slit from behind while watching a fight. The sorcerers stand away from the dock, blending as best they can with hoods up. They'd circled back to the shore after escaping their confrontation with the Tower, leaving them to find their two missing companions and deal with Vendar, who had nearly died from the effort of maintaining the cyclone that saved their lives. Peynter had heard of the fight in the arenas and made his way to the docks in the hopes that any survivors would meet back there. They'd found Malvin in the middle of a street near the docks, stabbed from behind with a spilled mug of ale at his side. Beta feels as though she's aged ten years in the past day. Losing her companion is a sobering reminder that not everyone worships the ground she walks on.

She's allowed herself to become careless and Malvin has paid the price. She tightens her jaw as the sails of their vessel grow smaller in the distance. She'd fought Vendar to let her go back with him, but in the end, he'd pulled rank, stating that they couldn't afford to fail their mission now more than ever. She hates that he left her behind. What if he dies and the battle-mage secrets die with him? Not to mention, now she's stuck finishing their mission with Peynter. He and Beta are the last hope of rescuing the sacrifice within the next four days before the ceremony.

Once the boat disappears into the fleet of other transports, Beta turns away. "First things first, we've got to find that light-house boy."

Peynter sighs wearily. "Jumping right back into it, are you? I need a moment to catch my breath, Beta."

"If you're hungry, eat some of that mix Xendia gave us. That kid said he knew the leemoah filly. If what he said is true, the girl's life is in danger and he may know where she is. We don't have time to catch our breath." She trudges up the Street of Angels with the reluctant water mage in tow. She can sense the heaviness in his shoulders. He is hurt badly by Malvin's death, despite how much he appeared to hate the stone mage in life. Beta also mourns, but this is the life they have chosen. Malvin often made reckless and idiotic choices, and that lifestyle was a dangerous and fatal one for them. She'll be thinking more critically of her decisions from now on.

"Where are we supposed to find him?" Peynter asks.

"We're not going to have to look." In her hand she holds the stem of the flower attached to the boy's tunic. She has also placed an idea in his mind that will bring him to the pub down the street in the next hour, something she'd done spur of the moment during their interview with him in the alley, in case things went wrong. Mind magic is tricky and often battlemages don't master it like those who bear the yellow scar. Thankfully,

Beta has proven time and again her adaptability when it comes to difficult magic. All they must do is wait and he will come to them. She can feel his pulse getting closer through the tracking petals even now. The question is whether he will be alone or escorted by Tower members. They will be keeping a close eye on him if they haven't killed him already.

They take seats inside where they can see the door clearly and order water in tankards. Peynter munches on the magical oat mix created by the Citadel chef to fill any stomach. The lighthouse boy is close now. Beta waves her hand over Peynter's face and her own to muddle them to the casual eye.

The boy enters the pub, accompanied by none other than their quarry—the leemoah A'Toa. She moves like water and she keeps her head down modestly. Ironhead is washed and the wounds he received from the arena patched. Her stomach churns just looking at him and knowing the way he looks at her. She gets his attention with a wave of her arm and he lights up with that blatant admiration she hates so much. The two of them join the sorcerers at the table.

"I did not expect you to bring a friend, Ironhead," Beta observes coolly.

The boy's eyes widen like a pup that has been praised. "I knew it would make you happy. After the fight, Reyder and the others were distracted and didn't seem to notice me slipping off. After that I managed to find Star thanks to a Tower agent I think is on our side. I don't know what drew me here, but it must be fate, because here you are. That's what you wanted, isn't it? Did I do it right?"

Beta is floored. Who is this confident man where she once saw a poxfaced slave boy? Peynter is chuckling into his water mug. "Looks like you can forget being a battlemage, Beta. This kid has got you beat for successful missions." He avoids the fork she throws at him.

"The star goddess nears every moment we wait. We can't

delay in returning to the Reef." Beta can sense coldness from A'Toa. She should be thanking the battlemage.

"Unfortunately, that's not going to be as easy as getting a boat back," Peynter says. "I spent a lot of time on the docks yesterday and was able to learn the Tower controls them and owns the ships that go back and forth. We'll be spotted right away, and as we've recently learned, the Tower is not a partner with the Citadel any longer. I suggest we head to the fisher towns on the southern part of the city. We can commandeer a boat there and have a much better chance of remaining out of their sight."

How has Beta never noticed how bright Peynter is? Perhaps it was always clouded by the company he kept. In the balance of magic and knowledge, his strengths leaned towards the latter. "Very well, a fisher boat it is. It will be easier if we travel with three instead of four, and technically we're being paid only to save the sacrifice—"

"The boy stays with us or I will remain in Nahem," the leemoah snaps. Beta liked her better when she thought she was docile.

"Very well. But if he slows us down for even a moment then we will leave him behind," Beta says. She stares into the leemoah's cold blue eyes. She will not allow this girl to command her. If all else fails, she can always put her into a magical sleep and drag her behind the boat the rest of the way to Uta'lihali. She keeps her opinion to herself and they get up from their seats.

"By Aryet, is that a battlemage?" A patron of the pub squints at Beta openly as though she is a jewel he cannot be certain is real.

She has allowed herself to be distracted and dropped the illusion spell. The man bears no Tower sigil and has a distinct odor that can only accompany a lifelong fisherman. She smiles politely. "Can I help you?"

He shakes his head in wonder. "Never thought I'd live to see one myself. You must be the young one, Vendar's apprentice?"

"Beta," she confirms. Peynter sighs audibly from behind her. His blue scar fades compared to Beta's yellow in the public's eye.

"We're busy here," Ironhead growls. His demeanor has changed at the arrival of another admirer. "Move along, citizen."

"Now hold on there, I thought battlemages were trained for the sole purpose of helping innocents. I'm an innocent, and I need help. That is, unless you're on some sort of top-secret mission."

Ironhead squares up to speak, but Beta beats him to it. "Are you a fisher by any chance?"

"That I am," he nods. Beta doesn't need his acknowledgement. He reeks of old fish guts and salt.

"We're in need of a boat. I will help you with your problem if we can take your vessel back to Elgireth. I'll see to it upon my return to the Citadel that you're sent one twice as nice."

"It'd be a great honor, Miss Beta! Something's been happening at my home. There's been earthquakes, and just yesterday the oddest thing happened—something of a magical nature."

Beta stretches. "I'll go with you to investigate. Peynter, when we get there, wait in the boat for me with them. If I'm not back by sunset, leave." Peynter knows better than to protest. Beta has a way of getting what she wants, and it is better not to challenge her.

"It could be unsafe," the boy says. Beta can feel a headache coming on.

"I can handle myself. Alright then, let's go."

They follow the fisherman down the gentle slope towards the fishing and industrial villages that cling to the edges of Nahem. He and Beta walk a few steps ahead of the others. He lowers his voice so only she can hear. "The situation may be a bit more peculiar than I let on, battlemage."

"What do you mean?" Her guard goes up instantly.

He remains silent as they cross the ridge, and the horizon opens before them.

Gafforah is undoubtedly a beautiful land with valleys like this one, reaching to the horizon where the inescapable cliffs cut the skies. The grass is as green as the trees and the air is thick with sea birds circling the tiny ships dotting the crescent-shaped bay. There is an unmistakable heaviness here, saturating the energy that makes up the world around her. Beta frowns and closes her eyes to the wind. "What is that? A kind of darkness?"

"It's something dark, Miss Beta. It all started with our new priest. My daughter is deathly ill when she was a healthy girl not yesterday. The fish have fled and the ones we do pull up are misshapen and sickly. We've told the town officials but all they say is that it's a sickness in the sea and it will go away on its own."

Beta sighs inwardly. It couldn't have been a cow stuck in mud or a child trapped on a mountainside. This power she feels is truly evil. "I suppose you believe otherwise. The priest, you say?"

"Aye, the priest. We have our own little temple to the fish spirits as well as a shrine to Deswana. Our old priest died of old age and a replacement was sent from the holy leaders in the city. At first, he seemed good enough, a little cold, but he would bless those that needed blessing. Then yesterday he stopped seeing people and the strange things started happening."

Beta can see the shrine standing high among the shacks of the water people. Colorful fish leap across the wooden walls and small bells chime in the breeze. She wants to take Peynter with her, but she cannot leave the lighthouse boy and A'Toa on their own. Besides, she has already given her orders. She cannot go back on them now. "If you would be so kind, take my friends to your vessel. I'll deal with the priest."

She heads off alone where the path breaks. There are no villagers on the streets. The windows are boarded up and the stalls abandoned. No livestock can be seen or heard. The only life is the seabirds. Beta shudders and takes a moment to take a deep breath. She feels magic flowing with renewed energy through her veins with each inhale and exhale. The earth is crying out, wrapping her in desperate tendrils of force. She becomes lightheaded and slips into a sort of trance that deepens her connection. Her heightened senses warn her that the danger is in the temple she's headed towards.

She enters the heavily blanketed doorway into darkness and summons a small flame on her palm to see by. The statues of the spirits leer at her through the dancing shadows. "Hello?" The braziers are full of ash, and her voice is swallowed by the darkness. Something stirs deeper within the hut. "Is there a priest here?"

"You came." She can make out someone dressed in a cloak with skin painted bright colors.

"You were expecting me?"

."I knew you wouldn't come on your own. I also knew that if I made enough of a fuss, someone would head into the city and find you." She cannot see his face, and that keeps her nervous.

"Can't we light a candle or two?"

"No. To see clearly you must see nothing. I have been sent specifically to find you, Betallia Arfore. It took me longer than I would have liked. I had to get your attention, and I killed a lot more people than I wanted to."

"Then tell me what you so desperately need to tell me." She slows her breathing and heartbeat to force her other senses into focus. She can smell old incense and layers of dust and mold. She can hear the shifting of the priest's robes and the bells from outside. She can feel the air currents, no matter how small, through the prickle of her skin. She closes her eyes to see the room. Every outline, every texture, every crack in the stone. She allows it to control her as Vendar had taught her.

"The gods speak to me in my dreams. Lately they have been screaming and driving me mad." He pauses and Beta remains silent, afraid to break her focus. She can see him as a silvery form among the crackle of energy surrounding them. "They tell me you are key in a very important event, yes, and that only you have the power to change the outcome they show me."

"What event? What outcome?" He has the droning tone of a soothsayer and she can feel her shoulders sagging. She hasn't had a good night's sleep in weeks.

"There is a star . . . a song . . . a dance. Yes, it will shatter."

"What will shatter?" She hates riddles and vague statements. This lunatic is asking for a swift ice blade to the heart to undo the damage he has done.

"Their greatest gift! There is blood, there is power, there is innocence destroyed and wicked steps. A betrayal. I thought when I left that place, the gods would let me be. Then I was called here, and they found me. They are angry! Andriel, Illiendiel, Heliendiel, Theliendiel, they are tipping, and they will fall and shatter."

"Where did you leave? You must give me more information. You're not making any sense." Her heart beats faster with the growing intensity of her surroundings as it feeds off her panic. She and it are locked in a cycle she was never taught how to break. She forces her breathing to become calm and steady despite the rasping sound that shudders through her lungs with each breath.

"I—I—" His silvery form shudders in Beta's magicked vision and she lights the braziers with swift snaps of her fingers. The priest's eyes are bleeding black blood and his body is deflating in front of her as though his bones are dissolving. She stares in horror as a shadow tears its way free of the remains and looms against the wall.

She can feel it instantly. This is a god.

"Betallia," the shadow says. It has eyes of red and sheds smoke.

She drops to her knees as visions dance before her. "Who are you?"

"A lesser spirit. There is no need for formalities. I have been looking forward to this meeting. Please, stand, so we may speak." She obeys. "That's better. I have limited time, so I will be brief. You are surrounded by deceit and greed, little battlemage, and while you are no priestess, you may be our last hope. The star, Ashlikani, is not what it seems. Its power has increased and cannot be contained by those that wish to use it for their own gains. Attempting to do so will result in Andriel shattering and your world coming to an end. The gods have sent me to intervene in hopes that some of the damage can be mitigated."

"What do you need me to do?" Her voice is barely a whisper.

"The ceremony must go on as it always has. It is up to you to ensure this is the case." The spirit starts to fade away. "If you need further proof, go to Saltspire. All your answers will be there."

The fires she has lit go out and the silence retakes the shrine. Beta shudders and exits into the warm sunlight.

"Are you alright?" Ironhead comes panting down the path, sweat glistening on his lumpy face. The sight of him is almost as revolting as his voice. "There was a cloud over the shrine, and now the curse is lifted."

Beta nods wearily. "Very good, at least that much was successful. Do we have a boat?"

He shakes his head as his face falls. "They sank, every single one. Whatever happened in there, it changed a lot of things out here."

"You have no idea," she grumbles. The energy of the world around her has vanished, leaving her feeling more lost and alone than ever before.

~ 21 ~

WENDWYNN
&
ZAVOSH

"Your Grace. It's time to come ashore." Grevin stood on the charred ground, holding a cloth to his face. Wen hesitated in the dinghy. She knew she had to join him on the sand eventually, but she would delay every second she could. The islands had been decimated just as Lekala had said. She had failed hundreds of people and it was time to face the consequences. Beyond the crumbled fishing huts on the beach and the charcoaled walkway, smoke still climbed into the sky like dark ribbons. The welcoming party watched her through hollow eyes. She hadn't visited most of these nations, not even after her conquest of Gafforah. She had her sights set on climbing the ladder and had swept past the bottom rungs without a second glance. Now, there was nothing left to do except face the consequences of her choices and see the damage they had caused.

Forcing a somber smile, she stepped off the dinghy and Grevin followed her to the dozen or so townspeople that had come to see their queen. An elderly woman wearing face paint and Gaffori pantaloons stepped forward and bowed. "Your Grace. My name is Glyan, I am the chieftain here. Welcome to Porfal, or what is left of it." She made no effort to hide the resentment in her voice.

Wen did her best to be respectful. "It is an honor to be here, Chieftain. I have brought supplies to help you rebuild and will spare no workforce to see your people back on their feet as soon as possible."

One of the men behind Clyan spat on the sand. Grevin shifted uncomfortably. He had insisted they bring guards of some sort, but Wen had turned him down. If the worst-case scenario did happen, she could defend herself, hopefully with no blood being spilled. The Chieftain was unconvinced. "With all due respect, Your Grace, there is nothing left to rebuild. Those that survived have either fled to Terrial or are biding their time until they can join the others."

Her words dug deep into Wen's heart. She kept the smooth mask of control over her features. She had known it could be bad. "Terrial? They are Gaffori, are they not? Why would they not find refuge in Gafforah?"

"War, Your Grace. It has already touched the island of Gafforah with the conflict in Ulden, and it is only a matter of time before it returns. The conflict with Mangzar cannot be won. They will keep coming back, until either every Gaffori is dead, or every Mangzarian is dead, and none of us are willing to take the bet that our nation of non-warriors will win against viprs and murderers. I will be boarding the last ship to Terrial myself. I agreed to meet with you to let you know the toll that you and your squabbles have taken on people that you hadn't bothered to visit when you first conquered our lands." Wen swallowed the incredibly hard lump of shame in her throat, glad that only Grevin was there to witness her beratement.

"Please, show me around, if you would be so kind." She had no excuse for her inability to care for the peasants of the

Gaffori colonies. She could only allow them to take out their frustrations and hope she could convince them to stay in her country. She could not live with the fact that she had made refugees.

Glyan bowed stiffly and the small crowd moved as one. Wen could feel silent eyes on her as she was led through a burnt forest of tropical flora. The plants and flowers must have been beautiful and lush where they were intact. The island would have made a perfect getaway if she had given them a chance. "We waited for you," Glyan stated, her ceremony dropped. "We thought we would meet the foreign queen who had destroyed the Puppetmaster—the man we thought would hold Gafforah in a chokehold forever. We slaughtered animals, grew extra crops, and bathed our children. We knew we were not first on your list of places to visit, but we were patient. Then the next news we heard is that you had started war with Mangzar."

Wen had left Hearthslayer on her wavecutter in favor of a dirk she kept up her oversized sleeve. She hadn't wanted to appear intimidating to the colonists. Now she wished she had the comfort of its cold metal nearby. "I assure you my failure of the colonies will go down as my greatest shame. I want you to show me everything, Chieftain Glydan. I don't want to be spared."

"You won't be," Glydan said sharply.

The winding path broke out of the forest into a small cluster of funeral pyres that were huts in another life. The homes had been converted into bonfires upon which wrapped bodies filled the air with the disturbingly tantalizing smell of charred flesh. Glydan had not exaggerated in her intention to show Wen the worst of their situation. There were dozens of bodies, young and old, and the signs that there had been a settlement were torched and scattered. There were three or four other citizens besides those who had met the queen, and they bore the same blank expressions.

"We were one of the lucky islands—if you can believe it.

Octaf, Wains, Urasth, and Cayff were not so lucky. There was no one left alive there. The Mangzarians came with the sole intention of sending you a message, Your Grace. The bloodiest, most horrendous message they could. By the time your navy arrived last night, the Mangzarians were preparing to leave. This is just the start if you continue the war. Their cruelty knows no bounds. Did you free the citizens of Gafforah to have them slaughtered at the hands of foreigners? At least Emperor Haldeen only controlled our minds, as opposed to allowing us to be butchered."

"That's enough," Grevin snapped. "Your words border on treason."

The Chieftain stood her ground. "And at what point does a ruler commit treason against their people? When we are all dead? Are we allowed to be angry then?"

Wen held out a hand to ease the growing tension. "Grevin, go back to the dinghy."

"Your Grace—" He began to protest. Wen's glare shut him up and he bowed before storming away.

"I apologize for my advisor. He cares deeply for me and always has. He has faith in me, as he has seen what I am capable of. Unfortunately, you don't even have that to base your opinion of me. You have slaughtered families, and a ruined home. They are equally my responsibility. It is because of what you have lost that I must fight Mangzar. I fight because they are brutal murderers who believe they can take whatever land they lay their eyes on. Do you think if we stopped the war that they would return to their black shores? They would swarm over us, and as you know, they do not take slaves. They see the entire word as inferior to them in every way. I have called for help from Terrial, from Nath'iki, and beyond. They are afraid to stand up to Mangzar and will only fight if the blood of their people is spilled. So, you see, Gafforah is all that stands before the Warleaders, and it must stand, to prove they are no different than we." She hoped the Chieftain could feel the urgent empathy in her words. The refusal of aid from nations that were considered allies had come as an unexpected and massive blow. Those who had joined her against Haldeen turned their backs on her when it came to fighting Mangzar. By the time she realized how alone she was, it was too late to change the course of the war.

"If what you say is true, then it is only a matter of time before death claims us all." Glyden showed no sign of fear or anguish in her voice—only acceptance.

Wen glanced at the desolation in the faces of her subjects. "May we speak privately, Chieftain?" She guided the older woman to an area where their voices would not carry. "You are correct. We will be destroyed if we continue the battle with Mangzar. I do not dispute that. They are better trained, better prepared, and their very existence revolves around war and death in a way we cannot equal. If you know this, you also know there is no surrendering. There is no scenario where the war can end with peace on both sides. But there is a hope. I have an elite force working to find a power that will ensure our victory and end the bloodshed. It is not fair to ask you to wait, and I won't. If you must flee to Terrial, you have every right to, and I will not stop you. But when we are victorious, I expect Gaffori to return to Gafforah, to their homes. And there will be homes. I will personally see to that."

The frustration tightening Glyden's face eased. Being spoken to as an equal was giving her some sort of control over her horrible situation. "This power you seek, how do you know it will guarantee your victory?"

Wen could not say too much. Even with a subject of hers, Glyden could still be turned or forced to give up the secrets whispered to her in confidence. The fewer people that knew Zavosh and Frej's quest, the better. "Yes."

"I have heard the rumors, as has the rest of Gafforah, Your

Grace, that you dabble in magics that someone born with no magical ability should not be able to access. Magics that have questionable natures. If your secret weapon is anything like that, I urge you to use caution. Andriel's balance is delicate, and those chosen by the gods to wield magic are chosen for a reason." She stopped in the middle of the path. "But I am not one to judge the spirits or their discretion when choosing who wields what kind of magic. If you can wield unnatural magic, then you may be the one I've been waiting for."

The Chieftain had caught Wen's interest. The old woman pulled a scroll from her belt pouch and handed it to the queen. "The spirits bless me with sight, and with finding things that otherwise do not wish to be found. The Well may be hidden, but it will not be so for long. They have given me this map for you, I believe." The remnants of her people had gathered their miserable belongings and looked to her for their next instructions. The Chieftain bowed once more and turned back to them. "We will wait in Terrial, Your Grace, for you to fulfill your promise to us."

Wen tried not to let the twinge of pain that her statement brought show through her features. She nodded respectfully to the Chieftain and watched them head down a different path towards the ships that would take them away from her queendom. The scroll weighed heavily in her hand as she walked back to the dinghy. Crevin waited for her there anxiously.

"Your Grace. How did it go?"

Wen lowered herself wearily into the boat and they pushed off into the water. She unfurled the scroll. It was a painting of what she could only imagine was a battlemage, in glorious Mangzarian detail. The paint was dull from age, but the spark of life still clung to the skin. Elements swirled around the battlemage's skin webbed with orange light. She let it snap back in a roll with a frustrated sigh. Yet another clue with no real answer. "With Halthax defeated, the war should be over, but my sources tell me our peace is only a respite. The new Warleader may be more ambitious and cunning than the old. We must make the time we have count as there is less of Gafforah to save every day. The one thing that can end the war now remains elusive, and my search only seems to widen instead of narrow. The Well is now either in Mangzar, or perhaps the Citadel. I had hoped to not alert the sorcerers to my search."

Her relationship with the sorcerers of Elgireth had been tentative at best, with the opinions on her conquest varying. Those that were loyalists and friends of Frejith would stand by her and assist her, but there were far too many unfriendly ears and eyes within the tower she had built as a gesture of good will towards the powerful magic users and the pirates that had been instrumental in her conquest. Together, they were supposed to represent the two sides of the moon, both working to protect Kaper's Bay. Things were never that simple when mortal minds were involved and her intentions for the groups had been twisted, leaving her to quash slavery as well as corruption once the war was won. It seemed no matter what she did, there would always be grumbling somewhere in her queendom.

"There may be those in the Citadel who do not personally support you, but there is one sorceress we both know would do anything to help you, and with discretion."

"And I have sent her into the jaws of my enemy." Wen gripped the scroll with a tight fist as though she could choke the secrets it held out of it.

"If you want to find the Gods' Blood soon, it may be time to take matters into your own hands. We cannot wait, you know that as well as I do. You have trained decoys and Seers to maintain the image that you are still leading the defense. The time for caution has passed."

Wen laughed despite herself. "What has the war come to, that you would suggest rash action before I do?" Her mirth was gone as quickly as it had appeared. "You are right, of course. I cannot trust another messenger with the one concrete clue I have." She rationalized the need to go to Mangzar and find Frej herself, but deep down she knew she was going to see her wife. Her stomach churned. It could be her greatest mistake in a long string of errors.

Fortress Blackfeather came alive in the days following the disappearance of Halthax ky Dzaxar. Duels filled the halls with the echoes of clashing steel as Warleader hopefuls battled to the death. Servants dragged bodies to the growing stack in the courtyard where the final victor would light them in a pyre to herald their new reign. The blood they left on the stones would soak into the masonry, strengthening the symbolism of the fortress's brutality. Zavosh could smell the influence of the queen in the air of chaos. If she had been the one to make Dzaxar disappear, he wondered if she knew the extent of the impact she had made on her enemies. Mount Thoyax might be at war, but there were some traditions that still took precedence. Sixth District was considerably weaker thanks to the loss of their warlord. Time that could be spent scheming against her was now used to fight amongst themselves, weakening their army and sowing chaos in their streets.

Zavosh avoided the bloodletting as best he could. The libraries were in shambles, long deserted except for the lone librarian who looked older than most of the dusty tomes. The ancient vipr had lost his mind as well as functional use of his body and spent most of his time muttering to himself in his chair when he wasn't tearing pages out of bindings. The works that were legible fell apart in Zavosh's hands or were full of battle tactics and warrior forms. The Mangzarians had no use for information that didn't heighten their abilities in war. It was one of the many reasons he had chosen to abandon the ways of his people; and yet remained his greatest pride in his heritage.

Shouts rang out from the rafters above his head, distracting him from his tedious investigations. Combined with the Var rantings of the librarian and the barely legible penmanship of ancient Mangzarians, he found his head throbbing on a consistent basis. He was almost glad when the door to the basement slammed, and he heard Frejith's fairy-like steps tap down the stairs. The sorceress was awash with excitement and the glow of chaos she thrived on. She wore pieces of armor over her servant's garb, a bold choice at a time when every able-bodied adult was a potential threat to a would-be Warleader. While not proficient enough in blade combat to join the festivities, there was still blood splattered across her chest.

"I thought I'd find you hiding down here."

The vipr barely glanced at her. "Where is your shadow?" Greysten had been a constant companion to Frejith, and the other way around. He could only hope that the stable boy had met his end on the point of an eager sword.

"You mean Grey? He's putting in actual effort instead of drowning in dust and paper mites. You really are the dullest vipr I've ever known." She glanced at the glossy-eyed librarian. "Can we speak in private?"

Zavosh shrugged. "He hasn't even been able to tell me his name. I wouldn't worry about the *intha*."

"Fine." She leaned in closer anyways. "There's been a change of plan, and I think you'll like it better than . . . whatever this is." She wrinkled her nose at the stacks of books on Zavosh's table.

"If it has anything to do with your new friend, I don't think I will." His excitement at being visited had faded to discontent.

"You've been down here long enough that you should have found something. We're treading water and our only choice is to follow my plan, which is evolving."

"Evolving?" Zavosh narrowed his eyes. He didn't want to appear too eager, but he was anxious for any idea that would get him into the soot-filtered sunlight above.

"Based on my experience, and certainly yours, Mangzarians don't write anything down. They kill, and they do art. So, let's find the answer through one of two languages they understand—violence."

Zavosh closed his book with a hesitant curiosity. If she'd come up with some hairbrained plan, he would have to shut it down. What the queen thought she could accomplish by sending her hot-headed wife here was beyond him. "I hope you're not suggesting what I think you are. You may be strong, but putting yourself in danger by fighting to be warqueen—"

"Oh, waves, no, not me. Greysten. You should talk to him. He knows what he's doing, and he's going to become Warlord."

Zavosh didn't like the light in her eyes. Whatever the foreigner had fed her, she had believed wholeheartedly and fallen prey to his promises. He growled and slammed the books to the floor in a dramatic sweep. "He is a foreigner and a human. What makes you think he can best viprs in combat?"

"He has his own tricks." Frejith grinned like someone who'd just heard a juicy secret.

"Take me to this stable boy," Zavosh demanded.

Frejith ignored the frustration in his voice and led him up the stairs. Zavosh fought the instinct to draw his weapons as they emerged to the stench of spilled blood and sweat. He may no longer identify as Mangzarian, but he was still a vipr, and had the urge to plunge his blade into flesh the same as his brethren. He reached for Frejith's hand in a panic. "I'm going to close my eyes. Lead me through." He wouldn't allow himself to be the one ultimately responsible for the demise of their plan because he couldn't resist drinking a soul. The loss of one sense did little to ease his withdrawal, but it was enough for them to get through the halls until the stone beneath his feet changed to the wood planks of the stable, and the smell of gore was replaced by animals.

He opened his eyes to see a smug Greysten wearing full plates, unmarked by battle scars. He wondered if the human knew he would be a laughingstock if he set foot in the fray with virgin armor. "I told you he'd come," Frejith said breathlessly. "Now tell him the plan."

Zavosh never should have taken the assignment in the library. He should have stayed close where he could monitor the foreigner and his relationship with the queen's wife. The stable hand nodded respectfully to Zavosh. "I hope you understand that I'm keeping it brief. Our window is small, and I have no intention of wasting it. I have a Terralian accent because I developed one specifically to hide my native voice. I am Qan, born and bred."

He had dropped into the lilt of the far southern island and Zavosh could see the dusky purple in the man's hair. When Zavosh had no reply, Greysten continued. "I'm sure you know our reputation with animals, and our magical abilities. I know you are also aware of the rules regarding a *milta*. I will be exercising a power well within my rights by summoning a creature that will guarantee my victory. And from my conversations with Frejith, an ally in Mangzar is something that is invaluable to a certain queen."

Every word was a punch to Zavosh's gut. He could see the guilt in Frejith's eyes. She hadn't blown their mission; she had shattered it and used the shards to stab him in the back. "No," he hissed. "You told him who we are?"

Greysten's expression didn't change. He had expected pushback. He allowed Frejith to come to his defense. "Qan is a neutral island and has no stake in our war. Since Mount Thoyax is alone in fighting Gafforah, he could become warlord and end the war with no consequences."

"No consequences? Every lava-blooded vipr will be at his

throat." Zavosh struggled to comprehend the reasoning behind the sorceress's choice.

"They won't be able to after today," Greysten responded calmly. He stood casually with a helmet slung in one arm. He wasn't afraid of the outcome of their conversation. "No one will be able to touch me. I'll have what I want, a warlord's title, and the war will be over. Dare I say, we could form something of an alliance."

"No, you may not dare to say," Zavosh snapped. "You are a stranger to Queen Wendwynn and a stranger to me."

"The truth is that I'm going to take these next steps regardless, vipr. The only question is whether you and Frejith will stand beside me. I tend to be more amicable towards those who choose to align with me."

Zavosh looked to Frejith and then back at Greysten. Was she afraid of him? What was he planning that had the greatest mind mage in Gafforah rattled? Perhaps her compliance to the potential warlord was more than misguided optimism. *Trust her*, he told himself over and over. He could learn to trust Frejith, but this stranger that acted as though he was an old friend? It was happening too fast. "Prove your loyalty and your power, and you shall have our cooperation." What else could he say? He was outnumbered and outvoted. And, if Greysten wasn't bluffing, outgunned.

Greysten gave the vipr a curt nod as though he'd had any real say in the matter. He strode out of the stables with full confidence, followed closely by Frejith and Zavosh. The Qan walked through the bloody fray to the center of the courtyard where he withdrew a fistful of summoning powder only his kind knew how to make from a silk pouch on his waist. He held out a hand to Frejith, who stepped forward and placed a palm-sized scale in it. Zavosh's breath caught in his throat. It belonged to a dragon. He meant to summon a dragon. The creatures were only native to Mangzar, and fast dwindling in numbers. How a Qan intended to control one and use it to his advantage without causing irreparable destruction to himself and everyone around him was something the vipr didn't want to discover for himself.

The harsh Qan words rang out over the sounds of battle as Greysten clashed the dragon scale and the summoning powder together in the air, causing a flash of light and a thunderclap that brought a sudden silence to the fortress. He had drawn the attention of the combatants and the events of the next few moments would determine the course of the future.

Through the ringing in his head, Zavosh saw Frejith, open faced and oblivious to the danger she had placed herself in. Her eyes were drawn in rapture to the skies where clouds were swirling in an unnatural vortex, laced with lightning. Zavosh was slack-jawed along with the rest of them. Had he done it? Had Greysten summoned the ultimate weapon in the bid for warlord?

If he had, Frejith was in the direct path of where it would land. She would die, crushed by her own curiosity. Zavosh cursed the queen yet again and dashed forward, knocking the sorceress out of the way just as the wind began to swirl furiously, and the result of the Qan spell landed with a heaviness that cracked the earth beneath it. Zavosh sheltered the sorceress as best he could while squinting against the stinging dirt and stone that whipped around their heads.

There it stood, a sight unseen by most living. With blue-back scales rippling in the weak light of torches and the distant volcano, screeching with a sound that caused ears to bleed and wings beating at the air, there was a dragon.

Zavosh screamed, knowing his cries would be drowned out by the dragon's wailing. He may not have been responsible for Ugden's death, but he would be devoured by the beast before he would lose Frejith as well.

~ 22 ~

KEYRA

How she came to be back on the docks, sewing for incoming merchants, she could not say. She remembers glimpses of the horrors at Erey's home. She had run, dragging Tilsman along behind her. She remembers sobbing in an alley for Aryet knows how long. She remembers the headaches returning with vicious force. Pushing back the memories of Erey's blood on her hands had relieved them, so push back she had. She thinks of him little more than she does her own breathing. It is never on her mind, but it is always there, pushing and pulling to keep her body alive. Now she barely speaks, leaving Tilsman to draw his own conclusions. He thinks she has finally snapped and become a feeble woman lost in the memories of the murders she had committed, but the truth is she can no longer muster the energy to take care of herself, much less the boy. She has regressed to what she knows best while using the least of her energy.

"What did you say?" she growls.

Tilsman glances up from the thread he is properly tangling. "What?"

"Why are you whispering over there?" She has considered leaving him behind many times. But every time the thought crosses her mind, she feels guilty and detached. It's as though there are two halves to her mind, and the duller, more comfortable one has become stronger.

"I haven't said a word, Granma Keyra. Are you sure you're alright? I've told you I think that leemoah did something to you. You wouldn't have killed those people on your own."

She knows he's right, but she's also irritated that he would worry about her. She has held her own for decades now. Here, Elgireth, Mangzar . . . she feels a stabbing pain in her head as memories she doesn't recognize are cut off before they can manifest. No. She was born and raised on Elgireth. Right? Her fingers continue to work the needle through the fabric that blurs in her eyes.

"Granma Keyra!" Tilsman yanks her hand away and Keyra blinks. Blood pools from where the needle has gone through her finger, pinning the fabric to her skin. She stares in horror as the feeling begins to return, and the pain with it.

She sees blood pooling on a tunic. There are screams and saltwater. She can hear Tilsman yelling from somewhere beyond her episode, but he is not much more than an echo. His slap across her face gives the jolt needed for her to break out of the spell. "You *impetuous* little bastard!" she shrieks, drawing attention from the onlookers.

The worry on Tilsman's face seems odd in such a young child as he examines her closely. "Let's get you in the shade."

She allows herself to be led out of the spotlight to a tattered awning shading a suspicious basket weaver that watches them carefully. "Tilsman, I think it's time to admit that I'm not quite myself."

"Not sure what gave that away," he mutters as he inspects the needle still impaled through her finger. "I'm going to have to yank this out. It's not going to feel pleasant."

She rolls her eyes. "I'm old, not an invalid. Rip it out and be done with it." She steels herself and doesn't allow him to see the tension in her jaw and shoulders. The longer he thinks her invincible, the longer she can order him around like a chubby servant. His pale fingers pinch the needle nervously and he yelps as he tugs, as though he is the wounded one. Keyra feels nothing. She calmly staunches the renewed blood flow with the now-useless fabric and stares into the distance. She sees ghosts there, hears whispers. Tears brim in her eyes and she doesn't realize how hard she's pressing on the cut until a jolt of pain races up her arm. "We need to go back to Elgireth. I need to find Tika."

"She could be one of those things, remember? Or she could have fled the country. It's not safe to go back there."

Keyra feels a smile play on her lips, more out of neurosis than amusement. "You underestimate her. I'm willing to bet she's immune to the affliction and that's why it killed Isah and not her."

"Even if that's true, we can't get to Elgireth. We probably won't be immune." Tilsman's panic makes his voice squeak.

"We'll figure it out when we get there. I could be wrong, but we must go. She's the only one that can help me." Yes. Her head is feeling better already as she makes the decision to return to Elgireth. That is where she is supposed to be.

Tilsman stands taller and helps her to her feet. "Tika, and me, Granma Keyra. If you think you need to get to Elgireth to get better, then that's what we're going to do." He pulls off a shoe triumphantly and a jewel the size of an eyeball drops out.

"What in the waves is *that*?" Keyra gapes.

"My mom and dad had me put it in my shoe for safekeeping before I left Waheth. They said to use it when there were no other options. I think it should be enough to convince a captain to take us to Hardock."

Keyra moves to slap him but is hit by another wave of nausea. "I'll deal with you when I'm back to myself."

She fades in and out of the present. The memories she does

have are gray and muddled, but there is undeniably something beyond the haze. Something she has experienced before.

At some point, Tilsman must have chartered a boat, because when she begins to regain control of her senses, saltwater sprays her face as the boat dips through the choppy waters. Elgireth breaks the horizon in chunks of rock and the ever-present cloud of seabirds.

Tilsman is curled up on the deck, moaning with each rock of the skiff. He does his best to hide the seasickness that overwhelms him. He is trying to be brave for her, Keyra realizes with a glow of warmth in her heart. After everything, he cares for her the same as she cares for him. Perhaps he isn't completely useless after all.

She notices the sailors on the rail whispering, their eyes glancing towards her. She frowns and does her best to ignore them. They may have accepted the jewel as payment, but they are still unhappy with the job. She should be grateful they didn't steal the gem and throw them off the side of the boat.

"Excuse me, lady." She nearly jumps out of her skirts at the voice behind her. It is the cabin boy, slick with salt and sweat and dressed in fabric not that much different from the sails. "We've been wondering why you would want to go to Elgireth. We know it's none of our business, but we've been told we're not allowed to go there."

"Who told you that?" Her eyes drift to the other crew members. Any one of them could mean her and Tilsman harm. They had witnessed the horrors of Elgireth firsthand, after all.

"An official decree from the Citadel. Everything's shut down. They said it was because of an outbreak of some kind, but everyone knows it's because of an experiment that went wrong."

"Aldin! Shut your mouth, you little seaslug." A burly sailor growls at the cabin boy, who scampers away before he gets in more trouble. The sailor turns his attention to Keyra. "Don't mind the kid, he gossips more than an old broad—no offense intended. You paid for passage to Elgireth, you're getting passage to Elgireth." He turns back to his work, chewing on a habalah stick.

Any other time, Keyra *would* have taken offense to his comparing her to an old broad, but she no longer has the energy, and the cold fact of the matter is that she can't deny his conclusion. The crew becomes quiet as they near Veden. Keyra has never seen the waters so empty here. There are murmurs as the crew turns their attention to the horizon.

"By the waves," she whispers. Hardock's normally bustling port town is full of people with hollow eyes, watching the ships silently. Keyra cannot believe what she sees. This is worse than the news that the people had all died. The Elgir sway as though there is no support except some powerful force holding them upright. Their faces turn towards the ships, but their eyes do not move.

"It's like Heliendiel got spat from the ocean and was named Hardock. What kind of spirit did they piss off to deserve that?" The sailor that speaks kisses a god amulet around his neck.

"Man the oars, boys, we're turning around." The captain is the first to look away. He shakes his head at Tilsman. "We can't take you any farther than this. You can swim or come back to Gafforah with us."

"What if there are people there who need help?"

The captain gives the chubby boy a sharp glare. "I'm a vegetable merchant, boy, not a hero. I will not die for a stranger."

Keyra would cuff Tilsman's ear later, but part of her was proud that he would stand up for Elgireth. "I'm afraid going back to Gafforah isn't an option for us, Captain. Can I buy a lifeboat from you so we can get ashore?"

He shakes his head in bewilderment. "If you had a death wish, a sword would be a much kinder fate. But if you insist on being eaten from the inside out by worms, then do so on your own." He sighs at the disappointment and fear on her face. "We'll take you as far as the southern peninsula. But we will not stop, and we will not get close enough to risk being affected."

The southern point would put them half a mile south of the city. "That's all I can ask from you, sir."

Tilsman whimpers but knows better than to voice an opinion against Keyra's plan. She will get her way eventually.

The crew remains silent as they work to direct the barge. Some of the other vessels have turned around. One tries to dock, but the walking bodies shuffle to greet it and its captain changes course. Keyra's sober expression causes Tilsman to worry. She gives him a wink. "There won't be any of those bastards around where we're going. Tika's not too far into town so we shouldn't run into any trouble."

"And if we do?"

Keyra taps the hilt of the dagger she had bought before they departed. She had no intention of being taken in for the murders she had committed against her will. "That's what this is for. Once we find Tika, her magic will protect us."

Tilsman is wide eyed as they near the deserted shore. "I sure hope we find her then."

"Now or never, we aren't slowing down," the captain barks.

Keyra takes Tilsman's hand before he can second guess himself and they jump into the lifeboat as it drops into the warm summer waters. Keyra curses to herself as she realizes they have left them no method for rowing. With the wind blowing west, they will have to swim. Already, the vessel is drifting farther away from land. "Can you swim?" she asks Tilsman.

"Kind of, it was never my strong point. I—ahhh!" Keyra pulls him into the water with her, knowing he will never go of his own free will. She looks back to the barge. It has turned tail and uses both sails and oars to get as far away from Elgireth as possible. There is no going back now.

At the midpoint of their half-mile swim, Keyra feels stitches in her ribs. She grits her teeth through the pain, wishing the water were colder to at least numb her. Tilsman manages to keep up with her by awkwardly dog paddling. His head goes under once, but he manages to fight the elements by spitting out the liquid as he swallows it.

Somehow, they reach shore and lie panting on the muddy sand as they catch their breath and let the sun dry what it can. "We're not dead yet. That's a good sign, right?" Tilsman gasps.

"I'd like to think so. If the curse doesn't take us, we have to worry about those magical sacks of death. They seemed a little too interested in our boat for my liking. Now get off your lazy ass, I'd rather not be caught sleeping on the beach by one of those things."

Keyra leads the way up the cliffside. The forced use of her legs has triggered something deep within her. She is exhausted and aching, but more alive than she has been in years. The headache has vanished and her sense of being has returned. She must be on the right path. Every step she takes now radiates with purpose.

Tilsman stops and tugs on her sleeve. They stand on top of the ragged cliffs that border Oldeville, preventing the muddy bottom of the island from draining. An Elgir with blackened eyes watches them from a far ridge. Her hackles raise as it moves towards them. Tilsman gasps as he points to more coming from the opposite side. They're cutting them off from the town.

Again, Keyra feels woefully unprepared with her six-inch dagger and an unarmed child as her arsenal. "I'm going to do something now, boy, and you're going to thank me for it later." She draws energy from an untapped well inside her. "Get to Tika's hut. I'm sure you remember it, it's the only one that looks livable in Oldeville. Get inside and barricade yourself.

If she's alive, she'll help you. If she's not there, at least you can hide. If she's not alive? Well, we're not going to think about that yet."

Keyra steels herself and knocks into Tilsman with her shoulder. The boy, caught off guard, tumbles down the ridge towards Oldeville, sliding and scrabbling to regain control of his descent. Keyra turns her attention to the advancing Elgir. They are completely silent in their movements, making it impossible to keep track of them all. From behind, a hand grabs her shoulder and yanks.

Keyra falls to one knee, turning and stabbing at the empty-eyed attacker. The knife punctures its skin like a sack of rotten wine. Dark liquid bursts from the incision and it crumbles to the ground in a sloughing heap. The seamstress vomits at the smell and sight but has time for little else before a second and a third descend on her. While easy to kill, they prove difficult to fend off long enough for her to retaliate. One goes for her knife hand and twists her wrist in an intelligent way meant to disarm her. Keyra buckles beneath the weight as nails dig into her skin and teeth search for purchase.

Just when panic swells in her throat as she fears the worst, they release her and step back. Keyra's heart thuds in her ears. She slashes forward and they move farther away, giving her enough space to head down the hill herself. Her joints creak in complaint as she sprints for Tika's hut through the muddy streets that suck at her shoes with every step. Eventually, they are left behind, and her bare feet slap the marshy path. She cannot hear pursuers, but she dares not stop long enough to check. Whatever possessed them to stop attacking her could wear off at any moment.

Keyra finds the door to the Seer's home ajar. The flowers that once marked the tiny oasis in the muck of Oldeville are dead and wilted. Keyra steels herself and adjusts her knife grip before pushing inside the rest of the way.

Tilsman cowers in the corner of the main room, tears streaming down his face. Across the table where Keyra used to have tea with her best friend, a gray-skinned woman with blackened eyes and golden tattoos sways, gaze locked hungrily on the chubby boy.

~ 23 ~
BETA
&
THE BOY

The boy watches Beta through half-closed eyes. He cannot help himself. He still doesn't trust that she is real and with him. She is a vision that has haunted his mind both asleep and awake for as long as he can remember. She is beautiful, more now than ever.

"I know you're not asleep," Star whispers.

Ironhead jumps despite himself. "Sorry. I, uh, what?"

The leemoah rolls her eyes and lies on her back to watch the stars. "You've been staring at the battlemage all night."

They are sailing at an impressive speed through the bay, spurred by Beta's control of the wind and some secret she would not share. Whatever happened in the fishing village, it has changed her. He has yet to see her sleep. "She needs to rest. She's the only protection we have." He glances at Peynter, who is slumped in the stern. He's seen the water mage work. Beta is their only hope.

"We have you," Star reminds him gently. "Ironhead, Warrior of the Arenas. I do not trust her intentions, nor the intentions of her people. I hear whispered warnings from the mists of prophecy."

Ironhead scoffs. "The mists of prophecy? What does that mean? You hear what you want to hear. As long as you get back to the Reef, why do you care who gets you there? You've only gotten as far as you have because of her."

"I'm here because of *you*. You were the one that found me and helped me escape. All she's done is steer the boat," she snaps loud enough for Beta to glance over. The leemoah lowers her voice. "Your feelings are clouded. You are simple, but capable of so much more than people like her will lead you to believe. She is different. She will destroy you."

Ironhead rolls over so his back is to Star. "Good night." He hears her sigh and settle again. Good. He glimpses Beta motioning him over and jumps to join her at the bow like an over-excited puppy. "Keep your head down," she hisses. "Your voice carries over the waves."

Ironhead drops down, glad of the darkness that hides his red cheeks. "Sorry. I didn't know there were enemies around."

"There are always enemies." She points to the horizon. "See that light?" The glowing in question winked chaotically.

"A ship?" The boy squints to see in the darkness.

"A decoy. Anyone pursuing us wouldn't risk a flame. They're going to ambush our boat, and soon."

"Who is?"

"Who else but the Tower? You stole their most valuable captive and put her in the care of the Citadel. They may be ragged excuses for pirates, but they can hold a grudge." She moves to rouse Peynter. The water mage groans and stretches. His face becomes serious when he sees what Beta points to.

"How long have they been following us?" he asks.

"I'd be willing to guess since we left Gafforah. The more important question is why they haven't made a move yet."

"Why would they?" Peynter sighs. "We're doing the

transportation work for them. It's so close to the ceremony that they wouldn't try to negotiate with us to get her back. They'll probably jump us when we get closer to Uta'lihali."

Beta grits her teeth and drums her fingers rapidly on the wood railing. "We can't let that happen."

"What do we do?" Ironhead blurts. Being in her presence is intimidating as well as intoxicating. His recent warrior status is laughable next to her lifetime of special training.

"She'll have to hide herself underwater and I'll do my best to disguise our faces. Be prepared to fight if we must," Beta orders.

She doesn't wait for him to acknowledge her. She is already rousing Star. There are tense words exchanged and then Beta raises her voice. "What do you mean, no?"

Star is sitting up in her blanket with a defiant look. Her face turns to meet Ironhead's eyes.

"We should go north, there's a leemoah village in the shallows. It's small and poor but they will escort me to the Reef in time for the ceremony. They won't expect that. Staying here will guarantee our capture."

Beta's short temper snaps. "Last time I checked, I was the one paid to be in charge here. Get in the damn water and let me handle it."

Peynter watches the unfolding fight with mild interest. "I'd listen to her if I were you, Star Shepherd. Beta doesn't like when people tell her no." He smirks.

Star jerks away from the sorceress as though she's on fire. "You're no fool. The only explanation is that you *want* to be caught. Is it because you want revenge? Or a fight? You—" She slumps forward as Beta pulls the blood from her head long enough to put the leemoah into unconsciousness. The orange veins in her arms glow.

Peynter is sitting up now. "Beta, you don't want a fight, right? We can't jeopardize—"

"Just shut up," Beta snarls. "Both of you. Let me think. I'm going to figure it out, but you have to trust me." Ironhead opens his mouth to speak but her twisted face of rage stops him. "Cover her with whatever you can. She'd be safer in the water, but we don't have time to convince her of that." Again, she assumes obedience and turns to scan the horizon.

Perhaps if Ironhead's obsession with the battlemage hadn't been so entrenched in what defined him, he wouldn't have spread blankets and packs over the leemoah. An hour passes during which neither of them talks. The shapes across the water that have been keeping their distance move closer. The skiff that pulls alongside them bears no flags and is full of serious-faced mercenaries. A hook secures the vessels together. Beta and Peynter move to stand between them and Star.

"That's far enough." Beta's voice is unwavering.

"You must be Vendar's apprentice, Beta, and the water mage whose name escapes me." Ironhead feels chills up his spine at El'rozai's voice. It brings back nothing but painful memories. The slaver steps from behind his soldiers, a smile on his face.

"Why is 'Peynter' so hard to remember?" The male sorcerer grumbles.

Beta's eyes narrow at the leemoah. "How did you know that?"

"I have a message for you from your master. Look at it before you shower me with those ice spikes." He glances above his head to the hovering cloud of glistening frozen water. Beta snatches the scroll and reads the words, keeping the spikes in place.

There is silence long enough for Ironhead to break out in a sweat. Finally, Beta speaks. "It's him, without a doubt. I'm just . . . not sure if I can trust you."

"He thought you would say that. You are as cautious as he is impulsive. You have both my and Vendar's promise for safe passage to the Reef."

"Last I checked, the Tower has always avoided having to answer to the law. How do I know you're not going to sell us into slavery?" Peynter questions Captain Zai.

"*Your* law is not *the* law. We are both private organizations and have had our alliances and differences in the past. But as far as gaining your trust in this moment?" He reaches between the boats to hand the sorcerers a heavy sack each. "Take this as a small token of peace from me and mine, along with our apologies for the incident in Nahem. It was impulsive and unnecessary." His reptilian eyes brush over Ironhead with mild interest. The boy feels chills up his spine.

Beta speaks slowly, careful with every word. "I see. There were mistakes made on both sides. The Citadel's history with the Tower has always been . . . cordial." Peynter nods his agreement eagerly. Whatever studious nature he usually utilizes has vanished with the presence of gold.

"A wise observation," the captain smirks. "Now gather your things and join us on the skiff so we can get the sacrifice to the Reef in time."

Ironhead looks up as a shadow passes overhead to see two figures standing over him with hands on weapons. One of them offers his free arm to the boy. When had they boarded? Now there were twelve of them, watching silently. "Nice and easy now. We don't want any trouble."

Faced with no choice, Ironhead allows them to lift Star and help him into the larger boat. The gloved hand never moves from his arm despite his lack of resistance. The sorcerers follow with only a brief hesitation.

The man holding the boy's arm releases him when the slaver leemoah shoots him a look. "We are all allies here, there is no reason to restrain anyone. We all have the same goals."

"What changed your mind?" Ironhead can't help asking.

The leemoah smiles as though Ironhead is an especially tasty morsel. "There is more to the world than black and white.

There is money, and there are compromises. Success is more often found with allies than with enemies."

"I do like allies," Ironhead agrees with an equally false smile. He cannot fight the unease as he watches the strangers place Star in a coffin-like box where she would sleep the rest of the journey. Something told him he would not be enjoying the same luxury.

By the time the sun has risen, Everlyn is visible from the tiny skiff, and Beta could not be more grateful. It is less than an hour's ride between the Citadel's island and the lighthouse to Uta'lihali where her mission will be complete, and she will finally be free to scrub the salt from her skin and hair. She wonders if Vendar has recovered, or if his physical appearance has changed altogether. Will she recognize him?

The Citadel towers over the rocky island like an eternal sentinel, its light shining brighter than the outdated lighthouse on the rocks a few islands over. The leemoah in charge maneuvers the skiff around the far side. Beta wants to ask if they can stop, but she knows the answer already. Not only is she a pawn in this new game, but the bonus pulling at her hip serves as an effective reminder that she has sold her right as leader of their group. Despite her new fortune, she feels just as much a captive as the men claim Star isn't.

"I wonder about him, too," Peynter says as though he can read her mind. "It's strange that our generation will see the end of the battlemages. Do you think they can ever be brought back?"

Beta averts her eyes. "You know how it works. Sorcerers must be descendants of other sorcerers, but even magical parents don't guarantee magical offspring. Having only one sorcerer parent lessens the chances, and battlemages are especially rare. I could have twenty children and none of them be a battlemage."

Peynter doesn't say what he's thinking but she knows it all the same. Her relationship with Vendar may be taboo and kept quiet, but there are no secrets in the Citadel—especially when it comes to the last two battlemages. She can't say she hasn't thought about having children with her master. If they did, the chances were still slim that one would be a battlemage. And what kind of life would she be forcing upon them? Vendar's days were numbered, now more than ever. Beta had maybe another twenty years to live—if she didn't die in combat first. The child would be raised by the Citadel, under immense pressure, only to die young. They wouldn't be saving the battlemage lineage. They would be dragging out its extinction for another generation or two. Peynter chews on his bottom lip as he does when he's thinking. "Nature has a way of balancing itself out. Genealogy class taught us that the traits for magic can be dormant for generations. Maybe there's someone out there about to have a battlemage child who doesn't even know it."

Beta smiles at his weak attempt to comfort her. There's nothing he can say that she hasn't told herself. "Get some rest, Peynter. We're close and this may be our last chance before we reach the Reef."

The water mage sags wearily. "I mean if you're going to twist my arm about it." He stretches and wanders off to find somewhere to curl up. The battlemage turns her attention to Ironhead. No matter how revolting he may be to her, there is something about him that is fascinating. He is focused on the dark lighthouse with nostalgia in his eyes. "Worried about your old man?"

She joins him at the rail, and he jumps at her presence. She wonders if he will ever grow accustomed to her.

"Not really, no. Just wondering who is keeping the

lighthouse now. It used to be me, and it can't be my father. He's either drunk in a puddle of his own piss or dead. Perhaps there's a new keeper now, and they've turned my bedroom into a parlor."

She laughs sharply and he beams as though she has handed him the key to her heart. "I suppose you won't be going back, then. What does your future hold after this?"

"I didn't expect to survive this ordeal, to be honest. I suppose I could go back to being a slave."

His dry humor is not lost on her. She is almost amused. "I don't think Gafforah is the place for you. Perhaps not for me, either." She frowns at what she has spoken aloud.

"Beta, a word." Captain Zai beckons the sorceress from the ship's stern. He points to a gray mass on the sea's horizon. "We are close."

"Finally," she confirms.

"I need you to remember who takes care of you when we reach the Reef. There may be some necessary action on your part."

Beta stares at the weak orange glow through the skin on her hand. "Let me ask, before we proceed. Are you working for the Citadel, or are we working for you?"

"There is mutual interest on both sides. Rest assured you will be satisfied with your payment. Our two groups aren't that different when it counts."

She doesn't like his comparing the pirate organization to the high-ranking sorcerers, but she doesn't know if she is in a position to counter his claim. "I've been trained to not go into a deal blindly. I deserve to know what changed between the attack in Nahem and now, and what's going to happen during the ceremony."

"You will know when it's time," El'rozai promises.

Her training has prepared her for many things. While most scenarios include physical tests, there is always a mental side.

He is avoiding something. "Have you been to the Citadel? Is Vendar healing?"

"He is well. He misses you." Lies. Beta falls silent as she accepts there will be no truth here. She kicks Peynter awake with a none-too-gentle boot as the water around them ripples unnaturally.

Leemoah guards are breaching beside the ship, glancing with sharp side eyes at the newcomers as they break the waves. The captain boards the vessel with a backflip on the deck. He approaches El'rozai, his gaze never leaving Star's still form. They speak in rapid e'likai with raised voices.

Beta stretches her hands and keeps the connection between her and nature hovering close like an expectant kiss. She will take any reason to unleash hell upon the Tower agents. Peynter moves to stand closer to the Star Shepherd, asleep in her unsettling coffin. Beta wonders what will happen when they reach the Reef. The Uta'lihali people will not be happy to know the condition of their sacrifice. An untrained eye would miss the package that passed from the captain's hands to that of the guard. The leemoah soldier disappears and their skiff is led to the tiny island dock that marks the last stop for air breathers without magical assistance. The sorcerers relax only slightly. Despite the uneasy circumstances, Beta feels excitement. She has never been to a leemoah city before. It is an honor not many humans receive. She wishes Vendar were there with her to experience it. Even Rolith would have been preferred over Peynter.

They dock to a greeting party of armed leemoahs with stern expressions and bubble-forged weapons. An old stallion with a thick head of feathers signifying his status as king busts through the line of men with nostrils flaring. He is old and flabby but moves like a viper. "What is the meaning of this? My daughter is not a slave to be sedated." He rushes to Star and Beta releases her from sleep.

A'Toa sucks in a sharp breath and sits up in her prison. The king embraces her as his daughter, as tradition dictates for those chosen as sacrifices. Captain Zai watches like a predator observing the insignificant actions of prey. "Apologies, we ran into some stressful situations—including traveling in this clearly inadequate vessel. Her dreams were filled with sweet magic and she slept in luxury instead."

Star keeps her mouth closed although her eyes tell a different story. Her future is out of her hands now—however brief.

"I didn't know she was a princess," Ironhead whispers to Beta. His breath smells like dried fish and lack of hygiene.

"She's not. When a sacrifice is chosen, she's temporarily adopted by the royal family. A fattening of a pig, you could say."

"So, they're going to kill her?" He sounds shocked.

Peynter interjects with a face that suggests he finds Ironhead's intelligence lacking. "No, she's going to be absorbed by the star that gives the Reef its unique magic. Did you never study leemoah culture? You were born yards from their civilization, for Aryet's sake."

"I never went to school." His tone gives away more than his vague answer.

"Of course not," Peynter grumbles. Unbidden, he continues the lecture on leemoah culture. "Ashlikani demands a new soul every thirty years. Only then do the stars align and the leemoahs dance to bring the star goddess beneath the waves. I've heard that it's so beautiful, anyone who witnesses it forgets to breathe, which is why land dwellers are usually banned. Too many accidental deaths. Then the sacrifice performs her solo, and the star form of Ashlikani absorbs her before returning to the sky, renewed and strong enough to command the tides for another three decades."

"She dies? That's horrible."

"Not really a death. She just takes on an ethereal form and the duties of the goddess. It is the greatest honor of their people. To become the power that sustains them is something envied by the leemoah. You know what? Just try to pay attention. It'll all make sense," Peynter says.

Beta smirks. "It's unusual for Peynter to become weary of explaining uninteresting subjects. Maybe you have some magical ability after all, Ironhead."

Peynter shoots her a glare but Ironhead beams at her praise, missing the sarcasm. He watches A'Toa as she is escorted by leemoahs and Tower agents alike. His expression goes dark. "Sounds like something they tell the sacrifices to make sure they don't try to escape."

"Their culture is unique," Beta says to herself. She doesn't have time to argue with an uneducated lighthouse keeper's son. She claps her hands together and holds them out to her companions. "Want to get drunk?"

~ 24 ~

WENDWYNN
&
ZAVOSH

"It's madness," Commander Nalag growled in his trademark gravelly voice. He crossed his arms disapprovingly as he stared at the queen's reflection. He wore the silver adornments of his new rank proudly along the plates of his armor.

Grevin tsked and adjusted Wen's head covering. "You have made your opinion clear, Sir. Your queen has taken your advice to heart but has decided to follow her own path, for her own reasons."

"Well, it's important enough to me that I must reiterate. You will be found out, before or after the spell wears off, and Gafforah will be left to the Mangzarian wolves. How can you justify taking such a risk when we are in the middle of a war?"

Wen appreciated the commander's honesty. Her personal relationship with Grevin sometimes had him feeding off her energy until he was as excited to make a move as she was. Sir Nalag had no such connections and was the voice of reason when she talked Grevin into seeing her side of rash actions.

"You do not need me to fight the war, Commander Nalag. You and my generals are more than capable of protecting our borders, especially with the securities put in place. Admiral Yo'aro's navy should be arriving soon with the rest of the leemoah force, and Saltspire will become a beacon of Gaffori strength in the bay. I trust you both completely."

The Chieftain Glyden and her feelings of betrayal had weighed heavily on Wen ever since her return from the colonies. The sights she had seen there were a wake-up call. There would be no victory without the God's Blood, and her sword alone would not make enough of a difference to change the tides. She hadn't expressed as much to her council. It was best they didn't know how dire their situation was.

"Some leemoah magic and barricades won't stop them, Your Grace. I don't trust them or their abilities." Nalag glanced suspiciously at the stallion standing near the door.

The envoy shifted uncomfortably at the slight and snorted disapproval. "Most Gaffori would have the decency to speak badly of my people while I'm not in the room. Our magic will be enough, and Ashlikani will defend her bay as she always has."

"My relationship with the leemoahs has always been strong. Thank you for your assistance in our time of need." Wen inclined her head respectfully. She swallowed the lump in her throat at the memory of Ip's exodus from her army. The leemoah mage had volunteered himself after it was clear his people would no longer fight for the queen. He promised his magic was powerful enough to protect her within Mount Thoyax, but any deeper into Mangzar and she would be too far from the bay to receive Ashlikani's protection. The salves he had applied on her face were cool on her skin.

"If Gafforah falls, we will not be far behind, Your Grace. Rest assured foreign magic is not as strong as local magic." He glared specifically at Nalag, who found himself more interested in the window tapestries.

Wen stared at the face in the mirror. It was not her own. The face was pale, the eyes dark, and her wild curls had been tamed. She felt shorter although she didn't think the spell was that strong. It wasn't a mind mage magic and would wear off within the next two days. She could only hope to have completed her mission by then or have found Frej and made her appearance more permanent. Her heart skipped a beat at the thought. She was going to see Frej again. Somehow that thought kept overtaking the seriousness of her mission. She had tried to push it down to keep her head level, but to no avail. Together, they would find the Gods' Blood. As it should be. And then they could end the war and finally find peace in Wen's reign. "One more time, gentlemen. Just so we can put the Commander's mind at ease."

"We will escort the queen through the water using our magic." The leemoah spoke first.

"Once there, I will stay behind to find Frejith and Zavosh." Wen finished for him. "With our combined knowledge, we should be able to interpret the map. When I return to Nahem, it will be in victory. My army will be ready to destroy Mangzar before they realize what's happening."

"*If* you can figure out what the drawing means, besides being a show of expert brushwork." Nalag's disagreements were starting to rub Wen the wrong way. There was skepticism, and then there was blatant lack of confidence in her leadership.

"Everyone out, please. Except for Sir Nalag." The queen's words were both quiet and definitive. She and the knight were alone within moments. She took a moment to study him. He was another comrade who'd stood by her since the beginning. When she'd first met him, he had patchy dirty blond stubble on cheeks that framed eyes that had yet to see the horrors of the world. Now, he was stronger and wiser, with a full beard kept neatly trimmed. He'd gone from being a pawn to a dictator to an instrumental member of her council and the leader of the *retyot* that claimed the center of Gafforah. "Is there a specific reason you are determined to make me look incompetent in front of my council?" Wen asked.

"Your Grace, you know as well as I how long I have stood by your side. From the beginnings of the rebellion, to storming Nahem. I even stood by you when you decided to fight against Mangzar aggression instead of apologizing to the nation for your inadvertent slights against their culture. I personally condemned the envoys from Nath'iki and Terrial when they denied your request for aid. You have long been an unstoppable boulder rolling down a hill at a breakneck pace, crushing anything in your path, and it is the reason I have nothing but the deepest respect for you. I know your humble beginnings, and I know what you have done and gone through to get where you are."

"Time is passing, Commander Nalag."

"You're making a mistake I cannot support, Your Grace. Going into Mangzar with nothing but the hope of finding your wife somewhere in the largest nation in Andriel , and nothing but a painting as a map and shoddy disguise spells is nothing short of suicide. You're going to throw everything away and I think you've been too successful in the past and are blind to your recklessness."

She turned to face him. They were eye to eye, equal in height. "Why do you think I do what I do? Ambition has always driven me, but I believe there have been other elements added over the years. I have seen the negative effects my reign has imposed on people I took for granted. I have seen the trust placed in me by those I care about, and those I have never met. I have not only learned to use an incredible magic ability despite my lack of connection, but I have used it safely and minimally. Whatever the people of Gafforah saw in me, whether it was simply someone freeing them from a tyrant, or something more, they see it in me now as we stand against an enemy that will most certainly destroy us if I am not successful. That, alone, is worth risking everything for. You don't have to agree with me, but you do have to support me. If you need to come with me to Mangzar to do that, so be it."

Her offer caught him off guard. "You want me to come with you?"

"Yes," she said with more finality. "Like you said, you have been by my side through nearly every trial that's come my way. I may not have as much history with you as I have with Grevin, but he is no warrior. Come as my bodyguard, or my confidant, whatever you choose. Watch me yourself and determine whether I have failed. Not only if I have failed Gafforah, but if I have failed you personally. If not, be reminded why you made the conscious choice to stand by me when things were their darkest."

She smiled at the multitude of expressions his face contorted through. He hated that she had pinned him, but he knew she was right. He could not change her mind, but he could ensure she didn't leave his sight. He finally bowed. "Then allow me to take my leave, Your Grace, and prepare for our journey into the land of fire mountains."

"Nothing would give me more pleasure, Sir Nalag."

As the knight left to prepare, the queen turned to Hearthslayer, laid out on the bed. She could only hope that her intentions were as pure as she insisted.

The fighting was over. The bodies of the hopeful Warleaders had been cleared, leaving behind the stains of battle. There was a distinct stench of dragon fire lingering in the air, mingling with the drying blood of the fallen.

Zavosh could only watch as the foreigner, Greysten, was

made Warlord, with Frej beaming by his side. She wore bright red that set her apart as a high-ranking member of the new court. The vipr noted that Greysten had been quick to fulfill his promise to ally with Frejith while Zavosh was mostly forgotten. He feared her bid to avoid making a dangerous enemy had evolved into something more. She truly believed in the Qan. She thought he could make a difference both in Mangzar and in Gafforah. It was hard to say, considering he hadn't had the chance to speak to her in private since the *milta* was declared won.

Instead, the vipr had taken advantage of her new position and an unprecedented freedom to wander Fortress Blackfeather, listening for clues and studying maps usually kept under lock and key in the council rooms. If the Warlord minded Zavosh helping himself to confidential material, he had yet to say anything about it. He'd been busy spending the days after his rise to power quelling any budding rebellions, replacing generals, and generally keeping visible astride his beast. He wanted word to travel quickly of his strength. There would be a meeting with the Conclave of Warleaders to solidify his claim and receive statements on his stance with the war.

Tensions were high as Mangzarians fought over the remaining positions—ones close to the new Warleader. Frejith was hard pressed to subdue those that coveted her rank when she wasn't joining Greysten on his flights. Zavosh grew impatient waiting for a chance to converse with her. If they were going to meet and plan, he'd have to make it happen.

He took matters into his own hands, waiting in her private chamber. Very few people resided inside the fortress with a Warlord. The more he surrounded himself with, the weaker he would seem. Most chose to roam the halls alone. The traditionalists took it so far as to hold meetings outside the walls and allow not even their family to step inside without threat of being cut down. Greysten had embraced the multitude of servants made available to him and kept his generals close in his halls.

Frejith's chamber was massive, but warm. There were very few cold places in the land of fire mountains. Murals depicted battles on the stones in place of tapestries or framed paintings. Zavosh recognized the spirits of death and war, the greatest Mangzarian deities, watching from above the carnage with bloodied spears and leering faces. The warriors at the forefront were no doubt heroes of some kind.

A soft knock on the door startled him out of his trance. "Ore'xi ky Maryin?" the small voice ventured.

Zavosh looked around for a moment of panic, wondering if he should hide. He decided against it. "Officer Ore'xi is unavailable at the moment, but I will receive you. Come in." He sat in the onyx chair by the dim fire, an excess ornamentation considering the weather in Mangzar was never drafty or cold.

The messenger that entered was clearly an *isilth* by the way she stared only at the stone floor and kept her hands on her chest. Holding extremities away from where weapons were readily available was like showing a throat to an alpha in vipr culture. "There are two people here to see her. Will she be back soon?"

"That is not of your concern. Show the visitors in. I will speak on behalf of Officer Ore'xi." Who could be searching out Frejith so soon in her new position?

The messenger bowed and stepped out of the chamber. Zavosh's hands touched the hilts of his various weapons for reassurance. The last thing he wanted to do was break his cover, but the vipr in him secretly hoped there would be a fight.

His anticipation was dashed when he saw the couple that entered and shut the door behind them. The man he recognized right away as Sir Nalag, despite the efforts to disguise his face by shaving his beard and donning a hood. He was not a famous-enough face to worry about recognition. But the other was an old woman, pale and stooped. The leemoah spells could not hide the queen's true identity from the vipr who had known her for years. He stood and bowed quickly. He dared not address her as the queen, even in their isolation from prying eyes. "May I help you two?"

Nalag moved to stand by the door while the queen threw back her hood and allowed herself to stand to her full height. She was taller than Zavosh, but it was not her physical stature that made him feel small. "Where is she?"

"I am unsure. We sent a message yesterday. It should be arriving at the keep by tonight. There is a new Warlord, and Maryin has been quick to solidify a relationship with him. I assume she is off helping him with some matter or other."

The confusion on her face was laced with suspicion and a touch of disappointment. "She has the attention span of a gnat. There have been some developments, and Commander Nalag and I are here to stay and assist you two in staying on mission."

"Your Grace," he spoke in a much quieter tone, "I could tell you were yourself the moment you stepped in. No spells can hide a queen's stature. This is far too risky."

The Commander smiled smugly from his position by the door. "I tried to tell her that myself. It's not going to work."

Wendwynn ignored their comments. She pulled a scroll from her belt and handed it to the vipr. "A clue, from a friend. To me it looks like any painting but there has to be a deeper meaning."

Zavosh studied the battlemage depiction with a careful eye. "Of course," he muttered. "Mangzarians know two things. Violence, and *art*."

The queen's eyes lit up. "It *is* a map?"

"Of sorts. A battlemage would know for certain."

Wendwynn was quick to brush over the topic. There were no more battlemages, and she had everything to do with it.

"Fre—Maryin should know, shouldn't she? She is the only sorceress I trust."

Zavosh sat again, letting his eyes roam the painting. "Mangzarians hold origins in high regard. It is why family names are so important, and why they do not actively take new lands without provocation. I would imagine, if this map is accurate, that it suggests looking where battlemages originated. Where is that?"

"It has to be somewhere in Mangzar," Wen said thoughtfully. "But that doesn't make sense. They use Gaffori magic. They dwell in Elgireth, which is a Gaffori territory."

"Who told you the Well was in Mangzar?" Zavosh couldn't help asking.

"Haldeen. With his dying breath. He couldn't have lied to me. He wouldn't gain anything from it."

Zavosh held his tongue and kept his opinion to himself. The overthrown emperor could have intended for her to run in circles, never finding the true power in Andriel. The distraction from her rule would make her weak and vulnerable.

"Your Grace, someone is approaching." Commander Nalag instinctively touched his sword hilt. Wen motioned for him to remain still. They waited with bated breath as the footsteps continued down the hall. "We are too exposed here. I must request that we wait elsewhere until we can meet with the sorceress."

Wen reluctantly nodded. At least she had that much sense. "Very well. Is there an inn nearby?"

The tightness in Zavosh's chest grew more intense by the moment. "Down the street. There's a blue sign. I recommend drawing as little attention to yourself as possible, Your Grace. Choose a backstory and stick with it."

There was nothing she wanted to do less than leave before seeing her wife. After a tense moment, she consented. "Tell her to find us there. Quickly. My spells will wear off soon and we will have a new set of problems."

They were gone in the next moment, leaving Zavosh with his mind reeling. What could have possessed the queen to come here, to the heart of enemy territory? And with half-cast spells, no less. Perhaps Frejith wasn't the only reckless one in their relationship. He waited for nearly an hour with nothing but his thoughts and the battlemage painting to keep him company before Frej finally returned. She was laughing, calling out to someone down the hall before entering her room. She jumped at the sight of the vipr in her chair. "What are you doing here?"

He bit back the anger he wanted to lash out at her with. "What am I doing here? What are you doing out there with the new Warlord? Are you so quick to forget our purpose?"

She wore the decorated armor of a Mangzarian soldier. Zavosh saw less and less of the Gaffori Frejith he knew as the days passed. "I have remembered more than you, it would seem. The connections I'm making are invaluable. Greysten hasn't officially declared the war with Gafforah over, but he will as soon as the Conclave confirms him. Meanwhile, I'm getting close to his generals and gaining every bit of information I can about Mount Thoyax and the way it works. If he does decide to destroy us, we'll be able to destroy them from within." She moved closer to speak in quiet tones. The excitement had returned to her eyes. "I'm going with him to the Conclave. I'll be able to get a read on the other Warleaders and know ahead of time if any of them plan to continue the war. It's the perfect plan. We're safe either way."

Zavosh shook his head. "There are too many variables. How do you know he trusts you and that he's not using you like you are him? We know nothing about him, and I can't give any insight since he's not Mangzarian."

"You think I'm stupid. You think I'm wasting my time. Meanwhile, you're sitting in my *private* chamber for Aryet knows how long, judging me instead of looking for the Well yourself."

Zavosh threw the painting angrily at Frejith. "Do you know what I was doing here? Speaking to your wife. Your queen. She was here, looking for you and for your help, but you were off playing general. She's waiting for you now at the inn nearby, with spells that will expose her within a day, holding on to the hope that she'll see you."

Frejith's face blanched and she held the painting with shaking hands. "She was here?"

"She stood where you stand and spoke of *the* mission. The one that we were supposed to stick to no matter the circumstances. The one that you came here to ensure happened."

"She was . . . here." Her voice was breathless. "I have to go to her." She shoved the painting in her belt and rushed out the door. Zavosh followed to ensure nothing else happened to distract the sorceress.

"Maryin!" The voice that called out belonged to the new Warlord, who had taken to the full regalia with vigor. Orange and black blades hung from his belt, and he had several new tattoos in bold black ink. Perhaps he would fit into the Mangzarian culture after all. He jogged to catch up to Frej with a look in his eye that Zavosh recognized instantly. He had taken to the sorceress—or wanted her to think he had. "I wanted to inform you the campaign was a success. The people have seen my abilities and accepted me as Warlord. The Conclave has agreed to legitimize my claim tomorrow."

"Great news, indeed." Frej didn't push further in hopes he would lose interest and move on.

"Aren't you going to offer me a congratulatory drink?" His charisma was annoyingly contagious. He glanced at Zavosh as an afterthought. "You can bring your friend, if you like."

"Later tonight, if it pleases you, Warlord. I imagine we both have work to do. Besides, you have the better salary, you should be buying the drinks."

Greysten cuffed her playfully on the shoulder. "My new

salary also comes with the benefits of doing what I want when I want. Come on, *General*, remember who gave you your new position."

Zavosh could see Frej screaming internally. Externally, she smiled cheekily. "If you insist. One drink now, and later we can truly celebrate."

Greysten wrapped an arm around her shoulders like an old war comrade—or a long-lost lover. "I'm thinking gold and red for my new banner colors. What do you think?"

"Why red and gold?" They were walking away from where Wen would be waiting. Zavosh could only watch her be led away.

"Red for the mountain fire, and gold for prosperity."

"You would be like every house in Terrial. Where is your creativity? What about black for your dragon and purple."

"Why purple? We have no royalty here."

"Why not? If ever there was to be a king of Mangzar, you would already have the colors." If there was one skill Frejith possessed, it was swelling the ego of rulers.

Greysten laughed as they passed through the yard to the private drinking hall of the fortress. Zavosh followed like a shadow, forgotten by both. Perhaps he could create an opportunity for the sorceress to sneak away—but how? He, unlike Frejith, was no one here. The Warlord took his seat on the throne at the head of a long table. The dais raised him slightly above the rest of the patrons. "Black and purple, eh?"

Frej took the chair to his right and Zavosh sat below her. He did not have a natural way with words like Frejith or the queen. He would have to be patient. Servers appeared out of nowhere with trays of drinks and food. The selection was only part Mangzarian, with Qan delicacies mixed in. They clinked glasses of ashberry wine and dined on spiced, buttery onions. "What are you going to say to the Conclave about the war?"

Greysten frowned at her question and wiped sparkfruit

juice from his chin. "Don't worry, General, I remember the terms of our deal. But I need your patience. If I decry the war during my confirmation, I could be seen as a weakling and an imposter. I can't risk my seat days after I've earned it."

And so, the betrayal began. Zavosh wondered if Frejith was starting to see his side of things now that her plan was unraveling. People craving power would say anything to get what they wanted—and then step on the heads of those who said they would help. He wondered if she'd had experience with that before. Wendwynn was an enigma of conquerors, someone who stood by her promises and left no one behind. It was starting to look like Greysten chose the path most followed.

The Warlord finished a tankard that was refilled almost before the empty mug touched the table. Frejith stared silently at the table, hands in her lap and food untouched. She was processing the new information. He noticed her unease and smiled, extending one arm to rub her on the back familiarly. While he was outwardly friendly, his grip on her shoulder tightened when he leaned in to whisper to her. "You'll get what you want, General, as soon as I get what I want."

Something clicked in Frejith's eyes. They relaxed from open and inviting to business. A servant carrying a tray of drinks provided her chance to escape the Warlord's attention. Distracted, the servant walked close to Frej's chair and she leaned back just as he passed. Mugs clattered on the stone and wine splashed in dramatic fashion. The servant's eyes opened with horror. Frej's robe was stained, and the Warlord's armor tainted.

The soldiers in the vicinity held their breath. Greysten released Frejith's shoulder and stood, dripping, his teeth bared as he decided how to react. Frejith took advantage of the breath before Greysten decided if he should unleash hell.

"I—I should change. Apologies, my Warlord." She sprinted off before further questioning could take place. Greysten was annoyed by her disappearance but made no move to follow her as the servants swarmed him with towels and whispered apologies. Zavosh took the opportunity to slip away after Frejith.

He traced their steps back down the hall towards her chamber. It was eerily quiet. A hooded figure knocked his shoulder headed the other direction. The face beneath the hood turned for a moment, showing little more than shadow. "Apologies. Under Akai." They were gone before Zavosh could press further. Dread filled his stomach. It had been years since he heard that greeting. He sped his pace to a jog until he saw Frejith, collapsed on the stone just past her doorway, blood pooling beneath her chest. He raced to her side, turning her over to see no puncture mark.

"Maryin?"

Her eyes fluttered open for only a moment. "Pain . . . I can't target it. Zavosh, you must tell Wen. Tell her. The battlemages are from Saltspire."

The pieces came together for Zavosh in that moment. Saltspire had long been a Mangzarian colony, validating Haldeen's statement. The sorcerers used to tell legends of how their power originated from the mysterious temple, and up until Wendwynn's reign, it had been occupied and protected by battlemages. The strongest of the magic users. Guardians of what could only be the Well deep within the island. The well that contained the blood of the gods, and consequently, the source of all mortal magic. The quarry for his quest.

~ 25 ~
KEYRA

Keyra somehow summons the strength to draw her blade. The shell of Tika turns its attention to her with an inhuman hiss. "This isn't you." Keyra's voice breaks as she tries to reason with the manifestation of death in front of her. She knows there is nothing left of her friend.

The shell growls and advances with arms stretched out. Keyra pushes a chair between them and Tika trips over the obstruction. The seamstress brings the knife down into the back of her best friend with a strangled sob. Tika gives a horrible screech and explodes with enough force to splatter the pair with the blackened juices inside her.

Keyra stares down at the remains with a strange peace. The people closest to her are dropping quickly, and she can't help feeling guiltily relieved. There are fewer to disappoint now. Everyone is gone except the boy sobbing uncontrollably behind her. She goes to him and wraps an arm around his shoulders, showing him comfort for the first time. The act of kindness opens the floodgates to the pressures and horrors the child has seen while in Keyra's care. Her head throbs for the first time since they have arrived on Veden and she pulls away quickly.

"That's enough of that now. She can't hurt you anymore."

Tilsman isn't reassured. "No, but we could turn into something like her. It was a bad idea to come here."

Had Keyra felt more herself, she would have smacked him across the mouth for such cowardice. Instead, she sags against the wall, still cradling Tika. "What in Heliendiel happened? She must have had some sort of warning. We have to look around and see if she left any clues."

Tilsman isn't excited about the prospect but nods all the same. Keyra pulls one of the many hanging blankets off the wall and covers her friend with it before heading to the Seer's laboratory in the back room. Everything is as she left it. There are shelves of inks in bottles and hanging brushes of varying sizes and materials. There is a liquid of every color, some shimmering with mystical light and others darker than the moonless night sky. The ingredients for her concoctions are contained in bins by the cauldron over the dead coals. Symbols and words in ancient languages decorate the hearth's bricks and the pot itself. As one of the most technical types of magics, Seer abilities are complicated and intricate in ways Keyra will never understand. Elgir magic is loose and based more on emotion by comparison.

She finds Tika's books on the far wall, under a map of the island chain. There are pins marking the Citadel, Uta'lihali, and somewhere off the coast to the west. Keyra instead turns to a volume lying open on the table in the center of her workspace. Her name is written in large, sparkling letters.

My dearest friend, I know you will make your way back here. You don't yet know why you are drawn back to Elgireth, but it will all be made clear soon. I don't have much time, but to understand what is happening, you're going to have to do a little magic. Don't worry, I've set it all up for you. All you must do is trace the symbols and say a few words.

I'm sorry I ran out of time. But after hiding and attempting to leave Veden, I realized escape was impossible. Now, I am trapped here, and I fear I will become like them. Good luck, Ra.

The next page is full of sketched symbols bordered by painted ones. The magic already trapped in the pages would substitute for Keyra's lack of power. She takes the tiny brush made of silky hairs with a driftwood handle and dips it in the red liquid beside the book. The smell is sickly sweet, like flowers on a grave. Keyra traces the symbols with a steady hand and repeats the phrase on the next page. *"Kraven za li."* Her Var is choppy, but it does the trick. The symbols she has written out glow faintly and then absorb into the paper.

"Well done, Ra. You may not only be good for sewing." The apparition beside Keyra is shadowy but her voice is clear. Keyra feels a new lump in her throat at seeing her friend once more.

"Ti?"

"I don't have much time, and you must know this isn't me. It's a message. I've never been a fast writer, so this will have to do." Keyra lowers herself into the chair to listen. "Ever since Isah died, I've been studying the epidemic and trying to put the pieces together. After you left, there were more and more sorcerers in the town and across the islands. They would never say what they were doing, but Elgir started going missing or showing up dead at an alarming rate. I managed to speak to one, an old-time mage. I was able to trade some services for some answers. The time of the star's dance is coming, and somehow Ashlikani's magic is connected. Her power is not just for the leemoahs. From what I can understand, the Elgir have long dismissed the lesser goddess, but she controls the magic on the islands as well as below them. What he wouldn't answer is whether the Citadel is involved, or how. I think they may have caused this, Ra, and they're trying to cover it up. Things got out of control and they're cutting their losses and retreating to Everlyn where they can protect themselves. Somehow, Ashlikani has been poisoned, or compromised, and as her power grows weaker, she's taking us with her. Hopefully by the time you get here, the worst will be past, and you won't be affected, or the ceremony would have taken place and things would be reset for now. If not, well, then you won't ever see this, will you?" The apparition goes silent and stares at the floor. "Either way. I can feel myself growing weaker. Be safe."

The magic wanes and the symbols go dark.

From the other room, Tilsman screeches and Keyra is forced out of her daze. She rushes to find him pressed against the wall, pointing to the door. The shells outside are scratching at the wood and it creaks from the pressure of their bodies. They're out of time. Keyra grabs the boy by his collar and drags him into the back room. Beneath a rug is a tunnel that leads to a frequent customer of Tika's services. Where they will go from there, she cannot say. She pulls Tilsman down the ladder into the darkness where they fumble forward.

Above them, the screams of the undead are intensifying. Dust rains from the many feet on the road. Keyra's grip tightens on Tilsman and they move faster in worried silence. Arms reach through the dust and dig furiously to get at the living beings.

"Run!" Keyra sprints and Tilsman follows suit. Dirt continues to fall until they are swimming more than walking. One hand grabs Keyra's shoulder and yanks her back. Tilsman is also thrown off balance and they fall backwards. They are pinned in seconds by the pressure of the falling ceiling and the presence of dozens of the magicked. Their horrifying faces are twisted in rage.

They ignore Tilsman to focus on Keyra, who cannot breathe beneath the pressure. The stress of the situation triggers images in her head. The shells are no longer screaming undead, but people about to die. Their hands reaching out to her are for mercy, for help, not for murder. Who are these people? Who is she, staring down at them with nothing but disdain in her heart?

Mercifully, the world goes black.

~ 26 ~
BETA
&
THE BOY

The floating inn, despite being only twenty yards from the shore, belongs to the leemoah world and not the human. The bar on the bottom level is open air and perches precariously on a makeshift driftwood raft. The rooms above are held up by massive stilts and sway with the tide. It is here that air breathers wait while business is handled in the city below. Beta feels her stomach churn from her stool. It is not made to be comfortable. The leemoahs seldom get an excuse to make landwalkers' lives miserable, and love using the inn as a mild torture method. Ironhead sits beside her, wincing with every sip of rum but too afraid of looking weak in front of her to stop drinking. She wonders if he's ever had a drop of alcohol before today. Peynter fights with the waves, practicing his connection with the water. From the amount of splashing and curses Beta can hear, it's not going well.

She finally speaks what's been on her mind since their arrival. "There's a boat or two that come through here daily. I've taken you this far because Star took a liking to you, but now that her mission is at an end, so is yours. You're going to stay here and hitch a ride wherever you like."

Ironhead can't hide how crestfallen he is. Did he expect her to bring him back to the Citadel with her? "Where am I supposed to go? I was a slave in Gafforah, and there's nothing left for me at home."

Beta forces herself to pat him on the back comfortingly. "You're a warrior now, remember? The Citadel works closely with the Tower. I could get you a job with them."

"As a pirate? You and I both know whatever the Tower used to be, they're little more than dirty thieves now." He sounds like a petulant child. Beta moves her arm away from him.

"Look, you're an adult, just like me. But you're not a sorcerer. I have a duty, and you have the world in front of you. Try not to waste the rest of your life." She snatches up her drink and goes to sit at the edge of the floating platform. The leemoahs and her charge have vanished beneath the waves. From here, the coral city is little more than blotches of color and the shimmer of passing scales.

Waving hands from an approaching vessel catch her eye. "Rolith!" She waves back. The stone mage in the boat fights with the sail rigging to slow his approach. Beta compels the water to nudge him into dock at the inn with a gentle tap on the raft. Rolith jumps from the deck, tumbling into Beta with a laugh. Peynter crosses his arms at the sight of their fellow sorcerer. "About time you showed up, team leader."

Beta helps Rolith up and they embrace shortly, ignoring the water mage. She holds him at arm's length, studying his face for any sign of bad news. "What are you doing here? How is Vendar? Do you know what's going on with the Citadel and the Tower?"

"Slow down, I need a drink first." Rolith drains her glass in a moment and ignores Ironhead, who is waving a greeting from his isolation at the bar.

"You're probably most concerned about Vendar. He's gaining strength and healing slowly, but it's hard to say how much longer he has. Without knowing how much magic he's used during his lifetime, it's impossible to tell exactly how many years he drained in Nahem. When this is over, it's going to be important that you spend as much time as possible with him." Beta takes the news in stride, waiting for further information. "As for the Citadel? They had a meeting with the Tower, including your new friend El'rozai. I wasn't invited, but I heard rumors. They're going to do something to Ashlikani. They're going to use the star somehow. All I know is there was a lot of money involved, and the promise of something powerful enough that the Citadel was willing to deal with them again."

Beta hadn't been born when the pact between the two organizations had been at its strongest. Were they hoping to rekindle the sort of symbiotic relationship that used to define them? The Tower acting as privateers for the sorcerers and Gafforah, and the Citadel taking the more prestigious contracts? Admittedly, the Citadel hadn't been immune to deterioration either. They had once been members of Gaffori court as established nobles and officers of the crown—when there was one. Even they weren't able to ignore the call of jewels from shadier dealings and black-market jobs.

"Why did they send you here?"

"Let's just say the Citadel isn't positive our new allies aren't going to double cross us. Which means we get to witness the ceremony."

Ironhead perks up at his announcement. "Do you think I could come, too?"

Beta rolls her eyes. It would save them all time if she pushed him into the water right then. She was willing to bet he didn't know how to swim. "You're neither Citadel nor Tower, as you so clearly stated. You'd just get in the way."

A leemoah jumps from the water, shaking droplets on

the sorcerers. He wears the bubbled armor of his people. "I thought I saw your vessel, sorcerer. My name is Ip'akala. I am here to escort you to the ceremony. The sun is setting so it will begin soon." He gestures towards Ironhead. "And him, as well. The sacrifice has requested your presence. You soothe her." He gets a good look at the boy's face as he approaches and his expression twists in disgust. "Although it's hard to say why. Hurry, humans, we need to get you ready to go underwater." Ip'akala's perky attitude only increases Beta's excitement. They step into the boat Rolith came on and the leemoah soldier hands each of them a collar of coral. "These will allow you to breathe underwater, but not forever. The more you move and the longer you are under, the faster they will expire. When the ceremony is over, follow the markers back to the inn and I'm sure there will be passage waiting for you."

The collar contracts to fit tightly around each of their necks. Beta suddenly feels claustrophobic but manages to swallow it. She is going to be a part of history. Why is she sick to her stomach?

Ironhead could not look away from Star. They were beneath the waves of the Reef, surrounded by coral left to grow for thousands of years and varieties of curious fish. The underwater world was unlike anything he could ever imagine. The leemoahs have unique vocal chords to communicate through the water, but besides their odd clicking language, the city is completely silent. The sun's rays play mildly over the stone and coral homes that twist together and build upon each other in natural formations that bend to the will of nature instead of the other way around. Beyond the clusters of the city are fields of seaweed that obstruct the rest of the ocean and protect the leemoahs from the dangers of the open sea. He can understand how most leemoahs never wish to venture to the overstimulating land above.

Star stands on a flat rock in the center of an open circle of sand just outside the city limits, surrounded by seven other leemoah fillies. They dress her in silk ribbons that make her look like a goddess. They themselves have donned pastel colors of matching varieties. He would ask Peynter about their meanings and purposes, but his words are useless within his bubble of air. All he can do is watch and wait. The sun casts blood red rays signaling the return of the night. Around him, a crowd begins to gather with solemn faces covered by tight hoods. He and Beta receive strange looks. El'rozai is nowhere to be seen.

A single, sweet note, distorted by the water, announces the official death of the sun. The handmaids swim to form a circle around the rock where Star remains the center. The stage is set in a massive clearing of sand surrounded by rocky outcrops and scattered coral. It is large enough to be a crater from some giant space rock. Or, as the boy sheepishly pieces together, a compacted star. Another voice joins the first in a seamless, unending harmony. One by one, every leemoah in the growing crowd joins with their unique notes. Ironhead closes his eyes, feeling as though there is a musical tapestry weaving around him. The beauty of Ashlikani's star song is one he will not soon forget.

The song ends abruptly when Star raises her arms. The handmaids dance to a silent beat. A veil falls across Ironhead's senses. His eyes refuse to close, and his fingertips hum numbly. The water's motion amplifies the magic that stirs at the handmaids' bidding until it's pressing all around him. Ribbons flutter in perfect unison, dragging him further under their enchantment. The night ocean lights up with increasing intensity as the song grows louder. The boy becomes petrified. Were they literally going to call a star from the heavens? Did they truly believe they could contain something so powerful?

A hooded figure among the crowd draws his attention. It's Captain Zai, his face covered. He isn't watching the dance. His eyes are fixated just over the ridge to the south. He looks away quickly as the leemoah to his left leans forward to whisper in his ear. There's a spark of light from the cliffside he had been watching. There's someone there, holding an object that glints dully in the darkness. He nudges Beta, who doesn't need words to understand what he's drawing her attention to. She nods curtly and fades back through the crowd. Ironhead follows three breaths later. Peynter and Rolith are positioned on the other side of the crowd, out of communication distance. It will be up to Ironhead to protect the battlemage. The water around them is bright as daylight as the ceremony continues.

Ironhead joins Beta behind a rock where she studies the movement on the ridge. Whoever those people are, they're not there to observe the ceremony. He is no detective, but he wonders if the sudden change in alliances with the Tower had ulterior motives to helping the leemoah population. But what could they be doing? Beta doesn't wait around to find out. She twists her arms to create a funnel of water that propels her forward, leaving Ironhead to catch up with his own pathetic excuse for swimming. What did the Tower and the Citadel have in common? Greed. If the leemoahs truly called a star and can contain it and harness it for their ceremony, as is becoming more believable as the light grows stronger, then it would be possible for one of the organizations to steal the magic for themselves.

Sometimes he impresses himself.

Lost in Beta's bubble trail, he is still swimming when there are flashes of conflict on the ridge. The spectators below are too blinded and entranced by the combination of intense light and the song of their magic. Are they all equally a part of the ritual? Can they alone feel the magic they summon?

The boy feels nothing but the throbbing cramp in his leg.

The battlemage has already reached the leemoahs on the ridge, and the churning of bubbles combined with arcing spears and flashes of magic confirms the boy's fears that these are enemies. Beta warps the liquid around her as though she is painting a violent masterpiece, putting her opponents to shame in their own element. It obeys every twitch of her hand, every command of her fingers. The orange glow within her veins pulses brightly. The leemoahs she fights wear the Tower symbol and struggle to defend themselves.

Peynter and Rolith make their way to the ridge as well, having seen the conflict. Rolith holds out a hand to stop Beta from attacking the Tower agents. He instead points to approaching leemoahs wearing Uta'lihali garb, wielding pikes and swords. Beta is confused. Ironhead imagines she would be arguing if her words could be heard. Why is she supposed to be attacking the protectors of the ceremony? Conflicted, she is forced to engage the advancing soldiers when one shoots a sort of water harpoon at the sorcerers. Beta turns on them without hesitation. One leemoah falls to a stone missile propelled in a water tornado. His blood blooms pink around him.

The water is becoming uncomfortably hot and Ironhead can no longer see. The sounds of the fight fade. He keeps swimming with one arm out, hoping he is still pointed in the right direction.

The dance comes to an abrupt halt. Complete darkness falls with an almost audible suddenness. There is only a small ray of silver light left, directly over Star's head. Colors burst in Ironhead's vision and he's forced to stop moving as nausea rocks him from the sudden change. Between desperate blinks, he can see Star beginning her part of the ritual. The handmaids call Ashlikani in its dying moments, but it would be Star's song that coaxes it beneath the waters with promise of new life.

She does not dance. Instead, she holds her arms up and sings. Ironhead is distracted by renewed violence from the ridge as leemoahs and sorcerers clash. One of the Tower lee-moahs is skewered by a pike, forcing him to drop the object in his hands. Beta scoops it up quickly while she defends her-self with her free hand. She sees Ironhead approaching and pushes the object towards him in a pocket of air. The boy grabs it and the sweet notes below echo his wonder. He holds a clear, strange crystal with jagged edges in no obvious pattern. It is heavy and large, reminding him of the sack Ayrek had deliv-ered at Predaya's. It hits him all at once. He has heard legends of the Magnium, the only device said to be strong enough to hold amounts of magic that would kill a lesser being. He could feel the hum of power where his skin touched the oddly warm surface. It is roughly hewn and clear, nothing at all like he ex-pected. He glances to Star, then back to the Magnium, then at Beta. They are using Star to summon Ashlikani and steal the magic before it can enter the leemoah. He isn't surprised that the Tower and maybe other members of the Citadel would be so greedy and careless, but what hurts the most is that Beta had been involved. No, he sees the look in her eyes and finds some-thing purer. She doesn't know what she's doing. She doesn't want to help those trying to use the goddess for their own self-ish gain. She is better than them. Different. She is trying to get his attention. He blinks away his musings.

Beta mouths for him to swim away. More leemoah soldiers are approaching by the moment. Gathering his wits, the boy begins swimming again. To his right, the silver orb of the star's soul is approaching the leemoah. Its surface looks alive with silver fire, contained by the leemoah magic and compressed into a ball the size of a ship. Star's head is back, and her arms outstretched. From the ridge, the water continues to turn red with blood.

Ironhead's heart skips a beat. Beta has stopped signal-ing him and her eyes are glossy. She is sinking as they flutter closed, a trail of blood following her ominously. He screams silently and goes to drop the crystal. Several events follow in the next heartbeat.

The orb touches Star's fingertips in a brilliant flash of light. She vanishes, but before the orb can ascend once more, the swimming mage on the ridge calls a bolt of magic fire that throws it off course. With the ritual interrupted, the star is pulled towards the most powerful object nearby—the Magnium. The crystal slips from his fingers but the star cannot change course. It hits Ironhead like a charged bolt. He is knocked unconscious instantly.

"Ironhead?"

Star stands in front of him. They are on dry land, surrounded by darkness above and below. "Star?" She stands before him in her ceremonial silk and ribbons, looking more like a goddess than ever before.

"My real name is A'Toa, or, as of a moment ago, the Star Ashlikani. Just as you are really Luthen, the lighthouse boy. There is no hiding from truths here."

"Am I dead? Is Beta alright?"

Her face twists painfully at the battlemage's name. "You are both alive, unlike me." She opens her hand to offer something to Luthen. It is a shell, soft pink in color and curled. "Take this. It is Ashlikani's Grace. It will bring aid when someone who is a leemoah or a friend to the leemoah is in their most desperate need. Ashlikani took it from the last human that used it, with no intention to allow another to handle it. But I think if anyone is worthy, it is you. Luthen, I never told you because I wanted you to realize your greatness without it, but you are magic. You have the blood of a goddess in your veins, one who has always protected you. It is why you have been chosen to carry Ashlikani's magic, and why you are physically capable of holding it."

Luthen's head pounds furiously. "What do you mean?"

"I don't have time to explain, but it's not just Ashlikani's burden you now carry. It is a cargo much more precious and has more lives at stake. Take the Grace and take the magic. I can entrust only you. Please, promise me you will protect my people, and when it is safe, you will return the powers to their rightful places—me to the sky, and the Blood to the Well."

He doesn't understand what she's saying, but he can feel his veins surging with power, every heartbeat an earthquake through his limbs. "I will. Beta and I both will."

Her face falls. "You will never forget her, will you? She will be the death of you one day. Stay away from her, Luthen. Carve your own path."

She fades and Luthen reaches out. "Wait! Please don't go."

The leemoah laughs in her last moments. "Of all the times for you to say that. Men have the worst timing."

And she was gone.

~ 27 ~
WENDWYNN
&
FREJITH

There was no doubt it was the hardest decision Wen had ever made. She could feel the spells as they wore off and the tingling as her skin became hers once more. Commander Nalag had become more tense by the moment until she finally made the call he was afraid he'd have to make. They would have to return empty handed, without seeing Frej. She would have to be satisfied with knowing they had been close. She felt more frustrated than ever. The walk back over the black ground to the smuggler that would take them back to Gafforah exhausted her mentally. She tried not to look at the various faces around her. She could see the determination in the eyes of the Mangzarians as they went about their daily tasks. Aggression seemed to be the dominant personality trait and she saw at least two disagreements that turned violent. What would happen to Gafforah when the districts inevitably banded together and began the attack that would decimate her islands? She wondered what was stopping them. Were they letting her sweat, knowing her defeat was oncoming? Did even Mangzarians require time to prepare a strategy? Perhaps Halthax had been more integral to the war than she knew.

"Hey, you!" Zavosh jogged to catch up to the couple headed towards shore. He held the painting in one hand. Wen couldn't help the disappointment when she saw it wasn't Frej. He stopped, breathless. "You forgot this. You must know. Maryin, she's in danger. There was an attempt on her life. They're doing what they can to save her."

Wen felt her heart stop. "I'm sorry to hear that. I imagine the healers here will do what they can." The voice that came from her mouth was methodical. It belonged to a regent with better things to do, not a wife fearing for her spouse's life.

"There's more. There's a Conclave summit tomorrow. They're going to decide to confirm the new Warlord and I fear the war will begin anew. But most importantly," he handed her the painting, "Saltspire. It's on Saltspire."

He jogged back towards the fortress without waiting for her response. Wen froze until Nalag shook her shoulder. They were being watched intently. Soldiers approached from either side. They headed for the boat at a speed that was supposed to remain unsuspicious until the soldiers drew their weapons and increased their pace. Wen began to run and Nalag followed suit. He drew his sword and Wen fought the urge to do the same. The dagger she had brought was less obvious than Hearthslayer and would do little against multiple Mangzarian attackers.

From behind, she could hear Zavosh shouting. "Leave them alone! They're following the Warlord's orders!" He was too late. Blades crossed as Nalag turned to take a stand against the Mangzaraian warriors. Once contact had been made, there was no honorable way for them to back off, even thinking they were infringing on their Warlord's orders.

Wen's feet kept moving though her breath stopped. She sloshed through the surf and the smuggler helped her into the boat. She turned to call for the knight, but found the words frozen in her throat. The speed and ferocity of the Mangzarian blades were equally frightening and beautiful. They moved as one organism, their desire for blood seemingly multiplied as it seamlessly connected their movements. She could not tear her eyes away as they cut Sir Nalag within a matter of seconds. He hadn't drawn any blood. She had a sudden and horrifying vision of the same thing happening to all her people.

The boat set off and the soldiers watched from the shore, too afraid of their Warlord's dragon to stop her, but questioning her motive all the same. The map in Wen's hand was wet and heavy.

"To Nahem, Your Grace?" the smuggler asked.

"I'm not going to Nahem." The news of Frejith's injury had settled like lead in her veins. Nothing and everything mattered more than ever. "Take me to Saltspire. Then go to the Keep and tell my council I've found it. Tell them to prepare for an attack."

The man was covered in ash, his body seared from long exposure to the elements of the sun and ocean. District Eleven was particularly famous for their ash storms where the flakes fell like snow in a frozen wasteland.

Warlord Lxan of Fortress Y'mal saw the shadow of a man limping towards his gates and frowned. If he was a challenger, it would be an insult to kill him in his state. The man passed through the gates with confidence despite his pathetic appearance. Warlord Lxan made his way down to the yard where sparring soldiers saw the look in his eye and moved respectfully to the sides.

The men faced each other across the yard to the silence of the onlookers. Warlord Lxan was short but stout, boasting more weight than two grown men. He wore no armor not because he wanted to prove his superiority, but because there was none forged that could encompass his muscled arms and chest. "Who enters my fortress?" Lxan asked in a booming voice.

"Warlord Halthax ky Dzaxar, of Mount Thoyax and Fortress Blackfeather."

Lxan gave a short laugh. It *was* the vipr, somewhere beneath the ruined remnants of a man before him. "District Six no longer acknowledges Warlord Halthax since his demise weeks ago. The Conclave is going to confirm Warlord Greysten Cordova. If you have a grievance with him, he can be found at Fortress Blackfeather. I'm sure you know how to get there."

"Greysten Cordova? I know that name. He is nothing more than a stable boy. My people would never accept a foreign Warlord. They are loyal to their nation, and our culture."

"You should take that up with them and leave my fortress before I'm forced to end your miserable existence." Lxan was aware of the many spectators. Warlords could never afford to look weak.

Halthax snarled, a spark of his previous ferocity coming through in his expression. He was not ready to give up. "I claim *xari'kai* for the purposes of *milta*."

Lxan's hackles raised in annoyance. His skull-sized fists clenched at his side, but he was forced to release them. Wounded Warleaders could claim amnesty to recover with the intent of challenging the current Warleader after their successful recovery. Such was the right of someone who had claimed a district. Since the new Warlord had yet to be confirmed, Halthax still held the privilege to be protected until he was back to his full strength.

"I will respect the laws of Mangzar and allow you to sleep in my fortress, eat my food, and be healed in security until the day you announce yourself ready for *milta*. Then I will crush your head like a fruit."

Halthax seemed to revel in the rapt attention the two Warlords garnered from their audience. Lxan knew as well as him that none of the weaklings would dare challenge Dzaxar even in his diminished state. Warleaders were a different breed of warrior. "There is one more matter to discuss, Warlord Lxan. I will go with you to the Conclave, as your honored guest and a current Warlord. I want to meet this Cordova that dared to take my seat without confirming my death. I want to speak to the other districts, and I want to begin the destruction of Gafforah and the foreign bitch that has claimed the throne there."

Lxan approached Halthax with heavy steps and held out an arm the size of a small tree trunk. Halthax clasped it with a strength that defied his condition. Lxan bared pointed teeth in a leering smile. "On that, Warlord Halthax, we can agree."

"Zavosh, is it?"

The sound of his real name jerked Zavosh out of his trance. He sat at Frejith's side as he had the entirety of the night, nothing disturbing her except the medical staff that drifted in and out. She was being treated with the respect of a commander. While serious wounding in battle would lead to minimal interference with what they considered natural forces, secretive attacks and shifty methods warranted healing the victim to allow them to exact their revenge. Zavosh turned his attention to the warlord in the doorway. He'd washed the silver out of his hair, exposing the pale lavender beneath. It made his gaunt face look sickly pale and drew attention to deep shadows beneath high cheekbones. The Qan weren't called the 'ghoul people' for nothing. "Excuse me?"

"I apologize, I know you are attempting to keep your identities a secret. Frej threatened my life if I ever spoke them aloud, and she can be quite frightening when she wants to be." He smiled crookedly as he glanced at the wounded woman in the bed. "I think we should use this chance to speak, you and I, if you are willing."

"Don't patronize me by acting like I have a choice," Zavosh grumbled.

The Warlord sat in the chair across the bed from Zavosh, holding Frejith's hand as though he was her closest friend. "I know you and she are equals here, in your secret quest. I apologize I have been so quick to brush you off in the past. I understand your suspicion of me and thought it wise to let you have your space while the sorceress and I cultivated our own relationship. However, things are about to change drastically, and I can no longer indulge you." His eyes flashed in an unfriendly manner. "In Qai we have a saying. *Memir foth saqet birel.* The hand you cannot see certainly holds a knife. We are distrusting people, and I am no different. I could see what Frejith was trying to do even before she came to the fortress. A vipr I had never seen before, who acted nothing like the viprs I served, asking questions. She was clever, I'll give her that. Not many would hear the pointed questions beneath her charismatic small talk. Who would expect a spy to dive so boldly into a life here? She is confident. It is something I find incredibly attractive about her. I daresay one of her few negative traits is that she's so powerful and confident that she expects mutual trust from everyone she meets." He chuckled at the frozen horror in Zavosh's face. "Don't fret, if I wanted to kill you or her, I have had every opportunity to do so."

Zavosh glanced at the miraculously nonfatal magical damage done to Frejith's chest. The internal bleeding had been enough to cause her incapacitation, but not enough to be irreparable. He swallowed the sinking feeling in his throat. "Did you do this to her?"

"From what I understand you found her directly after the

attack. What was it the assassin said as they brushed by you? Under Akai? That is a Tower saying, no? One of your own people." The playful light in his eyes was gone, a mask of stone clouding his true intentions.

If he had hired the assassin, it was a brilliant plan. Those that didn't know Frej's true identity would see it as yet another act of war on the part of the Gaffori, giving Greysten the ultimate excuse to continue Halthax's crusade. Besides that, a Tower agent was just greedy enough to take a contract with no question. "I'm assuming he didn't make it out?"

"Of course not. We would never let someone who has attacked one of us escape. He has been hung from the fortress walls for now and will be sent back to Gafforah with a message for your queen." He spat. So much for the alliance Frejith had hoped for. "Frejith will make a miraculous recovery and then have the chance to take her revenge on Gafforah and the Tower as any good Mangzarian, especially a vipr, would. And if she refuses, there will be no mercy from myself or anyone she has gotten used to calling friend here." Zavosh should have seen it coming. Frejith's hard work to create connections and build a name for herself was only solidifying Greysten's hold on her. The Warlord continued, "But for that to happen, I need your help, Zavosh. I need you to take the Tower agent to Wendwynn. I need you to send the message that after tomorrow, I will not be alone in my assault on her nation. Tell her how her wife has rallied to my cause. If she wants to avoid being annihilated, and wants to save Frejith's life, she must stand down." The false smile returned. "I am not without sympathy or mercy, Zavosh. I want the respect of my people, but I also don't want to slaughter innocents. Certainly, you can help her see my side of things."

If he could keep him talking, perhaps he could find a weakness. He had to kill the Qan. "Why do you want to be a warlord? It doesn't make sense to get so involved in foreign politics, especially in a nation so severe."

Greysten sighed. "You ask a lot of questions, but I am a patient man. Mangzar was always meant to be my home. Where else can you find a dragon to bond with? It very well may be the last one in existence. Continuing the cause against Gafforah is the fastest way to ensure my claim is solidified. It marks me as one of them. I have other ambitions, but they do not concern you or our current situation. Let me put it simply. I know the real reason you two are here. I know you're looking for the Gods' Blood and that it's in Mangzar. I can't have you finding it before I do. Go to Wendwynn with my offer or face my wrath when I become a god."

Zavosh had no choice. If he fought or refused Greysten, he would be killed and Frejith would still be used against Wen. If he agreed, Gafforah would fall, and this madman would control Andriel's magic. At least this way, he could speak to the queen face to face. "Very well."

Greysten smiled unpleasantly. "Good, because your boat is ready now."

Zavosh's heart sped as he followed Greysten out of the chamber down the hall to a waiting party of masked warriors. His mind raced. Wendwynn should have found the Well by now. If she had, why wasn't Gafforah launching the offensive against Mangzar? Perhaps it was just his vipr nature that assumed she would attack. Perhaps she had some other, deeper plan in the works. Either way, he could do no further good here. He would have to do the unthinkable and leave the queen's wife in enemy hands, praying she wouldn't cut him down with Hearthslayer on the spot for treason.

High above his head, the dragon's wings flapped ominously, mimicking his heavy heartbeats.

~ 28 ~

KEYRA

Keyra stands on a deserted island, feeling the familiar saltwater breeze blow her skirts playfully. The island is small and has sparse vegetation on an otherwise pristine sand bar. She sees a woman standing with her back to the seamstress. She wears pirate leathers, and has wild hair tied back in a loose braid. She holds a dirk in one hand and a whip in the other. "Excuse me?" Keyra calls out to her. Her feet are stuck in the sand. "Hello?" she says louder.

The woman ignores her. Out of the waves, leemoahs start to breach, bound and dejected. The first in the line approaches the woman, and she stabs the blade through their chest. The next approaches, and then the next, to the same fate. Tears brim in Keyra's eyes. "Stop! What are you doing?"

Her voice falls on deaf ears. There are dozens of leemoahs. None seem to know what is happening, and there is no sound as they collapse to the sand. Keyra screams and pulls at her feet. She digs furiously with her fingernails. She must do something. Who is this murderer? "Stop!" One foot pulls free, and she struggles to drag herself towards the pirate. The next person out of the water is no leemoah, but Erey. He falls the same as the others. Hot tears track down her face. "Why? Why are you doing this?"

The next one is someone that stirs a vague memory. A boy, ugly and lifeless as he falls to the sand. The wind stirs his badly cut hair as blood blooms beneath his chest. Finally, the carnage is over and Keyra collapses, sobbing. "What are you doing?"

The woman finally turns and the face that looks back is her own. "Why don't you ask him," the younger Keyra says with a distinct lack of emotion.

Keyra awakens in a home she does not recognize and Tilsman lighting a candle. She reaches out a hand to stop him. "We don't want to draw their attention."

"It's fine, Granma. I blocked the windows and made sure we weren't followed. I think we're safe for now."

Keyra forces herself to a sitting position. "What happened? I shouldn't be alive." Her dream has jogged some dark part of her memory. Though she cannot remember details, she knows deep down that the woman is her. Was her. The memories she had been so quick to repress were horrifying. She had killed, enslaved, and destroyed lives. Why? That she did not know—or rather she refused to investigate.

"I can't explain it. They were coming for you, and you were half buried. Then they just stopped. They watched me dig you out and followed when I took you here, but they didn't make any move to attack us."

"How in Heliendiel did you manage to get me out? I must weigh three of you. Well, one and a half of you at least." Keyra takes in the room around them. The man who earned himself a private tunnel to Tika's Seer hut lived lavishly for the tiny island. Imported rugs, statues, and paintings adorned otherwise humble walls. Everything sat forgotten where he had abandoned it.

"I don't know. I've felt stronger since we've been here. Those things probably aren't going to stay friendly for long. We need to get off Veden and out of Elgireth." He sounds mature and certain of his words. Where is the chubby, scared cabin boy she found a lifetime ago wandering the streets?

"We can't leave Elgireth yet. I'm so close." She closes her mouth when she sees his confusion. He cannot know the visions she's been having, or how much of the truth has been revealing itself. "We make quite a pair, don't we?" She struggles to smile reassuringly. "This island is doing strange things to us, and I for one would like to know why. Will you help me?" The boy doesn't answer as tears well in his eyes. The groans from outside have started again. The Elgir are becoming restless. Keyra can hear them scraping at the door and knocking at the windows. "We may not get out of this alive, Tilsman. I'm sorry I dragged you back here." He deserves the truth, not false reassurance. He has earned that much.

The boy forces his own smile through his tears. "You asked me to help you find out why we're both drawn here. As much as I may not like it, I think we're supposed to stay. I don't think we're going to die today."

The husks press onto the little house, their cries deafening Keyra. Her head throbs once more. "I'm glad you see it that way, but sometimes nature doesn't wait for humans to conclude their business in the mortal realm."

From the tunnel they entered through, there is banging and the trapdoor rattles. Tilsman moves to push the table over the entrance. The wood cracks and breaks on the wall where another hand forces its way through. "Granma—" Tilsman swallows a lump in his throat.

She no longer hides the tears. "We're completely surrounded, and the tunnel will be no safer. I wish you didn't have to die with an old lady like me." She grabs a candle and burns the face of the husk as it struggles to get its shoulder through the hole.

Tilsman's scream and sudden silence makes her turn to see a new hand clamping over his mouth, pinning him to the wall from behind. Keyra lunges forward with the candle armed but something grabs her leg and pulls her face first into the ground. They're coming through the tunnel. The hand grabbing Tilsman yanks his head painfully to the side. The chubby boy can only flail desperately.

All at once, the air is sucked from the room and time stops. Keyra and Tilsman wriggle free of frozen hands. A sorcerer in a silver cloak works his way through the townspeople, moving one aside to speak to them through the hole. "Hello, there! You seem to be in a bit of trouble. Perhaps I can help."

"Who are you?" Keyra stands between Tilsman and the newcomer protectively.

"Peterfer the Silver, my lady. I am a professor at the Citadel and, if you will have me, your rescuer. The nobre Seer said you would show up eventually."

Keyra drops the mangled remains of her weapon. She does her best to hide her relief at their rescue. She doesn't know yet if they can trust the Citadel. "Circumstances force me to let you help us, but we'll be on our way once we're safe. And I owe you nothing, you hear?" If Tika was right, the Citadel could have much to do with the horrors on Elgireth, placing Tilsman and Keyra into more trouble than they already are.

Peterfer bows gracefully. "Of course, my lady. Unfortunately, safety is relative these days. You should join me in going to the Citadel until we can find passage elsewhere. Perhaps I can see that you are fed before sending you on your way."

More red flags. Her mind told her if they entered the Citadel, they would never leave. Her gut told her this strange man meant no harm. "Take no offense, sir, but the sorcerers haven't exactly given me reason to feel secure lately. If we were to come with you, you'd have to answer some questions."

"I would sell the secret to magic itself for a moment of your time." Peterfer winks cheekily at her. "Follow me." He turns abruptly with a swoop of his cloak and they trail after him through the sea of magicked people, their faces twisted.

They head down a steep embankment to a tiny rowboat. It barely holds all three of them but even Tilsman doesn't complain. It is far preferable to the certain death they are leaving behind. Once they are a safe distance from shore, the howls return as time flows once more.

"I must warn you, my spells, while freezing time around us, will age you slightly more. Still, preferable to being the snack of one of these fellows."

"It's not like I had a lot of time left anyways." She is annoyed by the flood of relief that washes over her. They are far from safe; such intrusive feelings would make her weak. Thankfully, her head is clearer than it's been in weeks. Tilsman, on the other hand, is unblinkingly staring Peterfer down.

"Why were you in Hardock?" Tilsman asks abruptly, blurting it out before Keyra can stop him. She turns to eye the sorcerer suspiciously, waiting for him to answer the boy's question.

Peterfer smiles again. "What do you mean, Tilsman?"

"Why would a sorcerer come to Hardock knowing it's overrun by man-eating men?"

"To study them, of course. We need to know the extent of the damage they've caused here and be sure they aren't going to spread elsewhere. I certainly didn't expect to find survivors, or one so exquisite as yourself." If he is using charm to disarm Keyra, he is grossly overdoing it. Keyra blushes all the same.

"Stop calling me a lady. I'm Keyra. Also, this coward was the one screaming, not me."

"My apologies, Keyra. Clearly you could handle yourself." Tilsman rolls his eyes at the sorcerer's praise.

Peterfer laughs and shakes his head. "How entertaining! He is quite the little warrior at heart, I can tell. And from Waheth, correct?"

"I thought we were supposed to be the ones asking the questions," Keyra growls. She doesn't like how quickly she is falling into trusting the sorcerer. She blames her pinched stomach and weary bones.

Peterfer takes no offense to her suspicion or sharp words. "I love your spunk, Keyra. It's why I'm already fascinated by you."

Color comes to her cheeks and she finds something to avert her eyes over the horizon. "Have you learned anything in your studies? They seem easy enough to kill, but are you able to restore them to humans again?"

"Unfortunately, it's not that simple. While the transformations are horrifying, they are a symptom of something we have yet to understand. The magic seems to be localized to Elgireth, which is concerning as we must we discover the reasoning behind it. Otherwise, we cannot guarantee any assistance."

"Like a curse," Keyra whispers. Perhaps the Gaffori had been right to take her and Tilsman into custody.

Peterfer becomes deadly serious. "If it was a curse, the sorcerers would be affected as well. There is no known magic user powerful enough to cast a curse. This is either a good thing, or it means there is someone out there working from the shadows. That is what I am here to find out."

The Citadel looms large as Keyra tries to put the pieces together. Could her past have something to do with why she feels so connected to the magic here? Could Tilsman have something to do with it? The hull scrapes sand as they reach the shoreline. Runes scratch the surface of the massive marble tower with the pyramid-shaped roof. There had always been legends and whispers of what went on in that tower. It was in that top room that the most atrocities were supposedly committed. Up close, however, it has a clean, bright color that holds sunshine. The grounds are well kept and a brilliant green despite the rocky soil of the Elgir islands. On Everlyn, the temperature is pleasant and warm. The dreary gray of today's weather swirls around the perimeter, unable to penetrate.

If Keyra were a sorceress, she would never bother to leave the island. Peterfer laughs at their impressed faces. "Quite incredible, no? You're lucky. Most civilians never come here."

The grounds are empty. The guard at the door is alone in welcoming them inside. "Where is everybody?" Keyra's question echoes up through the center of the tower. It is open all the way to the top room, which blocks the direct light of the pink crystal. Staircases wind around it, creating a dizzying effect when looking straight up.

"They've been evacuated until we can guarantee they cannot catch the magic virus. There are only five of us here, including myself. We volunteered to fight this thing until it is safe for the Citadel to run again."

"How long have they been evacuated?" Keyra is impressed at Tilsman's interrogations. A week ago, he would have been grumbling for snacks.

Peterfer shakes his head in amusement. "I'm sorry, I can't tell you that. After all, I haven't ruled you two out as innocent in all of this yet. You were the only living people in Hardock, which means you may have already caught this thing, be it virus or magic. You could be the masterminds themselves, come to destroy any evidence of your existence."

"And for all we know, you are the one doing this." Tilsman gets a sharp glare from Keyra at his accusation. Any suspicions they may have should be kept secret for the time being.

Peterfer stops and kneels to look Tilsman in the eye. "Then let me prove I'm not right now. See this silver scar? It means I'm a time mage. It's a kind of sorcerer that breaks the rule of time and can manipulate it. I wish I were powerful enough to cast something like a curse, but I'm afraid what you saw in Hardock was the pinnacle of my abilities."

"I thought time mages could go back in time, too. Can't you fix everything that way?"

Keyra squeezes Tilsman's shoulder gently. "That'll be enough of that, Tilsman. Let's stop doubting the man that helped us survive."

"Suspicion is an irreplaceable trait for a warrior. While there have been some of my kind in history who could time travel, I fear my gifts are nowhere near as powerful. To be frank, my magical abilities have always been . . . elusive." He grumbles at some long-forgotten memory, then clears his throat. "I know you are eager to move on, but it is hard to say when we will be able to charter you a vessel. My rowboat won't make it anywhere near Gafforah. Why don't we eat, and we can discuss the questions you had for me? I'm certain you are frightened and as eager as I am to stop the deaths that plague our little islands."

Keyra wearily nods, left with no energy to fight his request.

~ 29 ~
BETA

Beta watches him with half-lowered lids. He looks the same as he always has—hair he cut himself, shoulders too broad and bony for his stout body. His teeth are still crooked, his chin still nonexistent. What has changed is beneath that. She can feel the magical energy within him, screaming to her. It pulses through his veins and grips the surface of his skin like a parasite. It will kill him eventually. The question is when.

Mages swarm around him with flashes of their own magic and physical instruments that they poke and prod with. She imagines they will eventually tear him apart to release the Gods' Blood and finally trap their quarry. Joining her at the edges of the chaos are the leemoah El'rozai, never far from the shadows, and Rolith. The stone mage is pale with shock, unable to look away. Beta should be helping the mages draw the magic out. It wants her, more than anything in that room, sensing her connection with it. It would kill her ten times as fast as it will kill Ironhead. The aching of staying away from the magic is stronger than the throb of her head. She had killed the leemoah that struck her from behind, but not before he'd given her a nasty concussion. There will be time for recovery later.

Beta jerks her head to catch Rolith's attention and he follows her to the stairs.

"Can you believe that?" he mutters once the din of the mages is behind them. "All that work, all those years, and it goes into that wreck of a kid instead of the Magnium. It's no wonder the Citadel has never been able to harness the Gods' Blood, it's unpredictable."

"Of course it is." Beta is in no mood for dumb comments, and it shows in her tone. "It's magic in its most pure form. It chooses who it gives power to, not the other way around."

"They're going to get it out eventually, you know. He's going to die."

Beta walks faster. Maybe wanting him to join her was a bad idea. "There's nothing we can do about that now. We've fulfilled our contract and it's time to move on."

Rolith grabs her arm as they descend, compelling her to stop and turn to face him. His dark eyes are full of concern. "Are you okay? You don't sound like yourself. You sound . . . like Vendar."

"I should hope so. He's been training me to become him one day." All heart has gone out of the defense of her master. The gold from the Tower weighs heavily on her belt, but it's not enough to distract from the distaste on her tongue. "If the Citadel isn't immune to being anything more than power-hungry mercenaries and murderers, then how are we supposed to take pride in it?"

The compassion in his eyes turns hard. "Careful, Beta. I'm still a high rank here."

Beta snatches her arm away from him with a scoff. "Don't embarrass yourself by threatening me. That's a fight you won't win."

She hears Rolith's steps behind her on the stairs. "If you won't listen to me, then come with me. There's someone who's been waiting to see you."

Beta's stomach does a flip. "You'd better not be talking about Peynter."

The mages stop, mouths open. "Shit," Rolith groans. "We forgot Peynter in Uta'lihali, didn't we?"

Beta couldn't even remember seeing their water mage partner. The events during and after the ceremony had been a blur. She had been yanked from the water and screamed at by Tower and Citadel alike for ruining their plans. The concussion had eliminated any chance of her retaining the information spewed at her until she saw a healing mage. The Citadel had blamed her for changing the magic's course, for interrupting their grand plans. How was she supposed to know they were stealing the power of Ashlikani instead of saving it by returning the sacrifice? El'rozai had been cryptic at best, and Rolith had been kept in the dark. Perhaps they were trying to avoid her screwing up their plans by telling her as little as possible. She hadn't even thought to ensure Peynter was with them when they were whisked back to Everlyn. The bitterness in her throat solidifies into anger. "We can't even take care of our own when it doesn't involve getting paid. I—"

Rolith wraps his arms around her shoulders in something of a friendly embrace. She allows it for a moment, relaxing into his warm hold, until she finally pulls away. She doesn't look behind her to see if he is hurt. She has never wanted anything but friendship and the occasional harmless flirt from him. "If it's not Peynter, it's Vendar," Beta whispers.

She doesn't need Rolith to lead her to the dormitory level and find Vendar's door. Rolith stands back as she knocks and a familiar voice commands them to enter. The elder battlemage sits at his writing desk, a cane resting against his chair. His skin glows undertones of orange except where there is visible cracking, where it shines brightly. Beta stands respectfully with her hands in front of her. "Master."

Vendar manages a smile but even the small effort is clearly

painful. "Welcome back. I hear you were somewhat successful in your mission."

"It's hard to be successful when you don't know who you work for. It doesn't *feel* like we've made any progress."

"Not for long," Vendar sighs. "I would be helping the sorcerers upstairs, but I fear the next ounce of magic I use will be my last. Where is Peynter?" Rolith and Beta exchange awkward glances. Vendar frowns disapprovingly. "Rolith, as team leader, you should be heading the search efforts, no?"

Rolith bows meekly. "I'll get on that." He hustles out of the chamber, leaving the battlemages alone.

Beta rushes to embrace Vendar, holding him tightly as though she can keep him from shattering. She leans forward to kiss him. He pulls away. His rejection hurts more than the confused emotions running through her mind. She stands rigidly. "What's going on here, Vendar? I thought the Citadel was supposed to help people. That's what made us better than the Tower." Her thoughts wander to the village she helped on Gafforah, and the warnings whispered to her in the dark. She refuses to fulfill the prophecy the spirit had given her.

"We *are* better than the Tower. We are magic, for waves' sake. When the pirates stole the Magnium, we started picking them off in the bay to remind them who is the more powerful organization. They must have realized how close they were to being wiped out when they attacked us in Nahern." His expression is carefully cultivated to show no emotion, as any good leader. But Beta recognizes the twitch of muscle behind the mask. He took pleasure in the fear inflicted on the Tower. "El'rozai called a summit with me and the other elders. It seems he'd seen our side and regretted going behind our back. We came to an agreement and decided to work together to protect the Gods' Blood. He acknowledged that only Citadel sorcerers were strong enough and able to protect it, and only requested that he be given some of the magic. You must stop thinking so small, Beta. Bad people have been trying to steal it for themselves for generations. It's not safe now that its existence is known. If we take it first, then no one can use it for evil."

"And what will we use it for? It seems to me that it was safe in Ashlikani, far from mortal hands."

"Where the leemoahs could take it for themselves at any time?" His eyes flash dangerously. Greedily. "They have been enslaved and trampled upon longer than anyone can remember. No, they would certainly use it to destroy us. It may begin as revenge, but then they would taste the power and become hungry. They would bring down retribution on Andriel by decimating those who have or would have done them wrong. No, in any other hands, the Gods' Blood will inevitably bring an apocalypse."

"Except for the Citadel?" Beta struggles to put the pieces together in a way that doesn't paint her comrades—her friends—as gluttonous. "What do you and the rest of the elders intend to use it for?"

Vendar's face twists into disapproval. "Your training is clearly not finished if you feel the need to continue this tiresome questioning." His eyes meet hers and his shoulders sag. "I can't stay mad at you, Beta. I don't think there's a man alive who can. We must put this behind us now. The Gods' Blood will land in the hands of the Citadel, and I will die before the end of the month. Shouldn't we spend that time doing things besides bickering?" He holds her fingertips with his.

Beta's heart yearns for his approval, his love. But her head feels sick and heavy. It's not just the concussion. "Of course. I have so much to learn from you, still."

He has other matters besides training on his mind. She can tell by the way he drapes invitingly over the chair. At one time, she would have felt her heart beating faster at the square shoulders and muscled arms, pulsing with power beneath the skin. But now all she sees is an old man cracking beneath his burden, gray and withering, his spark of greed borrowing time he no longer has. "Let us think of that on the morrow. Come, we have much to catch up on." He tugs on her hand to draw her towards him.

Beta shakes her head, stomach churning at the thought. "I don't know how you can think of that while there is a boy being tortured to death above our heads. I'm afraid this is where we part ways morally, master. I will speak to you tomorrow when you are ready for business."

She sweeps out of the room, afraid to look back and see the dejection in his eyes. He used to be such a massive presence to her. She wanted nothing more than to make him happy and prove to him that she was learning everything he could teach. Now, she wondered what other choices he had made in his life that were based off his own selfish interest. How much of the world the Citadel had built was a lie?

She finds her room with no difficulty. The inside is immaculate from lack of use and her bags have yet to be delivered. Sitting on the bed is a stranger. The woman has olive skin and thick dark curls in a braid. On her breast the sigil of the Tower. She stands when Beta assumes a defensive stance. "Sorceress, please, we need to talk." The woman has streaks of gray in her hair, and wrinkles from age on her otherwise handsome face. Beta relaxes. There is no magical aura around the woman, meaning any action she takes against the battlemage can be deterred easily.

"Who are you?" Although Beta has determined she isn't a threat, she remains in the doorway with the room's distance between them.

"Ayrek, an agent of the Tower. Please, I need to speak to you in private." She nods for Beta to close the door and the battlemage complies. "I saw you up there, with the others. You didn't participate, and you looked displeased. I recognized that expression. It was the same one on my face. You're disgusted by what they're doing. They're not helping anyone or protecting anything. They're using their power and status to claim magic for themselves."

Beta looks at the floor. "I'd be careful talking like that, agent. You don't know me, and you don't know my loyalty."

Ayrek sits back down on the bed, her own eyes downcast. "They've stopped trying for the night. They're going to let him sleep here, under guard. They're preparing spells for tomorrow and I can't imagine they're going to be gentle. I'm here because I can't do this anymore. I've done things that I can never live down. I've hurt people that I cared about most, I've killed innocents and I've taken slaves and bribes alike. I used to be able to keep my conscience separate from my work, but I'm old now. I can see the story of my life laid out behind me and there are very few moments I am proud of. I want at least one where I can say I did the right thing. I think getting that boy out of here will be that moment, and that my gut is right about you." Her arms tremble with the urgency in her voice.

Beta's shoulders grow heavy as she imagines which spells they plan to use on Ironhead. He may be a sniveling coward, but he deserves none of them. "How do you plan on doing that? They're not going to take their eyes off him for a second."

Ayrek smiles at Beta's answer despite their situation. "I thought as much. I was hoping you could help me with that. He has the Gods' Blood in him, doesn't he? That's where it's been hiding." Beta's silence is enough to confirm Ayrek's theory. She sighs. "I knew they looked for it in the Well, but it had been moved. Probably by someone who didn't want it to fall into the wrong hands. Someone who actually did the right thing. Well, it's time for us to take up that mantle. Even if the boy's not magical himself, there must be some way he can use it, right? With his own power, and yours, and them not knowing I'm a turncoat, we should be able to escape with our lives. Can you help me, sorceress? *Will* you help me?"

Beta stares out the window of her small room. The moon is massive tonight. The light seems so far away, yet so strong. She remembers the spirit from the fishing village. She had wondered when she would know what decision was right, and here Ayrek was, waiting for her. Her path couldn't be clearer. She sets her jaw and gives a brief nod.

~ 30 ~
WENDWYNN
&
ZAVOSH

Wen had left her heart in Mangzar, but duty and urgency called. She would send for Frejith and Zavosh shortly and they would be reunited at last. On Saltspire, priests tapped on walls and opened sealed doorways to find her quarry. They had been hesitant to search for the source of magic, something that had been forgotten even to the guardians. The secret of the Well had died with the battle-mages. But she could sense it, swirling around her like a thousand scents on a strange wind. There was deep, ancient magic here that called to her the closer she got. Every moment spent on Saltspire gave her a sense of purpose, of confident certainty.

She sat at the massive ebony desk reserved for the great philosophers and priests of the island, poring over ancient scrolls. There had to be a secret left untapped. Candles as tall as she was burned steadily. The shadows they cast seemed like living things to Wen, and she wondered if the whispers she heard from them were a result of her sleeplessness, or the magic that was deeply rooted here.

"Your Grace, I did not think you would still be here." Lekala stood in the stairway, hands tucked into oversized sleeves. He had been instrumental in helping Wen turn the temple into a fortress. She could see the sparkle of bloodlust in his eyes just like any good warrior, no matter how much he resisted at first. How long had he wasted his best years meditating and watching the waves?

"I could stay here for three lifetimes and still not know all the secrets Saltspire has to offer. How do you keep the island away from greedy hands?"

The priest smiled crookedly and sat across from the queen at the desk. "Except for yours, Your Grace? My apologies, you know I respect you immensely. There is a difference between your type of greed and men that seek the riches here. You have left our sacred items and statues untouched, including priceless jewels and ornaments. Instead, you came here, and have remained here, soaking in everything you can. That is a special and rare kind of greed, Your Grace, and one that I support. There is an old saying that magic is balanced by knowledge. Some ride the middle of the scales, like the sorcerers of Elgireth. Others lean completely towards the magic side and are nothing more than overpowered brutes. Then there are people like you, few and far between. People that crave knowledge, and as a result, find their own kind of magic. Those unlike you see nothing here but an isolated island and saltstone."

"And a strategic military position. I doubt every ruler has been so superstitious as to avoid claiming the fortress."

"Your Grace, the truth cannot be named superstition. I have convened with the gods myself, and I can confirm their existence. The land you come from, what is it called again?"

Wen caught herself glancing towards the floor. "It doesn't matter anymore. It is the past."

"The gods showed me mountains being swallowed by ice and birthing a demon drenched in chains. I thought it was the apocalypse of our world. It *was* an apocalypse, wasn't it? Just not Andriel's." His eyes strayed to the silver chains draped over the front of the queen's robes. "Now I believe *you* were the demon."

Wen stood to her full height, chills crawling up her spine. "You will not speak to me in a threatening manner, priest. You swore fealty to me, and I expect you to not press the matter further." She trapped his eyes in hers, unblinking.

He dropped to his knees in a moment, surprised by how much his words had affected her. "Y—Your Grace, I apologize, I didn't know—"

Wen's shoulders sank and her wrath subsided. "You couldn't have. I keep my past where it is for many reasons, none of them your concern. But I can tell you that if there is one thing I crave, it's knowledge." She motioned for the priest to return to his chair. "There is not a living soul that knows a fraction of what you just said. Killing you would be destroying a fount of information I have not yet tapped."

Lekala was wary but soon slipped back into his calm demeanor at Wen's wry smile. "I have seen more than you can imagine, Your Grace. Of course, I hope to share them all with you." There was something in the way he looked at her that was familiar and unpleasant. Something told her she didn't want to know *all* of his secrets.

"My wife is religious. I can only understand it as a coping mechanism for surviving the world in all its cruelty. I kneel with her at the altars of her gods, but I see only stone faces."

"Your wife? The mind mage, Frejith, no? A shame she has not graced us with her presence. She is a legend among us here for her abilities. Certainly, she has experienced the gods first-hand. Do you not believe her?"

"Magic works in strange ways and can bring visions. I think she sees metaphors, flashes into time and space that cannot be pinned down. Perhaps these metaphors manifest as deities. Who am I to know? I am no sorceress."

"I see a glimmer of magic in you, Your Grace, you give yourself no credit. In my humble opinion, while you are in Andriel you will experience the touch of the gods in some way. Whatever you worshipped in your homeland, here the spirits are involved. They walk the world among us and make mistakes just like mortals. Sometimes I see into Theliendiel and witness interactions. They feel as we do, hurt, happy, jealous, sad." He smiled as she fiddled with the edge of a scroll. Something about their topic of conversation and the essence of the priest made her feel childlike. "You still do not trust my words, Your Grace. I am not offended. I know that in time the magic of our land will reveal itself to you. They have noticed you and will not stand by idly forever as you sweep their creation like a typhoon."

"Then I welcome them with open arms. But for now, I must forge my own path, and it seems that lies behind sandstone gates I cannot find evidence even exist."

"Sandstone gates, Your Grace?"

"I see them in my dreams. They haunt me every time my eyes close. That is why I am here, instead of commanding my army for an invasion that will happen at any moment. They have inscriptions in a language I do not know, and behind them I can sense something truly incredible."

He stood taller at this statement. "And you do not trust in the intervention of gods! Your Grace, they are already working in your life. Those gates exist beneath this temple. They have long been sealed, and the inscriptions claim there is a tomb behind them. We always believed it was the original battlemage. Perhaps, instead, it is the power you seek."

"Perhaps, indeed," Wen breathed.

She was silent during the walk into the crypts. She heard whispers and saw faces in the shadows. They were curiously watching her. She did not belong here, but even the dead could not deny that her presence was demanding. Was it magic, or the gods? Perhaps they were the lesser spirits of the bay and Mangzar. Could the fire mountain spirits become rooted in the stone here when Mangzar stretched into Kaper's Bay? They would not be content with her conquest of their home. She was in a trance when Lekala stopped. There they were, just as she had seen in her dreams, down to the specific cracks on the frame. The High Priest bowed to Wen and handed her the dying torch, unwilling to break the tense silence. He headed back up the tunnel and Wen reached a tentative hand out to touch the frozen stone.

She closed her eyes and knelt on the ground, her hand still on the doors. The torch sputtered but she remained still. Something made her want to be as vulnerable as possible. She wanted the spirits, or the gods, or whatever watched her, to approach her. She wanted to know why she was here, why she had dreamed of the doors, and if her reign as queen would survive the week. She kept her eyes shut and took a deep breath, opening herself to the forces she could not understand.

It could have been days, or months, that she knelt there, head bowed, palm pressed to the stone. Her breathing matched the pulsing aura that surrounded her—invisible and demanding. She was caught in a trance that connected her to the rock beneath her hand, the dirt and sand beneath her feet. She was everything and nothing.

Footsteps stirred her from meditation. "Your Grace?" It was Grevin, out of breath with excitement. "They found translations in the library. I think you should look at this." The advisor set a stack of parchment beside her and another candle to read by. Wen blinked the cobwebs from her mind and smiled at him.

He stood back hesitantly, waiting for her to dismiss him or invite him to stay. She knew him better than anyone. He wanted nothing more than to stay and discover the mysteries with her.

Wen patted the ground beside her. "Then prove your worth, advisor, and ensure you have the correct translations."

Grevin tripped over his robe in excitement. Paper rustled and he cleared his throat several times. The queen allowed herself to slip back into meditation. There was an itch beyond her third eye that wasn't present during her first attempts. Could it be something was trying to come through now that they were closer to opening the doors? She may not believe in the gods, but she certainly believed there was something bigger than herself trying to send her a message.

"Light." Grevin's voice was nothing but a background noise. Wen's fingertips tingled as though she were close to touching something beyond the physical world. There was a crack forming in her own mental block.

"Growth." There was a rearing horse. It was jet black and had the glow of a god. Od Nedayeth, the High God? She had studied western lore—he was worshipped mostly in Terrial. Could this be a call to the powerful nation?

"Power." She saw a comet rushing towards her from the heavens. Faster and faster it fell. She was losing her grip on reality. Her instincts told her to pull back, to resist, but she had no desire to.

"Darkness." Emotions ran through her like water over rocks. Rage, agonizing loss, the warmth of love. Each was as torturous as the last.

"Chaos."

Wen fell face first into a vortex of colors, like fire but far more brilliant. Each flash of red was intoxicating, each ribbon of yellow moved tears.

There was a dragon, the color of ivory and the color of rainbows. He spoke to Wen in a language she would never understand. What he communicated, however, was not lost on her. There was incredible power behind those doors. The dragon warned against it, that once the gates were opened, they could never be resealed. She had a chance to walk away and allow the future to take its intended course.

Instead, she gave the dragon an all-knowing smile and stepped out of the vision. The real world was no less chaotic. Wind whipped from nowhere and Grevin was a petrified statue on the ground. Wen felt her heart in her throat as she went to him. A wrinkled hand stopped her. "He is gone. He could never have handled this kind of magic. He went painlessly and quickly, if that eases your pain." The voice was one she did not recognize.

"We are both from a land where magic does not exist. Why is he dead and not me?" Wen's voice cracked.

"What makes you think magic didn't exist in your land? Magic is everywhere. In the trees, the sky, the water . . . in knowledge. You crave knowledge, don't you? With it you were able to use Puppetmaster magic. With it you have kept Mangzar at bay when hundreds have fallen before you. It is because of magic that your homeland was suffocated into non-existence. My child, you are far from powerless." She looked up, half blinded by the light coming from the gates.

A hooded man stood between her and her prize. His robe was still despite the howling gale around them. There was no face beneath the hood, but a vibrant light. Wen knew he was a god no matter how much she wanted to deny it. His words fell on deaf ears as she tried to look past him. "Who are you?"

"Your final warning, foreign queen. The powers here are stronger than anything a mortal has touched before. The magic is delicate. Do not take what you cannot control."

"I must." Even as she spoke it, she knew the weight her words held. There was nothing she couldn't do, and until she challenged the stranger and the Well's existence, she would forever question herself. Knowledge may be magic, but without practicing it and pushing herself, she would become stagnant. She would become weak.

"I know," the god said sadly, "While history may carve a steady course through stone, sometimes it is necessary for someone to build a dam and see where it overflows." The vision vanished and she was left in the dark of the tunnel, a light extinguished. She could sense Grevin's corpse nearby and gritted her teeth. Whatever lay beyond the doors, she was damned if she wouldn't make it hers.

A gray cloud filled the entrance and she blinked to ensure it was not a trick of her eyes. "The future frightens you not, but your past does." The voice was different, softer, almost seductive. Her second test. Through the cloud she saw her homeland. There was peace, and children laughing. There were no weapons here nor danger to fight. Everything was delicate and welcoming, from the rolling hills to the lush forests that held no predators. She saw the anguish that had filled her father's heart at the death of her mother. She saw him fighting to create, to bring her back.

She knew what happened in the next scene and forced herself to watch. She saw the snow fall, innocent and silent at first. She remembered the awe. Then the panic crept in, as unassuming and constant as the spreading ice.

He was the apocalypse, and she the demon in chains who had arisen to pluck the followers from the snow and rebuild where she would eventually become queen. "The past cannot control those who do not allow it. This is no test I cannot pass."

The cloud dissipated with a great sigh.

"How about the present?" a gruff voice called from the darkness. "The future and the past hold no sway, little queen, but the present may. Shall I show you what your beloved is doing at this moment?"

Could she answer? She blamed her silence on the magic around her but could not prove it was her own reluctance to do so. "Very well, if it is necessary to open the gates."

A scene opened through the stone. A Mangzarian

bedchamber; not Frej's. Was that a Warlord crest above the headboard? At a small table, Frej and the young Warlord were breaking fast, exchanging jokes Wen could not hear and discussing politics that were not Gaffori. During their conversation, Frejith laughed out loud, and the Warlord gave her a roguish smile.

"He is not her type," Wen informed the oracle with only a small smile.

Frej's hand came to rest on his knee and stayed there. "Not all humans prefer one side or the other," the presence retorted.

"Enough," Wen snapped. "The present has no hold on me. Is that your final test?"

"You're not ready." The voice disappeared and Wen was yanked back to the dark tunnel, all light and magic gone.

Something felt off to Zavosh as the boat took him closer to Saltspire. He had never been there before, but even to his untrained eye, the green and gray flags of Gafforah looked unnatural and foreign. Guards patrolled the walls in place of the priests he imagined. One of them spotted the vessel and disappeared behind the battlements to report. What was Wen doing here, tempting the wrath of the gods? Certainly, the foreign queen laughed in the face of superstition, but her people remained religious. Taking Saltspire as a fortress was a bold move even for her and twisted the knife in Mangzar's ribs. He had to trust there was more to the story than first glance.

"Halt your vessel!" The command came from Peltet, a soldier he had drunk with after more than one battle.

"I'll stop when the waves stop crashing, you barrel-loving son of a crab!"

Peltet squinted and his expression changed to wonder.

"By Aryet, it's Zavosh!" He frowned when he saw the wrapped body in the boat with the vipr. It had begun to ripen considerably during the sun-saturated journey. "Is that . . . ?" Peltet trailed off.

Zavosh pulled back a corner of the fabric to reveal the face of the Tower agent. The soldier disappeared behind the battlements without another word.

When the boat grated onto the sandy shore, a dozen familiar faces were there to greet the vipr. Most were friends or comrades in arms, but any joyous reunion was on hold until they could assess why the sorceress hadn't accompanied him. Zavosh noted the queen was not among them.

Admiral Yo'aro, the only combatant to have fought Zavosh one on one and lived, nodded brusquely to him before shifting her attention to the body being unloaded from the boat. "I assume there's a story to tell here?"

"I'd rather discuss that with the queen. Where is she?"

Glances were exchanged and Zavosh's shoulders sagged further. If the queen was already distracted with ill tidings, his news would be a brutal blow. He repeated his question and Yo'aro took pity on him with an answer.

"She thinks she's found something in the catacombs. Some sort of power she won't speak to us about. Grevin went down to try and get her to come up for air, but now he's missing."

Zavosh's stomach churned. So, she had found the Well. Why was this bad news?

Smiles faded as Yo'aro led him inside the temple grounds. Zavosh could tell where well-tended gardens had been razed to create sparring space. Shipbuilders on the shore hammered the skeletons of skiffs. Priests who would otherwise be meditating or studying were fletching arrows and reinforcing walls. The most sobering sight was Prince Halthax, hanging from the battlements where approaching Mangzarians could see plainly. His body had decayed quickly, spurred by the heat and scavenging birds. Blood streaked the saltstone walls, enticing seagulls who watched hungrily. Soldiers drilled in front of ancient statues of gods whose candles had long gone out.

Yo'aro was silent as she led the vipr down a flight of stairs open to the elements. Here, glass crypts displayed deceased priests in all their untended, rotting glory. Most were broken and some had pieces missing. By then, Zavosh had become numb. The amount of holy desecration he had seen in his short time on Saltspire was horrifying. While never a friend to Mangzar, such disrespect was uncalled for. Saltspire had once been part of his homeland, and the Mangzarians honored the deities as required of mortals. This was asking for the wrath of the gods, from whom she sought to receive their greatest gift to Andriel.

Eventually Zavosh could see, as they walked deeper within the crypts, the corpses were untouched. No one bothered treading farther than the light reached. Perhaps there was still something left of their superstition. They passed a child's coffin guarded by the statue of a loyal pet, and the magic wall hit him squarely enough to knock the wind from his lungs. Yo'aro stopped with concern. "Are you alright?" While magically sensitive, Yo'aro was not as naturally in tune with the rhythm of magic as a vipr. "Zavosh?"

"Turn back. I'll go on from here alone."

The Admiral didn't object. She handed Zavosh the torch and briefly locked his eyes with her golden ones. "Do what you can, *cranle*. We need her back."

Zavosh nodded his understanding, inwardly touched at the use of the Nath'iki word for trusted comrade. Here was another example of how Wendwynn created friends out of former enemies. Now it was up to him to return the favor to his queen.

Zavosh took a moment to mentally prepare for the worst. If Grevin hadn't emerged, it could mean the advisor was dead, and he would have to tread lightly. Had Wen become consumed with the power of the Well? Was she dead within the boundaries, unable to hold the strength? "Your Grace," the vipr called through the barrier, sensing his words would be snatched away in the invisible winds.

He felt a response within his mind, a tickle of confusion and question. Wherever she was behind the barrier, she was alive. She had never been able to use magic before. Zavosh spoke to her mentally this time. "Are you alright?"

The answer was more a feeling than a word. She asked about Frejith. "She's been captured, Your Grace." There was no response and he spoke quickly to get it all out. "I don't know where to begin. The new Warlord, Greysten Cordova, he knows our true identities. He knows about the Well. He plans to find it for himself with Mangzar to back him up. He commands a dragon." The push from Wen's mind was stronger this time. She didn't care about the Warlord. She wanted to know about her wife. "He hired a Tower agent to wound her. He intends to blackmail her into standing with him, although I do not know the extent of his intentions. He sent me here with the assassin as a message to you. He wants you to back down in exchange for Frejith's life."

Zavosh took another step forward and his muscles seized up. She was angry, and he felt the intensity slamming into his body. "Your Grace! I need you to calm yourself." He shouted physically and mentally. The knives lessened enough for him to take another step. "You've found the Well, you've beaten him! You can use the power to take back Frejith and destroy Mangzar. Raze it to the ground." He clenched a fist. His nerves were on fire. "We can figure this out. *You* can figure this out. But you must come out and calm yourself. Gafforah needs you. Frejith needs you." Another step. He took advantage of a sudden release as the queen fought to control the energy surrounding her. Zavosh sprinted down the black hall, energy crackling at either side. He reached a section where the wall had been dug away and sandstone gates flung off their hinges.

He froze at a wall of pure magic. The intense amount of raw power was physically solid and through the churning depths he could see the fuzzy outline of Wendwynn.

Seeing her triggered a new tingle in the back of Zavosh's mind. There was another, competing, presence. It was Frejith. When Zavosh opened his mouth to speak, it was not his voice that came out.

"My love," Frejith whispered. Zavosh could feel the mind mage's yearning, and something deeper. Sorrowful. She was in pain. The shadow started and moved closer.

"Frej?" The queen's voice seemed small within the inferno of magical power. Zavosh could feel Frejith's grief and joy at hearing her voice again. Zavosh remembered that Wen was immune to mind magic, meaning Frejith could not speak with her telepathically. Of course. That's why Greysten needed him. He wanted to hurt the queen using her wife, but without a conduit he couldn't do it from afar. The vipr wanted to run, to fight his role in the Warlord's horrible game, but he could not bear to deny them their reunion, however false.

"Are you hurt?" the sorceress asked through the vipr, despite the physical anguish she herself was feeling.

"I—I don't know. I've awakened something, and I don't know how to put it back to sleep. It's . . . so powerful. It's the Well, Frejith. I've found it, and I'm going to take it."

Goosebumps prickled Zavosh's arms. "Can you control the barrier? Let me in and I will help you. You clearly aren't strong enough to get through this on your own."

"I can't. Whatever it is, it's alive. It's not something you can turn on and off. It's something I need to communicate with. I need to reason with it."

"Then let me in. Let me help you." Frej was fighting hard but there was little strength beyond what Zavosh could feel. This wasn't simply her recovering from her wounds. She was being tortured.

"You know I can't do that. Please, just wait for me. Grevin. He's dead. You're all I have left." Her voice cracked, betraying regret. Grevin had been her confidant, her protector, her guide, since before her arrival in Andriel. The intense emotion of his loss plus speaking to Frejith was a deadly combination.

"I can't. I must remain in Mangzar. The new Warlord is gracious. He will hear your surrender." Zavosh couldn't imagine Frejith expressing such an opinion without being coerced. Who was really whispering through his mind?

There was silence longer than he wanted to admit. "Surrender? Can I really be hearing this? I have the Gods' Blood at my fingertips. I just need a little more time, and I can use it, wield it. I'm strong enough. I know I am. How could you think I'm not?" She was growing angry again, the wind whipping up with an unnatural heat and sharpness.

"I don't—"

"Then come home. Fuck the new Warlord and the old. Be by my side where you belong."

"I'm where I belong." Frejith's voice faltered and Zavosh felt tears brimming in his eyes. It pained Frejith to speak such words almost as much as it hurt for Wen to hear them.

The barrier began to churn a dark color and crackle like oncoming lightning. "Fight him, Frej. I know your words aren't your own. I can sense your agony, your pain. Don't let him use you as a pawn against me. Escape, I know you can. Let us wipe the Warlord and the rest of Mangzar from the face of Andriel." She spoke with a thousand voices, resonating through the crypts.

"You won't surrender, then?"

Wen placed a hand against the barrier, resolved. "No."

~ 31 ~

KEYRA
&
TILSMAN

The dining hall is curved to match the architecture, as are the three tables that run the length of the room. The floor-to-ceiling windows open to the south where the sea stretches to the horizon. According to Peterfer, the room is normally abuzz with activity, from teachers to students. Today, it is silent as a tomb. The time mage brings them plates himself, and the spread is less than stellar. "I apologize for showing you the Citadel in such poor shape. Very few ships have been brave enough to come to Everlyn in our current trying time."

Keyra remembers the dead sloshing through the mud of Oldeville. Hardock had never been a destination sight, but now it is little more than a disheveled crypt. The Citadel's shining walls and silver plates are still a far cry from the horrors below. The food on her plate is humble but hearty. There is wine in her glass. She ignores Peterfer's out-of-touch comment. "It makes me nervous to admit, given where we are, but from what I understand, the sorcerers were involved from the beginning. Could you not have warned people, or evacuated them?"

"We weren't sure the extent of the damage that would cause. By evacuating, we could have spread the magic elsewhere. Elgireth is mostly contained and allowing people to panic wouldn't have fixed anything. What fascinates me is that you and your friend seem immune to the magic. I'm hoping that I can convince you to stay. Together, we could connect these pieces into something tangible."

Tilsman continues to glare at the man in a rude manner. His food is barely touched.

"When there is a boat ready, I will have them hold it for you in case you change your mind. I want you to feel comfortable here, Lady Keyra. As another gesture of goodwill, I invite you to the library once we finish eating. Usually, it is restricted to master sorcerers, but the circumstances demand extraordinary measures."

"It certainly does," Keyra agrees. She doesn't trust Peterfer or any of the other sorcerers' intentions when it comes to solving the problem at hand. But she shouldn't feel responsible, should she? The itch she cannot scratch has returned. She needs to see the library. She needs to know for herself.

The rest of the meal passes in relative silence. Even Tilsman manages to keep his mouth shut. When they finish, Peterfer offers Keyra a hand out of her chair. "Brace yourself, Lady Keyra. You are about to enter a room no non-sorcerer has ever entered."

The thrill seeker in Keyra feels her heart leap with anticipation.

The Citadel's library takes up an entire floor of the massive tower, shelves curved to match the walls. Tilsman feels as though he's gone around and around the never-ending rows, scanning the same books over and over. He rubs his eyes wearily. He cannot even read; why is he here? His stomach grumbles and he wonders why he didn't demand a second plate at lunch.

He peers around the shelves for Keyra, but she is nowhere to be found. She was quick to disappear with the time mage. He takes the opportunity to slip to the stairs, following his nose down to the dining hall level. He encounters no one, making him feel more unsettled than comfortable. The kitchen must be on the same level as the hall. He smells garlic, and fried fish with spices.

The curved nature of the rooms confuses the boy, and he ends up on a staircase winding downwards. He still smells the food, so he must be close. It doesn't make sense to put the kitchens below the dining hall, but the sorcerers must be able to magic the plates up with no effort.

He continues farther down the stairs where the air feels cooler and there are no more windows. He has yet to see an exit from the staircase and feels dizzy from the curvature of the tower. He doesn't know how people can live here on a daily basis without getting turned around.

The cool air has turned to cold by the time he reaches a landing. There are no torches here, but he can hear voices in the distance. The scents of food have been replaced by mold and dirty water. He imagines the beating Keyra will give him if he's caught and panics. He sprints for a barred door in the corner, slipping behind it before he can see where he's going. He is plunged into darkness. This is no exit. It is a closet. He steps backwards, the gloom closing in until his breath comes in ragged gasps.

His foot hits nothing but air, and he tumbles backwards with a shriek that would embarrass a small child. He plunges down, arms flailing as though he can swim through it. He slams into the floor on his shoulder, jarring it painfully. His ankle throbs as well, but he is more concerned with regaining the ability to breathe. He lies there on cold stone for what feels like a lifetime, gathering his wits and testing his bones for breaks. Once satisfied, he gets painfully to his feet and feels around for a torch of some sort.

His hand touches some sort of pressure plate and it crunches into the wall. The cracks between the stones light up with a soft orange glow, in the form of strange glyphs. He is in a sub-basement in a long tunnel now magically alight. He glances the way he has come, seeing a ladder half-broken as the only way back to the door. There is no hope of getting back to civilization that way.

Faced with no choice, he heads farther down the underpass. There are doors on either side. He opens one a crack. Inside, the glow from the tunnel reveals stains splattered on the walls and floor, disturbingly bloodlike. There are chains drilled into the stone and a chair half-rotted in the center. He closes the door quickly and doesn't open another. "Hello," he whispers in a squeak quieter than the mice that scurry around his feet, startled by the sudden disturbance. "I'm not trying to get anywhere I'm not supposed to be. I just fell, and I'd appreciate not being stuck down here. Hello?" There is no answer, so he keeps walking. The tunnel must go on forever. It doesn't seem to have any end, nor any sign of life besides the rodents. It feels as though this was abandoned long before the sorcerers fled the curse. The air is thick, and the dust-layered floor is undisturbed. Tilsman wrings his hands in worry. He is about to turn back and scream for the strangers he had heard earlier, no matter the consequence, when the hallway stops and reveals a massive underground chamber.

It is dark here, but Tilsman fumbles for another pressure plate and a calm, blue light weaves through the stones, illuminating the scene bit by bit. The ceiling is arched and at least twenty Tilsmans high. He dares not speak as his voice would echo like the stray drops of moisture he can hear reverberating through the chamber. There are statues of kings and queens he has never learned, paintings as massive as some houses, and rows upon rows of scrolls and books.

Heaped around the feet of the statues are piles of gold jewelry and sparkling gems that catch the azure light eerily. Their stone faces are serious, and most are holding swords of real metal. Tilsman finds himself drawn to them past the written knowledge he does not understand. He peers at the faces, recognizing some of the Western gods. Jallor is there in his shadow cloak; Aryet and Akai, the double faces of the moon, stand back-to-back, eyeing each other suspiciously. Salwynn holds a fistful of jewels, draped in a carved cape of a million feathers.

The kings and queens must be Gaffori, based on their puffy pants and draping tunics, open to bare their hairy chests. They are all the same, save one. He almost misses it, in the corner, arm broken and face chipped. She wears studs and chains, metal embedded into her stone shoulders and wrists. Is this a Gaffori queen? She looks more like a mercenary from some distant land. Around her neck is a square-framed amulet, carved from stone in incredible detail. Tilsman narrows his eyes then reaches for the amulet around his own neck. The stone version has the same sea stone center, the same thick, square casing with the tiny latch. Curious, that a long dead queen would have the same necklace as him. Perhaps it comes from a certain jewelry maker. He chooses not to read into it and turns his attention to the gifts around the statue's base.

~ 32 ~

THE BOY

Nighttime at the Citadel is clear, the stars' brightness enhanced by the magical weather that surrounds it. The moon shines so brightly in Luthen's window that he cannot hope to sleep. Perhaps it is a blessing; he has a chance to escape tonight, and he would expect to sleep through it if the moon would allow. What he is going to do, he cannot say yet. He knows nothing of his powers, and he is always guarded. Every move he makes is watched, meaning any attempt to test his abilities without suspicion is impossible.

He tosses and turns with a long sigh. He never wanted to be a hero. Being a slave again seems a much more realistic and appropriate status for him. Finally, he gives up on sleep and tosses his blankets to the side.

The guards tense as he pads barefoot to the door. "I would like to see Beta," he demands in the most authoritative voice he can muster.

"Sorry, you cannot leave the room. We can bring her here."

Now is the moment. He digs deep within to the strange new light burning within his gut. He can feel the star there, pulsing like a second heart. "You will let me pass."

The guard hesitates then steps to the side. "Very well. Have a good night, sir." The second guard never flinches, staring straight ahead under her own spell.

Luthen slides past them cautiously and then takes off running down the hall.

Beta's room is on the same floor, he can feel it. Luthen trusts himself to knock on the door he senses is hers. Sure enough, the battlemage opens it.

The hair she usually ties back or hides under a hood is loose and frames her small, orange-streaked face. Luthen is painfully aware of how thin her nightgown is and does his best to avert his eyes. "You're out of your room," she comments.

"Yes, I, uh, convinced them to let me pass."

She smiles wryly. "Look at you, becoming a true sorcerer. Come in before someone sees you."

He enters before she remembers she hates him. Once the door closes, he relaxes slightly. "My friend Ayrek mentioned she spoke to you about escaping tonight."

She perches on the edge of her bed and motions for him to join her. Her face, as perfect as it is, has taken on new worry lines. Something is weighing heavily on her. "If we don't, the Citadel is going to kill you and rip the Gods' Blood from your corpse."

"I know." He is as equally surprised by his blunt confidence as she is. "I can feel their intentions, their greed. I don't know what they plan to do with it. All I know is they have become obsessed. I wonder who between the Tower and the Citadel would win out in the battle to control it, or if they would actually share it equally."

"I think we both know sharing was never an option." She smiles at him in a way that's genuine for the first time. Luthen's heartbeat quickens. They're bonding. He can't screw this up.

"Let's just walk out of here, the two of us," he blurts. "We don't need Ayrek. I can command people to leave us alone, and anyone that doesn't listen, you can blast into the ocean."

He is close enough now to smell her scent, the same as the lock of hair he had kept under his pillow at the lighthouse and the cloak she had left on the rocks one day after a bayside swim. She smelled like the ocean and sandalwood and flowers all at once. Beta tenses as though she wants to back away but doesn't at the last moment. "You don't understand your power well enough, and we don't know how much longer you can use it before it kills you. It's too much for a mortal to handle. By all rights, you shouldn't be alive right now. Besides, Ayrek may have a more efficient plan than yours."

"Of course." His cheeks burn with his foolishness. He needs to trust her wisdom. When the silence drags on too long, he speaks again. "I think they want to use the star's power to revive battlemages. They're going to drain the rest of Vendar's magic to use as a seed for the next generation, and for themselves. If you don't come with me, you could be next." He winces at his own statement. All the magic in the world can't make him say the right thing to her.

The horror in her face suggests he has said something wrong, but she doesn't run away. Perhaps deep down she has known all along. She is the last of her kind, and the Citadel has made enough morally questionable decisions for her to doubt her place with them. "Thank you for your honesty."

His heart skips a beat. Had she truly thanked him? "What happens now?"

"We wait. Ayrek wants us to meet her on the north side of the tower in an hour." She is struggling with something internally. Ironhead can sense a memory but doesn't pry into her mind further. "How did you convince the guards to let you pass? Like anyone, I know so little about how the Gods' Blood works."

"I just asked them."

She leans forward until he can feel her breath on his neck. He goes rigid so as not to frighten her away. She studies him curiously. Luthen can sense she is prying for the extent of his power. She is also vulnerable. She has been betrayed, used, and watched her friend die in the past week. He can't imagine how much she is struggling.

"Then convince me of something. It shouldn't be too hard, right? I need to know you really can. I can sense the power in you. You've wanted me your entire life. More than anything. Now you have me alone, in my nightgown, sitting on a bed. Convince me to want you."

He freezes as her hand strays to his pants. She stops and pulls back.

He meets her eyes and digs within himself once more. "Stay."

She smiles. "That's more like it. Now tell me what you want me to do."

"Take off your gown," he commands.

She stands and obeys. Suddenly, the stars are not the brightest part of his night.

Ayrek breathes a sigh of relief as the apprentices slip out of the Citadel and make their way to meet her at the rowboat. They are going to make it out, unlike so many she had failed before. Perhaps now she can find peace with her past and the lives she has ruined or taken outright. She should have made this choice years ago, but the jewels had sparkled, and the wine flowed freely. Now, the jewels were nothing but rocks, and the wine tasted like ash and blood. She had spent nearly half a century destroying. Perhaps she would spend the rest of her life saving instead, after she made things right with Erey. One thing at a time. She must survive tonight first.

"Did anyone see you?" she whispers as they climb into the

boat. The boy shakes his head no and the girl remains silent. She is lost in her own thoughts and that makes Ayrek nervous. She should be scared or happy. "Alright, let's go."

They push out into the bay and Ayrek can taste freedom. "Where to?"

The boy is in especially high spirits. "Where to, Beta? We could go to Terrial and start a farm, or the Lerdin Islands and live on the beach. Anything you like." It's as though he doesn't even recognize the intense magical power within him.

The girl won't meet their eyes. "It doesn't matter where we go. You'll be dead in the week."

The boy is wounded but he gathers his wits. "We don't know that. Star said I could return the magic to the Well. I have to give Ashlikani's power back or there'll be nothing left for the next ceremony."

"You don't deserve it," the sorceress mutters.

Ayrek tenses. "If you're going to change your mind, then it's not too late for you to swim back to shore." They are only a few yards away from the dock. "Just leave me and the boy in peace."

Tears are brimming in her eyes. "You said they wanted to use the magic to save the battlemages, right? My people. They deserve a chance to be reborn. I don't deserve to be the last of my kind, right?"

Ayrek pulls the oars out of the water and touches the dirk on her waist. She doesn't know what she plans to do against a battlemage, but she's not going down without a fight. She sees the glowing in the girl's arms too late and the boat freezes in place. "What are you doing?"

The sorceress lowers her head until the hood covers her face completely. "I'm sorry. If the Citadel intends to resurrect the battlemages, then they deserve that chance. I can't be the betrayal the spirit warned me about."

Luthen looks at her with disbelief. "Did earlier mean

nothing? You wanted this, you wanted to get away. You promised me we would, and you took my amulet as a token."

"I *will* get away." She shudders and clutches the framed sea stone amulet around her neck. "I thought I knew what I wanted, but it turns out all the magic in Andriel won't make you less repulsive to me."

Ayrek can see in the boy's face that her words strike harder and more painfully than any knife. Luthen sobs and lifts his hand as though to do magic. Ayrek grips the side of the boat with white knuckles. Does he plan to kill her? No. He loves her, that much is plain. His hand drops. Even Ayrek doesn't see the rock until the battlemage has hit him over the head with it. She stares down at him, blood dripping from the weapon hovering above her palm, emotionless. "I hate you," she whispers.

Ayrek moves to disarm her, but the sorceress reacts quickly, calling the waves to wash Ayrek and the boy out of the boat. Ayrek flounders as the water pulls her down despite her desperate kicks. She fights until the magic releases her and she can surface with a desperate gasp for air. The battlemage is gone. A trail of disturbed water suggests where she has taken off into the distance. Luthen lies on a sheet of unnatural ice floating gently towards shore and the sorcerers that will destroy him. She is forced to swim after him and meet the party that gathers on the sand. She is pulled roughly to her feet and the boy is whisked back to the Citadel in a small mob. The stony faces around Ayrek are familiar. They are people she has fought with, people she has broken bread with. At one point she would have called them her friends. Now, they are another reminder of the horrible choices she has made through her life. Tears fill her eyes as they drag her back up the grassy hill. "Look at yourselves! What have we become, taking in one of our own because the damned magic users say so? We used to control them, not the other way around. Where is your pride?"

Vendar, the battlemage who had yet to recover from his

own conflict with the Tower, hobbles forward on a cane. His skin is cracking and peeling away, revealing orange light beneath. "It would seem you are the only traitor here. You should witness what we're about to do to fully understand why your people have abandoned you."

Ayrek hisses at him. "I am not the only one that was abandoned tonight. Your apprentice is gone, and I can't say I blame her. She saw what this organization was becoming."

There is a flicker in his features that suggests she has hit a nerve, but he betrays no further emotion. When he speaks again, his voice is flat and devoid of empathy. "Let's go."

They climb the massive circular staircase to the pyramid at the top. Here, the stars are visible through the slightly pink tint of the quartz. Luthen is strapped into a chair in the center of the room, beneath the channeled moonlight. He is still unconscious. The High Mages stand in a semicircle, faces draped by dark blue hoods. Vendar moves to stand beside Ayrek on the edge of the huddled mass. "You see, agent, all magic is pulled from a Well. There must be a source. A long time ago, the power was protected by people like me, battlemages, on an island called Saltspire. The last queen of Gafforah, who has been forgotten by history, changed that." He gives a small quirk of a smile, suggesting he has personal experience. Hands raise in unison and the hairs on Ayrek's arms stand on end. "We don't know how, and we don't know why, but someone disturbed the Well. It was broken, and the power stolen. We thought it lost forever." Different colors of light dance over the sorcerer's fingertips. Ayrek's body feels the pull of the magic from so many powerful users. "Then a leemoah agent discovered it had fused with the star Ashlikani. It only took a small amount of convincing to gain him as an ally."

It had to be Captain Zai. The sleazy leemoah had schemed his way up the ladder within the Tower, changing the very way they did business. Some of her most regrettable missions had been working alongside him and his hunger for power. "I wouldn't trust El'rozai, he has no friends, and he will use you and throw you out when he's done."

Luthen's head is pulled back, and masked incense priests draw patterns on his skin in ash. These are Seers, summoned from faraway Terrial specifically for the ceremony. The sorcerers will ensure precise magic this time. Vendar's eyes glint strangely in the magical light. "And he is a leemoah, barely able to summon a fish, going up against the entire power of the Citadel. It would be fitting if he went out the way he lived, no? Using people? Your friend here was the only thing we didn't predict."

The priests step back and the Magnium is rolled out on a cart. "Not this time," Vendar whispers. "This time it has nowhere else to go."

"What are they going to do with it?"

"What does it matter? You'll be dead long before then."

Ayrek falls silent as the Seers begin chanting. She pulls at her restraints. "Don't make me watch this. If you're going to kill me, why not get it over with?"

"Just in case. The Tower may have more use for you."

"What about you? You look worse for the wear. What did the Tower use you for?" She is desperate, but if she can keep him talking long enough, she may be able to free herself. The shiv in her hand is already sawing furiously at the ropes around her wrists.

"I put too much value on the next generation. I focused too much on what I could see in Beta, and lost sight of my true mission to help the new battlemages realize their powers."

"She left you, just like any other pupils you have will abandon you. They'll see the rot that is your soul," Ayrek spits. She's halfway through one of the ropes.

Luthen begins to glow from the inside out. The Seers and gathered sorcerers move closer until Ayrek can no longer see beyond the dark robes. The battlemage notes her interest in the ritual. "He's not going to survive," Vendar says matter-of-factly.

Luthen's eyes snap open. He has not been strapped down as he wasn't conscious, but now the sorcerers rush to hold him. He grabs something from his pocket. It's a shell, delicate and soft pink. He crushes it with a swift movement. Ayrek is blinded by a powerful wave of energy that bursts her ear drums and pops blood vessels in her nose. She is on the ground for what feels like an eternity, her muscles frozen, and her vision compromised. She can hear voices from somewhere beyond the physical impact. "Take it! Take it, Star, somewhere far away! Please, please give it to her." Luthen's voice fades. She can hear muffled screams from beyond the whiteness. Slowly and painfully, she regains her senses.

"But where did it go?" A panicked voice comes from what must be a sorceress. Ayrek sees Luthen slumped dead in the chair, his eyes burned through. His body looks as though there are no bones. While his light is gone, Ayrek's heart skips a beat when she sees the Magnium empty and glistening. Most of the pyramid crystal is gone, leaving behind nothing but jagged shards.

The sorcerers are in chaos. They argue, cast spells, and scour the sky to find the magic that has slipped between their fingers yet again. Ayrek's dragged to her feet and Vendar forces her to look him in the eyes. "Did you do this?"

"I wish I had."

The battlemage snarls and pushes her up against the wall. Her shiv clatters to the ground with the jerking motion. Vendar's eyes are full of fire despite the shattered skin surrounding them. "I don't think you understand what's happening here, but you're going to help me fix it."

"Looking at you, all I'll have to do is outwait you. You're crumbling like an abandoned statue." The battlemage towers over her physically without magical abilities. She shakes in his grip but refuses to let him see just how frightened she is.

"Perhaps, but I will ensure my legacy lives on. You're going to find where the magic went if it takes you the rest of your life. You're going to stay here on Elgireth until you find a lead and then you're going to pursue it. We'll be watching you every step of the way. You dedicated your life to the Tower, it's time to make good on that promise." The orange in his veins crackles. He's casting a spell. She can feel the cold rush under her skin. Mind magic? But he is no mind mage.

"Why tell me your plans?"

"Because you're not going to remember today. You're not going to remember me. You'll remember nothing except what I allow you to." The fierce determination in a face that fractures before her is the last thing she sees.

~ 33 ~

WENDWYNN

"**W**endwynn."

The faceless god's voice awakened the queen with a jolt. She sat up from her bed of cold stone painfully. Her bones ached from the days she had spent there now. Her only sustenance came from the power she absorbed from behind the doors. She wanted nothing more than to bathe and feel the sun on her face.

The old man emerged through the gates. "What do you want now?" She growled. "You have everything of me."

"I know. You have paid your penance in full, and you have earned the key to the gates." He pulled a literal key from his robe. It was made of some black metal she had never seen before. Despite its small size, the weight was considerable.

"Why now?" She was afraid to ask lest he change his mind. But she had to know. "I have been here days. I have rejected every visitor. Why let me in now? What changed?"

"You are quite the inquisitive one. Thankfully, I am not obliged to answer you. The next time a god hands you the key to the ultimate power in Andriel, do not question it. Just know that what you are about to witness is our ultimate gift to mortals. Drops of our own blood, magnified, and groomed, and then given to those great enough to deserve it. Good luck, Wendwynn, we will not meet again."

The old man vanished, and Wen was left kneeling with the key in her lap. Damn. She hated that Lekala was right. The gods had revealed themselves to her. Her fascination was outweighed by her glowing pride. Once again, she had defeated the obstacle in her path. Once again, she had proven to be strong enough.

She stood and slid the key in the lock. It turned of its own accord and the doors opened silently. She stepped blindly into the overwhelming light and waited for her weary eyes to adjust.

Eventually, she could see the outline of an orb suspended in a round cavern carved out of solid stone with runes covering the walls. She read them hungrily. They were a mix of ancient Var, Gathiori—the old Gaffori tongue—and one she did not recognize. She knew enough of Andreli magic to understand they were both sealing spells and opening spells. There were ancient incantations for strengthening and even older commands of containment. Everything was balanced and incredibly strong. Only when she was satisfied did she turn to the orb itself.

It was the size of a house, streaked with every distinct color of the rainbow. There were colors she had never known existed and more she could not focus on. The ones her brain could not process gave her a headache as much as the physical waves of power it gave off. She fell to her knees in rapture. The Blood of the Gods, the source of all magic.

"You are the first in many generations to lay eyes on the Well." Lekala stood in the doorway, arms crossed. "I did not think they would open the gates to you, to be honest. We knew from the teachings of the battlemages that used to be the guardians that the Well was here, but we assumed it had dissipated or would never be found by those who looked." He walked to the orb and tendrils of light played over his extended palm. "Our ancestors were tasked with keeping it safe and secret. Their duties have been passed down for generations to the priests on Saltspire. It is from here that all magic users pull their power from, no matter the type. The black magic of necromancers, the Holy magic of priests, witch magic, Seer magic, ones I do not know. The smallest and greatest spells begin here. As its guardians, the battlemages were offered whatever magic they wished. They chose to manipulate the world around them with their thoughts. An incredibly powerful and unique magic, yes, but also too strong for mortal bodies to contain over an entire lifespan."

"So, the gift was a curse. Balance." She was the reason there were no more battlemages. Could her discovery of magic's source be a way of regaining balance she'd destroyed?

"Always. Your Grace. I would love to give you more lessons, but I fear I am here for another reason. We have received confirmation that the new Warlord of Sixth District has been acknowledged by the Mangzarian Conclave. We do not know if Mangzar rallies behind him, but we have heard reports of Eleventh District gathering forces as well."

Wen felt empty in the presence of such power. Her emotions, her existence, had been replaced by something neutral. She extended a numb hand to the orb, offering it her body as a host. Let it become her, and she it. Let them be one in power and purpose. She whispered a prayer beneath her breath as the light stretched towards her. She had no magical abilities—it should be repelled by her. Instead, the light curled around her fingers and crawled up her arm until the Well was empty.

Wen didn't feel as though she had just gained the ultimate ascendency. She felt nothing but the hum of magic in her bones. "Then I should go. I have completed my mission here. It is time to destroy Mangzar." Lekala blinked in surprise, realizing he'd fallen to his knees in her presence. He stood at her command methodically.

As they exited the tunnels, it became clear that Wen's orders before her time in meditation had been followed to the letter. The newly dubbed Frejwynn Fortress was abuzz with activity. Nearly the entirety of her army drilled and prepared while her fleet grew by the moment around the island. She should have taken Saltspire for her own at the first sign of conflict. Establishing her dominance on the strategic island would have saved the colonies their destruction. She could add it to the list of her regrets. Each would make her stronger than the last.

Zavosh waited for the queen in the temple, where he wore Gaffori clothing and light vambraces as his only armor. He bowed stiffly. "Your Grace."

"I feel our time in the catacombs has enhanced our relationship, Zavosh. I thank you for your service and allowing me to speak to Frejith again. Now I ask that you help me save her and kill every Mangzarian in our path." She was eager to make her move. She had waited too long, and she wanted to see the look on the Warleaders' faces when she demolished their forces.

"It would be my honor."

"Thank you for your service, Captain. I am grateful that you decided to serve me despite our differences in the past."

She should have been worried for Frejith's life. She should have been mourning Grevin. But all she could feel was the rise of adrenaline in her body that was otherwise devoid of emotion. She decided against asking further questions and headed back down to the Well with long strides. All she wanted was the power. All she craved was the ability to change the present and the failures hanging over her head. And now? Now, she could.

Kaper's Bay was usually a calm water that held dangers below the shallow surface. Today was different. The skies churned with the gods' rage and the waves rustled in fear of the coming storm. Wen preferred to believe the weather had changed for her. She stood at the stern, dressed in her most impressive battle gear. Pointed metal studs traced the figure of a wave wrapping around a griffin. It was the first time she had worn a sigil from her native land with the Gaffori pattern. Her black and gray armor was made up of more pieces than the average set, giving her flexibility and range of motion. She wore the charcoal around her eyes and the black feathers in her hair as an homage to the leemoahs she ruled. Pressed beneath the armor against her undertunic was Frej's amulet for luck. Hearthslayer hung heavy on her waist.

Forty-three Gaffori vessels followed her, bristling with warriors. She feared no trap as Mangzarians would never give up the chance for open battle even if it meant surrendering their advantage. It was for this reason that she had never believed the Warlord's call for peace, and why she needed to end this now and bring her wife home.

Hearthslayer was in her hands before Mangzar's shores came into sight. There was no holding back today. There was only blood and the hope that it would be on her sword. Her veins sang with the magic pulsing through them. She had never been able to do magic. Now she was the very definition of the power. Unlimited.

She had reached to Frej through their connection to warn her of the attack with no reply. She hoped this was because the crafty sorceress was making last-minute preparations or somewhere far away where no enemy could use her against the Gaffori.

The shore came into sight. It was deserted. There weren't even fishermen making use of the stormy waters in hopes of a catch being forced into their net by the choppy waves. They knew they were coming.

"Admiral Yo'aro, keep the speed steady!" Somehow her voice carried over the wind. "Sound the signal!"

The horn of Gafforah was infamous for its unique sound. It mimicked a great sea beast and for good reason. Legends spoke of the Bay Beast, a creature that dwelled deep among the coral of the otherwise still waters. The horn was created by an ancient Gaffori king who had a special connection with the monster. Legends claimed he even rode it, although Wen could not attest to that. The stories had spread until the whole of the East knew the horn and the war of the waves it brought. It was said that if a worthy warrior sounded the horn, they could summon it to fight once more. It had adorned the walls of her audience chamber, but that day it would fill every Gaffori with bloodlust.

From the perch, the horn blower sounded a single note. It was the scream of a deep, massive throat, the cry of anger and rage. Wen felt goosebumps at its cry. She could only imagine how it made her enemies feel.

As they had been trained, her soldiers in all the ships began a chant of defiance. A chant that demanded victory or death. As if on cue, the rain began to fall. The storm would go on to be immortalized for its intensity, as would the queen that laughed in its face. Through the sheets of blackness, rocks of fire became visible in the air. "Brace for impact!" Wen screamed into the wind. Another storm of arrows ominously hovered, alight from the glow of the projectiles. "Shields! Keep the ship steady!"

There were soldiers on the beach. They became visible as the ship approached shore at breakneck speed. Wen crouched, riding the waves as easily as if they were a horse. Let anyone say she was not of Gaffori blood. Let anyone call her the foreign queen now.

"Battlemages!" To her sides, cloaked figures braced their feet with arms high. The priests had a long connection with Saltspire and the extinct battlemages that had guarded it. Giving them their powers had taken little more effort than a touch and a concentrated thought. There were three dozen in total.

The stone missiles froze in midair. The arrows hovered like a strange cloud of birds. The mortals held their breath while nature raged on. While most of the missiles were stopped, stray arrows broke through and continued their trajectory. Shields went up and the whistle of feathered shafts was followed swiftly by thuds. They hit wood, and there were half a dozen screams as they struck unsuspecting flesh.

The first blood had been drawn.

The ship hit the sand, cushioned by raised waves called by battlemages. Wen jumped, hitting the ground.

Orders barked in Var carried over the wind. They were watching the stones and arrows as they twisted and began falling towards those that had fired them. However, they were not the most renowned warriors in the world for nothing. Black magic users stepped forward in perfect unison, creating an impressive shield of dark smoke over their soldiers' heads. It hummed with incredibly powerful magic. Physical shields also went up in perfect unison as a backup. They would need it.

While Wen could not use physical magic herself, she controlled its existence. "*Algarath makton*," she whispered. She knew the words from her never-ending studies of Andreli magic. Knowledge truly was her greatest strength. The necromancers' connection to their magic shattered, as did their shields. Any lesser army would have dropped into chaos. Mangzar was no lesser army.

The physical shields did their jobs as the necromancers retreated until they could find the source of their collapse. The Gaffori swords followed their queen, never breaking stride as they raced to the enemy. The reversing of the arrows had done its job and no volleys followed. It would be a brief time before they gathered their wits and devised a new strategy.

The clash could be heard over the lightning. Wen was

among them, Zavosh by her side. She had insisted on giving him the honor. She had even sent her personal guard to join the vanguard without worry for her safety. She felt her body surging with power.

The legends had not over-exaggerated Mangzar. They fought with the intensity of those who wished for nothing but blood. A foot soldier found himself skewered on a Gaffori pike and dragged himself towards his enemy through the shaft until he was close enough to bite the Gaffori's neck. Then there were the viprs. They moved like shadows through the armies, unburdened by the massive cloaks that hid their existence until they were close enough to strike.

Wen had seen viprs take souls before and braced herself for the horrifying psychological impact they had, but felt chills all the same. The screams from the victims were disturbing to even the most seasoned warrior. Her men were shaken despite the advantages. They couldn't lose faith so soon.

Balance. The magic she had taken from the Mangzarians had to go somewhere. Wen channeled it back to her battle-mages. Their skin burned with orange cracks, but their magic intensified along with their confidence. As more of the army landed, the enemy found they were not only fighting men, but the sea itself. Fire, untouched by rain, bombarded the defenders mercilessly. They began pushing forward once more.

The Mangzarians broke lines without warning, creating pathways among their soldiers. The Gaffori filled in the cracks. Wen felt something was wrong. "Back up! Back up!"

Only a fraction of the soldiers had time to listen. From the darkened sky, a shadow sliced through the clouds. The dragon's jaws opened, and fire fell from its mouth through the open line. Dragon fire was something few had ever experienced. It was heavy, unlike normal fire, lavalike in nature. The Gaffori that were caught in the path didn't have time to scream. Astride the dragon was a man wearing Warleader armor. This had to be the Warlord Frej had spoken so highly of. Where was his call for peace now? Where was his understanding?

Where was Frej?

"Foreign queen!" He had spotted her. The dragon landed among the soldiers, the ground shaking beneath its weight. It swiped left and right with claws the size of broadswords as her warriors rushed to block the path to their commander. Wen held Hearthslayer at the ready, but the creature made no move to attack her as it came to a stop. "I hope I have your attention now," the Warleader called through the rain-soaked hair covering his eyes.

Wen raised her weapon as the dragon breathed heavily on her face. She could feel the heat from deep within its chest. "Where is Frejith?"

"Last I saw she was safe at the fortress with one of my new friends. He had much to say about you. You are a terrible hostess, from what I hear."

"What friend?" Terror settled into her chest. She had learned long ago to always kill her enemies. Ensure they could not live to strike back, because they would, and with renewed vengeance. She already knew the answer, but she wanted to hear him say it.

"You must have many enemies, to not remember Halthax ky Dzaxar the Elder."

She had become overconfident. It was one of her many weaknesses. She fought through the fray with renewed strength, Hearthslayer singing its baritone song as it sliced through the enemy.

"You'd better hurry, little queen! I do so enjoy a good lovers' reunion!" His laugh chased her into the thick of the enemy.

The harder she fought, the harder the Gaffori fought. They banded together against the dragon, whittling down its strength with pike, sword, and bow. Together they had pinned one of the wings and shredded the other, grounding it but also enraging it. Though it swatted at them like flies, there was always another soldier to take its place. Finally, a battlemage twisted the sand around its feet, trapping it in the ground. It made a horrendous screech as the sand filled its mouth and it disappeared below the surface.

The queen, while always a warrior, had never fought like this before. She had always been accompanied by guards or Grevin, or Frej, or all three. Now the only one who stood beside her was Zavosh, fast losing himself to the bloodlust of his kind. The solitude forced her to be aware of everything at once. She could block multiple swords at one time with Hearthslayer, then spin and cut clean through the exposed necks of the enemies with the momentum of her movements. The Mangzarians wore war masks, twisted faces of their spirits with grotesque bulging eyes and dripping fangs. They were everywhere, yet she was not afraid. This was her legend. She was a whirlwind, carving a path for her soldiers to follow, a small storm mimicking the large one above her head.

Perhaps it was her ferocity, or perhaps nature had its own, unrelated timing, but that day, the foreign queen was worthy.

The sea horn sounded, and she glanced back in confusion. The call did not come from the instrument, but from its namesake.

The Bay Beast's head broke through the waves as massive as two Gaffori warships side by side. It had the face and eyes of a dragon, with algae-encrusted horns twisting from its scalp. Its black and green scales were dotted with barnacles and more kelp. Countless tentacles the girth of a tree curled angrily. Crucifers were the rarest of creatures in Kaper's Bay, and this was the greatest of all. It stared directly at Wen. She laughed and cut down a soldier who thought he could take advantage of her distraction. "Warriors! Pull back to the sea! Bring our beast a meal! Battlemages, bring the ocean forward." The Mangzarians concentrated arrow fire on the beast but none met their mark as the battlemages protected their new ally.

The beast blinked sleepy eyes and opened massive jaws. Within were not fangs, but rows upon rows of smaller teeth lining the red maw. Tentacles arose from the waves, lashing out at Mangzarians and Gaffori alike.

Sir Seran grabbed Wen's arm with a blood-soaked glove. "Go, Your Grace. Find Frejith. We will handle the battle here."

Wen's voice froze in her throat as she tried to protest. It was only then that she realized how terrified she was of finding Frejith. She feared the worst after the words of the god had claimed she paid the ultimate price. Zavosh's hand on her shoulder brought her back to reality. The vipr gave her a nod and the queen lowered Hearthslayer. "Let's go." Together, they turned their gaze towards Blackfeather.

~ 34 ~
KEYRA

Being at the Citadel is affecting Keyra in strange ways. Everything she touches brings back flashes of memories, each less pleasant than the last. She has been here before. Something horrible happened and whatever has been holding it back all these years is deteriorating to expose the truth beneath. Peterfer's droning voice becomes background noise to the roar of her own thoughts. She can sense with renewing anxiety, as she scans the many titles in the grand library, that the answers she's looking for aren't here. She shouldn't be wasting her time with sorcerers she doesn't trust, but she can't seem to pull herself away. She's supposed to be here. The reason just hasn't been revealed to her yet.

She sees Tilsman coming around a bookcase and targets the boy vent her frustrations. "Where do you think you've been? Raiding the kitchens when you should be helping us do work?"

The boy is red-faced as though he has run some distance. She imagines the stairs must be as challenging for him as they are for her old bones. "Granma Keyra, I found something you should see. Well, two things."

He offers her a small, leather-bound journal and a

nondescript jewelry box. Keyra is drawn to them like a magnet. Peterfer watches curiously. "Where did you find those, Sir Tilsman?"

"Please don't ask that. I couldn't tell you and I definitely couldn't get back there on my own again."

Peterfer narrows his eyes at Tilsman. "The Citadel is full of many secret chambers and alcoves, little boy, and none of them are meant for you. You should be careful where you wander, or you may not make it back."

Keyra takes the objects from the boy and sits down on one of the overstuffed chairs that litter the library. Inside the box is a shattered pink shell. When she touches the pieces, she feels a hum that sings through her body. Like the dramatic pull of a wave before a tsunami's force, the hum turns to silence before it all comes crashing back. She remembers the boy, the battle-mages, the ceremony. She remembers the boy smashing a shell, *this* shell, that sent the Gods' Blood away before the sorcerers could capture it in the Magnium. She remembers her old name, her *real* name. Ayrek. Ayrek the Reaver, the agent of the Tower, a title she hasn't heard in three decades. Her hands shake and she drops the box. Peterfer rushes to examine them himself with an oversized monocle. "My goodness! I thought Ashlikani's Grace lost to Andriel. It is the most precious of leemoah artifacts. Legends say that when smashed, it calls upon the star to do the summoner's bidding for a short time. It is supposed to replenish after every ceremony, but it has been lost for decades. Where did you find it?" He turns to Tilsman with jaw slack.

The boy gives a rather impolite sigh of indignance. "Were you listening? I have no idea. There were lots of statues and random things like your shell. It was rather dusty, but these were the most interesting to me."

Keyra is silent, absorbing her realizations. Her previous life had been riddled with horrible choices and greed. Then, in her peace, she had been used by the sorcerers. She knows as well as anyone that the battlemage Vendar is long dead. She knows in her heart that he had either died after casting the spell on her, or shortly after. Peterfer could be one of the sorcerers sent to watch her. Of course, they would allow her into the Citadel. She must have found the magic without realizing it. Her heart drops as she looks to Tilsman. There is no doubt the boy has some strange connection to magic, but could it be a repeat of Luthen? How? He'd never even been to Kaper's Bay before she found him, and he was years too young to be present the night the Grace had been used. Why would Ashlikani give him the magic to protect?

Peterfer has cracked open the journal while Keyra digests. "Fascinating! This is an account from Frejith Aljez, a prominent figure in recent Gaffori history." The excitement in his voice is genuine. "There is so little information about her and Queen Wendwynn's rule before dictatorships were dissolved in favor of a Council leadership. I have researched her extensively, but almost every account has either been destroyed or wiped from memory." He turns the pages greedily.

"What happened to her?" Tilsman asks.

"No one really knows. We know there was a battle with Mangzar, but I have interviewed people that were alive during her reign, and even they cannot recall details. After that, there was the Council. It seems this diary is the accounts of her wife, Frejith, a rather powerful mind mage and a legend here at the Citadel."

Keyra had been alive during the reign of the last queen, and Peterfer must have been as well, considering his silver hair. She kept it to herself, but she recalled about as much as he claimed. There had been tension and bloodshed between Mangzar and Gafforah, and then as quickly as she had come, the queen was gone and the war with her. "You said there were more statues in the room, Tilsman? Perhaps there is more information about the forgotten queen."

Peterfer shrugs. "There absolutely could be. As I said, the

Citadel holds many secrets. If someone wanted her wiped from history, they would hide away the remnants of her rule. I can't help thinking this means something, don't you?"

Keyra agrees with him again. She wonders if she can trust Peterfer and his seemingly innocent exploration of information. He could be playing her, or he could genuinely be oblivious to the Citadel's conspiracy. "Do you think Wendwynn had something to do with the magic in Elgireth? If Ashlikani's Grace is here, and broken, then that must have something to do with what's been happening."

"Perhaps. It would seem our hero Tilsman has quite the connection to be drawn to these items in a room he shouldn't have been able to access. There is somewhere else we could check for further leemoah history. The King's Room will have records that may have slipped through the cracks of our attention here on land. The only problem is the key."

"It's locked?"

"Yes, and I'm afraid I'm on the outs with the sorceress who holds our fate in her hands. You see, Brielle—"

"Brielle what?" A tall woman with a pinched face stands at their table, her dark hair streaked with white and pulled back tightly. "There are strangers in my library," she states as she eyes the newcomers.

Peterfer jumps to his feet and opens his arms for an embrace. Brielle ignores him. "Ah, so good to see you, my little Bri. These are my companions and fellow knowledge hunters, Keyra and Tilsman. We have been here for quite some time. I apologize, I thought you would have noticed our presence in the library by now."

"I should hope nothing is out of place. Now don't play dumb, you need something. Spit it out."

"We need to get into the King's Room," Tilsman says before Peterfer can speak. "Ma'am," he adds quickly when Keyra pinches his earlobe.

Brielle lifts a thin eyebrow. "The King's Room? What could a child like yourself want in there? You hardly look like someone who does a lot of reading." She smiles at her cruel comment.

"Do you mind if we have a private word?" Peterfer asks with a strained smile. Keyra notices how he holds the sorceress with a familiar hand around the waist and walks her a short distance away. Their conversation is muted but she doesn't trust their body language.

"Tilsman, I need you to be ready in case we need to make a quick escape. We may be close to finding some sort of cure, but we may be even closer to stumbling on something more dangerous."

Tilsman opens his mouth to respond but the sorcerers have returned before he can. Brielle's lips are pressed in a disapproving line as she pulls the key from her robe. "You have five minutes. No more, do you hear? And if I notice anything out of place when you come out—"

"Yes, yes," Peterfer says impatiently. "You'll use my skin for book covers. It's nothing I haven't been threatened with before."

"I'm sure." Brielle narrows her eyes. The group follows the librarian to a marble door tucked between heavy bookcases. Keyra feels tears in her eyes as the sorceress unlocks the doors to the King's Room. Inside, even the air feels different. People did not pass through here, only memories. She wonders if she should remove her shoes to show respect.

Peterfer is surprisingly just as entranced. "I've never been in here before."

Brielle stands at the door with arms crossed. "And you won't get the chance again if you touch anything. Five minutes, and I'm going to wait right here."

Keyra tunes them out as her fingers itch to run over the displays. Each scroll left by a ruler is encased in glass and mounted on the wall beneath a portrait. She wishes she had years to truly study all of them. There are even the words of the first Gaffori king, Wavestrider, protected by magical spells that would keep the paper from aging. His portrait shows him much fatter than she would expect for someone with 'strider' in his name.

She is reminded of the little time they have and forces herself to look for leemoah faces. There are few, and they are significantly less ornate than their human counterparts. It seems even kings aren't immune to the tendency of humans to think of leemoahs as lesser beings. Keyra feels a twinge of guilt as the memories of her treatment of the water people were no different. Down at the end of the line, she stops at a watercolor portrait of a leemoah king. Gar'ithol. The last leemoah king before Uta'lihali was absorbed as a Gaffori colony along with Elgireth. His shrine has no candles or gold, but a book that Peterfer notices as he comes up beside her. "My goodness. This was supposed to have been returned to the leemoah people decades ago as a gesture of good will. Why would it be back at the Citadel?"

"Because of me," Keyra whispers. There is no hiding from her real memory now. She had sacked Uta'lihali in the name of Gafforah, using the Tower's affiliation as an excuse to further her own wealth and notoriety. She had given the order to take the book that held the majority of the leemoah culture and prophecies in its waterproof binding.

"There is no more queen, you cannot invoke her name!" Gar'ithol had been bloodied and shivering in the dry sun.

"Then she can stop me herself. The treaty between the Tower and the Citadel has been dissolved. The Bay belongs to us again and I don't see anyone here to tell me otherwise." She wasn't the only pirate that was taking advantage of the power shift in Kaper's Bay. Raiding parties had increased in number and brutality. Slaves were taken to be sold to Gaffori nobles who anticipated slavery becoming illegal. The progress made by the Forgotten Queen was unraveling before there was even confirmation that she was dead or alive. It didn't matter to

her. Leemoahs were weak, made to be slaves and rich in jewels they would do nothing with except hoard. She was doing them a favor.

Keyra turns away from the painting. The King had paid for his freedom with everything he had. Could she have unwittingly caused the damage in Elgireth? No, it didn't add up. Her attack on Uta'lihali had been decades ago. Why would they choose now to retaliate?

Peterfer notices her magnetism to the leemoah painting. "The Driftwood King. I hear he is still alive and as grumpy as always. I know leemoah live longer than humans, but I feel he has been ancient since I was a child." He chuckles and shifts his attention to another shrine.

Still alive. Keyra swallows hard. "He's alive? In Uta'lihali?" Something tells her the Reef is her next step.

"Outsiders are no longer allowed there. It seems they've had too many run-ins with pirates and, so the rumor goes, sorcerers." Peterfer clears his throat awkwardly.

"Granma." Tilsman stands by the stained-glass window and whispers sharply to Keyra. Far below, there is a ship arriving with a dozen sorcerers.

Brielle straightens. "Out, all of you. Your time is up."

"Keyra, take my hand." Peterfer touches her palm lightly and she grips hard. The world comes to a grinding halt around them.

"What are they doing here?" She knows she shouldn't trust the time mage, but she desperately hopes he is a true ally.

"I'm afraid there's more to the hospitality of myself and the Citadel than I told you. Your presence has stirred up interest from those who care more about your reason for being here than you as a person. If you think Gar'ithol has insight into the events on Elgireth, it is my duty to accompany you and discover what I can for myself. I must admit I have my own selfish reasons. Knowledge has always been an interest of mine, far outweighing my talents as a sorcerer. Firstly, it is imperative that we do not allow the newly arrived sorcerers to apprehend you. I may have a plan of action to ensure that."

Keyra hesitates as her head throbs. She has no choice. "What's your plan?"

"I'm going to throw you two out of the window. Brace yourself!" Time rushes forward. Keyra's stomach lurches with nausea.

She feels Peterfer lift her as though she is a child and lunge for the window. Before he tosses her through, he freezes time long enough to steal a quick kiss and drop her into thin air before she can slap him for his insolence. She sees Tilsman falling a split second later. She cannot scream as they plummet, nothing but water below them. She squeezes her eyes shut and braces for impact. When she opens them again, she is in Peterfer's arms on the ground. "How—"

He winks and in the same moment, she is standing on the grass and Tilsman is in the time mage's grasp. Brielle stands high above, screaming at Peterfer from the shattered window between calls to the sorcerers on the ship that their quarry is escaping. Peterfer helps Keyra onto the small boat that wasn't there a moment ago. His silver-marked face glows faintly and he pants from the exertion. "I have enough energy to freeze them for a few moments. If I may be so bold as to ask for your assistance, Lady Keyra, two rowers will get us farther than me by myself."

Keyra takes one oar and hands the other to Tilsman. "Me and the boy will do the physical work, you keep those bastards in one place for as long as you can. Ready to work off those tarts, boy?"

Tilsman whimpers but has little to say. He is still not himself.

Keyra's arms burn as each stroke of the paddle takes them farther away from the eerily still Citadel.

~ 35 ~

PEYNTER

When Peynter finally arrives at the Citadel after bartering passage back from Uta'lihali with a rather shifty looking merchant, he finds he has missed some great event. The peak of the Citadel's tower has been shattered, causing the jagged quartz to shoot light in random directions. The grounds, normally abuzz with students, are deserted. He hadn't expected a welcoming party, but some semblance of normalcy would be preferred. He grumbles to himself as he pays the merchant and hops ashore quickly before she can count the jewels and find his sum lacking. "What a nice greeting after failing to tell me they were going to attack the damn water people and then forgetting me in the underwater city." He marches towards the building with fists clenched. Rolith will get an earful for this, and Vendar too—if he hasn't died yet.

The first sorcerer he sees is Brielle, the nervous young librarian's assistant, darting through the main foyer. "Hello there! What's happened here?"

Annoyingly, she didn't seem to have noticed the water mage was missing. "What do you mean what's happened here? We tried to harness the source of all magic and it disappeared on us. Why don't you ask one of the first years? They can't seem to stop talking about it, and as you can see, I'm rather busy." She scurries off with her armful of books teetering precariously.

"Rude," Peynter mutters. He nabs the next student by the sleeve before he can disappear. "Where is Vendar? Beta? Rolith?"

"Who?" The boy crinkles his nose.

Peynter rolls his eyes and heads up the stairs to Beta's chamber. It seems that, again, he will have to do everything himself to get results. He finds her door flung open and her things scattered across the floor. A squarely built sorcerer wearing the tan scar of a fauna mage turns at the water mage's approach. His scent hound locks Peynter in golden eyes. "You're not allowed to be in here."

"If you're willing to help me, I'll gladly leave you alone. I've been gone for some time, and clearly, I've missed something. Where is Beta? Or Vendar? Perhaps you've heard of them? They're the only two battlemages left in existence. I would settle for Rolith, although he's never much help."

The sorcerer growls and the dog mimics. "I would be nicer to me if you need something. Vendar's dead, or at least damn close. Your friend Beta took off three nights ago and hasn't been seen since. Rolith was supposed to be looking for you but decided to go after her."

Every answer he got raised more questions. The water mage heads for the infirmary, holding true to his promise. He finds Vendar alone, shriveling in a bed. He looks like a ghost of the once great battlemage. His skin is mostly orange, glowing intensely. It would be beautiful if it didn't highlight the cracked, gray skin stretched across the withering man that flakes off by the second. He has lost enough weight to show the outline of his skeleton in garish detail. Peynter pauses, breathless. He has never seen the sorcerer like this. Battlemages had always seemed invincible, untouchable, and Vendar had been the pinnacle of strength. Peynter feels as though he should look away.

"Stop staring and come closer," Vendar calls. His voice is quiet but still commanding.

Peynter obeys. "They forgot me in Uta'lihali," he mutters. "Thankfully, I slipped away before the leemoahs caught me or they may have drowned me."

Vendar half laughs, half coughs. "Only you would face such a fate, Peynter. A water mage, being drowned by water people. Now stop thinking about only yourself for a moment. I need to tell you something while I still can."

"Hopefully, it's about what I missed?"

"Shut up, damn it. The Gods' Blood is gone, and we don't know where. The Citadel and the Tower will spend as much time as it takes looking for it, but it's not enough. I have my own power. A small taste I took for myself nearly thirty years ago. With it, I can influence minds in a way not even mind mages could imagine. It's been my secret weapon, and my heaviest burden. It is a magic not meant for mortals to wield. I have twisted it into a powerful mind-controlling power using knowledge of the Puppetmaster magic and my own battlemage abilities to create something of a personal curse. Unfortunately, it has made me fall apart faster than anticipated." Peynter is impressed into silence. How much has Vendar been influencing with his unprecedented abilities? He couldn't imagine someone who kept such power a secret would use it for good. It is no wonder Vendar is moments away from death. Such intense magic and knowledge were never meant to be used by the same person as it upset the delicate balance between the two. Vendar continues, "I want you to take it now and turn it into something less deadly. I want you to use it to find the Gods' Blood. Bring it back here to the Citadel where we can use it to help our own. Where it can save my kind."

Vendar is grasping Peynter's hand now, staring deeply at the water mage in a way that speaks more of desperation and hunger than the desire to do good. "You want me to take magic that is currently killing you?"

Vendar chuckles gratingly. "It has killed me already, Peynter. But I have abused it over the years. You are my choice because of your restraint, and your persistence. It will mold itself to best suit you. I know if anyone can find the source of all magic, it's you."

Peynter is skeptical. "What about your second favorite, Rolith? I can't be your first choice."

"Rolith is looking for Beta. I told him not to, but he insisted. He won't find her, and I don't believe he will return." Here, Vendar seems almost forlorn. "I can't sense my apprentice anymore. Either she's dead, or she has no intention of ever being found again. I blame myself. The last battlemage will fade from memory, as will I. But you have the chance to keep our legacy alive."

Peynter feels a pang of longing. The Citadel to him had always been home, made up of the people he cared about most. Beta, Vendar, Rolith, even the rockheaded Malvin. Without them, all he sees are greedy magic wielders living in a broken tower, surrounded by broken contracts with the privateers they were supposed to ally themselves with. "Of course."

Vendar closes his eyes and presses his lips into a line of a grimace. The orange in his skin glows like fire and Peynter feels a warmth through the hand holding his old mentor's. He wonders if Vendar feels as though he is burning from the inside out. "Do better," Vendar murmurs as the light fades and blinks out. The battlemage's hand falls limp, and the water mage is finally, completely, alone. Forgotten.

~ 36 ~
WENDWYNN

The capital of District Six was deserted. Every man, woman, and child capable of casting a spell or holding a sword would be fighting for Mangzar. The elderly and children were hidden in the secret bunkers beneath the city, prepared to fight to the death despite their disqualification from the Mangzarian army. Wen was not interested in them. She ducked to the shadows as a patrol passed by. Zavosh was beside her, breathing heavily as he tried to control the vipr bloodlust charging his veins. Being near her was enhancing his abilities and his desire for death. Wen tried to calm him with conversation while also distracting herself from what they may find in Fortress Blackfeather. "Do you remember the last time we fought against each other?"

The vipr's pupils were frighteningly small in his striped eyes. He grinned with bloodied fangs as they darted to the next building up. "I do. I fought Yo'aro. I remember defeating her and stopping myself from killing her because she lasted longer than anyone I'd fought before. It's a weakness of ours, to treasure excellent combatants as prize pets."

Wen smiled wryly. She'd been one such pet a lifetime ago.

They sprinted down the main road, not sensing any nearby enemies. "I'm glad you decided to join me—then and today."

The duo ducked behind a building at a sound farther down the street. Zavosh looked the queen over curiously. "You are distraught, Your Grace."

"I am worried. All the power of magic in the world, and if I can't save Frejith, then what is it for? Was I ever really strong?"

Zavosh's pupils started to expand the longer he went without battle. His breath was more even now. "Your Grace, pardon my frankness. But I know your story. You have come from less than nothing to the queen of a nation you aren't even a native of. You hold your own against an army that is supposed to be unbeatable. Not only did you find the source of Andreli magic, but you bound it to yourself and wield it despite having no natural connection to magic. You stand in enemy territory, beside a vipr that should want nothing more than to rip your head off. If that is not power, then perhaps only becoming a goddess would sate your thirst."

"You're lucky there was no one here to hear you say that, or I'd have to make an example out of you," Wen quipped as they made another press forward. "But since we are alone, and we may die in the next hour, I can finally admit something. I will never be happy." They took a moment in shadow, the queen's back pressed in exhaustion against the building that shielded them. She didn't care that there was intense sadness showing through her face, or that tears were welling in her eyes. "Each achievement sits like a rock in my stomach and comes with freshly horrible memories that do not disappear with success. Beneath it all, I am still the scared refugee from a land long forgotten. I will never have enough power to push past that."

Before Zavosh could respond, Wen moved forward. Her heart raced with anticipation as Blackfeather loomed closer with each step. Any other time, she would have taken a moment to examine the statues that led to the main gates. She would marvel at the architecture and at the murals that covered nearly every surface of nondescript stone. Instead, her vision was a tunnel. She could see nothing but the court-yard beyond the open doors and the distinct lack of guards. The new Warlord could be observing old traditions, or it could be a trap.

The emptiness became ominous as they stepped into the main yard where windows stared like black eyes surrounding them. There could be an assassin anywhere, but something told her this was not the case. The God's Blood pounded through her veins. She could feel her connection to the warriors back on the shore. She could feel their pain, their victory, their deaths. It was draining her at an alarming speed as the human body and mind was not equipped to handle such a burden.

"Wendwynn Forella." A chill went up her spine. She knew that voice. She never thought she'd hear it again. "You pride yourself on being a scholar, yet you consistently make mistakes when it comes to Mangzar. Never dishonor their dead by re-fusing to send them back to their homeland. Never leave one alive." Halthax ky Dzaxar stepped from the shadows around the yard with hands behind his back in a relaxed position. He wore Warlord armor and the colors of District Eleven.

"I'm glad to see you thriving. I assume you have claimed a new district for yourself. Although I couldn't tell there was more than one district present on the shore by the way we are carving through your ranks."

The Warlord breathed in deeply through his nostrils. "I can smell the magic on you, like a parasite. It's eating you alive and keeping you alive at the same time. I can't imagine how that must feel. Invigorating. Terrifying."

"Where is Frejith?" The queen could no longer hold back.

"Your wife, the spy? She has paid the price for her decep-tions." His eyes snapped to Zavosh. "Ah, and there is the other *isilth*. I recognize you. I should have known you would be clinging to the queen's skirts."

"Where is she?" Wendwynn's voice carried through the halls. She could not find the sorceress through their connection, even with the amplification of the God's Blood.

"Look behind you," Dzaxar snarled. Frejith hung from the battlements, wearing Mangzarian armor. "Did you truly think you could steal my son from me, humiliate me, and then allow me to live? I'm a vipr, foreigner! The only way we can be killed is by the sword." While he spoke, Wen remained calm. She felt the cold steel of Hearthslayer in her hands. She felt the prickle of the heat from the volcanic air and the harshness of each breath. She reached deep into the hot core of her stomach where magic brewed. She lent more strength to the soldiers on the front line.

Before she could move towards the Warlord, Zavosh did. Their swords crossed with a clang that reverberated through the yard. Wen could feel the rush of wind from the sharpness of their movements, their bodies cutting through the air like blades themselves.

The queen turned from the duel to climb the stairs to the wall with numb steps. Hearthslayer clattered to the stone as she knelt to pull Frejith up onto the ramparts and laid her head gently on her lap. She felt distant from the corpse in her hands. This was not her wife. This was some cruel prank played on her by the gods she had long denied existed. Even then she could not see the truth as it was. It disturbed her. Through all her successes, all she could see was how she had failed Grevin, and now Frejith.

As she clutched the sorceress's hand with white knuckles, she looked to the beach. The Bay Beast screeched over the wind. There were spears, swords and arrows protruding from its body. Finally, it had enough and slipped beneath the waves. In the yard, Zavosh was losing the fight to Halthax. Anger burned deep in her stomach and she lent her friend more power. The vipr's eyes glowed a strange shade of orange and he hissed like a rabid snake. The blows came so quickly they couldn't be followed with the naked eye.

Dzaxar stopped and his swords clattered from his hands. His eyes were open in disbelief. They turned to Wen, who met them with an unblinking gaze. She was glad her face was the last thing he would see. Blood ran from slashes through his armor, and he collapsed, dead.

Zavosh breathed heavily as he looked to his queen. She could see the pity in his eyes but wasted no time with it. "Your Grace—"

"We need to get her back. I can take her to Saltspire and have the gods heal her. I will use every last ounce of magic in Andriel if I have to."

He did his best to keep his expression neutral, but she could feel the disappointment cutting through. "Yes, Your Grace."

"When we return to the beach, be sure they have left that new Warlord alive. I would love to get to know him better. Oh, and Zavosh?"

"Yes?"

"Congratulations. You are rightfully the new Warlord of District Eleven."

His face was stone as he nodded his thanks.

~ 37 ~
KEYRA

The Reef has long been a symbol of leemoah success, from glowing flora to an array of sea life darting between corals. Even after she had sacked their city as Ayrek a lifetime ago, even when they had the source of their magic ripped from their star by the Citadel, they had moved forward without so much as a single act of retaliation. Is it weakness? A determination to keep their souls clean? She, like most landstriders, had never made much effort to understand the water people. Now she wonders if that disinterest has doomed them all.

Their little rowboat has moved slowly towards Uta'lihali, giving her ample time to study the journal Tilsman had found in the bowels of the Citadel's tower. At first Peterfer had been content to allow her to study in silence, but eventually his curiosity and frustration at being ignored had gotten the best of him and he had insisted on her reading aloud.

I have met someone. His name is Greysten and he is Qan. I have never met a Qan before, even in Nahem where dozens of cultures collide. He has a way with animals. He can coax a mouse from its hole or make an orven dance with a gentle request. That's another thing

I've learned, orvens are the mounts here in the fire land. No others can survive the harsh weather. I must admit, I find myself coughing much more often, and sometimes there is mysterious black substance in the bile.

I'm not writing to tell of my new and rather disgusting body habits. Greysten. He has worked in the stables for a few months now. He is the only one that can calm the orvens as their temperament is rather foul by nature. He also told me a secret. During his time here, he has been searching for a dragon. He found a scale it shed and intends to use it for a summoning spell.

"A dragon?" Tilsman pipes up. Keyra startles at his voice, having gone so long without hearing it.

"That's what I said, isn't it?" The annoyance at being interrupted is plain in her tone. "Now be quiet, I want to finish this before we get there."

He plans to use it to overthrow Halthax ky Dzaxar upon his return from the peace summit. He thinks he can usher these stubborn warrior people into an era of peace. I laughed at him, but he is serious. He is one to watch. We may have a potential ally here. I will continue cultivating a relationship with him in the hopes that if, by some miracle, he is able to overthrow Halthax, he will grant me access to information I otherwise wouldn't find.

"That name sounds familiar," Peterfer muses. "It could be . . . no, it's gone." He shakes his head in frustration. "Damn, why can't I shake these cobwebs?"

Keyra turns to the next entry.

Our conversation yesterday drifted to the war. He was surprisingly open with his condemnation of Mangzar's actions. He knows a lot about the Citadel and the culture of Kaper's Bay. He says he has friends there and has no intention of continuing the war if he were to become Warlord. I can't be certain, but he has said things that suggest he knows about the existence of the Gods' Blood. Any attempt to pry further without giving too much away has ended with him questioning my own honesty. He could be invaluable. But I believe I will have to tell him my true identity.

The next entry is nearly a week later and has an entirely new tone.

He let me ride the dragon today. Greysten named him Greywind. I teased him for it, but he was good natured as he always is. By Aryet, there is nothing more exhilarating and terrifying than riding a dragon! We were able to fly above the cloud cover and I saw the sun for the first time since I've been here. The days drag on when there is nothing to determine what hour it is, and no warmth to absorb from the air. I could have stayed up there for hours, but we had to land eventually. When we did, it was on a mountaintop above the black clouds. From there, it was as though we were floating above the mortal realm, untouchable.

I dropped my enchantments long enough to read his thoughts there, as he offered me wine and delicacies as though we were young lovers and not a warlord and a sorceress. He was thinking things about me . . . things that Wen would not approve of. He thought of the insurrections in the corners of his district, the ones he would have to quash before he could be confirmed as warlord. Even those thoughts faded when he looked into my eyes. I could see his intentions there without looking into his head.

What am I to make of this? I can manipulate his emotions to move our mission farther, yet Zavosh disapproves of my relationship with the warlord. He thinks the answers to our search can be found in a library. I find more purpose in people—books can be tampered with, but minds never lie. I tried to tell him I think Greysten is looking for the Blood as well. I can use what he's learned to help us. But Zavosh won't listen. He's written me off as spoiled royalty in over her head.

Keyra flips back a page to ensure she hadn't missed something. "She never explained how Greysten became warlord," she mused.

"Unfortunately, that's not uncommon for the more gifted sorcerers. They rely far less on reports and journals, instead choosing to use their power first and do paperwork later, if ever." Peterfer shakes his head in disgust. Keyra is willing to bet he isn't one of the 'more gifted' sorcerers.

We talked all night last night, drinking imported wine and swapping stories of our homelands. I tried to tell him I don't drink or swap the alcohol for water when he wasn't looking. But he insisted it was my duty as his general to partake and he never left the room. I have played along so far, hoping for the chance to pick his brain about the location of the Gods' Blood. Last night would have been a perfect opportunity if I hadn't drunk as well. While he knows my real name, I don't think he understands who I am to the queen, or why I came to Mangzar in the first place. I chose to keep my false story simple. I am here searching for the end to the war. That much is true. I told him I saw an ally in him, and that he would be a great warlord, and I wanted to support that. Also true. He said he made me a general for a reason. It would tie District Six and Gafforah together, ensuring a pact and transparency between our two nations. How could I tell him I don't want to stay here? I have become invested in his reign. I fear defying him will result in backlash. He could feel betrayed and grow angry. Then there is the added infatuation he has with me. That has increased significantly since he won the milta.

Last night, the wine and his silken words got to me. I let down my enchantments, allowing him to see the real me. I remember him touching my hair, now a bright yellow instead of the vipr black. His fingers are so damn gentle. He leaned forward to kiss me, but I stepped back and stumbled, him landing on me in a pile on the floor. He stared into my eyes for what seemed like ages, pressed close to me. They are a brilliant gray, not unlike Wen's, except darker. I have been gone from her for so long. Eventually I pushed him off me. My body had betrayed me at that point and my breath came in short gasps.

I became dizzy and laid down on his bed after emptying my stomach of the wine. He cleaned up the sick and must have joined me in the bed at some point after I had fallen asleep. I feel as though I have cheated on her. I feel dirty and alone, and so very homesick. I wish I could reach into Wen's mind to tell her how much I miss her, to summon her to me, to never let her out of my sight again. To untangle me from the mess of bedsheets I've found myself in.

This morning he had breakfast brought to his chamber and we laughed about the night before as comrades who had shared a night of heavy drinking. He will have me attend him to the confirmation hearing with the Conclave of Warleaders. Now that my mind has cleared, I find myself afraid. I cannot give up the opportunity to see what the rest of the Mangzarian leaders think about the Gaffori war. Wen will need to know every scrap of intelligence I will gather from them. That's why I'm here. To end the war.

Again, the tone changes in the next entry.

I woke up yesterday healing from a wound I do not remember receiving. There was an attempt on my life as I went to meet with a former associate. Warlord Greysten saved my life and came to my bedside, dressed in full regalia. Despite my injuries, he still wants me to join him at the Conclave. I am no longer physically fit enough to deny him his requests. For now, I am at his mercy while I heal.

As Mangzarian custom demands, the Warleaders came to Mount Thoyax to remind the inductee that they could take away his power whenever they wish before being confirmed. The Warleaders of Mangzar waited in the little-used council room.

I felt so small in their presence. I have been playing at this game without realizing how serious it is. An old vipr with tattoos that are almost as gray as his skin curled back his lips from his fangs. His orange eyes webbed with black found me with complete disdain. "Humans. Some would say you are lower than isilth."

Greysten nodded for me to stand beside his chair as he sat before the council. "Say what you will but refrain from doing so in my presence. My other associate is a dragon, although I didn't think I'd need to remind you."

"Don't think your luck at finding a dragon and binding it to you makes us respect you, human." The warqueen that spoke was Averix ky Her'ilth, leader of District Four. Wen made me memorize the Mangzarian Warleaders and their sigils on the boat to District Six. Her'ilth wore a black sun rising over a broken skull. "Let's get this over with. You have a dragon, and you think that makes you worthy of becoming Warlord."

Mangzarians are not known for ceremony or small talk. Warleaders have little patience for pomp. "I do," Greysten nodded, "but I am not fool enough to think that is enough proof for you all. I am also here to confirm my intention of using Mount Thoyax's strategic position to wage war against Gafforah."

Warlord Cerin was one of three humans in the room. His skin was the translucent ash color that confirms his family has been in the sunless land for generations. "We stood down while Warlord Halthax quibbled with the foreign queen. Why would you continue a war that is waged in the name of a vipr?"

I watched Greysten carefully. The Qan had been prepared for his takeover. But how far could he take it? "The slight against the previous warlord was a slight against all of us, including me. The Gaffori queen is our enemy. More than the internal wars that constantly plague this nation." I had known the more he tightened his grip on me, the less he showed interest in ending the war. But, to hear him request Mangzar unite against my wife was chilling. I feel like a fool for ever thinking I could manipulate him when I've limited my powers here. Had he thought the things he did about me to throw me off track? I could spend a lifetime analyzing what I did wrong during this mission.

"Be careful, boy, or you will find yourself the subject of one of our internal wars," Warqueen Meiy'ar ky Zeyra snapped.

"I mean no disrespect," Greysten said. "Mo'al'uri mestia Mo'al." Blood strengthens blood. "But to retake Saltspire, a sacred temple, there must be war. Do you know what the foreign queen is doing at this moment? She has taken the temple as a fortress. She trains priests to wage her war and she cuts down holy trees to form an abatis. Certainly, you cannot stand by while she desecrates holy ground." Greysten has been spying on Wendwynn. Nothing he says surprises me anymore.

Warlord Baa'rel is the only other foreign Warleader, hailing from Nath'iki. "If you are so concerned for our holy site, then why do you not destroy her armies with your dragon and claim it in the name of Mangzar once again?"

"I never thought I'd have to convince the great Warleaders of Mangzar to go to war against a small nation that has been a constant thorn in their side. I turn your attention to my general. She came to Mount Thoyax with the half-brother of the vipr killed by the foreign queen, left to be eaten by the fish, triggering the current conflict in the first place. They were both sent to my district to find the source of magic known as the Well of the Gods' Blood. During their time here, I have shown them my power and they have seen that there is no chance of the foreign queen's victory. Isn't that right, Maryin?"

He smiles at me. He keeps my real identity a secret for himself. I am certain he intends to use it another time, for another reason. "Yes, Warlord," I replied.

"I see no reason to deny the boy the seat. If he is set to defeat Gafforah, he will have earned it in blood. If not, we will demolish District Six," Warlord Gelvax spat. "I move to confirm Warlord Greysten, and to return Gafforah to the sea. Rath Noki Saryn."

"Mo'al thran ketar sa," the Warleaders muttered in unison.

"Very well, Warlord. You shall have our confirmation. But foreign Warleaders face more tests than any others, as Warlord Baa'rel can attest. Your first will be the war on Gafforah. We will not aid you, and we will respect the results as they are." Warqueen Zeyra leered at the humans. "There once was a time when only viprs could be Warleaders, and certainly only Mangzarians. There are those of us who would see that the old way returns. I cannot say I hope you succeed."

There was a chorus of agreements and each Warleader stood to say their piece. One by one, they announced their names, their districts, and confirmed Greysten as warlord. There was silence when they came to District Eleven. "Where is Warlord Lxan? He had the shortest distance to travel," Warqueen Tyveliv said impatiently.

"He is also the fattest," Gelvax noted. "We cannot vote without a unanimous approval. We will have to wait for him."

"I'm afraid the previous warlord of District Eleven won't be coming," a familiar voice purred as a ghost stepped from the shadows. Halthax ky Dzaxar limped heavily and was worse for the wear, but there was no doubt it was him. Greysten reached for his weapon, but Dzaxar waved it away. "Don't trouble yourself, I have no need for my old land. District Eleven gets a nice breeze from the south."

"You have defeated Warlord Lxan in combat?" Cerin was suspicious given the warlord's ragged appearance. "I don't have to tell you that anything less is an insult to our way of life."

"I know no other way," Dzaxar smiled as he tossed a head on the table in the middle of the Warleaders. Lxan's neck was nearly as thick as his skull. I don't trust for a second that Dzaxar had earned his title honorably. Lxan was one of the greatest warriors and would be hard pressed to lose to someone who had been floating in the bay for days. With no witness present, however, there was little to challenge his claim. "I, Halthax ky Dzaxar, present myself as Warlord of District Eleven, and endorse the war on Gafforah. The foreign queen left me adrift instead of taking my life, throwing another insult at Mangzar and our beliefs. Confirm me here, and District Eleven shall fight alongside District Six. Rath Noki Saryn."

"Mo'al thran ketar sa!" Their synchronized growl gave me chills.

Keyra flips through empty pages. That can't be it. What happened to the sorceress? Why didn't she use her magic to escape the Warlord? Keyra's head throbs and she shuts both her eyes and the journal. Perhaps finding the leemoahs will produce some answers and give her peace of mind at last.

~ 38 ~

WENDWYNN

The queen that returned to Mount Thoyax's beach was not the same one that had left it. The air stirred around Wen from the push and pull of magic inside her. Behind her was an orven carrying Frejith's body. Zavosh walked a few paces behind, holding Halthax ky Dzaxar's head.

The silence that met them was deafening. The Mangzarians would never surrender, but they had done their equivalent, standing in one place with weapons drawn. The Gaffori army waited around them for orders. Any move forward would be met with volcanic forged steel. Any step backwards wound signal the Mangzarians to go on the offensive once more. Tradition dictated they would remain that way until the last of them died, or until the enemy left their shores. Their Warlord's dragon was dead, its wings torn to shreds by the jaws of the Bay Beast after it had clawed its way out of the ground. She caught sight of Greysten himself, holding the same stance as his people. Wen allowed Sir Embyr to take the orven and Frejith with instructions to place them on the nearest skiff. The queen walked through the crowds that parted like the rippling of a ship's wake. She stood at a distance from the Warlord and raised her voice above the ocean breeze. "You have been defeated,

Warlord Greysten. Your ally is dead, and District Eleven has a new leader. The other districts are not here, which means they do not support your war. Your army has lost their magic, and you have lost your dragon. Gafforah is victorious." The words tasted bitter and bland in her mouth. "I can restore their powers, but only under specific restrictions. You will come with me to Saltspire and allow a *milta* to take place to replace you as Warleader. Mangzar, specifically District Six, will abandon the war with Gafforah. Saltspire will remain part of Gaffori territory. In return, I want only the foreign, former warlord as a prisoner of war. Normal trade operations will resume between Mangzar and Gafforah, and borders will be respected. If you agree to these terms, warriors of the fire mountains, stand your ground as we leave."

There was no answer from the enemy, as expected. No one stopped the Gaffori that approached and subdued Greysten with little struggle. He was no warrior without his animal, and no warlord without his people. The Gaffori began retreating to their vessels little by little. It was impossible for the queen to gauge their exact feelings on her actions, but there would be time to discuss that and their future once they were back in familiar territory. She knew without a doubt there would be controversy.

Wen was the last one to step off Mangzarian soil. She waited for a moment with the bay at her back, watching the soldiers, waiting for a challenge. Hearthslayer hung heavy on her back. No challenge came. She nodded to Zavosh, standing once again among his own people. He would have to prove himself worthy of his new status, but such was the way of Mangzar. There was nothing more she could do for him. Then she was gone.

Once on board her ship, the storm came. "Your Grace, you cannot expect Mangzar to respect the terms of their surrender. They have no morals. They respect no contracts."

Wen looked wearily at Yo'aro. She wished she had Grevin's

council and Frejith's strength to guide her words. Even Commander Nalag had been lost to her. "They are warriors, not soulless murderers, Admiral. They will respect the terms because at their core they are honorable, and everyone who had a quarrel with me is dead or captured. They have no reason to continue violence towards Gafforah now."

The Admiral was unappeased. "You have sentenced Zavosh to death, Your Grace. He will not last as warlord, especially with his history of being an *isilth* and supporting your cause. We could have used him in Gafforah."

"That may be correct, Admiral, but I saw him cut down Halthax ky Dzaxar myself. When I asked whether it was a task he was up to, he wanted nothing more than to accept it. He may be Gaffori, but he is a vipr at heart, and he will only find real peace within his own nation. If it puts your mind at ease, however, I wouldn't worry too much about his Warlord career." She had promised to restore magical abilities, not remove extra power given to Zavosh.

Yo'aro accepted the look of finality she gave her. There would be no more discussion of the matter. The queen turned to address the rest of the leaders on her ship. "I will give further instruction on the future once we return to Saltspire. We may have won the war, but there are many changes that must happen within our own nation to ensure peace and prosperity."

Once they were satisfied, Wen retired to her cabin to wait out the rest of the trip. Frejith was there, laid out on the bed, covered with a white sheet. Safe in the confines of the cabin and alone with her wife, Wen finally allowed herself to cry.

By the time they reached Saltspire, her eyes were dry, and the puffiness gone. It was time to don the mask of queen once again. The priests greeted her with cheers and there were congratulations for all. Wen did her part to accept praises and gifts. She made her way through the crowd to the small room where

Greysten waited for her. He was bound and had received quite a beating either during the battle or after at the hands of the queen's guards. She could not tell for certain.

He looked up at her entrance, eyes glossy from a head wound. "Congratulations, Your Grace. You won the race."

"You mean the war?" She chose her words carefully.

"We both know that was a byproduct. I knew as soon as I saw your ships on the horizon. You found the Gods' Blood and have harnessed it for yourself."

Her face betrayed nothing. "How does a Qan come to know of the Gods' Blood?"

"It affects us the same as it does everyone in Andriel. Of course, if you were from our world, you would understand that. Like most, I imagined it an abstract concept rather than a physical entity. Imagine my surprise when a young sorcerer from your own Citadel fled to Qai, looking for an ally in overthrowing you. He promised power incarnate, the ability to control all magic, in return."

"A young sorcerer?" Wen had many enemies and few friends among the magic users of Elgireth. Most resented her for destroying the battlemages. What they didn't know was she hadn't killed them all. One she had spared and exiled, but she had been female. The only other sorcerer she knew who would harbor such a grudge and had managed to slip through her fingers was one she would dismember if she ever saw again.

"He had orange streaks and quite an ambitious thirst. You would have liked him."

"I used to," Wen admitted. It was him. Vendar. There was no doubt. "So, you partnered up with the battlemage, and you decided to wage war on me through Mangzar?"

"It was flawless—or should have been. With Dzaxar starting the war, all I had to do was get rid of him. Then you did that for me. I hadn't planned on you finding the Gods' Blood so quickly or turning the temple into a fortress. I, like you, assumed it was on the mainland of Mangzar. I had heard stories of your tendency to become obsessed. I had hoped that the death of your wife would send you into a spiral. I still think it's possible."

She didn't like his confident attitude and reckless smile. He was too comfortable, even now. "This sorcerer, where is he now?"

"I could not tell you that if I wanted to. He is probably halfway to Lizaq by now, or at the Well himself. I'm beginning to think he undersold you on purpose. It seems there are quite a few battlemages around here now."

"Not for long." Wen frowned. She had no intention of allowing such powerful sorcerers to exist again. "One last matter. I saw you and Frejith together among my visions. I saw how much she trusted you." She swallowed touching on her suspicions of adultery. There was no place for that now. "You betrayed her, and you murdered her. The question is how am I to adequately punish you before I take your life?"

She took pleasure in the fading amusement on the warlord's face. "It wasn't my original intention. Halthax insisted on her death as a condition of our alliance. He was not immune to a father's love, it would seem, or the desire for vengeance. I much liked Frejith, to be honest. She was full of fire and tasted like summer."

Wen saw red. Her hand closed around his neck. She could feel his lifeforce there, pounding through his veins. "I've always had a problem with killing my enemies. When I have taken lives, it hasn't felt like enough. Why should someone who's done me wrong be granted permission to rest forever, in blissful ignorance of their actions? But I've also seen what happens when I don't ensure they're never a problem for me again." Wen felt thirsty. She wanted to drink his lifeforce, the sensation stemming from the vipr magic she had absorbed. "Usually, viprs consume souls when their victims are in their last moments of life. I wonder what happens when your body is healthy? I imagine it would be incredibly painful, leaving you helpless and broken." Her hand tightened around Greysten's neck. The Qan's eyes opened in horror. Wen leaned close, whispering a breath away from his lips. "I imagine it will cause a slow death." She breathed in deeply, the air tasting like warm dirt and metallic sunshine on the roof of her mouth. She could feel his soul charging her, causing her mind to swirl. It was easy. It was satisfying. And she had no control over it.

When she shook the feeling enough to control her own thoughts, Greysten was dead. His twisted face suggested he had perished in agony, the fibers of his being shredded. The queen left the chamber with gritted teeth and a new headache. She wondered if it was more from withdrawal or the fact that even killing Greysten had been bittersweet. She couldn't think about her own emotions now. Her council would be waiting for her. There was too much to be done, and all she could picture was Frejith's blue face decaying by the moment. She was running out of time.

Lekala caught up to her long strides as she passed down the hall. "Your Grace, I wanted to reiterate that we of Saltspire will continue to back you as long as you require. Remaining a Gaffori stronghold will be our highest priority."

"You're not keeping your battlemage powers," Wen snapped grumpily. She wanted another soul to quell the thirst in her gut. It was no wonder the viprs constantly sought out violence. "I have kept the council waiting this long, they will not mind another few moments. Has Frejith been taken to the catacombs?"

"Yes, Your Grace, as you instructed. Although, it is tradition to embalm the body or at least wrap it before burial." If Lekala was disappointed about losing his magic, he didn't let on. He was wise not to irk her further.

"She is not going to be buried." Wen turned down the tunnel that would take her to the Well. There were no guards or other barriers. Wen was the only one who could pass through the doors besides the guardians as she had paid the price in full. "I'm going to heal her."

Lekala paused as they made their way into the cold underbelly of the island. "Your Grace, you can't be serious. She has been dead for some time now."

"Know your place, priest. As a sworn ally to me, you cannot question my instructions. It is not you that wields the power of the Well."

Lekala bowed respectfully as they reached the doors where Frejith was laid out on a white sheet per the queen's sharp instruction. "Of course, Your Grace, but I do hope to impose with some advice for someone as powerful as yourself. The dead are not meant to be raised. It is not natural."

"Do you dare test me?" Her voice was just as powerful despite being laced with grief.

"Never." The High Priest stood back as the queen touched her wife's cold cheek.

"You may go now." The fire had gone from Wen's voice. The next step was for her and Frejith alone. When he had left, Wen closed her eyes to feel the sensations around her. The darkness and the tingle of electricity was strong, but she was no longer afraid. This power was hers now. The whispers welcomed her instead of warning her.

She lifted Frej like a child. The sorceress was nearly a foot shorter than the queen in life, and now she seemed smaller than ever. They passed through the stone doors and entered the grotto. Instantly, Wen felt the push back. "Get out," the walls whispered. The empty Well left a menacing presence within the cavern. Devoid of color, it was nothing more than another cave within the catacombs traced with strange writings and runes.

"You can't stop me." Wen grimaced. She closed her eyes. She would have to return the magic to the Well. She would have to release the power she had gained and the power she had given.

Everything for Frejith. She reached her left hand out and called back the power of her artificial battlemages. She reached her right hand out and released the Mangzarian dark and vipr magic to its rightful owners. She raised them both above her head and there was a second of silence. Colors danced around her fingertips and tugged greedily at her curls. She could release it all back to the Well, where it belonged. She could bury Frejith and set things back the way they were. Her eyes filled with tears as she looked at the sorceress's face. It was her fault she had died, so why shouldn't she be willing to sacrifice everything to set it right? She wondered what Grevin would say. He would warn her of her father's tendency to become obsessed. He would tell her to be different, to break the cycle. He would tell her to make the harder choice because it was right. Then he would tell her it would be alright. That she had always been better than her blood.

Her shoulders shook as her arms dropped to her side. She felt more alone than ever. "I'm sorry," she murmured to the corpse. "I'm sorry I sent you away, and that even when I have the power to, I can't save you." She closed her eyes as she held out her arm to the Well. The magic glowed as it danced to its place. The cave shimmered with an immortal light that burned the tears from her cheeks.

Wendwynn stood there for what felt like a lifetime, watching the colors dance eternally. If she had found it, someone else would. There would be more heartache, more death, and more greed that followed her. She reached for the cord around her neck, bearing a curly seashell in a soft shade of pink. Ashlikani's Grace was an artifact that belonged to the leemoah but had been gifted to her in a different time. She was supposed to give it back. She sent a quick prayer that they would forgive her for using it once more. The queen dropped the shell on the stone, smashing it with the heel of her boot.

There was a flash of light and a sudden gust of wind.

Ashlikani's Grace could only be used once every thirty years and was reforged after each Star Shepherd ceremony. It was meant for the most dire of circumstances where the goddess of the star would control a situation long enough to protect the summoner. With no imminent danger sensed, the magic essence tugged hard on Wendwynn's clothes and hair before it settled into the form of a leemoah mare, young and cloaked in waves. "What is this?" she asked in an ethereal voice. "Surely a human would not disregard our culture enough to waste my Grace for no reason."

Wendwynn fell to her knees. She wasn't sure why. She didn't respect the gods. But she was asking something massive of Ashlikani. It felt right. "Your power has saved me once before, in the end of the previous cycle. Now I fear I must abuse it once again. The Gods' Blood is not safe here, goddess. If I could find it and be found worthy to wield it, others can as well. I fear the purposes they will use it for, and the consequences. Please, I beg you to take it. Hold it within the star and protect it where it cannot be reached by mortal means."

She bowed her head, afraid to look up at the silent star. Finally, Ashlikani spoke. "You ask something of me that I cannot guarantee. The Gods' Blood is meant to be held here and protected by battlemages. Ah, but there are no more battlemages, are there, Wendwynn Forella?"

Wen flinched. "I do not regret wiping out the battlemages. And if you know I was responsible, you will know why I did it."

The goddess's voice softened. "Yes, I do know. I also know that you could have abused this power yourself. You could have brought your wife back and kept it. Perhaps you would have wielded it wisely and justly. Perhaps you would have brought the apocalypse on Andriel, as your father brought it on Alayada."

Wen sucked in a sharp breath. Hearing the name of her continent spoken aloud brought back sharp pains in her heart.

Ashlikani continued, "I may not be a goddess recognized by many, but that doesn't make me any less powerful. I will grant your request, little mortal. Not because I agree with you, or I want to help you. But because I want to protect my people, the leemoahs. They have seen enough hardships for lifetimes and the Gods' Blood will be yet another weapon in the world's arsenal against them. I want them to feel safe in their peaceful ways. I will hold it."

"Thank you," Wendwynn whispered. "One more thing, please. There are books detailing a magic for those who were not born with the gift." Her eyes were glued to Frejith, who had fought so fervently to warn the queen of the dangers of magic. "They call it the Puppetmaster. I want it wiped from the face of Andriel. I don't want anyone else to suffer because of it."

The goddess frowned deeply. "I can take the ability from you and nothing more. It is up to you to destroy the physical connections to the Puppetmaster magic. I will warn you—I don't know the effect it will have. Magic from knowledge is not meant to mix with raw magic."

"Of course. Thank you." Wen closed her eyes.

"It will take some time," Ashlikani said not unkindly. "My power is incredibly delicate and must maintain balance. You will have to protect the Well for a while longer." Wen nodded her agreement. "What will you do now?" The goddess was genuinely curious. There were some characteristics not unique to mortals.

"I have done my damage here." She took a long pause, pondering the question and her answer. "I think I will go home."

She shut her eyes tight and covered her face with her arm as the cavern glowed with a powerful light. There was a sound like a stormy gale passing around a thousand windchimes, and then darkness.

~ 39 ~

KEYRA

She can see abnormalities in the water that suggest they are no longer alone. The boat lurches as they are pushed forward by a leemoah beneath them. It comes to a sudden stop a few moments later and the oars are wrenched out of Peterfer's hands.

"Everyone stay calm," the time mage commands with a shaky voice. "The last thing we need is to scare our hosts."

A head pops out of the waves, slick with seawater and glistening blue. The leemoah looks at each of them fiercely. "We no longer accept landstriders around our capital city. We will push you to the nearest island and you will leave us forever. Do you understand?"

Being here has triggered more of Keyra's memories. She feels ashamed for intruding. "I will be glad to accept any terms you have for us. But I must ask that I meet with the king first about an urgent matter."

The guard tilts his head curiously. "You look like an Elgir and speak like an Elgir, but you cannot be one of our neighbors. Last I heard, they were dead or held upright with dark magic." His tone suggests he has lost no sleep over the matter.

"That is exactly what we're here to discuss, my good sir," Peterfer pipes up.

The guard frowns deeply. "I will pass your message to the king, but I guarantee no audience. He may decide for us to drown you here in your boat." He gives a snort and vanishes beneath the surface. Keyra starts to feel lightheaded. Whatever truth they're getting close to, she isn't supposed to know it.

For what seems like an eternity baking in the unforgiving sun, the humans wait in the boat. The vessel lurches forward at an unsettling speed with no warning. Tilsman is nearly thrown over the side and Keyra grips the railing with renewed terror. They are rushing out towards the sea and out of the swimming distance of the nearest land. Are the leemoahs going to drown them? She is seized with sudden guilt at dragging Tilsman here. She should have left him on one of the islands where he could eat his fill of sweets and be somewhat safe.

As suddenly as they start, the boat comes to a halt. They have pulled up to a large raft with sawed-off posts on each corner as though it had held a raised building at one point. The leemoah guard pops his head out of the water. "Get out and wait."

Faced with no other choice, the humans obey. Peterfer offers Keyra his hand to step out and Tilsman struggles to half-roll, half-pull himself out of the boat. In the middle of the sea, there is no respite from the autumn sun. Keyra sweats but refuses to complain if Tilsman isn't. The poor Wahethian is as red as his curls.

From the waves around them, six guards emerge and land neatly on the raft. Between them, the water bulges and breaks around the massive form of King Gar'ithol. The stallion is ancient, his scales a dull shade of gray and his body flabby from lack of swimming. His head feathers are thinning and have been replaced with golden chains. He squints angrily at the sun while attendants struggle to spread an awning over their king's head as quickly as possible. "I am too old to be above the water," he grumbles as the visitors bow respectfully. He only acknowledges them once his shade has been established. "You three don't look like assassins or warriors. Although, I've learned that sorcerers cannot be trusted." He squints at Peterfer. "You stay in the boat and take the child with you." He waves dismissively at the boy and the time mage.

Only when they have been shuffled away does the king turn back to Keyra. "You are much older and fatter, but do not think I've forgotten you. So, tell me, Ayrek the Reaver, what brings you back to my Reef? Speak quickly so I may kill you and be done with it."

Keyra's throat is dry. She hadn't expected to be recognized. "I understand you're upset about the past. I am too. I'm hoping we can work together and discover the source of the magic currently plaguing Elgireth."

Gar'ithol chuckles in raw amusement. "You think we don't know what's happening? You humans are all the same. You think you can use us and trick us into helping with your cause and then toss us aside like an empty shell. Disgusting." He scrapes the wooden raft with his webbed foot, a cultural sign of distaste. "I have lived a long time, Ayrek, and I have trusted landstriders on more than one occasion, and every time it ends with our traditions being trampled and our cities ransacked."

Keyra wishes Peterfer was close to pass along the information she would learn here in case of her untimely murder. "The leemoahs weren't the ones to cause the magic, were they?"

"We cannot take full credit, although I would like to. It would seem the greed of the landstriders has come back to bite them. For the past two cycles of the Star Shepherd's ceremony, there has been human interference. Thirty years ago, members of your Citadel sought to steal her power through deception, and her power waned. Ashlikani's magic was stolen away, along with the Gods' Blood she had been tasked to protect. Leemoahs may be the main worshippers of the star goddess, but we are not the only ones affected. Like the faces of Aryet and Akai, without Ashlikani's magic, the dark side of our power gathered in the sky. We saw it, and we renewed our sacrifices and our prayers to protect those of us under the waves. The ceremony was supposed to take place a month ago, but Ashlikani wasn't strong enough to even tell us who the next sacrifice would be. Now, her power is gone, and the darkness has seeped into the people that used to be protected by her. I'm sure you have seen the effect on the islands. Why it has affected your people in such a horrific way is beyond our knowledge. Something has twisted the power inexplicably. What we do know is that we are finally free, even if we wither away with our star. We could have warned someone, we could have done something, but as history has repeated over and over, it would have ended with us being betrayed and enslaved, just like the last cycle. Instead, we decided to let the humans reap the consequences of their actions against us and against our magic. Let them see what happens when they take advantage of Ashlikani and her people." He spits on the raft contemptuously.

"Even now, it has taken weeks for someone to approach us to find the cause. If anything, it shows how little we mean to the human world, and how stupid they are to think themselves separate. We are all connected, Ayrek the Reaver, and while leemoahs have been accepting of this fact for centuries, somehow landstriders have managed to blatantly ignore it." He jerks his head at Tilsman in the boat. "I can sense Ashlikani within your friend. He carries her, and the Gods' Blood, I'd bet my fins on it. I'm guessing he appeared in Elgireth right as the dark magic started taking effect? He is a conduit, directing the lightning strike of divine karma towards your own."

Keyra remembers Tilsman's immunity to the dark magic, his appearance, and the sudden change in Elgireth's atmosphere. Her head throbs but she can tell it is her own pain, not caused by any spell. "You are angry, I can tell, Your Majesty. I am sorry for the anguish your people have gone through, and I know I am more than partly to blame for it. But I cannot let everyone I know die. Please, tell me if there is a way to reverse this and set things as they should be."

"Disgusting," Gar'ithol growls, "That you would even ask that of me. I owe you nothing."

Keyra reaches in her robe for the box containing the shattered pieces of Ashlikani's Grace. "Of course not. I owe *you* everything. I will set it right as I can, starting with returning this."

The guards tense their grips on spears as the king accepts the box. He sucks in a breath at the sight within. "Ashlikani's Grace. She was a gift to a long-lost queen, a gift meant to be temporary. We haven't seen it since." He holds a withered hand over the pieces, and they tremble before fusing together in one quick movement. Gar'ithol breathes in deeply as though enjoying a pleasant scent. "It is good for her to be home once again." The suspicion returns to his face once more. "How did you come across it? Did you steal it as you did our ancient texts?"

"I found it. In the Citadel," Keyra inclines her head respectfully. "Along with many other artifacts that belong to the Reef. I cannot atone for all the sins of my people against yours, but I hope Ashlikani's Grace is a start. Please, tell me how to heal the land and water."

The king hands the shell to one of his guards, who vanishes beneath the ocean's surface with it. "*Alip erdall ga eseen.* What has been wronged must be made right. Whatever magic that was brought to Elgireth to disturb the skies must be put back. Ashlikani must be restored to her former glory. Only then will the land and water be given a chance to heal."

"And what magic is that?"

"We do not know. We will not help you find what went wrong, it is the problem of the landstriders. We only have enough power for ourselves."

Keyra looks deep into the rheumy eyes of the ancient stallion. She sees a spark of anger there, but also sympathy. Unlike his guards, he almost speaks kindness. "Your people have suffered greatly at the hands of humans and even your own kind. I can't imagine how you must feel, being asked to help someone who has caused you nothing but pain."

Gar'ithol clears his throat wetly. "I have lived through many generations, Ayrek the Reaver. I have seen great people turn bad and bad people turn angelic. There is no sense to the timeline we exist in and there is no reason to try to understand it. All we leemoah can do is trust in the balance Ashlikani promises our region. We are still here, after the horrors we have experienced, and we are not going anywhere. Now do some good to atone for the bad that has defined your past."

The king doesn't wait for a response and hobbles to the raft's edge where his guards help lower him into the water. Keyra watches them disappear one by one until they have all vanished, leaving behind the oars and a heavy burden of shame on her shoulders.

Their tiny group is silent as they return to their boat and leave the Reef. Tilsman has retreated into himself and ignores the snacks in his pockets. He doesn't seem to mind the rocking of the water. Even Peterfer's cheerful nature has been clouded. In another reality, they would dock in Denali and regroup, but the undead are visible even from their position in the water.

Keyra watches Peterfer, who is lost in thought. "You're a time mage, aren't you? Can't you help us set things right by looking at what was done wrong in the past?"

The silver scarred man can't make eye contact with her. "I can't; using magic has always been difficult for me. My personal pride has come from being knowledgeable, but it would seem even that is inadequate. Although, I don't need to see into the past. I was there. I am part of the problem, I fear, which is something I had hoped to avoid telling you." Keyra waits patiently for him to continue. She is in no position to judge someone for their past. "I was not always a time mage, and my name was not always Peterfer. It was Peynter, and I was a water mage. I was gifted some of the Gods' Blood by an old mentor and used it to change my abilities. If I had fully understood that being a time mage meant I would age faster than nature intended, I may have considered my options more seriously."

Was there anyone blameless in the destruction of Elgireth? "A small portion? What happened to the rest of it?" There is time later to delve into the moral decisions her ally had made.

"I don't know, but I know it used to be on Saltspire Island."

Tilsman perks up at the mention of the name. "That's where the battlemages came from, isn't it? My mom used to tell me stories about them. They were the most powerful sorcerers."

"We're going to need a bigger boat, preferably with sails, if we're going to make it nearly to Mangzar," Keyra comments wearily. Her shoulders are sore, and her hands are covered in blisters. Aging was supposed to mean she didn't have to do manual labor anymore.

Peterfer looks longingly towards the Citadel. "They have plenty of good ships on Everlyn. I suppose it's too much of a risk to go back there. Very well, if I am part of the problem, I should be part of the solution. Sit back and relax, you two. I will get us there."

She blinks, and they are off the western coast of Gafforah. Peterfer is noticeably thinner, and his hands are cracked and bleeding. He droops in exhaustion. "This is as far as I could get us in one go. Saltspire is on the horizon, but I'm afraid we may not be alone. Someone has beat us here."

There are ships blocking their path. Keyra recognizes the banners as Tower. They make no move to attack but circle the stranded raft curiously. Keyra sees the face of the leemoah sla-ver, Captain Zai, among those on board. "Can you get us out of here?" she whispers to Peterfer. The time mage shakes his head wearily, unable to find the strength to speak.

Keyra curses as the waverunner nears. El'rozai smiles coldly down at them. "Will you look at this. It's the beginning of a bad joke. A sorcerer, an old woman, and a redheaded child are floating in the bay. Care for a lift?"

"We don't need your help, thank you," Keyra snaps. "Your help has never been beneficial for me or mine."

"It seems someone is getting their memory back. Under Akai, Ayrek the Reaver. Last I checked, a contract with the Tower was for life. It's time to come back to work now."

"If you know me, then you know what I'm capable of," she bluffs, "so you'd do well to leave us alone and be on your way."

"I don't think so." The waverunner pulls up alongside their raft and ropes are lowered. "Come on up and we will consider allowing you your life despite your betrayal of your brotherhood." There are crossbows lowered at Tilsman. Keyra's mouth goes dry, and she feels helpless. They have no choice but to be hoisted onto the ship where they are promptly surrounded by curious Tower agents. Keyra feels eyes examining her especially closely. The pirates whisper amongst themselves.

"That can't be her, can it? She's old and fat."

"That's what happens when you let yourself go soft."

"I heard they wiped her memory and made her simple."

Finally, she has enough. "If you keep it up, you'll find out just what I'm capable of, even as a fat old lady." Her growl silences the curious voices.

Captain Zai turns to address the sailors. "Lady Ayrek is a celebrity among us and will be treated as such. We're going to help her get where she's going and if I hear of anyone showing her anything less than the utmost respect, there will be consequences." The crew bows at his words but the tension in the air remains. Keyra feels for the comforting outline of the knife under her waistline. Her reputation and her current condition are too tempting for an ambitious recruit to solidify their fame. Peterfer would be of no use, he is slumped against the railing of the ship, looking as pale as his scar.

El'rozai approaches her as his crew disperses to their duties. "Tell me, Lady Ayrek, where is it that you need to go today? We are at your disposal."

"You can drop us off in Ulden, and no more. I would rather not spend more time with the Tower than absolutely necessary."

"I will try not to take offense to that," the leemoah says indignantly. "But we both know Ulden isn't your final destination. May I venture a guess? Saltspire is especially beautiful this time of year."

"Perhaps we should speak in your cabin," Keyra says levelly, showing as little emotion as possible. The Captain leads her to the small box that serves as the captain's cabin on the waverunner, too cramped to hold anything except a chest of scrolls and a small desk. There isn't even a chair to sit on while studying maps.

When they are alone, the leemoah drops the friendly ruse. "I'm no fool, Ayrek, or whatever you call yourself these days. You remember, don't you? You remember everything. Something has changed since the last time we met at your son's home in Nahem."

"Yes, I remember. I remember who I was before I was spelled, and the cruelty of the Citadel. I remember the Tower working closely with the sorcerers and the shady deals that were made. I remember how I am to be used, and how you all managed to lose the source of all magic in Andriel on more than one occasion." She smirks. It is the singular pleasure she gets out of the entire situation.

El'rozai's eyes glint dangerously. "Then you will remember that we can take your life as easily as we gave it to you. If you're looking for the Gods' Blood as you were instructed, you're not going to find it on Saltspire Island. It hasn't been there for decades."

"It's a good as any place to start. Do you have a better idea?"

The captain's tail flicks beneath his cloak as he pours salt ale for them both. "I do. I think you've already completed your mission, and that's why the memories are returning. I think you've been lugging him around with you everywhere because the spell makes it impossible for you to leave him behind. I can sense it on him, like I did on that boy thirty years ago. What I couldn't determine is why the boy is so young if he absorbed the power so long ago, and why him? It took quite a bit of digging, cashing in favors, and asking for new ones, but my Wahethian connections were able to tell me about a strange woman who came from the East glowing orange. She was pregnant for years, they said, holed up sick and dying. There were healers, Seers, witches, and all manner of magic users called to try and heal her, or at least speed along the pregnancy. In the end, after nearly two decades, she died, but the child lived. My contact said he was spelled at birth to carry the traits of a Wahethian. Rare, powerful, and permanent. They have been researching how it was done ever since with no luck. That was twelve years ago." Keyra is silent as the meaning of his words absorb and he continues speaking. "I can't imagine the pain she went through, her body fighting the immense pressure within her. A fetus bearing the Gods' Blood in nearly its entirety would have killed anyone lesser. As a battlemage, and with the assistance of the hordes of magical staff, she was somehow able to survive long enough to give birth. They say the event caused every fire in Waheth from the smallest candle to the largest forge to flare with the intensity of a thousand suns. Whatever happened, they worked especially hard to cover it up, but too many people knew for it to remain a secret forever. When my suspicions were confirmed, I knew it was only a matter of time before I ran into you and your ward again."

Keyra's cup of ale is forgotten in her hand. Everything she thought she knew about herself is slipping away into more lies. Her attachment to Tilsman is nothing more than another spell, another aspect of the bindings that had been placed on her so long ago. That's why she had lost herself and killed Erey. He had been an obstacle in her forced goal. She feels guilty when she wonders if she ever felt anything for Tilsman that wasn't false. Did she even care? No, there are some things that they could not take from her. "Say Tilsman is the vessel, and you finally have what you've been spending what I imagine is most of your life looking for. Now what? You can't kill him, or you'll lose track of it again."

"I have not spent six decades without thinking about the next step." He seems amused at her counterpoint. "We will take you to Saltspire, as you intend."

He drinks as though the conversation is over. Keyra will get no more information out of him, but she doesn't have to. If Saltspire is where the magic originated, then killing Tilsman there will ensure it is attracted back to its most natural state. Once there, they can do what they want with it without worry of more interference. Her and the boy's days are numbered. Peterfer could have already been killed.

She stares into the cloudy contents of her cup. She had never been a fan of salt ale. Ale was bitter enough without adding another abrasive flavor. "You acknowledge that I am still a member of the Tower, correct? And I hold all the rights of one? Especially since the time spent away was technically for a mission, whether or not I was aware of it."

He narrows his eyes suspiciously but nods. "Correct."

"Then I challenge you for your position as captain of this ship, as is my right." She crosses her arms definitively.

The leemoah snarls, baring fangs. "We are not in Mangzar, and that rule has been abolished for decades as part of the Tower. Besides, fighting you would be an insult to us both."

"We were both members when challenges were a part of our way of life. I have been absent for some time, but I know that means we're grandfathered out, correct? The challenge stands, you are to face me or face disgrace. Under Akai, Captain."

She smiles smugly although her small victory here will do nothing to save her during the actual confrontation. She doesn't imagine she'll last more than a few seconds. El'rozai inclines his head. "Fine, we shall have it your way. I will slaughter Ayrek the Reaver in front of dozens of witnesses. Under Akai."

Keyra feels another headache coming on. She wonders if the memories that have trickled back include muscle. As they exit the cabin, she looks desperately at Peterfer. The time mage is pale and slumped. Captain Zai holds out his arms to gain the attention of those around them.

"Wretches and warriors, we have a real treat for you today. Ayrek the Reaver has challenged me for my posting. While this tradition has been barred in recent years, she and I come from a different era of the Tower, and her challenge will be honored. We shall fight to the death, on the deck of the incumbent captain's ship, in the presence of his crew."

There are subtle and less-than-subtle reactions from the spectators. Some murmur, somem shake their haeds, others outright point and laugh. Keyra feels her hackles raise. She is nothing but an amusement to them, and to the leemoah. They expect her to die quickly and horribly. Tilsman moans from where he sits against the railing, looking green around the gills. Of course, he would choose to be seasick now. Before she can turn back to El'rozai, however, the captain holds out his hands for silence once more. "As we are working with rules that no longer exist, there is one more stipulation. Ayrek has brought along a time mage and a boy whose magical abilities are yet to be understood. Such an unprecedented move may seem like a threat to a lesser man than me. As a precaution to ensure the fight goes smoothly, they will have their heads held underwater until the conclusion of the battle. I'm sure fighting for their lives will distract them from any intent to interfere."

There are cheers and jeers from the crew and Keyra snaps in horror. "You can't do that! They're not a part of this. You could actually kill them."

As she protests, two buckets of seawater are pulled onto the main deck and Peterfer and Tilsman are grabbed by pirates. "Then I suggest you defeat me quickly," El'rozai says as he pulls a sea-forged scimitar from his belt sash.

If she felt woefully unprepared before, Keyra is a helpless child now. The boy and the sorcerer are pushed to their knees in front of the buckets with little opposition considering one is a frightened boy and the other is an exhausted old man. Keyra feels a bubble of rage building in her gut. The Tower was supposed to be a family to her, a unit that protected her no matter what. Instead, they had used her to pillage countless innocents, and when the price had been right, they had sold her out to the sorcerers, trading the rest of her years away. She grits her teeth.

Off the bow, Saltspire Island becomes visible on the horizon, the pinnacles of the temple cutting sharply into the sky. The sight charges her with a new energy, something deep and primal. Could she have some of the Gods' Blood? She hadn't been affected by Elgireth's dark magic despite being exposed to it. She reaches deep inside herself even as she reaches for her knife. The weapon looks acutely pathetic next to the scimitar.

Whatever had been dormant for thirty years awakes once more. If Peterfer could use his magic to change himself from a water mage into a time mage, who was to say she couldn't weaponize hers? The crew frenzies as Tilsman and Peterfer have their faces pushed into the water.

Whether or not she has magical abilities, she is committed. Keyra lunges for the leemoah, and he dodges easily. His scimitar is lowered as he sidesteps. He's going to drag it out in order to torment her. She knows he cannot afford to kill Tilsman now, but there are no such restraints necessary for her new sorcerer ally.

Keyra lunges again, and at the last second feels a tingling on the back of her neck. She can see his sword arcing towards her and moves to block it seconds before it happens. It gives her time to reach forward with her other hand, grasping the fist that holds his weapon. She twists his palm away from his thumb, forcing him to drop the scimitar.

There is a roar from the crowd that temporarily drowns out the floundered splashing from her friends. Keyra senses Captain Zai reaching for his scimitar and snaps her foot into his face as he bends. It connects solidly with his skull and he hisses as blood is drawn. He backs up as she picks up his weapon.

Armed with the scimitar and the knife, Keyra advances. El'rozai bounces back and takes an offered sword from one of his crew. The seamstress has no time to comment on his use of assistance while hers is drowning. Again, she feels the tickle on the back of her neck and sees the blade from behind before it strikes. She catches the interfering cutlass between her weapons and yanks it from the crewmember's hands. "That's twice you've breached the rules, Captain. If you don't have to adhere to the guidelines, then I don't." She trusts her new strength and throws her knife, sending it spinning into the eye of the pirate holding Peterfer's head underwater. There is dead silence as he falls backwards onto the deck and the time mage lifts his head with a massive gasp for air. He shakes water from his face, cheeks red with rage. "How *dare* you, you ragged, seawater drinking, sunfried—" He splutters as he has forgotten to take a breath between nearly drowning and insulting his captors. Time freezes around Keyra and Tilsman, who has tears mixing with the water on his face. He pulls away from the pirate holding him and kicks him several times.

Peterfer nods to Keyra. "We can get our rowboat back in the

water before I have to slow us back down. We have to hurry, though."

"No," Keyra says defiantly, "I'm done running from the Tower. I am about to rightfully become the captain of this ship, and I intend to do so. El'rozai is right. I will always be a member of the Tower. It's time I embraced it instead of fighting it."

Peterfer's face suggests he disapproves, but he relents. "Very well, have it your way. But I will reserve some energy in case the boy and I want to escape when your plan goes horribly awry. I suggest you use these last few seconds to make a mark on your opponent before things balance back in his favor."

Keyra shoulders El'rozai squarely in the chest as time re-starts. Her stomach lurches at the motion and the leemoah flies backwards, delayed by the shift. He has no chance to catch his balance as he flies backwards into the crowd. His weight causes a chain reaction of collapsing pirates and enough of a diversion for Keyra to advance and press the sword tip onto the scales of his neck. "Yield," she says coldly.

Captain Zai hisses through his fangs. "You use dirty tactics, and your age and weight are shown through your weapon movements." Then he chuckles suddenly. "Just like any good Tower agent. You may have my surrender and my ship, but if you are foolish enough to leave me alive, there will be consequences."

She hesitates. She should kill him, otherwise he will betray them the second they reach Saltspire, and potentially take Tilsman's life. "First things first. My name is Keyra, not Ayrek the Reaver." She lowers her blade. While Ayrek would have taken his life, Keyra is her own person. "Secure him in the hold and hold course for Saltspire Island." The crew jumps to obey their new captain.

~ 40 ~
EL'ROZAI

Captain Zai found himself among the elite of Gafforah. To his left stood Captain Seran of the Royal Guard. To his right, the Nath'iki Admiral of the Navy, Yo'aro the Tigress. There were other nobles whose faces were familiar but the leemoah could not determine their names. He recognized chiefs from the colony islands, and Gar'ithol, the King of the Reef. Across from the aging leemoah was Romansi, the Head Sorcerer of the Citadel. At the head of the table was Queen Wendwynn Forella herself. She was as fierce as the tales, earning the multitude of titles that she had gathered during her short reign. Black charcoal streaked around eyes that looked like the heart of ice. Her dark hair was curly and wild, untamed beneath a simple circlet. Her features were unique in Andriel, heralding she was not of their world. The differences stopped at her physical structure and impressive height. Her clothing was Gaffori through and through, from her dark green tunic to her billowing harem pants and slippered feet. She sat in silence as the nobles murmured amongst themselves.

When she stood, she cast a spell of silence. "Thank you all for coming today. I understand it is short notice, and celebrations for our victory in Mangzar are in full swing across our nation." She waited for the cheers to die down. "However, the war was not without casualties. As you all know, my wife, the mind mage Frejith, was killed in the line of duty, along with countless other Gaffori and Elgir soldiers and citizens. I cannot hide the truth that they died for me. They died because of my negligence, my hardheadedness. I have been forced to step back and look at myself and my reign with newly discovered humility. I have acknowledged to myself that I had become obsessed with power, with ambition, and found no satisfaction in victory." She turned her eyes to stare at the table. "I have decided to dedicate the next part of my life to finding my homeland and restoring damage that was done by my father. I do not wish to turn Andriel into another disaster at the hands of a Forella." She paused, but there was not even a breath from the enraptured audience. "I have also decided to renounce my position as Queen and return Gafforah into the hands of its own. Not an emperor, empress, king, or queen, but a council. *This* council. Monarchies are outdated and it is time Gafforah helped forge the path to a more democratic process. I have drafted papers that will set guidelines for voting, terms, powers, and new law for Gafforah, the first of which is that slavery will not return after my exit. You will all hold each other accountable, and the next members voted in, to ensure dictatorship remains a thing of the past."

Romansi cleared his throat. "And where does that leave the Citadel and the Tower, Your Grace? You established the relationship we have, where we answer to the pirates. The structure has been tentative at best, and it cannot sustain without your oversight."

El'rozai recognized the tired expression in the queen's face. Whatever happened in Mangzar had broken her. Now was his chance. "Your Grace, I have risen in the Tower's ranks quickly despite my youth. This is partly because of my strong ties with the Citadel. I respect them, and they respect me. Let me handle the contract between our organizations and I promise I will not let you down."

Her eyes were distant as she nodded. "Under probationary considerations, I will allow it if there is no protest. I want you to analyze the Tower and how it operates, and Romansi will do the same for the Citadel. No questionable contracts, no foreign interference. We have had enough of that in this war." The leemoah nodded his agreement. The queen turned to the next addressee. "The next matter concerns the High Priest of Saltspire."

El'rozai fought the smile at the ease of his victory. An afterthought, a brush aside, to the queen, but a solidifying of his career to him. High Priest Lekala stood. "It is no secret now that the source of all magic lies within the catacombs of Saltspire Temple. We have dedicated the fortress to protecting the Well and will do so as we have protected the temple for generations. As requested by the queen, we will seal it up without resurrecting the battlemages or utilizing the Gods' Blood in any way. Reportedly it will be absorbed into a new source, far from mortal reach. Until that time, the priests of Saltspire will hold our duties to the highest standards."

"That sounds like a matter for the Citadel," Romansi bristled. His puffed-up chest suggested he hadn't been happy with the announcement that the sorcerers would still be held accountable to the Tower, especially to a stallion who had just grown his head feathers. "Your Grace, it seems you forget we hold the most power and abilities in Gafforah."

"I have not forgotten," Wendwynn snapped. "It is because of your power that you must be given less authority and be held accountable for what you do have. The priests of Saltspire are the guardians of the Well, and therefore have the right to handle the Blood as they see fit. The assignment is a temporary one, and the Blood will be gone from the mortal realm within the month."

The flora mage shut his mouth in a thin line but even Captain Zai could see the unrest bubbling beneath the surface. He wondered if the queen knew the chaos she would cause by leaving, and if she did, he wasn't certain she cared.

"There is one more matter to take care of," the queen whispered with eyes still downturned. "Please, join me on the balcony."

The air was cool as summer melted into the early autumn season. Saltspire's main balcony was large enough to hold a crowd of pilgrims, but now it was full of half-finished catapults. On the horizon, there were eleven ships bearing eleven different Mangzarian flags. El'rozai recognized each as a different district. Queen Wendwynn stood in front of her new council and raised her hands to the brisk breeze. "I offer a final gift, and a final warning, to those that will guide Gafforah from here on. To ensure Mangzar never rises against us again, to guarantee peace with our neighbors to the west, I have determined there must be new Warleaders chosen. Mount Thoyax technically belongs to me, and District Eleven is under the guidance of Erdendaz isilth Zavosh. But the others are potential threats who could prey on my people when they smell weakness, to restore Mangzar's name or seek their own fortune. I cannot let that happen."

Warleaders stood at the bows of their vessels in full armor. El'rozai felt a sickening weight in his stomach. He recognized the cold determination in Queen Wendwynn's face. Ice from eyes to mouth, a golden glow faint beneath her skin. While it was hard to see the expressions on the faces of the Warleaders, their synchronicity and lurching movements suggested they were not themselves. Puppets. One by one, they jumped into the bay and none surfaced.

The silence over the council turned to a dark weight on each of their shoulders. Wendwynn turned back to them. "This is the gift. New Warleaders will be chosen, and they will promise peace with Gafforah. Zavosh will oversee the process as he is now the most powerful vipr in the nation. This is the warning; I did not gain the Puppetmaster magic from the Well. I carved it out for myself, by myself. I have burned the books that detailed the process to ensure no one ever uses it against their own people again, making me the last and only Puppetmaster. As quickly as I have given power here, I can take it away. And I will."

There was no denying the impact of her words as the council watched the ships turn silently back to Mangzar.

They dispersed shortly after her show. Each councilmember had her papers to study and become familiar with. She herself said nothing upon her exit. El'rozai expected she would slip away into the night like a cat that knew its time to die with dignity had come. For the leemoah, work was just beginning.

He made his way through the temple to where he could see the entrance to the catacombs. There were guards wielding spears traced with holy magic runes. It would not stop someone who was especially determined.

"We never would have imagined it was here, so close to home." The boy that moved to stand beside the stallion was barely fifteen, his orange scar small and bright. He wore a cloak to hide his face here. El'rozai guessed he wouldn't have to worry about the wrath of the queen much longer. Beneath his cloak, a book wrapped in cloth rested on his belt. One of the Puppetmaster tomes? No, why would he need to know Puppetmaster magic when he had the Gods' Blood at his fingertips?

"Can you get through?" The captain watched the tunnel greedily. He was so close to becoming more than he could ever imagine. The power filled his lungs like the sweet scent of flowers. "We have limited time, and the guard will only increase from here on out."

Vendar snorted. "I'm a battlemage, leemoah. Don't embarrass yourself."

"I'm not the one that will be killed on sight here. Remember our deal. You will bring us both magic enough to command our own factions unquestionably. I brought you here through the heart of the queen's territory. I've upheld my end." They had agreed to only take a small amount, enough to amplify their power but not enough to draw suspicion.

"You've done beautifully," Vendar agreed. "But I'm afraid that means you've used up your worth to me."

El'rozai reached for the scimitar at his side, somehow unsurprised at the battlemage's betrayal. He didn't think to look for the rock that flew towards his head. The last thing he saw as consciousness faded was the leering face of Vendar the battlemage.

~ 41 ~

KEYRA

Saltspire has been abandoned for some years, its priests gone, and its towers left to crumble. Without the magic, and without a war with Mangzar, the otherwise priceless piece of land is nothing more than a sandy lump in the middle of Kaper's Bay. The rumors surrounding the old temple have kept curious travelers away, and the Tower is no different. The crew chooses to remain on the ship while Keyra and her companions step onto the shore. The sand here is smooth from disuse and there is evidence that there was a sandstone path before the elements reclaimed it. Walking towards the temple, the wind whispers eerily through the empty windows and she feels as though she is being watched. Thorny vines have reclaimed most of the stone and reached into the many cracks. All three are silent as they walk, although it is impossible to tell whether it is out of reverence or unease. Whatever ghosts haunt these halls won't be friendly.

Somewhere along the line, Keyra allows Tilsman to lead them. His face is far away but his feet guide them directly to a large tunnel guarded by statues of sorcerers wearing stone hoods. He blinks strangely. "Where do you think this goes, Granma Keyra?"

"I think know that," she says grimly. She doesn't know what will happen once they are inside. Will Tilsman die without the magic inside him? Will the spell on her vanish and she crumble to dust? Or will it blind them all and leave them to the mercy of the ghosts and the waiting pirates? She doesn't imagine their nonexistent loyalty will be enough to guarantee their safety. She is already regretting leaving the disgraced former Captain Zai on board with them, but she didn't have much of a choice. To bring him along would be to invite trouble, and to kill him would be to go back on her word.

She mulls over the choices she has made as the sun disappears behind them and the blackness of the tunnel takes over. Tilsman moves closer to her when he realizes they are in catacombs.

The glass coffins are unsettling. Keyra chooses to keep her eyes on the floor instead of the grisly remains on display in the see-through cages. The deeper they go, the colder the air and the less disturbed the dead. She hears whispers and feels chills across her spine. Her hair prickles when she sees a shadow dart across the wall. Whether it is from a member of their party or a ghost, she cannot say.

They travel until it is cold enough to shiver, and the dead are no more than bone. A section of the tunnel has been covered and then blown away. Stone rubble scatters across the ground and there are long-rotted bodies contorted from a blast decades ago. Tilsman stops here and rubs his arms. "Do you hear that? A whisper of some kind? It wants us to go in there."

Keyra remains silent as the boy steps forward. The Tilsman she knows would have wet his pants before following an unknown voice into frigid darkness. Whatever has taken ahold of him is stronger now more than ever. Peterfer and Keyra follow him into the grotto beyond.

They are on a ridge above a small lake that glitters with its own light. The reflections dance on the walls and ceiling around them, lighting up the thousands of runes carved into the stone. The cavern is large and echoes their breaths. An empty pedestal dominates the center of the lake. Tilsman sits down as though he can no longer support his own weight. There is a stirring of impossible wind at their presence. Tilsman closes his eyes. When he opens them again, they are glowing with an unearthly light. "The Blood has made its way home at last." The voice that speaks is of a thousand deities, deep and ancient. "You have done well."

"Who are you?" Peterfer asks breathlessly.

"Someone who has waited too long for the Blood to return. I will spare the child as thanks. But when you leave this place, you will ensure it is forgotten to the mortal realm. Too long it has been used for personal gain."

Tilsman stands and a shimmering vapor rises from his body like a mist. It thickens and becomes colorful as it returns to the Well, a rainbow of shades that mix and churn like a living thing. Keyra and Peterfer watch in awe, unable to look away. The light thickens until it is as solid as paint yet glowing and pulsing with a heartbeat. Keyra doesn't just hear singing but *feels* it, inside her and around her, the voices of the gods. From her own skin, a small tendril wisps up to join the rest of the magic. The spell, her own personal curse, is leaving her forever. She feels lighter, realizing that was the reason she hadn't been affected by the dark magic in Elgireth. Vendar's magic had been a parasite for decades, but it had also ironically been her shield in the end.

There are tears in her eyes by the time the Gods' Blood has completely exited Tilsman. He sinks and she catches him. She pushes back sweaty hair from his forehead and slaps his cheek gently until he opens his eyes. Now the tears are of relief. She still cares about him. That is real, not some malicious spell. "You're alright now, Tilsman. You'll be okay."

Peterfer's eyes are still on the Well. "I was there when they tried to take it. Why this boy? Why the boy, Luthen, thirty years ago?"

"The child is the son of a battlemage, and the grandson of Thentil," the voices whisper back.

"The lesser goddess of weaving?" Peterfer scoffs. Then his brow furrows in thought. "A battlemage? It couldn't be Beta, could it?"

"A demigod is a demigod," the voice answers. "His father, Luthen, requested the battlemage Beta take the Gods' Blood, as well as Ashlikani's power. The Shepherd obliged, and the child inherited it from his mother."

As Tilsman wakes, his face begins to change. His red curls turn dark, and his blue eyes change to green. The spells placed on him at birth are fading with the magic. He looks up at Keyra, still a lost child at heart, no matter his appearance. Keyra sniffles. "All those spells wearing off and you're still chubby."

"I feel so different now, Granma Keyra. Lighter."

"Well I don't know if I'd say that. But it's a start."

"I knew your mind was getting weak in your old age, but I never expected you to lead me straight to the source." El'rozai steps out of the tunnel entrance, a familiar crystal the size of an infant in his hands.

"Peterfer!" Keyra calls, turning to the time mage to find his silver scar has faded and been replaced with a deep blue color.

"My magic returned with Tilsman's," he says mournfully. "I am Peynter the water mage yet again."

"And you, Keyra, are officially nothing more than an old woman," El'rozai sneers. There is splashing from the lake below and shouts. Pirates are beating at the base of the pedestal with clubs and rams, shattering the delicate stone. The orb shudders with each strike, its resting place becoming less stable every moment.

"No!" Keyra shouts as it crumbles. She can only watch as the orb is drawn towards the Magnium with unquestionable clarity. It fills the glass with warm light that is both pale and every color at once. El'rozai laughs and holds it high above his head.

The grotto shakes as a deep growl fills the air and reverberates through the stone. "You mortals never deserved the Gods' Blood!" Those on the ridge are unable to stand and those in the lake scream as water churns and consumes them like a ravenous beast. The Magnium begins to hum and crescendos into a piercing shriek. The glass glows brighter and brighter. "Never again shall one have access to the entirety of its power!" The symbols on the walls ripple sharply. Magic pulls into the stone from all sides of the cavern, followed by the screams of thousands of wielders. The gods are reclaiming their gift from mortals.

Then, with the sound of a dying star, the Magnium shatters. There are several individual pieces that spin in midair like rabid fairies. They sing unique songs before shooting through the roof of the grotto faster than any arrow. El'rozai is left staring at his empty hands. "By Akai!" he screeches like an unearthly thing. "All those decades, all that work! I deserved this!" He stamps his foot like a spoiled child. "The conniving, the dealing, the murders and the sacrifices I have made! It cannot be all for nothing. I refuse to acknowledge it was all for nothing!" He throws back his head and screams at the gods.

Peterfer approaches the distracted slaver with a deep frown. "I remember you now, leemoah. You are a slaver, a fiend, and a greedy bastard. You have killed and threatened people I care about for too long. Return to the water you came from!" He shoves El'rozai with a strength that defies his age. The leemoah struggles to catch his footing on the ledge. Keyra steps forward confidently, placing a hand squarely in El'rozai's chest.

"No," the leemoah growls, meeting Keyra's eyes. "You said you wanted to be better than Ayrek the Reaver. You were going to spare me." Beneath him, pebbles fall from the ledge to smash into the shallow water far below.

"Maybe I'm not quite done being Ayrek. She will die with you." Keyra gives a small push, enough for him to lose his balance. The gods must have agreed with her decision as a tidal wave rises with a roar from the grotto floor, wrapping El'rozai in an embrace so fierce that he vanishes instantly with nothing but a gargled scream. The water below turns to solid ice, encasing El'rozai and the rest of his followers in a clear coffin.

The three of them are left standing on the ridge, alone in the dark grotto. The silence is too much for Keyra to take. "Now what?"

Tilsman whimpers from beneath his shaggy dark hair. "Can we go home now? I'm famished."

There is a long pause that Peterfer breaks with raucous laughter. Keyra can't help but follow suit, relief flooding her. She is glad her face is wet so they cannot see the tears there. "That's the best idea I've heard all day."

~ One Month Later ~

Hardock has never been impressive as a dock town, but now the sailors that come aren't just stopping on their way to Gafforah. They are there to trade with the renewed leemoah markets in the town. They are there to speak to the Elgir, a people whose reputation precedes them throughout Andriel. They bear strange markings on their eyelids and their skin hangs loose on their bones as a reminder of the horrors they have overcome. The people are eager to tell tales about their experiences as they have little else to do except swap stories and talk visitors out of their jewel shards. Those who travel through the southern island of Everlyn find exceptional lodgings at the Citadel, once a monument to the local magic users, and now a museum and comfortable room to stay. There are no sorcerers now and the Elgir have an array of tales about the end of magic born. Those that travel share similar tales. Magic has all but disappeared in Andriel, with various reasonings but no solutions.

Keyra likes to believe that perhaps they have entered a new age. Those she knew that used magic used it for their own selfish gain, whether consciously or not. They considered themselves above the average person with disastrous results. Perhaps in this new world, there will be less divide between classes and types. Perhaps now, they can learn to live in peace as she has, surrounded by her adopted grandchild and the love of the last part of her life, sewing ripped sails for traders and warning youngsters of the dangers of Elgir magic.

Perhaps now, the world can be at rest.

~ EPILOGUE ~

Thousands of miles away, the heart of Terrial is nothing but hot sand and the unblinking eye of the sun. Small villages dot the landscape, offering little respite for any travelers passing through.

Sari does as the other desert dwellers have to, making a meager living on simple wares and hoping for a better life amongst green lands. Until then, food is scavenged from scraps, and water is pulled from a well outside of town.

It is on one such trip to the well that she hears a strange humming, tantalizingly magical in nature.

If you enjoyed this book, please consider leaving a review at your favorite book retailer's website. Reviews from enthusiastic readers are vital to authors everywhere!

GLOSSARY

CHARACTERS:

A'Toa: Also known as Star. The leemoah sacrifice for their religious ceremony in 30 BEM (Before End of Magic)

Ayrek the Reaver: A senior ranking member of the Tower. Member from 70 BEM to 30 BEM.

Betallia Arfour: Also known as Beta. A young battlemage apprentice to Vendar in 30 BEM and member of the Citadel.

El'rozai: Also known as Captain Zai. A leemoah slaver and member of the Tower. Advanced to leader of the Tower in 60 BEM.

Sir Embyr: One of Queen Wendwynn's personal guard in 60 BEM.

Erey Anwave: Son of Keyra Anwave and factory supervisor in 1 BEM.

Frejith Aljez: Also known as Frej. Powerful mind mage and wife to Queen Wendwynn in 60 BEM.

Gar'ithol: King of the Reef leemoahs from 80 BEM to 15 AEM (After End of Magic).

Greysten Cordova: Qai native and Warlord of District Six in 60 BEM.

Halthax ky Dzaxar the Greater: Warlord of Mount Thoyax (District Six) of Mangzar in 60 BEM.

Halthax ky Dzaxar the Lesser: Son of the Warlord of District Six and general of his army in 60 BEM.

Isah: Elgir baker in 1 BEM.

Ip'akala: General of the Reef army from 60 BEM to 15 AEM.

Keyra Anwave: A seamstress citizen of Elgireth who has strange flashbacks and a desire to

discover her mysterious origins in 1 BEM.

High Priest Lekala: Head of the Saltspire priests in 60 BEM.

Luthen: Also known as the boy, Eight, and Ironhead. The son of the Elgir lighthouse keeper and the lesser goddess of weaving. Arena Champion in 30 BEM.

Malvin: Stone mage prodigy and member of the Citadel in 30 BEM.

Sir Nalag: Commander of the Gaffori army and personal guard to Wendwynn Forella in 60 BEM.

Peterfer: Old time mage and member of the Citadel in 1 BEM.

Peynter: Young water mage apprentice, member of the Citadel, and scholar in 30 BEM.

Rolith: A stone mage and team leader in 30 BEM.

Sir Syver Seran: Member of Queen Wendwynn's personal guard in 60 BEM.

Tika: Nobre Seer specializing in sexually transmitted diseases and Elgireth resident in 1 BEM.

Tilsman: Abandoned Wahethian boy and companion of Keyra in 1 BEM.

Wendwynn Forella: Also known as Wen. Queen of Gafforah in 60 BEM.

Vendar: A battlemage master to Beta and high-ranking member of the Citadel in 30 BEM.

Yo'aro: Admiral of the Gaffori Navy and member of the Nath'iki Tigress faction in 60 BEM.

Zavosh: Agent of the Gaffori army during Queen Wendwynn's reign. Vipr *isilth* and former customs agent in 60 BEM.

DEITIES:

Akai: The dark side of the moon god/goddess worshipped in Kaper's Bay.

Aryet: The light side of the moon god/goddess worshipped in Kaper's Bay.

Ashlikani: Takes the form of a star that is worshipped by the leemoah people of Kaper's Bay. Weakens over 3 decades and needs to receive a sacrifice to be replenished.

Jallor: The Terralian god of shadow.

Od Nedayeth: The Terralian High God.

Salwynn: The god of the eliives and decadence.

Deswana: The Kaper's Bay goddess of the ocean

VAR TRANSLATIONS:

Ruth Noki Saryn: Traditional Mangzarian greeting in the Var language. Translation: "I will hold them down for you." The traditional response is *Mo'al thran ketar sa.* Translation: "And there will be blood."

Milta: Traditional Mangzarian battle royal for the title of a district's Warleader.

Xari'kai: Traditional Mangzarian rehabilitation through fighting methods for the purpose of exacting revenge.

Intha/inthae: An elder/elders.

ABOUT THE AUTHOR

Tides of Gafforah is Sena Andeo's second novel, and the first in the *Blood of the Gods* series. There are currently two more titles in the works with many more to follow. Outside of writing, she enjoys playing piano, live music, dive bars, and working in the humanitarian field.

NEF HOUSE PUBLISHING

Check out more awesome books at
www.nefhousepublishing.com and find your next favorite
author today!

www.ingramcontent.com/pod-product-compliance
Lightning Source LLC
Chambersburg PA
CBHW020506260626
47156CB00006B/1888